UNBOUND

© Five Points Press 2021

Cover design by Sarah Anderson and Lisa Amowitz

Edited by Emily Colin and Madeline Dyer

This is a work of fiction. Names, characters, businesses, places, events, and incidents are either the products of the authors' imaginations or used in a fictitious manner. Any resemblance to persons, living or dead, or actual events is entirely coincidental.

Hardcover ISBN: 978-1-0879-4689-4

Paperback ISBN: 978-1-0879-4098-4

eBook ISBN: 978-1-3934-8561-2

ASIN: B08VGK3ZP32

EDITED BY
EMILY COLIN
& MADELINE DYER

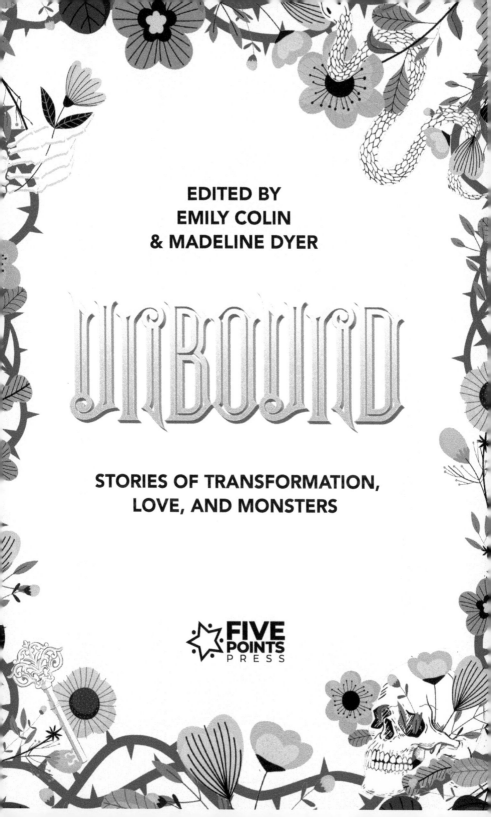

UNBOUND

STORIES OF TRANSFORMATION, LOVE, AND MONSTERS

FIVE
POINTS
PRESS

TO FRIENDSHIP, AND TO THE

ENDURING POWER OF

CREATIVITY TO TRIUMPH

OVER LOSS.

ABOUT FIVE POINTS PRESS

FIVE POINTS PRESS was formed by five authors living in four different countries with a shared experience of one pandemic and way too much time at home. 2020 was a year of transformation, and for this group, it became a time of creation and support. This creative safehouse was something we wanted to share with others.

All of us reached out to writers we appreciate—because of their work and because of who they are. We chose them for a reason, the central criterion being OwnVoices, inspired stories to remind us of the connection we have to one another in what can seem like a fragmented world.

From the chaos of a year of uncertainty, quarantines, and never-ending online meetings, UNBOUND was born: a collaborative creation, a collection of twelve stories, a gathering of the mysteries each author lives, each trying to make sense of their world.

Few books come into the world without a great many people helping move them along the way. UNBOUND is no exception. This is a collective effort with special thanks to the contributing writers, designers (Sarah Anderson and Lisa Amowitz), editors (Emily Colin and Madeline Dyer), and now you . . . the reader. Thank you for joining us on this journey.

TABLE OF CONTENTS

WASHING DISHES
HRISHIKA MUTHUKRISHNAN

Water poured out of the faucet

Washed off the surface-level grime

The friends that were no longer

She pulled the dirt out from under her fingernails

The words they said behind her back

She wiped her tears across her sleeve

The altered perception of herself

That people convinced her out to be

"Semi-attractive"

"A 2 out of 10"

And then she scrubbed

The underlying layer of mud, grime, dirt, grease

The insecurities

Her nose that sat too largely on her face

Her height,

not quite 5'5

but not quite 5'4 either

Her lack of curves

"Fat in all the wrong places"

She washed

And she scrubbed

Till all that was washed off was no longer

What remained?

A clean sink.

Remnants of what was

But most importantly,

Her.

Her in her purest form.

Acceptance of who she is

Confidence in what she is capable of

THE THINGS LEFT BEHIND
HEIDI AYARBE

THE WALL
NOW

Evie.

Swoopy E with a heart over the i, instead of a normal dot, which probably seems obnoxious to everybody, except those who know Evie.

Yeah. I think it's obnoxious.

Two years ago, the wall was bare. Evie was the first to sign it in thick black Sharpie, putting the date underneath. Now, it's a "thing." The hostel's been written up for it in all the good guides and blogs. A wall of names—Evie, dead center.

Dead center.

Write your name and the date you passed through. Nothing more. No message. Your name is enough.

And they come.

They look at her name and feel part of the mystery. They like the uncertainty. Then they leave their mark, as if their names mean something.

Evie made it happen.

I'M SITTING WITH DOROTHY ON MY BREAK.
Dorothy from Germany who orders a double espresso with toast and says everything is okay. She travels for a month every year. Alone. I'd like to think I could be that brave. But maybe it's not bravery. Maybe she's looking for more than okay.

I always get a break between the breakfast rush and cleaning the rooms. It's short but appreciated. La Escala is this town's hottest hostel.

Just look at the wall.

I usually sit alone, but when my break started, Dorothy motioned to an empty chair at her table. I sip on my latte and watch her. She's not like the other backpackers who pass through here. She sits with her back stick-straight. She doesn't try to fill the place with conversation. She swims in that place of awkward silence. She's an intermittent blinker and stares at me over her thimble-sized cup of espresso. Her thick, black hair is pulled back in a ponytail at the base of her neck. You can see where the ponytail is so tight, it pulls on her skin.

She tells me about her travels around the world like you'd imagine someone describing their daily bus ride to work. I look through the photos on her phone. She's the human Travel Channel. With every image I point out—of sunsets over ancient cities, lush jungle walks, full moons over desert dunes— she nods and says, "It was okay."

I test her. "Have you been to Tikal?" I ask.

"Yes."

"How were the Mayan temples?"

"They were okay."

"Have you been to Nepal?"

"Annapurna Basecamp, yes."

"And?"

"It was okay."

I think I like Dorothy.

I'll remember her.

I LEAVE DOROTHY WHEN THE FIRST backpackers come into view, straggling in after a twenty-plus-hour bus ride from *somewhere*.

It's crazy to think that the existence of this tired, forgotten town is because of a logistical glitch of bus schedules—a glitch that makes it impossible for travelers to move on, on the same day.

Dorothy watches the new arrivals check in. She should've been gone days ago, but here she is. Besides me and the occasional wanderer that sticks around to do some work for board, nobody stays longer than two nights.

Maybe Dorothy wants a job.

Breakfast is always a rush. We lay out a table of fresh-baked rolls and discount sliced-bread for toast, cheese portions, fresh-cut fruit, carton orange juice, and pretty shitty coffee with powdered creamer and packets of sugar to mask the bitter taste. Except for those who want to pay extra for espresso or lattes.

Dorothy always does.

I like making the specialty coffees.

Backpackers pile their packs in the hallway and sit down, talking about the next place to go. By the time they are ready to move on, Evie's signature has become white noise. The newness of the wall, the mystery of the missing girl, is gone. The hum of conversation buries the lost girl. She has faded in their memories because they've seen the signature, taken the photo, and hiked to see the sunrise. Only the ones who get up extra early for the sunrise walk stay an extra night. They come back awed and pretend it was important—this hike to see the sunrise.

There's a sheer drop from the lookout spot. Not because the sunrise looks better from that spot, but because it adds to the drama.

It's freakish scary, but I'd gotten to the point where I could sit on the edge and dangle my feet over, until the local authorities built a fence to keep everyone safe.

I suppose they didn't want anyone else to go missing.

BY 10 A.M., MOST BACKPACKERS ARE TIRED AND bored. In the den, the spattering of stragglers gathers—people playing cards, sharing travel stories, swapping telephone numbers, hooking up. They laugh at the VCR and put in an old movie because it's quaint.

Everything is posted, shared, liked.

I sometimes wonder about the soul of places. When do they stop being the places they are and turn into the places others expect to see?

Dorothy sits at one of the front tables and sips on her double espresso.

"How was the sunrise?" I ask Dorothy from my counter.

I hike to the sunrise spot every day. This morning, I saw Dorothy there. She took a couple of photos. It was incredible. Clouds pressed down on us, promising rain. Light didn't come. I felt the darkness grow inside me when zig-zags of light cracked open the clouds, punching through the blue-black. It was extraordinary.

She blinks. "It was okay."

I smile. *It was okay.* I like those words. There's something comforting about everything always being 'okay.' I'll miss Dorothy.

"Are you leaving tomorrow? Like everyone?" I ask.

She shakes her head. "Are you? Leaving?"

"I can't," I say and rub my wrist. I pass her another double espresso.

WAITING
THEN

I'd been sitting in La Escala Hostel for two days, just staring at Evie's backpack propped up on the lumpy pillows of the bed next to mine. Backpackers came and went—most didn't bother to stay for the sunrise.

Sunrises happened everywhere, right?

There was a quiet rap on the door. The girl from reception pushed it open and peeked in. She had greasy, lank hair and rough elbows. "Martina wants to talk to you."

I pulled my buds from my ears and pretended I hadn't heard her. "Sorry?"

"Martina. She owns this place. She wants to talk to you."

I couldn't work out where her accent was from. When I'd checked in the other day, she'd seemed nicer. She'd said she was working here until she saved up enough money to move on.

Momentum is a big deal in the backpacking world.

I followed the girl down the hall. She nodded toward Martina's office. I crowded in the cupboard-sized office and squeezed in the chair facing Martina. She had thick eyebrows and broad cheeks. Her lips had been colored in with salmon-colored gloss. She smiled. Some of the gloss was stuck on one of her crooked incisors.

Our knees brushed under the desk. I tried to scoot back but couldn't. It felt hot, and the room smelled like burned coffee and floral perfume.

I turned to my side, and my knees banged into the door.

Martina knotted her eyebrows, leaned her chin on her knuckles, and said, "Tell me about your friend? She wrote on my wall." She nodded toward the wall. "Evie."

When I first saw it there, shortly after I'd arrived, I almost added my name next to hers. I imagined Evie walking up to the wall the second she'd gotten there, pulling out her pen and signing—in front of everyone. Unapologetic. I held the pen in my hand, hovered over the wall. When a couple of backpackers came in, I felt a rush of shame and put the pen away.

"I'm waiting for Evie," I said.

"You are in contact?"

I shook my head.

"She is in contact with her family?"

My stomach clenched as I thought about Evie's mom. Evie sometimes did this disappearing act. She'd get pouty and just . . . drop away. "It's a thing she does. She'll come back." It was hard to explain that Evie was a pixel person who didn't exist outside the realm of Instagram. So, as soon as she was left with her 3D self for too long, she'd come back and BAM! Instagram-palooza.

With Evie, if it wasn't posted, it hadn't happened.

"It's been a few days. You say this is normal?"

I nodded, trying to swallow the chalky mass that lined my throat. "Absolutely."

"You will pay for her bed?"

I shook my head. I barely had enough money to get through the rest of this trip. Plus, it wasn't like this place was ever full.

"I need her bed," said Martina. The scowl lines between her eyebrows were like train tracks.

I couldn't give up her bed. I was waiting for Evie to return. The knot in my stomach grew. I made a fist, digging my fingernails into my palms. "Did you see her on the morning she did the sunrise tour? Does someone have a list of all the others who went with her?"

Something changed in Martina. She gnawed on her bottom lip. That salmon-gloss stained her front teeth now. She shifted in her chair. "This Evie—she is eighteen?"

"Just turned it a week ago." I counted days on my fingers. "We celebrated with a group of other backpackers. We drank a couple bottles of wine that made me sick. I don't drink. You know in the States you can't drink until you're twenty-one." I looked around the cramped office for a calendar. "Do you know what day it is?"

"I need the bed. It is not a closet. Find your friend."

I STARED UP AT THE CEILING, AT A WATER STAIN shaped a little like the Italian peninsula—another place I'd rather visit in a book than in person. I browsed through Evie's Instagram. She got over 800 likes on "Going to see the sunrise."

I read through the comments then typed: *Where are you?*

Those three words made it all too real, though, so I erased the message. Someone else could ask.

My phone vibrated, the ring shrill. I jumped and stared at the unfamiliar number on the screen. "Hello?"

"Do you know where Evie is?"

The connection was crystal. It sounded like Mrs. Yates, Evie's mom, was sitting next to me. My stomach tightened. A tingling rushed through my body, a jolt of electricity in my bloodstream, fire everywhere, inside and out. Then the tingling stopped, and it was like I'd been unplugged, drained of energy. I reached out and touched Evie's backpack, still propped against the pillows.

"Mrs. Yates? Hello!"

"Why didn't you call?"

The crackers I'd eaten for breakfast solidified in a ball of cement, settling at the base of my stomach. I'd been doing the sunrise hike every morning. I headed out before everyone, because it was about a thirty-minute walk to get to the trailhead.

I mean, it was kind of silly to pay to walk up a bluff—public space—and sit on the edge of a cliff for a sunrise show.

But backpackers paid. They wrote about it on their blogs, about how sublime the sunrise was. Instead of walking to the trailhead, clusters of them hopped in the Jeep—holding onto the back, feeling the wind in their hair. The sun rose. The selfie orgy commenced. Then they got served hot chocolate with chili pepper and fresh pastries and headed back to the hostel to sleep most of the morning away.

They sell it as authentic, the local transportation. When, really, the Jeep guy makes bank using a Jeep he imported from Colombia. It's totally not 'authentic.' He sells a story, and backpackers buy it because they want things like a sunrise and Jeep ride to mean something.

Evie bought it, too.

Weirdly, I felt like the sunrise got better each day. It was something that made sense. Light always comes.

"I'm waiting for her," I explained to Mrs. Yates. She'd understand that. We all waited for Evie.

"We have a flight tonight. We're coming to you." Her voice quivered. She choked on a sob. "Have you looked for her? Is anyone looking for her?"

Did almost writing a message on Evie's Instagram feed count?

IT WAS WEIRD TO STILL BE HERE IN THIS revolving-door hostel. People stayed one or two nights, tops. I watched them come and go. La Escala—the Layover. The name fit. The staff was layover, too. Martina hired random backpackers who were strapped for cash and needed to save up for the next leg of their trip.

I wondered if I could get a job here.

I didn't know what happened to time, but when Martina tapped on the door, it was already evening. I looked out the square window at the bruise-colored sky.

"You have a phone call."

I pulled out my cellphone. After the call with Mrs. Yates, I'd turned it off. I looked from the phone to Martina.

"In the office," Martina said and scowled.

I followed her back to her closet-office. She handed me the phone.

"Hello," I said, holding the phone tightly against my ear.

"Good evening. My name is Carla Morales. I work with the American Embassy here in the capital, and we've received a call from the family of Evelyn Yates and are just following up."

"Okay."

"Is Evelyn with you?"

"No."

"Do you know where she is?"

"Her backpack's here."

"When was the last time you saw her?"

"I don't know," I said. "Maybe a couple of days ago."

"Her family is concerned. Is there reason for them to be concerned?"

"Her backpack's here."

There was silence on the other end of the line. I heard the clicking of a computer keyboard.

"I've pulled up her Instagram," Carla Morales said. "There's a pretty decent stretch between Evelyn's last post and today. It seems like she liked to post new content quite a bit. Do you think it's strange she hasn't added a new photo?"

"Yes."

"I tried calling you," she said. She dictated my phone number. "Please confirm this is your number."

"Yes. I, um, turned off my phone."

"You turned off your phone?" she asked. "So, how do you keep in touch with Evelyn?"

"We weren't supposed to get separated. My phone isn't great."

She didn't respond.

"I can turn it on. It needs to be charged, anyway. I don't actually do that stuff—Instagram, social media stuff. I mean, if I'm taking a photo, I was there, right? I don't need to post it."

"Have you been in touch with your family?"

"I email my mom and dad every week. I send them WhatsApp notes."

"On a phone that isn't on or charged?"

"It's only been a couple of days. They work a lot."

"Charge your phone. We'll call again."

THE THINGS LEFT BEHIND
NOW

My arms and back ache. It's new, this ache, after stripping the beds, disinfecting everything. Even though I've done it every day for the last two years. Every single day, every room gets cleaned, laundry washed. It's a re-set. A re-do.

And every day, there's this blink of time that feels like I could walk into the dorm, see Evie's backpack, and she'll be back.

Except for the sunrise hikers, almost nobody stays more than one night—definitely no more than two.

The rooms always smell like sweaty socks.

I sweep under the beds and pile the things left behind in a box. We used to save the not-totally-gross things, but more people come now.

More do the hike. They leave in the morning. They come back, check out.

More things get left behind. For a while, the linen closet was filled with jackets, Teva sandals with frayed straps, scratched-up sunglasses, socks. Lots of socks. Now we trash most of it and divvy up the rest among ourselves, if anything's worth having.

I keep all the journals, stashing random backpackers' memories under my bed. Their lives fill the room. At night, I can feel their words pressing against the mattress, spilling onto the floor.

AFTER CLEANING THE ROOMS AND CHECKING in the new guests, the afternoons are quiet. I got my GED online last year, trading cleaning the Internet café for free access to the computers. Mom and Dad were proud.

I still clean so I can connect with my parents whenever I want.

They ask me about college, but I don't know how to do that, how to think past this place. It's been my home for two years, now. I stare at the wall of names.

Maybe people sign not because they want to leave something behind, but instead, because they think they matter. Their names and stories matter.

I *exist*, I think.

I pick up a Sharpie that someone dropped on the floor. There's a small space by the floorboard, a place where I could sign. I look over to see Martina watching me. I slip the Sharpie into my pocket.

MISSING
THEN

There was a rushed calm about everything. Two police officers came in—local authorities. They didn't look particularly concerned.

One of the officers stepped forward, tilted her head to the side. "I am Officer Calvet." She shook my hand. Firm and dry. Efficient. Posture perfect, she paced around the room. Her hair was pulled back in a loose, gray-streaked ponytail. "How many days ago did you see—" She looked down at her notebook. "Your friend Evelyn Yates?" She had just a hint of an accent.

Travel days got blurry. Everything was so basic—food, a place to stay, catching a bus or a train or a boat or whatever. Going to see something that's in the book. Photos, upload to Instagram (if you were Evie), counting how much money you had left to string along (if you were me). It was hard to keep track. The hostels all felt the same, the backpackers the same, the smells the same.

Dirty socks.

Evie's backpack was on her made bed, leaning against the lumpy pillows, just as she had left it.

I shrugged. "I don't know. Maybe two. Maybe three." I counted back the days. "Definitely three."

The officer clicked her tongue and nodded at Evie's backpack. "Can we have a look?"

"Of course." I sat down in the bunk facing her empty bed, and all I could think was I hoped the hostel wouldn't add Evie's charges for all these nights to my bill.

I knew that was the wrong thing to think.

The officer took out Evie's belongings, one at a time. She flipped through the pages of a worn journal, pausing on the last page, looking from the journal to me.

I hadn't realized Evie kept a journal. She wasn't the type to have private thoughts. She was more of an *if-it-isn't-posted-it-didn't-happen* kind of person. Officer Calvet noticed me staring at the journal. I pulled my gaze away.

"Evie's cellphone?" she asked me.

I shook my head. "Not here. It'll be with her. She would never leave her cellphone."

"Anything else?"

"She signed the wall. In the dining room."

They followed me to the wall. Calvet leaned in and traced Evie's name with her forefinger. She looked at the date, squinted.

"Has she called? Left a message?"

"No."

"Where would she leave a message, if she did?"

Evie wouldn't message me privately. No audience. "Probably on Instagram."

"May I have a look?" Officer Calvet asked.

I went back to the bedroom and got my phone. It was dead. Again. "Bad battery," I said and shrugged. The hostel had a charging station. I plugged my phone in.

"So maybe Evelyn has messaged you, but your phone was dead?"

"Maybe," I said.

Officer Calvet watched me.

I shrugged. "Evie didn't ever message me, though." Sometimes, things were just too hard to explain.

We both stared at my phone. When a bar popped up, I turned it on and, after an agonizing wait, loaded my Instagram. I followed precisely one person: Evie.

"Evie has a public account," I said. "This is her last post. *Going to see the sunrise.*"

Calvet read. "That was eight days ago." She continued to scan through Evie's feed. Then she handed me my phone and returned to the wall where the other police officer was taking

20

pictures of Evie's signature. Officer Calvet squinted and looked at the date. "No, nine days ago," she said, counting back on her fingers.

Darkness clapped down over me—everywhere. Nine days. My stomach tightened. I unplugged the phone and stuck it in my pocket.

We returned to the cramped dorm room.

Calvet sat on Evie's bed, shoving the backpack's contents aside. "Can I see your phone again?"

I handed it to her. "It just has one bar. Of battery."

She nodded and skimmed through Evie's Instagram feed. She took out her cell. "I will follow her now, too." She handed back my phone, using her own to look at Evie's feed.

Officer Calvet's gray eyes were completely expressionless as she looked from photo to photo. Then she showed the feed to her partner, who had yet to say a word. I wondered if, in this country, it was a good-cop-silent-cop-schtick.

She turned back to me. "It looks like Evelyn was having a great trip. And you? I don't see you in any of these posts. That's strange."

I shrugged. "I don't like traveling much. Even Evie didn't like it sometimes. But you can't tell from Instagram."

Calvet looked from the feed to me.

"Nobody lives an Instagram life," I explained.

"Your account is private?" Calvet nodded to the feed.

"I don't post. I just follow . . ."

"Evelyn."

"Evie."

Calvet typed a few searches. Clicked her tongue and continued to look through the posts. "Evelyn always wears this beautiful bracelet."

"Yes. It was from her mom. She never takes it off."

She looked to my wrists. I pulled up my sleeve.

"Do you wear jewelry?"

"No. I'm allergic. To gold. It gives me a rash."

"So, you were here when she signed the wall?"

I shook my head. "No. We separated for a night last week."

"Why?"

Evie left me.

"I got sick. Evie liked schedules and plans. Everything 'just so.'"

"Your friend left you when you were sick?"

"Hungover." I felt my face get hot. "I don't drink."

There was a pause.

"We brought the wine to our last hostel and drank with everyone else there," I explained. "I think it's okay, right? I'm technically an adult, so . . ."

"You're eighteen?" she asked.

I nodded.

"It is not illegal in this country for young women of your age to drink."

I exhaled.

"That doesn't seem like a good friend—leaving you behind?"

It was hard to explain Evie. When you were in her light, it was like walking in the sun. Incredible. But her shadow was ice. You could tell when she got bored of someone—something. Everyone was disposable.

I learned to be in the place in between, always in the place she needed me. I think I was the only real thing in Evie's life. I became essential.

We were supposed to be hiking this week. Or seeing an important statue in some plaza. Her life was a checklist—everything from being senior class president to the volunteer work we did for the first two weeks of this trip.

How exhausting to be Evie. I picked a hangnail and tasted the coppery blood.

"Evelyn's parents contacted the Embassy a few days ago. She hasn't used her credit cards. No posts on Instagram. Poof!" Calvet snapped her fingers.

"Poof," I echoed. "Her backpack's here." I nodded to the bed.

She leaned her elbows on her knees. "I think it is strange you did not think to contact anybody about her being missing."

Something had changed. The way she looked at me. There was that familiar tingling rush of fire in my veins. It surged through me. My muscles tensed, and my jaw ached. I gnawed on the hangnail. It stung. I tried to remember to breathe.

Officer Calvet talked to her partner for a moment. Then she turned to me and said, "Do you have anybody at home you can contact?"

THE NEXT DAY, EVIE'S PARENTS SHOWED UP.

"Mrs. Yates!" I sat up from the bed. For a split second, I thought they'd come to take me home.

Officer Calvet stood with Mr. and Mrs. Yates. I moved toward Evie's mom.

She rushed past me in rumpled clothes. Her usual news-anchor hair was limp, tied in a sloppy bun. Really, she looked like shit. She didn't acknowledge me. She looked at Evie's backpack and hugged it in her arms.

"She'll be back," I said. "It's Evie. She does this."

Evie's mom turned to me. She usually hugged me. She wasn't a warm hugger—not like my own mom—but she mostly made an effort to show some kind of affection. Until now. "How could you not look for her?" Her bottom lip quivered. "And not call? We've lost so many days."

Mr. Yates stood in the doorway, blocking all light. He was one of the only dads without an aging-guy gut. He was also one of the few who had hair. It was black with streaks of silver. His face was scruffy, stubbly—total aftershave-commercial material.

23

He didn't acknowledge me. But he was always good at that—pretending I didn't exist. Officer Calvet stood next to him, her head tilted to the side. She watched me.

Mrs. Yates set the backpack down next to the door. She turned to the bed and stripped it—the pillowcases, sheets, and sheet protector, shaking everything out.

Officer Calvet stepped forward. "We need to have forensics go through this," she said.

My stomach did flip-flops. My mouth felt chalky-dry.

Mrs. Yates fell to her knees. I got on my knees as well, and we both looked under the bed.

"What are you looking for?" I asked. Our foreheads bumped.

Mrs. Yates sat back on her heels. We faced each other. She took my face in her hands. "Please," she said. I tried to pull away, but she had a vise grip on my face. It hurt. "Please."

THAT MORNING, AFTER THE YATESES AND Officer Calvet left, Martina moved me to another room that wasn't meant to be a room for anybody. The mattress was on the floor. It smelled like mildew. A dusty, bare bulb stuck out of the wall with a rusted chain to click the light on-and-off. It was tiny and cramped with a high, triangular window where the ceiling slanted. Muted light slipped through greasy glass panes.

Evie and my room had been taped off. All day, police officers came and went. Heavy boots, walkie-talkies, the click of cameras, bagged sheets and pillows.

I could tell Martina didn't know what to do with me. She felt sorry and annoyed, and I didn't have the words I needed. So, I just sat in the cramped room and waited, until it felt like the walls would fold in on me.

I took what money I had left and found an Internet café, just a couple blocks from La Escala. I didn't need the Internet. I just needed somewhere to go. There, I took out my phone and crouched in the corner, knees tucked to my chest, working on steadying my breathing as I listened to the ringing. Even the ringtone was different.

I felt so far away.

"Hello?"

"Mom?" There was a pause, and I could tell she was crying. "Mom, it's okay."

"Where is Evie?" Her voice was strained, faint. The line was crackly. I pressed the phone so hard against my ear that it ached.

"You know Evie," I said. "She's like this. She'll come back."

"Dad and I can't be there with you. It's too far."

I knew that. Everything in our lives revolved around distance. Most people looked for school districts—we looked for homes based on proximity to the nearest hospital.

"Maybe they have a unit here," I said. "You could come and—" Then I caught myself. I couldn't wish them here; I wouldn't do that to them.

"Oh, babe," Mom said. "I'm sorry."

I stared out the window, waiting to sort out all the thoughts banging around my head. I had to order them, say the right thing, to keep Mom from worrying. It was hot again—the kind of air-bending heat that left everything hazy. I dried my sweaty palm on my shorts, cradling my cellphone between my shoulder and ear. "I'm just talking. You know I'm okay. Are you okay? Are you keeping up with treatments?"

"Do you—" Mom started to say but interrupted herself. "We can't be there," she repeated.

That was one of the reasons Mom hadn't wanted me to travel. She kept saying, *What if something happens and we can't get to you?* That and Evie. Mom and Dad never liked Evie.

"We've called the Embassy," she said, and she was back to herself, even over the shitty connection.

Calling the Embassy seemed like a thing to do.

"Why?" I asked. "Evie's parents already did."

Mom cut in. "They sent us a list—of attorneys. I've contacted one. The Embassy can't do more than that. Just listen to the attorney. Do what he tells you to."

"What for?" I tried to keep my voice as even as possible. "Mom, I haven't done anything wrong."

"You need a lawyer. We can't come."

I felt the sting of tears in my eyes. I cleared my throat. "I'm okay. I'll be home as soon as I can." Mom and Dad didn't need another worry on their plate.

"They have to find Evie," Mom said.

My heart felt like it was being squeezed in a vise. "I'll wait for her here. When she returns, I'll come home. Mom?"

"I'm okay, babe. We're just a phone call away."

But the connection was shit, and her voice faded.

THE CRAWL OF TIME
NOW

Dorothy has gone for the day. I don't know where. I scrub tables and mop the floor, pausing to read the signatures on the wall, trying to match names with the backpackers over the last couple of years. But most blur into the same memory.

Except Dorothy. She's different. She hasn't signed.

My stomach knots.

Maybe Dorothy's another PI. They used to come all the time. Evie's mom and dad spent thousands of dollars on investigators, searching, searching.

Dorothy could be a reporter. They've fizzled out, though. The missing girl—two years later—doesn't really grab your attention.

When Dorothy's here, I watch her, but she doesn't watch me. She hasn't looked at the wall at all.

Maybe she doesn't know about Evie, about me.

Maybe she doesn't care.

Maybe she's staying because this place—this in-between stopover place—is okay. Maybe there's nothing more than this, than okay.

BEFORE EVIE, THIS PLACE WAS A PAUSE, A cheap bed to get from one place that matters to another place that matters.

After Evie, this place mattered.

It's funny how we prescribe meaning to places like that.

The Mountain Condor Hostel had set up a sunrise hike where backpackers could ride in an 'authentic' Jeep and eat 'authentic' foods grown from local farms blah blah blah. But then Evie happened.

Bam!

This place became the Times Square of the backpacker route. New hostels popped up.

El Descanso changed its name to Desaparecido and started advertising a mysterious sunrise tour-turned-murder-mystery, which is in pretty bad taste.

Instead of being a layover, this place became a destination. The biggest group was *Church Groups Forming Search Groups*. There weren't enough hostels for them, so they camped on the edge of town and combed through the valley floor.

They held sunrise and candlelight vigils. Mrs. Yates came many times. She never talked to me, not after that first visit with Mr. Yates and Calvet.

On the third search mission, the eco-botany students from a nearby university protested because the *Church Groups Forming Search Groups* were damaging millions of years of evolution, trampling flowers and plants endemic to this delicate ecosystem.

That's one of the things I really love about deserts. A tiny plant can take thousands of years to grow. At the hottest desert temperatures, a carcass gets mummified, the skin growing tough from the dry air. Unless vultures come first.

It can take months for a skeleton to get exposed and bleach in the relentless sun.

The daintiest flower means everything in a desert—so often overlooked. Most people don't understand the desert's lethal, slow beauty.

The eco-botanists made their cause international.

Then there were protests about protests. Lots of confusion.

Nobody ever found anything. Evie just . . . disappeared.

Numbers have dwindled over the past year or so. Facts get messed up. I'm often in jail or have gone into hiding or never existed.

Evie's missing.

I'm the one who disappeared.

INTERVIEW 1
THEN

"We'll be recording this."

I nodded. Everything was shockingly scripted. The dingy table and uncomfortable chairs. The small room with a mirror. I wondered if there were internationally-approved interrogation design standards.

The attorney Mom and Dad contacted was here. He was bigger than the room. Sweat-rings stained his shirt collar and armpits. He sat on an uncomfortable-looking chair, his knees no doubt angled up, brushing the bottom of the metal table. "Your parents couldn't come," he said.

"You look uncomfortable," I said.

He brushed it off. "This is a one-size-fits-all world that most of us don't fit in."

I smiled. I liked him. "Thank you for coming."

"Your mom is worried."

"It's okay." I blinked back tears. "I want to go home."

The attorney's eyes softened. "Answer their questions."

Evie's parents had left that day with Officer Calvet and never came back for me. They didn't pay Martina either.

There was a click. A red light blinked on the camera.

"We're recording," said Officer Calvet.

I looked from the camera to her. "Okay."

"Can we start from the beginning?" she asked.

"Which beginning?" There were so many.

WE WERE EIGHT, IN MRS. VELEZ'S THIRD-GRADE classroom. Evie raised her hand to be class representative. She mouthed, Vote for me.

She smiled, and it felt like I mattered. It was the first time she'd talked to me. We'd been in the same class since Mrs. Maple's kindergarten class.

Mrs. Velez called for a show of hands for each candidate.

I voted for Manuela.

Evie lost. By one vote.

She followed me out to recess, mad and stomping, tears streaming down red-flushed cheeks. "A real friend wouldn't do that," she said.

"But we're not real friends," I said and walked away and sat alone on the swings.

She came over to me, and I thought she was going to kick dirt at me or take my swing, but she didn't. She sat in the swing next to me and took out a bag of grapes. "Do you want some?"

"Thanks." I bit down on a crunchy, green grape; its sweet tartness burst in my mouth.

After that, we were real friends.

Almost always.

"ALMOST?"

"Yes."

"Why *almost*?"

"Always only exists on the Disney Channel."

The room smelled stale, like spilled coffee.

Officer Calvet drummed her fingers on the table, then leaned back. Silence filled the room, pressed against the walls. I waited for them to crack and crumble beneath the strain of the words not said. In the upper-left corner, dingy white paint was peeling. Streaks of even dingier gray showed behind it. I looked at the clock.

My lawyer cleared his throat. "Do you have anything else to ask?"

Officer Calvet leaned forward, elbows on the table. She pulled out sheets of printed Instagram posts. She pushed them toward me. "You're not in a single picture. Not one."

I skimmed through the pages and shrugged.

"Not one photo of you. Not one mention of you. It's like you don't exist."

"I exist," I said.

Officer Calvet scowled. "She left you behind when you were sick—"

"Hungover," I corrected her. "It's not the same thing."

"Evelyn wasn't a good friend."

"She actually is," I said. How could I explain friendship? How could I explain Evie?

EVIE'S UNTOUCHABLE.

Evie is light.

People just wanted to be with Evie. She's the incarnation of social media—an Instagram life, right?

She used to turn it off at home. Back in middle school. I was the only one she ever invited back to her place. I get why. Her dad is this billboard lawyer. He calls himself The Justice Crusader—and puts the 't' like a cross on his billboards.

I'm not kidding.

They are Christians on steroids. Evie goes to all-day Sunday services, even now.

And her mom, she's the old-person version of Evie, you know. The right hair and clothes and house and friends. She makes sure they live an Instagram life—without the social media accounts.

Back in elementary and middle school, I'd go to Evie's place in the afternoons. She was more fun then. She knew the difference.

"THE DIFFERENCE?"

"Yeah. The difference between that—" I pointed to the piles of printouts of Evie's Instagram feed. "And this." I pointed to the room.

31

"What is this?" Officer Calvet waved her arm around the room.

"Real," I said.

"What else is real?"

"Kidney failure and dialysis are real."

Officer Calvet scowled. "Did Evelyn ever go to your home?"

"Once."

"Just once? You've been friends . . ." She shuffled through her notes. "For ten years."

"My house isn't like her house."

I pulled a memory out for them.

WE WERE IN SEVENTH GRADE AND WERE partners in a social studies project. We were supposed to do an infomercial for the Aztec Empire, sell ourselves as the top chinampas engineers for your sewage needs.

I invited her to the house. And reminded Evie to take off her shoes when we walked in the door.

"Why would I do that?"

"It's cleaner," I said. I walked down the hall and knocked on Mom's bedroom door. "I'm home."

Mom hollered through the door, "Snacks are in the fridge."

I took out a little plate of cheeses—cut up in triangles—and saltines. I felt a little embarrassed because I knew how hard Mom worked to make everything look nice for Evie. She knew I cared too much about what Evie thought.

Evie stared at the cheeses and saltines. I served her water from the tap. She glanced toward the bedroom. "Is your mom sick?"

"No," I lied. "I'll be right back. Help yourself, and we can work on the project."

Dad and I were both trained to help with the hemodialysis, and we alternated days. It worked well. Mom could do it, pretty much, on her own. But it's important to have someone there.

When we finished the treatment, I came out, and Evie was standing at the front door.

"I called my parents to pick me up," she said. "I forgot I had stuff to do."

"Okay." I glanced at the plate of cheeses and saltines. She hadn't touched them, and my embarrassment slipped away. I felt sorry for Evie.

"We'll work on it at my house tomorrow, okay?" She was itching to leave.

"Okay," I said and waited with her on the porch.

We didn't talk until she asked, "What's wrong with your mom?"

"Kidney disease. But she has machines to get her body to work. She's like a bionic woman."

Evie laughed, that kind of embarrassed laugh. "I'm sorry."

She was. But not about my mom. She was sorry about her reaction.

GIMMICKS
NOW

Travel gimmicks are big.

Freja, the Danish girl, nineteen years old, won't fly. She travels everywhere by land or sea. She signs her name in cramped letters.

The Spanish Tuna group—three brothers and their best friend—spends a month every year traveling, paying their way with music. They sign their names in cartoony-drawn instruments.

Charlotte from New Zealand takes a stuffed bear, Santana, everywhere. Which, at first, was kind of cute until she took out her Instagram feed and showed me the 317 posts of Santana, then Santana's passport that she'd made border officials stamp, which is probably illegal somehow. She even placed Santana's paw in an inkpad and pressed it on the wall.

The American rock climbers are sponsored by some big-name brands. They're traveling from Alaska to Ushuaia in a refurbished fire truck that uses cooking oil as gas. They climb when they can. There's something magnetic about them, the way everybody wants part of them.

The American rock climbers take up so much space with their story. So loud.

They go to the sunrise hike and aren't impressed.

That makes me sad for them because you know you've hit bottom when you can't feel wonder at the rising sun.

They sign the wall in big signatures, cover others' names, marks.

The YouTuber that only eats and reviews street food; the photographer who takes only one photo a day; the motorcyclist who is doing gravestone rubbings of his favorite dead people all over the world. They all sign the wall.

Except for Dorothy.

GIMMICKS.

They sort of defeat the purpose of going out to see the world and being humble and awed by the crawl of glaciers and the thunderous crack they make when they fall away; the infinite salt flats that, when there's a thin layer of rainwater, reflect the sky so perfectly it looks like you're soaring; ancient cities built from stones that came from quarries hundreds of miles away; a post office at the end of the world to mail a letter.

A sunrise.

I wipe down tables, sticky with jelly from this morning's breakfast. A man always passes the hostel, selling cakes his wife made. I talk to him sometimes. The cakes are always dry. There's something reliable about dry, homemade cakes. They're not trying to be anything else.

I don't know why that's become a bad thing—living a normal, unremarkable, okay life.

I look at the clock. I wonder where Dorothy went, when she is coming back.

AT NIGHT, IT GETS TOO LOUD. THERE ARE TOO many memories under the bed from the journals that I've kept. Moonlight cuts through the high window and dribbles onto the floor.

I sweep under the bed and pull out the journals. I pick and choose and piece together the life I want from snippets of memories of others, tossing everything else out.

Now, I have stories to tell about memories that I will never have. It makes it easier to wait.

35

INTERVIEW 2
THEN

"Evie isn't a bad friend. She's just kind of broken inside. So, when you're broken inside, you can't stand if things are broken outside. Does that make sense?"

We were back in the same room as the day before. It smelled the same. My lawyer wore the same tie. The red light blinked on the camera.

Officer Calvet didn't respond. She waited for me to talk more.

"She doesn't realize that she's enough, you know?"

"Enough what?" Officer Calvet asked.

"Just . . . enough."

"Evelyn's parents don't like you."

I shook my head. "No," I explained. "To people like Evie's family—who care so much about what others think—someone like me is hard to accept. My family is hard to accept."

"Why?"

"Sick people make others uncomfortable. Haven't you noticed?"

"In what way?"

"The smells, mostly, I think. That perma-ammonia, antiseptic smell. Sometimes a little sour, too."

"So, her family can't accept your family because—"

"We don't make for good social media posts."

Officer Calvet scowled.

I cleared my throat and swallowed. "I'm sorry her parents are so sad right now."

"You say—" Officer Calvet read back through her notes. "Evelyn used to know the difference."

I shook my head. "I didn't say that."

Officer Calvet flipped through the transcript of the recording from the first interview. "Yes. Look here."

"Not Evelyn," I said. It was weird she wouldn't call her Evie. Evie hated when people called her Evelyn. "I said 'Evie.'"

"Does it matter?"

"Everything matters," I said.

Officer Calvet tapped her pen on the table. "So, do you think Evie doesn't know the difference anymore?"

I nodded and motioned to the Instagram pictures and the comments. "That became everything."

"Do you think something bad has happened to Evelyn?" Officer Calvet asked.

I couldn't let my brain go there. I rubbed my eyes. "I think she's okay."

She scribbled something in her notebook.

"Why do you think Evelyn has not contacted anyone?"

"Maybe." I studied the grain of the wood on the table, its swirls and knots. "Maybe she's tired of it all. Of the lie."

My attorney shifted uncomfortably in his chair.

"She does this sometimes," I explained. "Ask her parents."

"We have. Her parents are worried."

"Evie does this, though."

"Does what?"

"Leaves."

"Leaves to go where?"

"She's always looking for something."

"Can you explain?"

"Once, she hid at her family's lakeside cabin for a week. I was the only one who knew. She said she needed space to collect her thoughts, find herself. She was big into that stuff. She ended up finding herself by having a party. She called the party 'Missing' and pasted her face all over the walls." I traced the swirls of the wood with my finger. "Missing," I muttered.

Officer Calvet looked at my lawyer and back at me. She waited. She was good at this.

I exhaled. "She got caught and escorted home by the police. Her parents considered Evie's disappearance a call for help and gave her a new car. I think they missed the point of it. *Missing*."

"Missing," Officer Calvet said and wrote something in her notebook. "Why do you think Evelyn did that?"

"I think she's lonely. And *missing* gives her a distraction from that."

"And you think this might be one of those times?"

I shrugged. The red light on the camera blinked.

"What about other times Evelyn went missing?"

"Not counting now?" I asked.

"Not counting now."

"I don't know. She'd just leave, but after *Missing*, people stopped paying attention."

"Did you stop paying attention?"

"No. She was my friend."

"Were you her friend?"

"I'm here."

"Where do you think she is?" Officer Calvet tilted her head to the side.

"Maybe with the backpackers we met before."

"They are not with her. We caught up to them."

My stomach tightened.

"What do you think happened to Evelyn?"

"I don't," I said.

"You don't?" Officer Calvet asked.

"I don't think *anything* happened," I said. "It's Evie. *Poof.*"

We slipped into that silence again. I closed my eyes and imagined the way Evie looked when the morning light split open the darkness. So calm and happy. Enough.

Officer Calvet tapped her pen. "You see, people just don't *poof*. They leave things behind." She placed the pen on the table. "And I find those things."

She spread out the pages full of Evie's Instagram in front of me. "Why this trip? Why travel with you if you're not even here?"

"She wanted to be extraordinary. That's not hard to do next to me," I explained. And there it was: Officer Calvet gave me the *she-needs-some-major-counseling* look. I was fine, though, with me.

"Traveling was another checkmark on her list of ways to be extraordinary. With Evie, sometimes, it was just easier to go along with things."

"It sounds like Evelyn always got what she wanted."

I shrugged. "I don't think she knows what she wants."

"What do you want?"

"To go home. That's what I've wanted from the time we got on the airplane."

Something sparked in Officer Calvet's eyes. "Your mom and dad are worried."

"Yes." I thought of my dad, the only one to help my mom now. For as far back as I could remember, I'd helped with her care. We couldn't afford to bring in a nurse. I wondered how Dad was organizing his work schedule. My trip here was a logistical feat on his part.

I shouldn't have come.

I leaned my forehead on the table. It was cool and smelled a little bit like lemon pine cleaner.

"Are you okay?" Officer Calvet asked.

I sat up. "Sorry. Yes."

"The thing is . . . There was no sunrise tour the day Evie posted that post—*Going to see the sunrise*—on Instagram. You see, the tour is pretty off-and-on, depending on whether the Jeep is working, whether anybody signs up."

I shrugged. "She could've walked. I walk every morning, to watch the sunrise."

Officer Calvet looked at the pages again. "Evelyn doesn't seem the type of girl to do things on her own."

"Evie wanted to stick to a schedule. No cancelled tour would change that."

"You're saying she did the sunrise on her own?"

"I guess. Or with the others. She's the one who posted on Instagram that she was going."

Officer Calvet looked at Evie's post and sighed.

I picked at a hangnail and felt the weight of sadness build up in me. "She was convinced that this trip would matter . . . would change things."

"Did it?" Officer Calvet asked.

That was a stupid question. "Yes. Yes, it did."

"What did it change?"

"Everything."

"Can you be more specific?"

I'd never felt so tired before in my life. The air in the room pressed down on me, my shoulders, the base of my neck. "I think the places we've seen on this trip are extraordinary and some people are, too. Very few people, though. I think Evie finally got it on this trip."

"Got what?"

"The difference between real and Instagram."

PRESUMED DEAD
NOW

I t's like backpackers' *Where's Waldo?* Evie's signature is hard to find. Signature after signature cover the walls.

Martina was interviewed so many times—bloggers, YouTubers, serious journalists, and even a high-brow camera team came down from the States to do one of those in-depth, investigative journalism shows.

They retraced Evie's and my steps.

They posted my high school photo and made it sound like I was a tag-along friend.

I refused the interviews—still do. Mostly, because all the reporters ask the same thing: *What keeps you here? Guilt? Loyalty? Hope?*

Being stuck isn't really newsworthy. It's hard to explain waiting. Even I forget why sometimes.

Also, my lawyer said until I am no longer a person of interest, it's best to stay out of the news.

At one point, Martina blocked a space on the wall with this weird clear enamel, so nobody could write their name too close to Evie's. But then somebody wrote a blog post about how the hostel had capitalized on tragedy.

"You can't win for losing," Martina said, shrugged, and stopped giving a shit. But she let me stay here and work for room and board. Keeping me on here was good for business.

Until people started to forget about me, too.

MARTINA PAYS ME BETTER NOW. I THINK IT'S because she feels sorry for me. Or she thinks it's time I moved on.

There aren't as many backpackers as before. The Desaparecido shut down. Most of the new hostels only made it a year.

A while ago, maybe a year and a half after Evie went missing, she moved from missing to presumed dead. I thought they couldn't do that for seven years, but I guess there's a way to fast-track the missing to dead. Anyway, the church searches stopped. No feds got involved. There was no suspected kidnapping, no ransom requests. I'm no longer a 'person of interest.'

But here I am.

Waiting.

Officer Calvet still stops in every now and again. She's stuck, too. I'd like to talk to her about Evie. But she just asks the wrong questions, and I don't have the energy anymore.

She orders an Americano and watches the backpackers slump in the door, sign their name. She takes her coffee with cream.

There aren't as many backpackers as before.

'Presumed dead' isn't as good for business as missing. I guess there's a line, right?

Here at La Escala, we still get a steady stream of backpackers. They order lattes with extra sugar and stare at the wall. They pretend they're not looking, but they hug their dog-eared guidebooks to their chests, highlighters out, ready to take the photo so they can check something else off their list.

They scroll through photos people have posted of the wall and try to locate Evie's signature. They pretend they think it's a joke. When they sign, they pretend it's an obligation, like kissing the Blarney Stone or something. But you can tell by the way they take care to sign just-so that they think it matters.

Signatures crowd every space of the wall.

The heart over Evie's i has been turned into a scrotum, shockingly accurate, from some guy's 'graphic signature.' It's the way of things. Kind of like bird shit on a monument.

Sometimes they'll ask me *which one is hers? or is it true? or did they ever find . . . ?* and I can tell they're embarrassed. But there's the excitement, the thrill, the mystery.

I shrug and pretend I don't know, then get sick in the bathroom.

Lore. Legend. The fading fame of the lost girl.

Even permanent marker washes out over time. Maybe when her signature fades, I can go, too.

I TALK TO MY PARENTS EVERY WEEK. IT'S A scheduled call. Martina lends me her phone if the Internet café's connection is shit or if they've closed. My phone's coverage is almost nonexistent now and its WiFi stopped working over a year ago. The café has regularly irregular hours, depending on how many backpackers spill out of the buses that arrive.

After that first conversation, after the questioning and the whole person-of-interest deal, Mom and Dad never asked me about Evie again. Mom talks about work and gardening. She tells me she's doing fine. At Christmas, they send a package of my favorite things. For my birthday, they send a card with a long letter.

Dad's usually too busy to come to the phone. But when he does, he asks if I need money.

Today, Mom sounds sad, like her words are in bubbles that float up and pop. Empty and fragile. I hold out my hand and expect one to slip through the receiver.

I tell her about the latest backpacker gimmicks, and she laughs. I talk about how they come and go—constant movement. Nobody can be still anymore, except for Dorothy. I tell her about Dorothy and how everything's 'okay.'

"When?" she asks. I can tell she's asking about me coming home.

"She's fading here," I say.

I think Mom understands I'm talking about Evie. And it scares us both that somebody can fade away, even in memory.

I say, "Mom, how are you?"

"Okay," she says, and we laugh and home tugs at me.

INTERVIEW 3
THEN

Officer Calvet clicked on the camera, introduced the people in the room, and looked at her watch. "August 13. Evelyn Yates disappeared eighteen days ago."

Eighteen days was a lifetime. I could feel my jaw tightening, temples thrumming. Tears burned my eyes. I still hadn't paid Martina for room and board. I'd missed my flight home.

Nobody spoke.

I watched Officer Calvet look through Evie's Instagram feed on her phone. You could tell it was something she'd done many times. Her expression never changed. She could've been shopping for underwear, looking at real estate prices.

"We found this two-week volunteer program at an institute for kids in foster care," I said, trying to fill the silence, imagine what she was seeing. "We'd make mud pies, jump rope. I liked being there. More than Evie."

Officer Calvet scanned the photos, paused, then returned to something she'd passed. "Here you are." She slid the phone across the desk. "I didn't realize it was you until now. You look different," she said.

My heart leapt when I looked at the picture. I was jumping rope, laughing. I hardly recognized myself, either.

"That day, it felt like forever was possible. We were free." I showed the picture to my lawyer.

"Free?" Officer Calvet asked.

"That's the thing about living with someone who's sick. It's always there."

"What's always there?" she asked.

"The end."

"The end?"

"Everything in our lives depends on time, machines, treatments. If we miss any of those, my mom's body stops working." I bit down on my lower lip. "She would've loved to go on a trip like this." I ached with guilt. How could I blow an opportunity like this? "For being stuck at home, Mom is better at living than anyone I know."

Officer Calvet pointed out the side-by-side photos. The one of me jumping rope, and next to it was the same exact pose, with Evie jumping.

She posted it on Instagram with the caption: *This is real.*

It was pathetic. My eyes burned with tears. The two photos were identical. Hers first, the lie, distorted—the second, mine, the truth. I looked at the expressions on the faces of the girls swinging the rope in Evie's picture—everything staged. Calvet had to see that.

These pictures of Evie, pretending to care, to be invested in someone else's life for once. It was too much, even for Evie. "These kids needed something Evie can't give. She broke at that place. It's hard when you realize that you simply aren't."

"Aren't what?" Officer Calvet interrupted.

I looked at my lawyer. His shirt had yellow sweat-rings from the day before. I took a sip of water that tasted like metal. My head throbbed.

Officer Calvet put the photos in front of me. "Aren't what?"

"Just . . . aren't," I said. I leaned my head on the palm of my hands. My cheeks were wet with tears. I was so ashamed for Evie.

"Why didn't you go to the authorities when she didn't show up?"

Why would I?

"When did you last talk to her?"

I thought back to the day after her birthday.

"I DON'T WANT TO MISS THE BUS." EVIE stood outside the bathroom door. I could hear the tick-tock in the tap of her toes.

"Real backpackers don't necessarily have a schedule for everything," I said through the door, hugging my knees to my chest. She was into being a 'real backpacker,' and she'd mastered it—the not-quite-filthy, not-quite-clean look with her hair pulled back in that just-right tousled way.

"You didn't drink that much wine." Only Evie could be irritated at someone for getting sick. My hangover wasn't on her travel calendar. My stomach cramped. I hated this trip.

There was silence. "I'm sorry. It's just I was so excited to head out today with the guys. We're going to do the sunrise hike tomorrow. It's supposed to be incredible."

A sunrise hike in a nowhere place . . . Check. *No doubt Evie would turn it into a divine experience.*

"Go without me. I'll meet you there. I don't need to see the sunrise. I've heard that happens every place in the world anyway."

Evie laughed—real. "You are such a grouch. It's—"

"—in the book," I interrupted. My stomach seized, and I pressed my head against the cool tile of the wall. "I will never drink again."

"Lightweight," Evie said through another laugh. "You don't mind?"

Now she was asking for permission to ditch me.

"No."

Rule #1: Don't get separated.

"Don't miss the bus tomorrow! I don't want to wait forever," she said through the door.

I felt too sick to answer.

"I'll post a picture of the sunrise. Try to get there, so we can do it together."

Silence.

"The bus leaves in fifteen. Are you sure you're okay?"

"Fine."

"You're the best."

I listened to her walk away.

"IT'S FUNNY," I SAID.

"What's funny?" Officer Calvet asked.

"I'm the one who's waiting."

There's a beat of time when we all sit with that.

Officer Calvet said, "She never posted a picture of the sunrise. You see, nobody remembers you staying behind. Youth hostels keep solid records of those who come and go. And it looks like you checked out that day. With Evelyn."

My lawyer cleared his throat. "*Looks like* doesn't sound like proof. And do you have witnesses placing my client on the bus with Evelyn Yates?"

Officer Calvet didn't flinch.

I exhaled. "I am remarkably unremarkable."

Officer Calvet paused, leaned into the table. Spider-web lines stretched from the corners of her dark eyes. She scowled in this way that her brows furrowed together and looked like they'd self-tie a knot.

"I think you know where Evelyn is."

"I don't." This was true—technically speaking.

"I think you want to tell me where Evelyn is."

I picked at a hangnail. "I think," I said, and my lawyer shook his head ever-so-slightly. "I think she's where she wants to be."

I LEANED AGAINST THE BATHROOM COUNTER and splashed water on my face. The toilet paper consisted of these scratchy, non-absorbent squares that I had to pull out of a contraption on the wall.

No three-ply.

A police officer waited outside and escorted me back to the room where everyone else waited. It smelled sour, felt stuffy. The fan on the wall moved hot air around.

"Have you seen Evelyn's journal?" Officer Calvet asked.

"Her mom and dad took everything," I said. "You were there."

"Yes, but the journal was not among her belongings."

I looked over at the blinking red light on the camera in the corner. The room swelled with silence. It felt like I was in a fish tank, trapped underwater. The pressure built, and my ears throbbed.

"The journal?" Officer Calvet repeated.

I watched as the silence slipped under the door with a hiss. "I do not have Evie's journal." This was my first lie.

"Do you have anything else to ask?" my lawyer asked the officers. "From all accounts, my client was not with her friend at the time of her disappearance. All you have is an Instagram feed of a typical teenager who loves to take selfies."

I loved how he present-tensed her. I wanted to hug him.

Calvet leveled me with her stare. "You don't call anyone. You don't look for her. You sit in that cramped hostel room. Why?"

"I'm waiting," I said, "for her to come back."

"Things simply don't add up. I will ask you again. Do you know where Evelyn has gone?"

"No," I said. This was the truth. "I do not."

Officer Calvet flinched.

My lawyer leaned on the table. "Tell me, Officer. What is the right reaction for a young woman whose friend has gone missing? Someone whose parents cannot come because of—" He paused. I didn't know if it was for effect or if he was really searching for the word. I waited, remembered to breathe. "Because of pretty serious health issues. Someone who isn't running but waiting? What else would you have my client do? Perhaps you can give us a checklist of appropriate responses according to pop psychology, and I'll make sure my client and I go through them together."

Officer Calvet looked at him, total poker face. She was back to this impassive, neutral place. She turned to me. "Evelyn's passport and phone were not in her backpack either. Do you have her phone and passport?"

"No." I ached for that phone, to see if there were more photos of me, photos that she hadn't uploaded.

"Have you seen Evelyn's passport? Her family is looking for it."

I shook my head. It was like they thought I was going to Mr. Ripley her or something.

"Have you called her?"

"No," I said.

A TIMER BUZZED. I COULDN'T EVEN SAY HOW long I'd been there in that square little room, that timeless place.

My lawyer looked at his watch, even though there was a clock hanging right in front of us. My stomach growled.

Officer Calvet turned off the recording. "We want to find Evelyn," she said. "I won't rest until we do."

That was fair, and it was the right response from a police officer. Maybe my lawyer was right. I could've asked for that checklist of ways I should've acted.

I've never been good at playing games.

"Do not leave the country."

"Under what jurisdiction?" my lawyer asked.

"I won't," I said. "I think I missed my flight." My stomach tightened again.

My lawyer looked from me to Officer Calvet. "We are done." He scooted his chair from the table and pushed himself up. He nodded at me, and I stood up.

Outside the station, he handed me his card. "Call me if you need something. Do not speak to them on your own. Ever."

"So, see you tomorrow?"

He shook his head. "We're done. They have no evidence."

Poof, I thought.

"Do you need a ride?"

I shook my head. "I like to walk."

"In this heat?" He wiped his arm across his sweaty forehead.

"Thank you." I pulled out a wad of sweaty money from my pocket. "How much?"

He wrapped my fingers around the money. He looked at me, in my eyes, for a long time. I didn't know what he wanted to see. But we just stood like that for a long time until a truck barreled past, spraying us with dust. He let go of my hand and folded himself inside his car, never looking back.

#REVIVEEVIE
NOW

That first lie, about her journal, was the hardest.

It gets easier.

This morning, it pissed rain on the way back from the sunrise. The Jeep ripped past, spraying me with muddy water. Back at the hostel, Martina fumed because I was late for checkout, and she had to do it.

She's gotten used to me now. I'm more than marketing.

When she first hired me, it was half pity, half need.

I had returned from that last interview with Officer Calvet. Martina was staring at my room, bed unpaid for, arms crossed, and I said, "What if I work for my space? Like that other girl did."

"You really are waiting for Evie?"

I shrugged.

"You know how to make those sweet coffee drinks Americans like so much?"

I nodded. "Pumpkin spice latte."

She visibly cringed. I got the job.

Being a person of interest is good for business. At least, it was.

I STRIP OFF MY WET CLOTHES, SERVE MYSELF A hot coffee.

A watery sun pushes through the clouds. I go through the rooms, stripping the beds, shaking out sheets, pillowcases. Pale light hits the dust mites, and for a moment, the room explodes with stars.

A folded, faded picture falls to the floor. It was tucked in an envelope with a letter. I open the letter. There are words that look more like art than language.

I squint at the picture. It's the Israeli girl who stayed here the past two nights. She has her arms wrapped around two friends. They're in their army uniforms, the foamy sea behind them.

They traveled together with others—all of them recently out of the army. They huddled at breakfast, early before the sunrise. There was something impenetrable about them, like being part of them would've been safe.

They scoffed at the wall, pointed to Evie's name. Someone said something. They laughed.

Evie meant nothing to them.

Evie has started to not matter, and it leaves a deep ache.

The girl saw me watching them. She looked at the name and shook her head. She half-smiled at me. An apology?

They didn't pay for the sunrise tour. Like me, they walked to the trailhead. I followed behind. The girl waited for me when I stopped to tie my shoe, and they let me catch up. When we got to the bluff, we made our way past the tourists and sat, waiting for the sun to rise.

Before, you could sit right at the edge, feet dangling into nothingness. We edged as close as we could to the fence and waited.

There's always a moment that I think it might not happen, when I think the darkness will stay forever.

Then fingers of light stretch across the canyon floor. The sun breaks through the darkness and glows orange on my face.

I breathe again.

Extraordinary.

This morning, the guide from the Jeep was a little flashier than normal, passing around the hot chocolate and fresh pastries. He hates when people just go to the sunrise. He hates losing business and thinks I tell others they can just walk.

I don't. Because I usually like to do this alone.

But this morning, it felt different being with others—others who didn't care about her. I pulled out some fruit and offered it to the group of Israelis.

They shared what they had—mostly leftovers from this morning's breakfast. But it was perfect. Everything tasted better.

Then they left. The girl waved goodbye, and they were gone. *Poof.*

The tour group stayed longer than usual. We all watched the way light filled everything. I smelled the storm first. Across the canyon, streaks of gray poured from black clouds. I shrugged on an old rain jacket and started back. Walking as fast as I could.

But you can't outrun a storm.

BACK IN MY ROOM, I TAKE THE LETTER OUT OF the envelope and unfold it next to the faded picture of the Israeli girls. I read it without reading it. Whoever wrote it didn't push their pen so hard that the words bubbled up. Every space on the page is filled with words, but it doesn't look urgent. Just peaceful.

I think she'll miss this, regret leaving it behind.

It's a treasure.

I trace the letters of the Hebrew alphabet. They feel like another world, another possibility.

I tuck the letter and photo in my notebook and slip them back under the loose floorboard, next to Evie's journal. I never gave the journal to Evie's family or the Embassy. How can you put someone's truth in an evidence bag?

"DIDN'T YOU GO TO CARSON HIGH?" THE girl signs in at the reception desk. She's vaguely familiar. But everybody kind of feels familiar when they're backpackers.

It's been a while, though, since somebody pretends to know me. She hands me her passport, and I feel the familiar tightening at the base of my neck, clenching every nerve, working its way up, squeezing my temples.

"I'm Caitlyn. With a C," she says, which is unnecessary. I have her passport.

I steady my breathing and hand her a fresh towel. "Checkout is at 11 A.M. You can sign up for the sunrise tour here. Here's the price." My voice is steady.

"You were Evie Yates's friend, right?"

"Am," I say.

"No way. You're the one who traveled with her, right?"

"Yes." I scowl.

"You're still here."

"Yes."

She looks like she's found the Lost City of Atlantis. She takes out her phone and snaps a picture of me. "That's kind of cheating, but I can get extra points." She looks really pleased with herself.

"Please, don't," I say.

"Oh. Sorry. Do you mind?" She's so wrapped up in her phone, posting something, scanning, laughing, she doesn't notice I slip an extra bill out of her wallet. "There are lots who do the route now. It's a thing."

"What route?" I ask. My face feels hot. "Extra points?" I'm trying to see her phone but not see.

"The Revive Route." She shows me her feed, and it's like looking into Evie's feed from a couple years ago—the same photos, same poses, hashtags, clothes.

#ReviveEvie.

"Jesus," I mutter. My throat aches.

"That volunteer place with those kids has stopped taking volunteers. I'll be one of the last to complete the circuit. 'Hashtag CloneEvie.'"

"Clone Evie?"

Dorothy walks in the front door. A gust of wind rips the door from her hand and bangs it against the wall. Martina steps out of her office and scowls. The glass chatters, settles. Nothing is broken.

Dorothy is completely unperturbed. She shrugs her daypack off and sits at the café counter. She half-waves and takes out a thick book to read.

I exhale and turn my attention back to Caitlyn. With a C.

"How does it end?" I ask, feeling like my nerves are on fire.

"What?" Caitlyn asks.

"The route?"

Caitlyn's lost in her feed again. "Extra points," she says. She smiles wide and clicks off her phone.

"How does the route end?" I ask again.

"You won't tell?" She leans over the counter, and I can smell tuna fish on her breath.

"Who would I tell?"

She shrugs. She looks at her phone, and I can tell she wants to look at the feed and likes and shares. "When you get back to Carson, you've got to spend the night in a coffin. They buried her a couple of months ago."

"Buried what?"

"Air. I dunno. Maybe wanted closure or something." Her phone is back on—the screen reflected in her glasses. She turns on her heel and heads toward the wall.

I barely make it to the bathroom before I get sick.

But something lifts when I lean against the wall, sink down to the floor. "Evie is back," I say to myself. "A feed of reviving Evie. She's never even gone." Hundreds of others keeping her trending, alive. I half-laugh, half-cry, and curl up into a ball. The wait is over.

"ARE YOU OKAY?" DOROTHY ASKS ME AFTER I return from the bathroom.

"I'm okay." Okay isn't such a bad thing. Maybe Dorothy's onto something.

"Your wrist looks like it hurts."

There's a blistery rash. I nod. "Just an allergy." I pull down my sleeve and serve her a double espresso. "Do you like this drink a lot?"

She shrugs. "It's okay."

God, I love Dorothy.

THE NEXT MORNING, DOROTHY'S BACKPACK IS leaning against the reception counter.

"Why did you stay so long?" I ask.

"It's a thing I do."

"What do you mean?"

"I stay in places most don't . . . just to feel them. The okay places."

A gimmick. Dorothy has a gimmick.

"Where to?" I ask.

"Following the route," she says.

"North or south?"

"North."

"Have an okay trip," I say.

She doesn't catch on, so I'm left laughing on my own.

She turns to leave then pauses. She signs her name on the wall, which surprises me. Maybe, though, she's worried that she'll be forgotten like everybody else. Her signature is small, precise. She checks her watch and dates the signature.

A gimmick. A signature. Just like everyone else.

THE TRUTH
THEN

I watched my lawyer drive away, tires spitting gravel on a strip of infinite highway. His car became a dot on the horizon. *Poof.*

His card was rounded at the corners, fuzzy, like it'd been stuck in his wallet for ages. I looked at his name. I hadn't even bothered to learn it.

Other than his name and a phone number, it was blank. There was no sage advice, no pithy quote. I wanted to ask him how to live with the truth. If anybody knew, it would be a lawyer.

Officer Calvet stood inside the station, watching me through dusty windows.

I was alone with this now, with what I knew.

IT WAS ALREADY ALMOST NINETY DEGREES, and the sun wasn't even up. The air shimmered with heat.

"I knew you'd make it." Evie smiled and nodded toward the horizon.

Light punched through purple clouds in orange streaks. Evie spread her arms wide, like she was capable of holding the sunrise. Her face was bright and peaceful. "This is everything," she said. She looked to me and pressed her forefinger to her lips.

Her eyes betrayed her surprise before she closed them. Her bracelet snagged on scrub brush in her silent descent.

I pressed myself against the cliff wall and swallowed the scream, swallowed what happened, and what I was going to have to do.

ERASING EVIE
NOW

Evie.

Swoopy E with a heart over the i, instead of a normal dot, which probably seems obnoxious to everybody, except those who knew Evie.

A sliver of fiery sun cuts through the purple dawn.

The first brushstroke is hard, like a betrayal. But then it gets easier, pushing the roller across the wall, paint covering everything, erasing Evie.

I don't need to sign to exist. My story matters.

I clasp the bracelet on my wrist, shrug my backpack on, and walk into the morning—the air already bending with a haze of heat. The sun will rise. It always does.

Light fills me as I walk away.

NOTHING BEGINS UNTIL YOU GROW
KAYE HART

The first three times the boy visited the garden, he didn't notice how there was always a convenient patch of moss to sit on, or how the flowers bloomed a little extra brightly when he came near. It didn't seem extraordinary, or strange, how the vines moved in the wind as if they were trying to reach out to him. Or how the leaves rustling could almost be a voice, if he listened close enough.

He wasn't listening. Or he was, but to endless streams of music on old tinny headphones that had seen their best days two years ago. And beyond that, he was listening with his soul to songs much darker than the garden's.

". . . Back again, V," he said.

The boy didn't know why he'd taken to calling the garden V. He wasn't even entirely sure he was talking to the garden at all. Just to *someone*. To the universe, perhaps. To himself, most likely. But each day he'd find himself drawn back, ditching friends that laughed a little too loud and drank a little too much. Friends who cared more about their laughter than his struggle.

"Do you ever feel . . . like you're changing?" he asked the garden. "Even when you thought you were done? Like . . . for some reason all the things that made so much sense to you, don't make sense anymore?"

There was no reply, of course. He sat among the flowerbeds and looked out onto the street and sighed, running a hand through his newly-cropped hair. Underneath the old band shirt he wore, his binder dug in just below his ribs. He'd wanted to get something full-length. Might have done, if he hadn't had very sudden other expenses.

"Yeah. Me too, V. Me too," he said, as if the garden had heard him, and understood.

It would be so easy if that was how it was. If every time he spoke, people just . . . got it. Got why he used different pronouns now. Or why he couldn't go back home like everyone else at the end of a long day of too much of nothing at all.

No sixteen-year-old expected to lose their home so suddenly. Or if they prepared for it, as he had . . . even then, the blow was harsh and unrelenting, not just once with a clean cut, but over and over again as all of the little things he couldn't do now struck him.

Sometimes it felt like those strikes were the only thing keeping him rooted to the rest of the world. Reminders that they hurt because he was still human, not the monstrous thing his parents considered him to be.

A stray gust of wind blew one of the trailing vines from the garden wall across his shoulder in an awkward, one-armed hug, but he detached from it gently, pushing it away.

"I'm not the sort of person that's made to be touched. I'm not solid enough. I'll only crumble."

No more wind. No more vines. Just sad sighs as air rushed through the gaps in the trellis. He felt like joining them, and yet he hadn't cried a single tear since his parents had thrown him out. Boys didn't cry, and he was allowed to be a boy now.

And yet he wasn't allowed to be anything else.

Certainly not a child.

He stood, looking at a garden that wasn't made for the likes of him, and turned away. That was all he had now. Stolen moments and things that belonged to other people. Worn sofas and leftovers and pitying stares from overprotective mothers. He never knew if they pitied him for his parents' rejection or his parents for having a 'broken' child.

A deep breath brought him to the edge of the garden, where the sanctuary became the real world. For a moment he stood with a foot in both, feeling so distinctly the separation between the two that he could have sworn he'd stepped through a portal to another dimension.

"See you again, V. Same time next week? I'm sorry we've had to cut down. I miss seeing you on weekdays."

If he survived to next week. If the bits of food he scrounged from friends and the nights he managed to wrangle an invite to stay over were enough.

His father had always warned him against finding a man that couldn't stand on his own two feet. That couldn't provide for himself, and was always waiting for someone to come and save him, do the laundry for him, cook and clean. He hadn't wanted a son-in-law that was a waste of space, he'd said.

He never said anything about having a son that was.

Of course he could do those things. But they got a lot harder when there was no washing machine to put the laundry in, and no stove for the cooking.

Slowly, reluctantly, he stepped away from the plants and their accepting looks, and back into the world where the looks became harsher and more concerned, and even the kind people had something to say, some opinion on who he was.

It wasn't an opinion.

It was a fact.

THE WORLD DID ITS THING. BIT BY BIT, IT ATE him up, stealing a word here and a word there, or that little smile he'd always thought would never leave him. The love of things left him, too. The hobbies he had no money to fund anymore. The friends who slowly drifted away from him as they realized he wasn't what he used to be.

They thought it was him coming out.

'You've changed.' Over and over again. *You've changed.* And he had. He'd changed so much, become so bitter and jaded and not the person he'd been before. But it had nothing to do with his gender, and everything to do with all of the times the world twisted and molded him into their perfect vision of a trans man.

The Gender Identity Clinic, that wanted a piece of his soul for every visit. That asked him what toys he played with as a child and how he liked to dress and whether he wore makeup, as if any of that had anything to do with what being a man was. The woman from the housing place that wanted him to confirm, over and over again, the story of how his parents had told him to never darken their doorstep again. The mental health team, that quizzed and quizzed him about the difference between gender dysphoria and a child simply playing pretend. That asked him delicately about trauma he'd never experienced and that, even if he had, would have no bearing on him knowing in his heart that this body was the wrong one.

He wanted to scream at all of them until his lungs gave out that this wasn't how it was supposed to be. That it wasn't who he was that caused him pain, but the world's refusal to accept it.

And through it all, there was the garden, V. The peace and tranquility. The way it always felt as though it was there for him, though the trees and the vines and the flowers had existed long before him and would exist long after. He walked through the gates and checked on the flowers, not daring to pull any weeds, but bringing a little watering can that he filled from the water fountain near the park. And it felt like V was waiting. Listening willingly to his endless rambling about school and the many teams that claimed to be there to protect his welfare and yet left him feeling more empty and broken, appointment by appointment.

In autumn, he got a temporary placement in a flat. And there was no one left to tell. There was no one left to laugh with him, to show around the flat proudly as he fixed it up with some bad DIY and even worse furniture. There was no one to laugh, or at least cringe with when he discovered a pair of lace panties down the drain that was stopping the water going through, presumably from the previous owner.

So he wadded up the underwear without a single ounce of awkward laughter and threw them in with the rest of the rubbish, washing his hands repeatedly until they felt clean again. The underwear would give his new neighbor, the guy who couldn't seem to figure out whether to check him out or fist-bump him when they met, something to think about.

"I wish you were here, V."

That wasn't quite true, but the truth was something he couldn't really say aloud—he wished he was there, with V, instead. He wished he could build a home among the flowers and vines and the trees, and have a friend that he could sit and talk to, day in, day out. Instead of the rattle of an old washing machine and the low hum of a heater that did absolutely nothing to heat the room. He'd gotten rid of the staff that helped him find the place now, thankfully, only to replace the small bossy woman with a thirty-year-old man who thought he was 'down with the kids' because he asked what boybands they liked and knew a bunch of skateboarding terms that he used incorrectly.

There was something about being an adult way before your time that felt like skipping a step on a set of instructions. Sure, you could get to the end, but there'd always be that one part of the structure that wobbled a bit every now and again, because there was nothing to fill the gap where it should have been.

He spent a few nights in the new flat before he went to see V again. It felt different, somehow. The leaves were turning orange on the trees, and different plants showed their heads compared to the ones there in summer. But the soul of the place was the same.

"How do you do that, V?" He sat down on a rock that he could have sworn wasn't there last time and looked around. No litter, no kids hanging out. Just him and the garden. Same as always. "How do you keep your soul the same when the outside changes?"

People looked at V and saw all the different plants. The yellowing leaves. The change of the seasons drifting past, and forgot to see how V moved the same way in the wind. How the peace was the same. How even when every plant that grew right that second was replaced, V would still be the garden.

It was the same for him. He hadn't changed, he'd always been this. Only no one could see it before.

A flower bloomed near him. Blue, with white closer to the center. He didn't know what it was called. But he knew enough to know it shouldn't bloom that fast, all of a sudden.

He looked up, glancing about the trees for some trick, or trap, or some street magician toying with him. It would be just his luck to come to his only safe place and find it invaded by the rest of the world. But cameras hidden in the trees would still give themselves away with a flash of the lens, or a light indicating they were on. There was none of that. And the only people he caught sight of were far away, distracted by phones or conversations.

"If you're messing with me, you can come out now. I'm not in the mood. And I don't give permission for you to use this on some stupid TV show. My father's a lawyer."

The last part was true, but had no bearing on the subject. No one watching needed to know that, however. His father had taught him that. It didn't matter what you actually had up your sleeve, only what people thought was up there. A dangerous game, but it paid off for his father in the courtroom over and over again as witnesses confessed vital information and criminals fell over their own feet to tell lies.

But there was silence. No apologetic cameramen. No overly chirpy host trying to play things up for the camera. So he slowly looked down at the flower. It stayed in full bloom, defying him, daring him to pretend it wasn't real.

Gently, not wanting to disturb the beauty of the garden, he touched the petals, checking for invisible string or . . . whatever else could be there.

He'd never touched a part of the garden like this before. Sure, he'd brushed leaves from his jacket, or felt the grass under his bare feet in the summer when he needed to feel connected to something, anything. But to touch the flowers had felt like sacrilege. They were so beautiful, and so fragile. Not made for clumsy hands like his.

Now he did, though, and held back his amazement at the softness of it under his fingertips. The way he could have sworn it trembled slightly in the breeze. It was so delicate that he could see and feel the tiny little veins in the leaves, see the little marks on the petals where the light had absorbed a little differently and edited the color.

It was real, then. There was no way that something with this much detail could be fake.

Feeling beyond stupid, he took a breath.

"Is that okay, V? I don't want to hurt you."

No reply. But he could have sworn the vine that hesitated over his shoulder was held there by something other than the wind and a piece of trellis it was stuck on.

" . . . I feel a bit stupid." Saying it out loud helped a little. Even if there was a camera filming somewhere nearby, hopefully they'd take pity on the poor mentally ill kid talking to the garden and think no one would want to watch the footage after all. "You can't hear me. But I like talking to you anyway. I like sharing my day. And sometimes I imagine what you'd say back. Like, just now you'd say something warm and comforting. Like 'If it helps, you should keep on doing it.'" He paused. "But better than that, since I figure you're way smarter than me."

Wouldn't be that hard to achieve that, though. At least not according to his teachers. Bit by bit since the first year of school his grades had dropped further and further, to the point where every piece of homework now came back with the ominous two words written on it. There was nothing quite like the fear, at first, of 'See Me' in red pen . . . But now he thought he'd be more afraid if something came back without it.

At least they'd stopped asking him if there were problems at home. Because, of course, everyone knew there were. Everyone knew that he was the freak kid, the guy whose parents didn't even want him. Or at least only wanted him under specific circumstances that he couldn't meet.

The argument in the counselor's office about switching schools had been hard. The desperation, way before he gave up on ever having the help he needed, back when he thought if he just said the right words and behaved the right way they might do something to help him. Being told over and over that he couldn't change schools. He couldn't leave the place where everyone called him by the wrong name and there was still a mocking tone to it when they were forced to use the right one . . . Why? Because he needed to focus on his exams. It was the wrong time to switch schools. Didn't he care about his education?

The honest answer to that had always been no. But they wouldn't hear that, either. No one wanted to know that the idea of following in his father's illustrious footsteps made him want to gag, that he preferred taking things apart and fixing them to filling out paperwork and harassing people into telling him the truth.

"Most people are smarter than me. They used to deny it, my parents . . . But that all went out of the window when they didn't give a damn about my feelings anymore."

He pulled a face, sitting back, careful to avoid damaging any of the plant life.

"I know you'd probably say something like 'that's not them telling the truth, that's them being cruel' . . . But the thing is, they're my parents, you know? They're supposed to know me better than anyone else. They're supposed to have seen me grow up, and they think they get it. They think they get it and they just don't."

V got it. But V was a collection of plants with no voice and no ability to yell at everyone for him. He had to do that himself. Make people see, all alone. Make them realize he was just a guy trying to live his life.

He didn't want to perform masculinity for a crowd waiting to poke holes in everything he did. He didn't want to have to explain repeatedly that that one picture of him in a dress for a school recital didn't mean that he'd been a girl and changed his mind one day. He didn't even want to explain that he wouldn't even be sure that that was some terrible crime. Who said gender was fixed forever in one place, unchanging? And who said gender had anything to do with his clothes?

. . . *They* did.

As he'd come out, slowly his wardrobe had melted into grays and blacks and dark depths that reflected the life around him. Because that was what he had to be, to make them listen. To let them know that he was really who he said he was.

He picked at the edge of his shirt, a ratty gray t-shirt that he wouldn't have been caught dead in before, but that guarded him better than anything he would actually want to wear could have. It was a trade-off. It always would be. Did he want to be respected for the gender he was, or did he want to be respected for who he was as a person? His personality.

"V, if you had the choice, what would you do? Would you still bloom like you always did? Would you be yourself? Or would you hide all of your color to be taken seriously?"

With his eyes squeezed tightly shut, he didn't see the movement. And it was too light to hear.

But when he looked up, the world had stopped. Amongst the autumn leaves, the changing of the seasons, grew endless blooming flowers. The colors swirled before his eyes, turning like a kaleidoscope. If he'd have thought properly, he would have liked his last words before he blacked out to be something a little more profound, but as it was, he heard his own voice murmur:

"I swear to God if someone spiked me somehow . . ."

And then nothing.

If he'd fainted in the flat, he would have woken up surrounded by fussing and ambulance staff, most likely. They kept an eye on the tenants in the building. Most of them were prone to committing crimes of some sort. But for him all it meant was that if he got into trouble, it was pretty certain someone would find him.

So it did feel a bit strange when he regained consciousness not to noise and fuss, but incredible calmness and peace.

"Well, I know I'm not dead . . ."

He didn't, but even if the experiences after death reflected those in life, he always figured that they'd be a little more fire and brimstone-y. And not really involve V.

He sat up. The flowers, all of the blooms had gone. But now there was something new entirely. Fruit, juicy and big, of all kinds, growing on the branches of each tree. His mouth watered.

If he'd been thinking straight, if his mind hadn't felt so hazy, he would have been too uncomfortable to so much as touch any of the fruit, let alone pluck a piece from the nearby tree and take a bite. But when he did . . .

It was beyond sweet. The kind of fruit that made him doubt the convictions of his five-year-old self, who had proudly proclaimed that Eve was really stupid, giving up peace and happiness for a bit of fruit.

"Is this how I become eternally damned or something? Is that what this is?"

He wasn't sure if he cared. He ate, quietly, savoring the fruit.

"Well, thanks, anyway. I . . . uhh . . . I don't get much to eat, you know? In general? I mean, people's mothers fed me before, but I think now I've got a flat, they assume it's okay, because I'm not having to stay on their sofas. Anyway, it's not like I can live on fruit, but . . . it's nice to have something." He paused. "Don't get me wrong. I have food. At the food bank, and things. But half of it is in tins and my tin opener only works half of the time. And the other half needs cooking. Haven't paid my electric yet since my money didn't come in. So they cut it off."

It felt as natural as it ever did, telling the garden about his life. And yet somehow it was more personal. As strange as it felt, he had a response. A reply. The garden wasn't just an empty object to pour all of his bizarre thoughts and ideas into . . . it was listening.

That should have felt dangerous. It should have made him feel watched. That he had told all of his personal fears and thoughts to what he had assumed was an inanimate object, only to be known, truly and deeply, by it instead. But all of his usual fears and wariness battled within him, fighting a much larger enemy they could never defeat: loneliness.

He had never understood how people could latch on to anyone and anything the way so many of his friends had done. How a brief fling with someone they didn't even like turned into intense fear that such a person would ever leave them. But he did, more than anything, understand how all of the frightening, scary things—like the prospect of being hurt or killed—paled in comparison to the all-encompassing, yawning pit of emptiness inside him. Holes that should have been filled by people, communication, love, companionship . . . were left empty and gaping.

"V?"

This time his question was met with a gentle rustle. A quiet confirmation: *I'm here.*

"If you don't have anyone in the world you interact with . . . if you're drifting through, never really having an impact on anyone, or letting them have an impact on you . . . Does it really matter if you're real or not? How do you tell? How do I know if I'm real, V?"

71

The tears fell, wet on his cheeks. Boys don't cry. But people did. Scared people, broken people. Alone people. He tried to wipe them away, the shame driving his hand. But when he did, he met with quiet resistance. A vine. Not forcing, not trapping, but in his way.

He swore softly and moved away, but even as he did so he felt a stab of guilt. The garden was his friend.

"I'm sorry. I . . . I think sometimes when people touch me, it's like I'm suddenly aware of how real they are. And how intangible I am. It feels like I've got to keep up the illusion. To be so grounded and so real and not at all fantastical that they can't possibly doubt me." He snorted softly. "The counselor said I might be overcompensating, but I'm pretty sure she didn't realize quite how much."

Everything was so abstract, in his mind. Even now, as he brushed his growing hair out of his eyes—he'd have to get that cut soon—the world was distant and strange. If he narrated it all, bit by bit, he wouldn't have to live it.

. . . And there he was, doing it again.

Aloud was better. Aloud at least meant some implication of someone, somewhere, hearing. Not some bizarre internal pantomime where even the pretend voices with their exaggerated expressions couldn't make it out into the real world.

The one with the garden that listened to him, and gave him fruit and tried to offer its own, strange form of comfort.

He really was going mad.

"V . . ." He was laughing before he even got to the rest of the question, but V didn't seem to mind. "Would you tell me if I was going mad?"

The answer, of course, was 'no.' How would the poor collection of plants even know what a mad human looked like compared to a sane one? And beyond that, how would it know how to express such a judgment if it had one?

Bizarrely, the thought was reassuring. He could be as strange as he liked, here, with no psychological assessments, no unnecessary labels. No opinions imprinted on his heart from well-meaning, concerned stares. It didn't matter what he was.

He reached up a hand to pet the vine nearest him, feeling it shiver happily under his touch. There was no explanation for that feeling. Why it should feel so real, so solid, when it was just leaf matter and stem.

"I think I am, you know. Going mad. But I also think everyone does. Maybe that's what the world does to everyone who doesn't fit in. I've never met a single person who wasn't weird in some way, and yet we're all trying to fit these impossible standards. But I think I'm losing it. I think I'm really losing it this time, and the only thing tethering me to earth is a garden that shouldn't even be able to do half of the things it does."

The vine slowly and gently petted him back.

He could have laughed. All of the appointments, all of the chaos, and he was losing his mind in a garden.

THIS TIME, AS HE ENTERED HIS BUILDING, turned the key in the battered lock, and tried not to snag his foot on the equally battered doormat, he didn't walk in empty. Confused. Scared. But not empty.

And when he ran into the guy in the flat next door, the look was the same. That same little crease between eyebrows that were surprisingly light compared to dark hair. The same confusion.

But somehow, it no longer looked like a glare, or anything sinister. Just . . . a guy.

For the first time, he quietly lifted his hand in greeting. There was an awkward moment where neither of them did anything, but then a sort of startled delight came into the other guy's eyes.

They had to be around the same age.

"Uhh . . . hey man. The . . . the door's kind of been a bit janky, but the caretaker said he'd sort it out? Wouldn't count on anything though." The guy ran a hand through his hair awkwardly.

It was the most mundane conversation in the world, but outside of official appointments and planned responses, he hadn't said a word to anyone in weeks, perhaps months. And now, here the opportunity was. Connection. With a human being.

And he couldn't find the words. All of the sounds stuck in his throat, so he just stood there, staring blankly at the guy in his jeans and ratty old Converse. He watched the delight fade into awkwardness across the guy's face, and felt a familiar surge of shame rise up in his chest, sickening him.

The guy began to turn away, awkwardly, apologetically, as if the act of talking had been an unforgivable mistake. Watching the awkwardness and confusion was too much, so he looked away. If he spoke now it would only make him look ridiculous.

". . . Uhh. If you don't understand English or something I could mime?"

There it was again. The guy's voice. Breaking through the chaos in his brain with a delicate touch.

He remembered the flowers in V's garden unfolding their petals, the riot of color. Their answer: Be You.

"If I didn't understand English, to be fair, I probably wouldn't understand what you were offering, either." The murmured words came out of his mouth involuntarily, pulled by unseen forces, and heat rose to his cheeks. He tried to get away, walk up the stairs. If he could avoid ever seeing this guy again, that would be great.

Then he saw the relief flash across the other guy's face.

"Thank God. My miming is shit. I'm Oscar."

There was a collection of letters that existed on his forms. There was another collection of letters he had been so excited to choose for himself, that he had thought long and hard about and felt connected to in a way he never had the first set. But the excitement had faded. The connection had faded. He wasn't anything now. Names were for real things.

". . . Kyran."

He couldn't say the 'I'm' in front of it. Couldn't commit to that, although he had many times before, in the moments before he'd stopped existing.

"Uhh . . . not being like, weird or anything, but are you alright?"

"I'm . . ."

Fine. Fine. Just say fine. Just keep this conversation friendly and normal and go back to your flat with the knowledge that some guy doesn't forever think you're a weirdo.

The silence stretched between them, and Oscar looked more uncomfortable as it grew. It was that discomfort that saved him from having to give a reply, as Oscar blurted out:

"Sorry if I make you feel weird. I make people feel weird. Like, I'm pretty sure that's why I'm in this hole, you know? Like if I'd just been a bit more normal then maybe I wouldn't need all of this and maybe there'd be a better place for me."

His laugh sounded empty and strange, echoing in his ears like something long-forgotten. "Oscar? . . . I don't think you're the one that has to worry about weird."

Oscar stalled for a moment. "You sure? Because, I mean. I can totally understand if you want to just . . . pretend this isn't happening. Hasn't happened. If I weird you out, it's totally fine. Totally."

The number of 'totally's in that sentence should have been a linguistic nightmare, but actually it felt sort of endearing. And reassuring. Someone else, who was a little more than just shy of perfect.

Kyran shook his head.

"No, I . . . this is the most normal interaction I've had . . . in a long time, actually."

The way Oscar's face lit up, it was as if Kyran had paid him the biggest compliment of his life. And perhaps he had. The flats were for the unwanted kids. Always had been. Too old for anyone to care much about their plight, too young for them to fight back by themselves. Briefly, he wondered what darkness had to exist in someone's soul for them to reject something as soft and delicate as Oscar.

He took a deep breath, considered his options. Normal conversation, check. Someone not looking at him like they needed to fix him, check.

" . . . Oscar? Do you want to come inside a moment?"

Not the wisest move, really. Who knew why the guy was here, what terrible crime had forced him away from his family. But still, Kyran's heart sank as Oscar shook his head slowly, his face twisted into an apologetic grimace.

"Can't. My sister's coming in a bit. She broke up with this guy . . . well, he was kind of married so it was bound to happen anyway, but . . . Yeah."

The silence stretched. Kyran tested out his own name in his mind as though it was entirely new to him. It felt entirely new.

"That's alright. I don't want to get in the way of . . . family things."

There might have been a hint of bitterness in his reply, and that could have been why Oscar's discomfort grew. All of Kyran's ability to read normal human emotion seemed to have left him, leaving him to improvise.

Oscar cleared his throat. "Well, I . . . I just mean . . . I'd like to? At some point? If the offer's open? Like, I don't really know anyone here yet and the girl downstairs looks like she'll stab me if I ask her about any of it."

Kyran had thought the same about Oscar, but he didn't mention it. Even he knew that wasn't the way to make friends. Instead he thought of the girl in question, and stifled a laugh. He could definitely see where Oscar was coming from.

"Yeah, the offer's open. Just . . . knock? If you're free. I'm out a lot, but . . ."

'I'm out a lot' evidently sounded better than 'I can't stand the endless emptiness of my flat so I escape to a garden I'm not even sure I'm supposed to be in,' since Oscar looked mildly impressed. He nodded eagerly. "I don't want to disturb you . . . but . . . I can knock? There's a peephole so if you . . . you know, change your mind, you could just ignore the knocking."

What, he wondered, had made Oscar so sure to tell him that? As though somehow he, Oscar, wasn't worthy to be in Kyran's presence except as an afterthought? As he let himself into his flat, he kept wondering about it. What did Oscar see that he didn't? Was all of the kindness a misunderstanding that would fall down around their ears once Oscar realized that he wasn't some popular socialite, but an oddity who could barely hold down his own identity?

He asked V as much on his next visit, as he placed himself not on the grass in the center for once, but among the flowers, careful not to disrupt any of them. Poured out his soul the way he always did.

"I met a guy the other day, V. After I left. Well, I knew him before, but we actually spoke this time. And perhaps you can't really know someone until you speak to them. Or . . . I guess . . . communicate? It must be easier being a plant. Never having to find the right words, no misunderstandings . . . just survival. In the end, all you have to do is grow."

His last words echoed around the space. He wondered absently why it was so different for plants. Why they could pare down their basic needs in a science class with a silly acronym of only a few letters, while human psychology seemed to require knowledge beyond any logical capability.

"Is it really that much better to be human? They always say so, those scientists. Greater forms of life, greater intelligence. But I want to know what's so intelligent about a race with so much confusion in it that half of us don't even know what we need. You seem pretty smart to me, V. Living your life, not bothering anyone."

He found himself leaning against the trunk of a tree. It no longer bore fruit, and in fact, there was no evidence of his little escapade that day at all. Not in the blooms, or the way the garden moved. But somehow he knew in his heart it was still there. Listening.

"I don't even know what to do when someone talks to me, anymore. They should have scripts for those things, that we can read and learn in advance so that when someone says something we don't stumble through the conversation, leaving destruction everywhere."

He traced the veins on a nearby leaf with a gentle finger. The words felt strange, out loud. Maybe that was it. That notion that when he spoke, it could be heard. Not endless monologues in his own mind, but out loud. Having a voice. Having a say.

"Do you ever miss not having a voice, V? Is it different for you, or do you sometimes have something you want to say and wonder why the words won't quite come out? Here I am, talking about how difficult it is to get my intentions across, and you don't have any of that at all. Perhaps you're stuck, frustrated, wanting to express something really important, and I just can't hear you."

The usual movement in the garden—wind, leaves rustling, and so on—seemed to cease. In his mind he imagined V, holding itself so very still.

". . . I'm sorry, V. I didn't even think of it being hard for you. I didn't think that—"

The vine wrapped around his wrist gently, much like a human would put a hand on him to stop him. His father had done that, when he was a child. When the thoughts became too much, and he began babbling nonsense, his father would reach out and hold onto him, as though the pressure could keep the words inside.

And all of a sudden, it was too much again. Flashing images of the disgust on his father's face assaulted his vision, making it impossible to think of anything else. He imagined what it would take to make others reject him too. Some people were already there. His old friends . . . gone. Therapists . . . well, they were just doing their jobs. Oscar . . . there was time yet.

V . . .

Nothing in the world felt big enough to make this incredible force of nature hate him. And yet a little part of him worried that it would.

The vine hadn't let go of his arm. If it had been a person, this would have kept the memories flooding in. But slowly, he focused on the differences. The feeling of leaves instead of fingers, the thin winding strand that seemed to have some sort of grip. Slowly, he calmed and considered his options.

"V . . ." He phrased his words carefully, bit by bit, as the counselor had taught him. "When you do that, it brings up memories that make me sad. And a little scared. Is it okay if we try something different?"

He'd never seen V move so quickly before. The vine was gone in an instant. Releasing him.

I'm sorry.

He would have thought it was his own voice, had it not been older, had it not sounded so ageless and ethereal. Masculine, but only in places.

"V?"

The shock barely allowed him to so much as suggest it, but all of the evidence pointed in that direction.

Yes. I did not intend harm. Only comfort. I will not do it again.

Bizarrely, a collection of plants was more respectful of his wishes than 90 percent of the people in his life. He almost laughed at that, but there were more pressing matters.

"You have a voice?"

Yes. I do now.

There were so many questions to ask, but he managed to hold them in for a moment, long enough to sort through them and prioritize into something that at least vaguely made sense.

"I don't think I quite realized how . . . conscious you were. I'm sorry if I bothered you with all of my rambling. I do that. Ramble. But usually in my head."

His cheeks heated as he thought of Oscar, who did all of his rambling to other people. Kyran's rambling had always been internal.

. . . Except to V, apparently.

"I know I've been calling you V, but . . . do you have a name?"

There was a sound, a little like a chuckle. Or rather, what a chuckle might have sounded like had it been made from the rustling of leaves.

That is an odd question. I have a name. You just said it. Surely a name of something is often decided by someone else? It is a very human action to decide upon one's own name, as you have.

"I . . . did I even tell you my name?" He couldn't remember. He had a distinct feeling that his first 'conversation' with V had primarily consisted of venting about the day's troubles. The thought made his cheeks redden further.

I am a collection of plants. People rarely tell me their names. And I cannot say I have ever had need of one, before this. Humans are odd creatures.

His brain felt as though it was firing far faster than he could keep up with. So many questions that they all became jumbled into a cacophony of thoughts.

"How can you speak?"

There went that chuckle again. *How can you?*

It was a good question, and not entirely one he could answer. Though perhaps some team of child psychologists somewhere could. He absentmindedly traced the markings on the nearest tree.

"Well, I suppose I knew you were listening? So this shouldn't be such a shock. Not after the . . . responses. The flowers, the fruit."

You are not very good at getting the correct nutrients, it seems.

"Are you a plant or my mother?"

The comment came out of his mouth before he truly considered it, but thankfully, the laughter came again.

I don't suppose either would truly be correct, or incorrect. But then we are becoming . . . philosophical, as you seem to refer to it. I am afraid much of my language is still limited. I am learning, but it is not an instant process.

"You, me, and the rest of the world, V. None of us can ever properly express what we mean. It's why humans screw up with it so much."

That is reassuring. Thank you for the reassurance.

It was a little like talking to a robot, or some creature that hadn't quite gotten the hang of language yet. So formal, and rigid in ways that human speech wasn't. And yet when he listened, he could hear genuine feeling in it that he had rarely heard from humans.

"That's alright, V. I sort of feel like we're already friends, you know? You know more about me than anyone else, even if I don't know you all that well."

I know facts about your life, it is true. And I know the thoughts you express. In that sense, we must be. I don't suppose I have had a friend before.

And yet somehow, without knowing at all what to do, V had managed to become one of the best friends he had ever had.

"You know, V . . . The vine thing you did . . . if you give me warning, I don't think I would mind it so much? If I know it's coming."

There was a quiet, thoughtful rustle, and V's voice came again.

I have no arms. But I do have vines. I recall that you were missing hugs. I may be a poor substitute, but . . .

"—Please, V. I would love a hug from you. More than anything. That you even care enough to offer . . . means a lot."

Incoming.

He almost chuckled, but he didn't have time to. The vines wrapped around him gently in the strangest semblance of a hug, and it didn't matter. It didn't matter that V wasn't even close to human, just that he had contact, that he was grounded in the universe for a single moment. He was real enough to touch, and so was V.

THE FEELING LASTED DAYS. EVEN AT HOME, HE would wander around his flat and momentarily feel the touch of those strong vines wrapping around him, cradling him, keeping him safe. Human hugs were so fleeting. Moments of happiness shared, but so often hollow. So often fake, out of obligation. He had hugged his parents because that was what he was supposed to do, and it seemed as though they hugged him with the same reasoning. V had actually *wanted* to. And that made all of the difference.

He was lost in one such moment when Oscar knocked on his door for the first time. He'd been waiting for the event, or at least hoping for it, but when it came he found himself startled and confused. How should he look? Was his flat tidy? Was it *too* tidy? Did it look weird, unlived in?

He couldn't stand and debate forever, so instead he pushed his thoughts aside to answer the door, trying to look like he hadn't been waiting for the knock.

He had what he hoped was a smile on his face when he opened the door, and Oscar seemed to respond to it well enough, so that counted for something. They went through the usual motions, the ones Kyran had never engaged in before but had seen his parents enact multiple times. That scripted interaction.

"You have a lovely home."

It was such a bizarre thing to say, since they both knew no one in this building truly had a home anything close to lovely. But it was a home, a roof over their heads, and that was what mattered.

"Well, you know, they check it over a lot to make sure I'm not causing trouble . . . or hiding drugs, or something," Kyran found himself saying. "So it's not like it could get into a total mess. My room in my parents' house was always chaos, though."

Oscar grinned, a hint of mischievousness in it. "They can't check if you don't answer the door to them."

Kyran offered the other boy a seat. "Well, I can't really take the risk of being kicked out." He shrugged. "I'm . . . sort of running out of other places I could stay. They don't give away flats for free, you know."

That prompted a moment of consideration from Oscar. "I think they're pretty used to me not answering. It's on my file, you know? 'Isolated, strange, unused to people.' That sort of thing. You know how they are. I mostly just see them in their offices anyway. It feels safer than having people in my space."

Well, that part was relatable, at least. But Kyran wasn't entirely ready to go into that yet.

"So, you came?"

Oscar nodded, awkwardly. "Sorry I took so long. Or, you know. Maybe it doesn't matter. I guess you're pretty busy. But there's lots of . . . stuff. Life's weird, you know?"

A sentient garden had fed him fruit and hugged him. Kyran was pretty sure he knew a bit about life being weird.

"I'm not really that busy, actually," he blurted, unable to stop himself. "There's just this garden that I hang out with, and—"

He cut off, realizing he'd said 'with,' not 'in.' He tried to hide his horror at the slip, but Oscar didn't seem to notice. His eyes were alight with interest, and rather wistful.

"I used to love gardening. I did it with my grandpa in the Phoenix Garden not far from here, and we spent hours getting it all just right. All of the weeds away, keeping the plants cared for. It was really rewarding." He paused. "But it's not like we get gardens in these flats. And Grandpa didn't make it through the hospital, so . . ."

All of the normal platitudes failed Kyran. He opened his mouth, but no sound came out. Instead, Oscar spoke again.

"It's alright though. It's . . . like, it's part of life, isn't it? When that happens? . . . Sorry, I'm weird like this. This is why people don't talk to me. I just say things that go through my head without thinking of how stupid it sounds or whether you're supposed to say that. You can tell me to shut up if you want. In fact, please tell me to shut up, or I'll just keep rambling at you."

Kyran spoke quietly. "You don't have to shut up. That's the very worst thing you can do."

Oscar stared in confusion. "That's . . . not the usual response I get."

"The problem with shutting up is that, after a while, you start to forget that you ever had anything to say at all. And even when there's something you want to say, you forget how to get the words out right. Eventually it doesn't matter and you have no voice at all. At least if you're talking, you're real. You're having an impact on someone else, you can be understood . . ."

He found himself trailing off awkwardly. People didn't usually make impassioned speeches about things that didn't personally affect them. Not even Oscar was oblivious enough not to see that.

"That sounds pretty hard," Oscar said at last. "I . . . think I'm the opposite of that. I say so many words that none of them really get through to anyone what I was actually trying to say. Like how when you play a bunch of songs all at once they don't sound like any sort of music at all, just noise."

Oscar might have said they were opposites, but to Kyran, their ultimate experience sounded exactly the same. Isolation.

"All of my friends left when I got kicked out of the house. Slowly, but they left. I guess I wasn't right for them anymore."

Kyran had said all sorts of things to therapists, counselors, professionals, gone through every detail of it, but that was new. He'd never said those words aloud before, and somehow saying them made him realize how very real they were. The thought was a little overwhelming. But Oscar just nodded.

"I don't think I had any in the first place. But . . . it definitely didn't help me find any." Oscar paused, flushed. "Or . . . I don't know? Maybe it did?"

It took Kyran a moment to realize what he was being asked. It wasn't the way he'd made other friends, gravitating together through shared interests and the enforced time shared within the school grounds. It was endearing, like a child in a playground.

"I think it did."

V WAS WAITING FOR HIM THE NEXT DAY. AND there were a million questions he wanted to ask.

He had no one else to talk to about Oscar. No parents, no friends. But he had V.

You look troubled, Kyran.

"The guy I told you about? He's . . . actually really sort of sweet. He came in, and we talked . . . We ended up talking for hours, actually. It was good to talk like that. Made me feel real again. But now I'm a fool because instead of leaving it at that and being happy . . . I've been having other feelings."

You humans do seem to have a lot of feelings. The complexity seems rather a hindrance.

That was an understatement. He almost laughed.

"V . . . if I was back at my parents' house, and everything was okay . . . I mean, I'd be talking to my parents about this.

85

Eventually, at least. Maybe friends first." He paused. "Alright, definitely friends first. I'd want to see how people felt about him, getting to know him. And I mean . . . I don't even know if he's into guys."

. . . Or even if, once Oscar realized, that he would consider Kyran a guy. But that was even more difficult to think of, and saying it aloud would be too much.

Well, you cannot control the type of human he prefers. But you can ask.

"It's . . . complicated. You know. The gender thing. I never know if they're looking for me, or they're looking for . . . well, someone very different."

You are a 'guy,' Kyran. If he is interested in that particular subtype of human, it would seem logical that he would be interested in you.

If only it was that simple.

Kyran sighed. "Well, there are . . . differences. That some people don't accept. And you can never know that about someone really until you tell them. Not for sure." He knew what V was going to say before the garden said it. "And it's not as easy as just telling them. It's a risk. There's . . . violence. Spreading rumors. People can . . . destroy your life."

I was about to suggest that you bring him here.

That startled Kyran enough to halt his spiraling mind. "Here? What would that do?"

You said you would have people . . . meet him. I am not people, but I am capable of meeting someone.

It was true, V was the closest he had got right now to a community, a family, someone to look out for him. But 'hey, I want to introduce you to a talking garden' wasn't exactly how he usually attracted people. Not to mention V's bluntness didn't exactly suggest they would be subtle about the assessment process.

"I'll think about it, V. He might be a little intimidated. He's very shy."

He avoided mentioning that most people were shy of large gardens that started to talk to them when they entered.

Understandable. I hope he regains confidence. I understand it is unusual for humans to leave their growing area so very soon. Perhaps that explains his fears.

The thing was . . . Kyran found he did want to bring Oscar here. The thought of Oscar being threatened or uncomfortable was unbearable, but the thought that Kyran might be able to share this experience with another person . . .

V was his rather more leafy version of a guardian angel, and had brought him, piece by piece, into a place where he was even able to talk to Oscar in the first place. But it would have to be very carefully done.

"V, is it too early to be bringing him home to meet my family? That seems a bit like a . . . thing you do when you know someone is actually interested. And a long way in. Not . . . right this second."

There was a confused pause on V's end, which Kyran had never heard before. The rustling that followed was as though the garden was clearing its throat.

Is it entirely wise to revisit your parents? I didn't think that was very safe for you. At the very least emotionally.

"I didn't mean them, V. They gave up being my family when they threw me out of their house. By family, well . . . I sort of meant . . . you."

How to stun a garden wasn't something he'd ever learned in school, or come across in a textbook. Apparently it was a skill of the more intuitive kind.

". . . V? Are you going to say anything, or will I just stand here like a fool wondering if you're ever going to allow me back here?"

The voice that came back to him was softer, and full of whatever passed for emotion. V had no need to mimic it, and it didn't feel even the slightest bit the same as the human emotion Kyran had heard in others. But there was no denying it or what it meant.

I don't think I've had plants that have walked on two legs before. You are such beautiful creatures, when you wish to be, it seems.

And so was V. Something more than Kyran could truly understand, but something that he felt he understood nonetheless. Family.

"You know what, V? . . . I'll bring him. If he doesn't like you, well, that's a pretty instant sign that he isn't the right person for me."

THE STRONG ASSERTION HAD FELT RIGHT AT the time, but when it came to asking Oscar to join him, it felt rather as though Kyran's insides had shriveled up. They sat across from each other, having just finished their coffee, when he managed to clear his throat.

". . . Oscar? You remember I said I spent a lot of time in that garden? . . . Perhaps you'd like to come with me?"

He'd been intending to tell Oscar everything. But as his mouth formed the words . . . he couldn't. Better for Oscar to see for himself, decide by himself, than think Kyran was mad.

Of course, there was the possibility he would think that anyway, Kyran realized, his stomach sinking. Perhaps no one else could even hear V. In fact, perhaps he was mad and no one had been there to tell him.

But Oscar's eyes lit up at the invitation. "I don't think I've been in a garden in a while, of any kind. The last one was the Phoenix Gardens, you know? Plants are so beautiful. I'd love to." He paused. "I mean, if that's okay. I know you invited me, but I don't want to impose or presume or . . ."

"It's fine, Oscar." Kyran smiled, already used to exactly when to cut Oscar off before he started spiraling. "I'd like you to. I'll just put these coffee cups in the sink."

Who washed dishes when there was a garden to see? And to be quite fair, Oscar seemed to be of the same opinion. The walk to V was filled with nothing but Oscar's eager questions about the plant life, any care needs, what type of soil there was in the area.

All of which, Kyran began to realize, he had no answer to.

When they arrived, V was waiting, the vines that Kyran thought of like arms since the hug swaying in a nonexistent breeze. No one else would notice it, but to Kyran, knowing V was quite awake and aware of them, it felt like the garden was dancing.

Oscar's eyes were shining. He moved quickly to the flowerbeds, and to the trees, looking closely at the patterns and colors.

"Look at you." Kyran hid a smile as Oscar addressed the plants. ". . . Aren't you beautiful? And so well-maintained. I don't think I've ever seen a wild garden that was quite so cared for. Not to mention the diversity of plant life! I could stay here forever."

I am not entirely sure that I could give either of you the best of care with no modern human appliances, however I certainly appreciate the company.

The moment of truth. Oscar froze, halfway through inspecting a flower that was in the process of growing new leaves. Kyran watched him, crossing his fingers, toes, and any other part of his body he could remember to cross that this wouldn't end badly.

". . . Did you hear that?"

While Oscar seemed to be doubting his own sanity, Kyran felt more reassured in his. That gave him the courage to speak.

"Oscar . . . I'd like you to meet V. V, this is Oscar."

Oscar looked around at the garden, as if searching for something. "This is a beautiful garden, but . . . Kyran, there's no one here."

Kyran almost chuckled. "No human, maybe. V is the garden. The one you were just looking at adoringly."

Oscar leapt back, and Kyran thought for a moment it was from fear or disgust, but then he saw a familiar flush creep into the other boy's cheeks.

"I'm so sorry. That must have been really uncomfortable for you, V. I . . . I meant no harm. I just . . . you were beautiful and . . . and I didn't know you could hear me. I mean, most gardens can't. Or maybe they can, and I just . . . I don't know. Maybe I'm not normally worth talking to."

There was an amused rustle from the branches.

It's quite alright. I am not concerned by your attentions. As for other gardens, many of us are aware on different levels and communicate between ourselves, but it is unlikely we will attempt to communicate with any human guest. I cannot say it often goes well, nor is it within the capability of most.

Oscar took all of that in. No doubt, Kyran thought, thinking of the garden he had tended with his grandfather. He was quiet for a while, but then approached the flowerbeds again as he had before.

"Pleased to meet you, V. I don't think I've met anyone quite so different before."

And then he stopped. Kyran stared at him, waiting for the next sentence, the babbling. But for once, Oscar didn't seem quite as nervous that something would go wrong, should he not explain every last detail of his intentions.

"I think we have our answer, V," Kyran said out loud. "He likes you. Maybe he's allowed to stick around, then."

I am glad. I believe you humans find romance so very stimulating.

It was Kyran's turn to go bright red as Oscar looked at him. "Romance?" Oscar asked, baffled.

"I don't . . . they . . ." It felt easier to refer to V as they, with no indication of their gender. "They're not familiar with humans," he managed at last. "They just mean . . . friendship."

Oscar stopped. "Oh." He sounded, bizarrely, disappointed. "I mean, that's fine too. But for the record, I do . . . well, I do like guys. So if that's a problem . . ."

A small blink was all it took for Kyran to realize the monumental tangle they'd gotten themselves into.

"That . . . would not be a problem. But . . . not everyone who likes guys is into me."

Oscar's babbling was back. "Of course not. I mean, no one is everyone's type, and personalities, and clashes, and confusion, and things might not work and . . ."

". . . And I'm trans," Kyran interrupted. "So that's often a turn-off for some."

Oscar looked from Kyran to the plants above him. ". . . Is he serious, V? Kyran, you just introduced me to a talking garden and I was fine. Why should I give a damn what some doctor decided you were based on a cursory glance at you as a baby?"

That wasn't babbling. The message of that was very clear.

Kyran had heard that in the moments before death, a person's life flashed before their eyes. But actually, for him, it was that moment. All of the people who wouldn't listen, all of the rejection, judgment, hate . . . And then that.

"So . . . that wouldn't be an obstacle?"

Oscar may have been continually anxious, but there was something firm and certain in the way he brought his lips to Kyran's and tangled his hands in Kyran's hair. As they kissed, the rustling of V's branches almost sounded like applause.

Finally, Phoenix. V sent a pulse across the city to another garden that was eagerly awaiting updates. *They certainly took their time. No garden has ever had to learn human communication to get people together before, but there's a first time for everything.*

JOLLY FATS DIES TONIGHT
ANGELA SIERRA

They're talking about a party, my cousins. Yelling, more like, because they're costeños and 'loud' is their default volume setting. It's their defining characteristic, along with an obsession with Kola Roman that I cannot, for the life of me, understand.

I don't even know why they call themselves costeños. I mean, they weren't born anywhere near either of Colombia's coasts. Their parents were, though, and according to them and every other costeño I've met, the sea stays in your blood for generations. Apparently, this holds true even if you're 8,530 feet above the sea, in Bogotá, which is where this annoying yell-fest is taking place.

I close my eyes, trying to block out my stupid cousins talking about their stupid party. I mean, it's not like I want to go. It's not like they want me there, either. I know that, which is why it comes as a shock when I hear Samir, my oldest cousin, say, "Do you want to come?"

Since Samir's not yelling, it takes a moment for it to register that he means me.

"What?" I say.

My other cousins are twins—Diana and Nadia, otherwise known as Dee and Nee. They're nineteen, only two years my senior, but you'd think I'm still in diapers the way they roll their eyes and snicker every time I talk. They do it now, until Samir gives them a look that shuts them up.

"I asked if you want to go to the party tonight," he says again, patient, kind, like he's a hundred years older than me instead of ten.

"I'm a minor," I say.

I think this is the end of the conversation, so I go back to looking at my phone, but Samir smiles and slides over a flyer for the party, his finger pointing to a small icon on the bottom. There's a carrot, which means it's a "Zanahoria" party: no alcohol.

"No booze," says Nadia, as if reading my thoughts. "And no drugs," she adds, giving me a look.

Suddenly the baggie full of pills is heavy in my jeans pocket. I remember the time we went out, when I tried to be so smooth taking out the stash of molly—still in the bag I found circling the toilet in the girls' bathroom at my high school back home in Miami—and showing it to my slightly older, way cooler cousins. I thought for sure this would earn me some street cred, but it backfired. Big time. I got a long lecture on drugs and how could I and what was I thinking, and didn't I know how that shit could kill me?

I cried so they wouldn't tell my parents, but they held it over me like a net over a fish.

"What's this other thing mean?" I deflect, pointing to an icon of a clothes iron.

"Plancha music," Nadia says.

Plancha, so called because it's what maids and housewives listen to while ironing, is basically ballads for the lonely, the broken-hearted, and the poor, played by the likes of Yuri, Daniela Romo, Selena—not Gomez—and Juan Gabriel. I think the name is sexist, classist, and wrong on so many levels, but we've had this discussion before so why bother? It'll only end in a variation of *what the hell do I know?*

"So?" Samir singsongs. "You can come with me to my studio for a while and then go help with the preparations for the party."

For most girls my age this would probably sound tempting, but I shake my head. "I'll just stay and practice my violin."

"For your audition?" Dee asks. She's the nicer twin, though not by much. She's the only one I talk to, except right now I ignore her so that I don't have to tell anyone what I've known for three days: my audition was a bust, my chances of ever getting into Juilliard have gone down the drain, and my dream has been shattered.

When it's clear I'm not going to respond, Nee says, "Well, you can't stay here. Nene is busy making the food for her costurero."

Nene, our grandmother, has a weekly knitting gathering that is the highlight of her social life. When it's her turn to host she makes kibbe, tabuleh and hummus, pita bread, sweet greibes, plenty of baclava, and her special blend of coffee with spices. She told me once food had been the salvation of our ancestors when they came to Colombia. They'd been shunned as heathens and devil-worshipers until the locals tasted the food. Since then, in any respectable Turk household, people expect to find good food and lots of it.

Anyway, it makes sense now, Samir asking me to tag along. It's a pity ask.

"Look," he says, tapping the flyer like it's a toy and I'm a bored kitty, "the party is in the hotel near El Salto de Bochica. It's rumored to be haunted by the souls that plunged to their death in the falls."

I raise a mildly interested eyebrow.

"It's true," Dee says, and Nee nods. "The waterfall was a holy place for the Indians."

I purse my lips and whip out my phone, having learned to Google before I speak.

I find El Salto de Bochica easily. It's a waterfall more than five hundred feet high, and near it is a century-old house, once a railroad station, then a hotel for the first-class passengers on the cross-country trains. For several centuries, the falls have been a hot spot for suicidal jumpers.

"It's a museum now?" I say, reading the description.

"It's been a lot of things. It was a restaurant in the '80s, but it was abandoned and all but fell apart. They're trying to rebrand it but so far it hasn't been a great success. So they hired me," Samir says.

When he was fresh out of college, Samir started with a small recording studio, making jingles mostly. He's slowly expanded into the events gig. I think of him as a glorified party planner.

"Anyway," he says, "I've been doing a series of Haunted Parties in the scariest places all over town, and this is going to be the biggest one yet. Wanna come?" He wiggles his eyebrows, which are full and dark like his ridiculously long eyelashes. They frame his greenish eyes like tiny moustaches. I smile at this thought, and they all take the gesture to mean I'm saying yes.

"You're going? Yay!" Nadia claps excitedly, and I can't find a trace of her usual sarcasm in her happy dance.

"I'm so glad you decided to come," Dee says. "I'll help with your costume. Assuming you don't have one, that is."

"Um, no, I don't. But that's okay. I can just wear jeans and a crew t-shirt," I say.

"Oh, come on. Me and Nee are going as genies, and three is way better than two," Diana says, almost begging.

"And why is that?" I ask.

"Because," Nee says, "whenever Dee and I match, people think it's a twin thing, that we're just doing it to look alike."

"They focus on how alike we are and not on how awesome we are," Dee says.

They share a look and nod.

Nee and Dee dream of creating their own fashion empire and have been tinkering with Nene's sewing machines since they were in preschool.

"And you think you can make me look good?" I say.

"We can certainly make you look *better*," Nee says.

My lips move to form a rude reply, but Dee speaks first.

"Tell you what, Jolly," she says, "we'll supply the right clothes if you supply the right attitude."

My head shoots up, my eyes boring into hers. I had the right attitude when I got here, five weeks ago, doing my best not to act like this would be the worst summer vacation of my life. I want to say so, but I don't. It doesn't matter.

Nothing matters anymore.

I take another look at the waterfall on my phone. Five hundred meters. Six seconds to reach the bottom. Six seconds and it's all over. Six seconds.

"Tell you what, Dee: don't call me Jolly and we've got a deal."

I see her face fall but I'm not sure why until Samir clears his throat and says softly, "You don't want us to call you Jolly anymore?"

That's when I understand what's bothering them. It's the way he says 'us,' like it hurts that I'm not allowing them to use my pet name, like I don't think them worthy or something.

Instantly, I feel bad. I hate it when anybody calls me 'Jolly,' not just them, but they don't know that, so I say, "Nobody back home ever says my name right. They say it like Yo-leema or Jolly-maw. And don't get me started on our last name. Fat-Tammy."

Put it together and you get Jolly Fats, which is exactly what my sixth-grade English teacher did. I tried to explain to Mrs. Flynn that it was Joe-Lee-Muh, but she said the nickname suited me. She must've thought it was cute or clever, but it was really a death sentence. Once I got stuck being Jolly Fats, I became everyone's smiling fat idiot best friend, the one who always consoles the pretty girls when they have to break a boy's heart, but never once gets to be the heartbreaker.

I hate the name and what it means and what it stands for.

And I hate myself. I hate myself so much.

But I don't say that. I say, "Just call me Yolima. Please."

Maybe it's the 'please' that gets her, but Nee looks at me a little differently. "Yeah, people made fun of my name when I was little. They called me Doña Nadie. I'll show them who's a Miss Nobody!" she says, waving her fist dramatically in the air and getting a giggle out of all three of us. She looks back at me with something resembling understanding. "Yolima it is, then."

Dee and Samir nod slowly, understanding and maybe even a little respect in their eyes as they look at me.

I smile back. I can do this. I can play nice with them, if it'll get me to the waterfall.

After all, being nice to my cousins won't kill me.

That's what the pills in my pocket are for.

I BLAME MY PARENTS.

Everyone blames their parents, I guess, but mine chose my cursed name. They could have given me a beautiful name, like my sister. Adira, the Most Beautiful. That's really all you need to know.

My parents tell Adira's story a lot.

It begins when they were just a couple of teenagers.

My mother had been pageant-pretty, fair and blond, a face begging to be carved in marble. Groomed since infancy to be Señorita Cartagena like a proper well-to-do girl, she was committed to bringing home the gold.

The gold scepter, that is.

Marina, her name and eyes a tribute to the sea, was in Bogotá as part of her preparations when she first laid eyes on the quietly handsome Mahmoud.

Mahmoud, my father, was a waiter at his uncle's restaurant, working to pay his way through college. His grandmother had moved with her five children to Bogotá from Riohacha when his grandfather had been shot down in what was probably a drug-related payback. Yadira, a Wayúu that had learned to weave from her mother and cook from her suegra, used both of her talents to put food on the table for the six of them, and now the second generation of Fatamis distributed their talents equally among the kilim trade and the restaurant business.

One night, Marina was dipping her flatbread in hummus and chatting with the other beauty queens when she and my father locked eyes. Mahmoud slipped a note under the coaster of her orange blossom lemonade, and she left him her number written on a lipstick-smeared napkin (she would first deny and later confirm that the lip mark was made on purpose).

They fell in love.

But Marina was an Emiliani, Cartagena royalty. Her father was a successful merchant, her only brother had died at sea in the line of duty, and she had barely said the name of the boy she loved when her mother forbade her to see him ever again under threat of disownment.

Alas, the threat came five weeks too late. Adira was on her way.

They wed in secret, lived in Yadira's house until Mahmoud finished school, and left for Miami with Adira still in diapers. There, Mahmoud opened a branch of the family's kilim emporium. Marina, still a beauty, smiled her way into the hearts of every client. They were a golden family, Moodie, Marina, and Adira.

Adira was their miracle.

And ten years later, I was their accident.

They tell my story often too, but when they do, I'm always the punchline.

JOLLY FATS DIES TONIGHT

I THINK ABOUT MY NAME, YOLIMA, THE MODEST
violet, as Nee and Dee doll me up for tonight's party. We're at
Samir's studio and they've wheeled out a portable makeup case
that's three levels high. They even set up studio lights and
everything. I'm sitting on a stool and they're fussing over me,
spritzing and smearing and dabbing things from a dozen
bottles all over my face.

They've been fairly nice, for the most part. I was expecting
them to tell me my pores are too big, my nose is too wide, my
eyes are too far apart.

Instead, they tell me I should use this eyeliner to bring out
this color and that bronzer to highlight that feature.

It's great until Nee says, "I can't believe how different you
and your sister are."

"I know. She got all my mom's good European genes," I snicker,
thinking self-deprecating humor will be our common ground.

"And you got the inferior genes of our side of the family?"
Nee says, biting every word.

"I didn't mean it like that. It's just . . . I got dealt a bad hand
from a deck stacked in her favor. I mean, I play the game with
the cards I've got, but we all know it's not aces."

I mean to be funny, but it comes out so bitter that I barely
recognize my own voice. I sound petty and jealous, which I
guess I am.

But I'm also tired. I'm so tired. I just want them to be done,
all of this to be done so we can get to the party and I can slip
away, slip under, and then . . . just slip.

I have it all planned out. I'll take the pills, so it won't hurt, so
I'll be happy and high as I swan dive off the waterfall.

Over and out.

I smile at my own joke.

"You shouldn't be so mean to yourself," Dee says.

"Or us," Nee says under her breath.

"I'm not mean; I'm realistic. Do you think I would be
happier if I lied to myself? Told myself that I was beautiful,

only to find out that other people don't share my delusion? I know the truth. I'm a short, fat, busty tapioca pudding."

Silence again, and then Nee pulls on my hair a little harder than she needs to and says, "You know you're wearing my clothes, right? So what does that mean? Huh? I'm fat? Is that what you're saying?"

"No. Of course not." Why were they making everything about them? "You're curvy. That's totally different. You've got that whole Latina fatale thing going for you."

"So do you," Dee says.

I don't even bother correcting her. I know she's just trying to be nice. I don't have to agree with her, but I won't argue either.

"If you don't believe me, look for yourself," Dee says, rolling a full-length mirror my way.

The mirror shows someone I've never met. The girl in the mirror has long wavy hair that looks nothing like my usual mousy-brown sensible shoulder-length tresses. They've done something to it, and now it tumbles in waves, framing my face.

Except it doesn't look like my face.

My eyes, normally puddle-brown, now have flecks of green and gold like the sand under the sea. My eyelashes go on for miles, and each eyebrow is an elegant arch instead of a dead caterpillar.

I stand up, and immediately wish I hadn't. I'm wearing harem pants and a small vestlike shirt that ends in a wide sash, hugging my waist. I've never worn anything so tight and I feel exposed and foolish.

"This is too small on me," I say, tugging at the shirt.

"That's it? No 'thank you, dear cousins, I look amazing, you guys rock'?" Nee says, tossing a sponge into the kit.

"Thank you, dear cousins, you guys rock and this is too small on me."

"That's how it's supposed to look. See?" Dee says, removing her jacket and showing me her own costume. It falls on her waist, making her hourglass figure stand out.

"You look nice," I say quietly. "I look ridiculous."

"Well, tough. It's all we've got. If you want to go wash it all off, go right ahead. I'm not wasting another second on you," Nee says, throwing everything back into the suitcase.

It's plain to see that I've hurt her, and I don't know how to fix it. Words run through my head, but none seem right. I end up not saying anything and because I don't know what else to do with myself, I start picking things up, putting the lids back on the bottles and wiping the brushes off on a tissue.

After a while, Dee says softly, "She didn't mean it like that. It's not a waste of time to help you."

Nee starts to contradict her, but she holds up her hand. "But it is frustrating. It might not feel like it to you, but we've tried to be nice. We've asked you out, introduced you to our friends, taken you to our design studio. I mean, sure, to you it's a spare bedroom at our parents' house, but to us it's our dream."

I think back to that day when the twins had taken me to their house, shown me their clothes. I said it was neat that they liked to sew. But they weren't just showing me their little projects; they were sharing something important, and I didn't see it then.

"I'm sorry," I say, looking at the floor because it's easier than looking them in the eye.

I sit on the couch and Dee sits next to me.

"Look, we know you'd rather practice your violin than talk to us mere mortals, but you're here now. Make the best of it. Or at least, don't make it worse for us," Nee says.

Nee's phone beeps. She gives Dee a look and they both leave me alone with my thoughts, and my thoughts are these: I'm here now, but it's not where I want to be.

And I don't just mean the studio.

My parents shipped me off to Colombia because they wanted to be with Adira at her graduation. They said they wanted to make this summer all about her, and I had to laugh because everything is always about her.

Dee walks back in, alone, holding several bags, which she places on the low, rectangular coffee table in front of the couch. She sits cross-legged on the floor.

"Sushi and poke bowls," she says, taking small boxes out of the bags and spreading them around the table.

I slide off the couch to sit on the floor across from her.

"Try this one," she says, spearing a piece with a chopstick and offering it to me.

I take it and shove it in my mouth. "This is delicious," I say, and mean it.

"That one has mango biche. I remembered you like it," Dee says.

I realize that I don't know what she likes or doesn't like, if she has allergies, if she has a boyfriend or a girlfriend or a goldfish. I don't know this about any of them.

"I'm going to text Juancho to come in before it's all gone," Dee says.

Juancho is Samir's assistant here at BeatWeaver Studio. I met him soon after I arrived. We hit it off right away. Juancho has an easy smile and soft brown eyes and can talk about music for hours. He came over to the house a few times and we hung out, but then Samir said he was looking for someone to handle the studio side of things while he focused on expanding the events angle and asked me if I wanted the job. I turned Samir down and felt guilty about it, so I avoided Juancho and didn't come back to the studio again. Instead, I spent the summer locked up in my father's old room in my grandmother's big house, drawing tired notes from my shiny violin, making video after video of myself playing the classics to prove that I had what it takes. Only to fail.

Smart. Very smart.

Juancho comes in, eyes zeroing in on the sushi and making himself comfortable next to Dee. He goes straight for the mango sushi and when he finally looks at me, he stops, sushi an inch from his open mouth.

I stare back at him, unsure of what to say or do. Nobody says anything for what feels like a long time, and then Dee giggles and says, "Juancho, you remember our cousin Yolima? From Miami? Who plays the violin?"

Juancho nods, his eyes still on me, and I feel my face go red. He's probably heard terrible things about me all summer and is now afraid to talk to me at all.

"Hey," I say, "nice to see you again."

Dee cracks up and Juancho looks mortified, probably wishing he'd ignored the text, thinking no sushi is worth having to sit with me.

"Hey," he says. A few seconds pass before he speaks again. "You look, um, different."

Of course. The makeup, the costume. That's why they're laughing. I look down at my sushi, breathing through my nose, the red slowly receding. "Dee and Nee did it. For the party tonight."

"You're coming to the party?" he says, his face lighting up.

Again Dee snickers and I hate feeling like the butt of a joke I don't get. I scowl at my sushi and say nothing.

Juancho doesn't care or doesn't notice that I don't answer. "That's great. I'm glad. That's cool. You'll like it. And you look good. The costume. It's good. Dee and Nee did a good job," he says, and by the time he stops talking he's red in the face because he hasn't taken a breath.

Dee keeps laughing and I don't understand what's so funny but I'm sure it's something I've said or done and I'm too tired to figure it out.

So tired.

I think again of the pills and I realize they are still in my pants, the ones I took off to get into this costume, and I'm trying to sort out how I will grab them and the note I wrote explaining why without anyone seeing and where I will hide them in this skimpy outfit when Nee comes in.

She sits on the other side of the table, between me and Juancho, and we all start to pass different types of sushi to her at the same time, but she shakes her head.

"First things first," she says, and hands me a plastic bag.

My hands take the bag as my mind comes up with a million reasons not to (everything from *it's a gag gift* to *there's a snake inside*). I open it before I say anything, which is good because as I look at Nee she smiles and says, "It's a peace offering."

Inside the bag is a bottle, beautifully decorated with tiny mirrors and golden accents. It matches my costume.

"You made this?" I say, truly impressed.

Nee nods.

"Wow. It looks store-bought. I mean that as a compliment, even if it doesn't sound like one," I say hurriedly, before it can backfire. "I mean, I know to you two, store-bought and off-the-rack are the death of good taste, but cut me some slack. I'm from Miami. I was raised in Walmart. Come to think of it, I was probably conceived at Walmart, too."

The joke lands. Juancho starts to giggle and the others follow.

"Well, every genie needs a bottle," Nee says.

"I wonder what happens if someone rubs the bottle and makes a wish?" Dee says, raising her eyebrows at Nee.

"Yeah, Juancho. What do you think would happen?" Nee says, wiggling her eyebrows.

Juancho chokes on a piece of sushi and I stare at the bottle for a moment, wishing I could blink myself inside it, away from them, away from everything.

Juancho looks mortified and tries to say something, chokes again, and drinks water while Nee slaps his back. When he's done coughing, he wipes his mouth and pushes the rest of the sushi away. "I, um, I think I—" His phone vibrates, and relief etches across his face. He looks up at me for some reason and says, "I have to go. Samir needs me."

Juancho walks out of the room and I turn to the others. "You don't have to be so mean to him," I say.

I get ready for a fight, but instead they both laugh at me.

"Us? You're the one who's mean. Poor kid," Nee says.

"Yeah, Yolima. Throw him a bone," Dee says.

"What?" I say, but Nee and Dee just laugh harder.

I turn to Nee, eyebrows raised. "What is it with you two?"

"Seriously?" she says.

"Yes, seriously. I know it's a pain to have to explain everything to your dumb gringa cousin, but you'll probably get to go to heaven for putting up with me."

Nee's eyes darken for a moment and I think she's going to hit me with an acid retort, but she breathes once, twice, three times, in and out. She touches a medallion of the Virgin Mary she always wears and seems to think about the going-to-heaven thing before saying, almost sweetly, "He's into you."

"Who? Juancho?" My voice is all high and squeaky, and she must think it's cute or something because she smiles, not with malice or anger, but really, truly smiles.

"Yes, Juancho. Poor boy could barely keep his eyes off you. He's liked you since the first time we saw you. He begged us to get you to go out with him for weeks because he was too shy to ask you out himself. We tried to play matchmaker and get you to go out with us as a group, but you never said yes, and we got tired of making up excuses for him. We finally told him that you were too busy practicing your violin."

"She said that," Dee cuts in, and smiles. "I said that you were going to become a nun. A violin-playing nun."

They both smile and I'm shocked, not just because that was probably the most words Nee has ever said to me at once but because it makes no sense.

"Why would he like me?"

The giggling stops suddenly, like someone pressed the mute button.

"Beats me," Nee says bitterly, "because it's not as if you go out of your way to be nice to him. Or any of us."

Dee punches her in the arm but doesn't disagree.

There's not a lot I can say to that.

Truth is, before this visit, all I'd known of Colombia were the combed beaches and practiced smiles of Cartagena. We visited my mother's side of the family every year, and every year the weight of what my mother could have been was suffocating. My grandparents displayed their wealth on every occasion to show her what she'd given up. They regarded Bogotá as a cesspool, the city where my mother had been ruined, where she had leapt from grace into my father's arms.

In Cartagena, the Fatamis were described as mafiosos, snake oil salesmen, con artists, and whores. It was partly why I hated my name, so much so that I had asked my father for permission to change it. He'd asked only that I visit his family once before I erased them from my life forever.

That was the reason they sent me to Bogotá instead of Cartagena this year. I had come here to gather evidence against them, so I could convince myself that they were unworthy of me because I was tired of being a Fatami, but really, I was tired of being me. Of being Jolly Fats.

When Adira heard I wanted to change my name, she defended the Fatamis and urged me to come and meet this side of our family. And of course my cousins all loved Adira and made no effort to disguise the fact that they wished she were here instead of me. This was just another room where I wasn't the favorite.

So, no. I hadn't been very nice at all.

"I really was practicing my violin," I say.

"No wonder. I think you like your violin more than you like any human," Nee says.

"Maybe we could hear you play?" Dee says, placating as ever.

Playing hurts now. Physically, because my fingers have barely recovered from the beating I gave them for my audition video; and emotionally, because I know I'm not good enough, and this was the only thing I was ever good at.

Also, I don't have my sheet music and I feel weird playing without it, but I don't want to come off as difficult. I might as well play for an audience before my swan song hits the last note.

I reach for my case and take my violin. Franke Henner, an upgrade from my Fiddlerman, supposed to prepare me for the future. I was so excited when I got it for my Sweet Sixteen (I refused to celebrate my Quince, as was the Colombian tradition; Adira had, of course) and still remembered my hands trembling as I first rosined up my bow. Now I rosin the Mongolian horsehair bow that seems too good for me, and I bring the ebony chin rest up to my face with shame.

I play my audition song, *The Last Rose of Summer*, because I know it by heart. The first notes leave the strings and I feel my face tighten, my toes curl inside my shoes, my eyes snap shut, and my entire body clench from the effort. The execution is perfect, note for note, but I open my eyes and see their blank faces and know that this was what the judges looked like when they saw my audition video.

I can't go on. I stop, wanting to call them ignorant fools because they don't appreciate H.W. Ernst, but I don't have it in me. I let the violin sag at my feet and look down at my shoes.

Dee speaks first. "Wow, Yolima. That was . . . that piece sounds really hard."

"Yeah," Nee says, "that thing with the strings where you . . ." she makes a plucking motion with his fingers.

"Pizzicato," I say softly, "it's called pizzicato."

"That," she says. "Looks really difficult."

"It is. It's one of the hardest pieces ever written for the violin," I say. There's no triumph in my voice, no admiration in theirs.

"Why?" Nee asks.

"Partly because of the complex variations—" I begin, but Nee interrupts me.

"No, I mean why did you pick that song? I get that it's hard but that's no reason to pick something. It doesn't sound like you're having fun playing it," she says.

She's right, too. Playing the violin hasn't been fun for me for a while, not since I decided that I had to get into Juilliard, that I had to be the best, had to be the one who made my parents proud.

And I did only pick the song because it was hard. I wanted to show mastery of my craft, but forgot that music was supposed to be beautiful, not just difficult.

I sit back on the couch.

The twins start putting the leftover sushi away in silence. On an impulse, I pick up the violin again and the first few bars of *Bittersweet Symphony* begin to fill the room.

I mean it as a joke, because it was one of the first songs Nee ever asked me to play (I refused, thinking it was beneath me), but it comes out rich and nuanced. This time as I play, I don't close my eyes. I look straight at Nee and all but sing to her that I can't change, I can't change, and she nods ever so slightly, to me or to the words I don't know but I can feel the weight of each note and I'm almost on my knees and I look at Dee and she smiles, she smiles at the pain she sees, not like she's laughing at it but because she sees it for what it is, part of a symphony. I hear the lyrics in my head and I feel them in my fingers, I close my eyes and let each vibration of the string whisper gently that we are all sharing something here, now.

I open my eyes again and I look at Dee who is nodding as I play, looking like she feels every note deep inside.

I close my eyes again, sawing on my violin, twelve notes over and over, each one carrying pain and release, pain and release, over and over until I reach the final note and look up to see Juancho standing there, mouth open, eyes wide, looking at me like he's never seen anyone with a violin before.

"That was deep," he says.

"Yeah. I felt that," Nee says, and to my surprise, adds, "thanks."

"Too many feels," Dee says softly. She looks up at me, a small fire in her eyes. "Got anything with a little more pep?"

It sounds like a dare, and maybe I'm high on rosin but I smile as the notes from Luis Fonsi's *Despacito* make their way out of my violin. It's Adira's favorite and a shameless crowd pleaser, but it works. They recognize the song instantly and start tapping their feet, the mood lifting. The sounds, now golden and light, bounce around like a playful gust of wind, caressing Dee's hair, rustling Nee's shirt, making them both a little tipsy.

Not surprisingly, the words are in my head, having gotten stuck there from hearing the song dozens of times. I hear the words gather around me like a cloud, saying *I want to kiss your clothes off,* and I look at Juancho. He turns bright red as I take the tempo down and make sure that *des . . . pa . . . cito* is nice. And. Slow.

Juancho suddenly jumps up, leaves the room and comes back with his laptop, a set of headphones, a sampler, and a microphone.

"Keep going," he says to me, "I have an idea."

Juancho fiddles around with his software and points the mic at me, but by then I've lost the thread.

I do some scales, hoping inspiration will strike. I've concentrated on classical music for so long I'm not exactly up to speed on what the cool kids are listening to because, duh, I'm not a cool kid. I land on *Smooth Criminal,* my dad's signature party tune. Juancho's face is all smiles as he starts a loop with the notes from my violin.

"Alright," he calls out, "we've got eight bars. Now we loop it, and you add to it."

"I beg your pardon?" I say, bow hovering over the strings. Add to Michael Jackson? Add to greatness?

"Yeah. Like this," he says, and starts playing the loop, waiting for an opening and adding sounds with a digital drum kit. He slows the beat down until there's space for a snare drum, soft and vibrant, snaking around the notes of my violin. It's shy at first, but as the two sounds blend Juancho turns it up and adds a vibraphone, making the tune brighter but still sharp. My cousins' heads snap at once towards the sound and they move towards me, moths drawn to the moon.

We play around with the chords (Am, G, F, A) until I stay on the G for a few beats and segue into *We Will Rock You* with a G D C G Em that Juancho grabs out of the air and mixes with a marimba and kick drum that turn the familiar notes into a new experience.

I lose them when I try some Mozart, but I try again, this time without clenching my jaw, and sway, letting my arms move on their own, fusing snippets of songs I barely remember hearing with something new. Something me.

Juancho adds a beat that is slow and sexy, and I savor it, breaking it apart, separating the sensations, like trying to find the caramel filling in a bite of chocolate.

Then there's a kick drum and a trumpet and I feel dizzy with the notes of *Titanium*, and my violin catches up and it's magical, time holding its breath while I find myself inside the beat and everyone in the room is there with me.

It's not always magic. We rise and fall, we hit and miss, but there are moments in which the room is mine and I feel powerful and brave and mighty and strong.

And when I open my eyes, Samir is there, clapping and watching his cousins dance and his smile is so bright I can't help but smile along.

I remember Adira telling me about his smile and Dee and Nee giggling as they told me about the two of them, Adira and Samir, about how they dated in secret and how I didn't believe them, called them gossips and worse.

"They're cousins, for goodness' sake!" I said, indignant.

They laughed, and Dee said, "Second cousins. Doesn't count."

And Nee said, "Entre más primo, más me arrimo."

I hadn't known what that meant at the time, something about cousins getting a little too close or something like that, but I see it now, how she could have felt something for him. I realize, too, that if Dee and Nee were right, it would explain why my mother never let Adira come back and had shipped her off to Europe, to make sure she would find someone else, anyone else, not another Fatami she would have to defend at every Cartagena polite society dinner.

Samir smiles at me, sweetly, with fondness, like he cares. I see that the others are looking at me, too, and their smiles match his. They're sweaty and happy and their eyes are shining with admiration and I bask in it.

"You really can play," Juancho says. "I guess all that practice paid off after all."

"You're not so bad yourself," I say, pointing to his setup with my bow. "Where'd you learn to mix like that?"

"La Ponti," he says, and when I don't react, he clarifies, "the Pontificia Javeriana university. Top-notch music program. We've got great violin teachers, if you're interested."

"You should totally check it out, Yolima," Dee says, a smile both wicked and sweet dominating her features.

"Yeah, since you didn't get into Juilliard," Nee says.

Dee jabs her with a death stare, but it's too late.

They know.

I can't breathe. The room grows eerily quiet and I feel the temperature drop.

Samir takes a few steps towards me, and it's only when I see him kneel down that I realize I'm sitting on the floor.

"Hey, Yolima, it's okay. He . . . we didn't mean for you to feel bad."

"When did she tell you?" I ask. No point in pretending it wasn't Adira.

"Yesterday," Samir says.

"She just wanted to make sure you felt, you know, supported. By your family. By us," Dee says.

I should've known. Adira told me she had friends at Juilliard. She has friends everywhere.

Did everyone know? Did she tell my parents? If they know, why haven't they called? No, she wouldn't have said anything to ruin their trip.

Pieces start falling into place. That's why my cousins invited me to the party. It wasn't just pity, it was pity that Adira had bartered for me.

I start to laugh. I can't help it. I laugh and they think it's a happy laugh so they laugh along with me and I feel like I'm dying inside, like my heart is turning to stone, like my hands are crow's feet, gnarled and stiff, and I will never again play anything worth listening to.

I laugh until tears streak my face and I sound manic even to my own ears, but I can't stop. The others have gone silent, unsure of what level of crazy they're witnessing. Samir puts his hand on my shoulder, makes sure my eyes meet his, and says, "It's going to be okay, Yolima. This hurt? It won't last forever."

Oh, he's right about that.

I nod and wipe my nose with the edge of my costume. I see Nee cringe, but she doesn't say a thing.

Samir checks his watch and informs us that we need to leave in five.

I reach for my pants, but Dee tells me we are to leave everything here because there's not much space in the van. I walk out, holding my violin, and Juancho walks with me.

"You gonna play that thing at the party?" he asks.

I look at my violin and turn back to the office without saying a word.

I place the case on the sofa and, before I lose my nerve, take the pills and the note out of my jeans' pocket and stuff them into the genie bottle Nee gave me, suddenly grateful for the accessory.

Magic bottle, indeed.

THE TEQUENDAMA FALLS ARE PROBABLY beautiful, but I can't tell. Between the grayish sky that usually covers the Bogotá savannah and the mist generated by the fall itself, I can't see much beyond the house.

The house, though, is majestic. Republican-style chic, the Castillo de Bochica lives up to its name, a true castle in the midst of lush, almost jungle-like greenery. From the Muisca-Greco Roman accents in the foyer to the French-inspired moldings all around the house, it's breathtaking.

And loud. So loud.

The party isn't for a few hours and we're just setting up, but there's a bunch of people and, of course, they're costeños. Birds of a feather, I guess. Especially sea birds.

Everybody greets me and my cousins with kisses on the cheek, Colombian-style, and the whole time Juancho is never more than a few feet away. He keeps sneaking glances at me, smiling at me whenever our eyes meet.

I smile back.

Objectively speaking, Juancho is pretty hot. I'm flattered that he likes me. He seems to be flirting more openly, like we've shared something now, like it's out there.

It's nice, but it's not enough. It's not nearly enough because I'm not the girl who rethinks her entire existence because a boy likes her.

Not after her One Dream has been shattered. No crush could outweigh that.

"Juancho, have you been here before?" I ask, once we're done putting things away and there's a lull in the activities.

"Just a few times, when we were scouting this place for the party. Why? You want a tour?"

I nod, and he blushes slightly as he says, "The, um, the rooms are really nice. I mean, the upstairs in general is really pretty."

I giggle. "I meant outside, actually. The waterfall? I'd like to see it. It's famous, right?"

He looks stricken for a moment, like he's afraid he offended me, but I smile and add, "Maybe you could show me the upstairs later."

His grin nearly lifts the fog and we grab our jackets to head outside.

THE GORGE IS CUT BY A RIVER THAT DROWNS out the noise from inside. The hotel sits almost opposite the falls, and the walk there would take longer than we have now, so we sit at the edge of the property near the stone balustrade and dangle our feet off the edge. From here we have a perfect view of the forested area near the falls, all covered in green.

I'm not sure how I feel about this. On the one hand, a lot could get in the way of a nice clean fall; on the other hand, better not to be a visible splat from above.

Juancho is feeling chatty and tells me about the history of the place, the meaning of the word Tequendama in Chibcha ('he who precipitated downward') and that according to the Muiscas, the falls were created by the hero Bochica when he used his staff to break the rocks and unleash the waters all over the savannah.

"Did he jump?" I ask.

"No, that came later, when the conquistadors came and started imposing their religion on the natives. Many of them preferred to jump off rather than turn their backs on their gods, their beliefs. They say the natives believed they would turn into eagles and fly to freedom. They leapt from there," he says, pointing toward the falls. "Suicide Rock."

Suicide Rock sounds like a bad band name, but I keep the thought to myself and think instead of natives jumping and turning into eagles mid-fall. I like that idea. Fly and be free. I wonder if I have any Chibcha blood in me.

"What do you think?" I ask.

"About religion or suicide?" he asks with a laugh.

"Either. Both."

His eyebrows rise, but he smiles.

"First, I'm an atheist; second, I don't think suicide sets you free."

"Why not?" I say, maybe louder than I need to.

He gives me a look I can't decipher and says, "Because once you die, you let go."

"Letting go doesn't sound so bad."

"Depends. I don't like the idea of letting go of choice."

"Dying is a choice."

"Yeah, but what comes after that may not be."

I think about that for a beat. "What if you're out of choices? Or out of good ones, at least."

Juancho shakes his head vigorously. "In that case, I understand."

I smirk with a triumphant nod, but he doesn't stop there.

"But I think that if you're mostly young and fairly healthy, you have time; and if you have time, you have choices," he says.

That's a bit naïve, I think, but I don't say anything.

We sit in silence for a while, letting the mist and the lull of the falls envelop us. I look down, trying to find a good spot, and Juancho sees me looking.

"Are you trying to see the Virgin?"

"What?"

He laughs and points to the river. "La Virgen de los Suicidas? A statue of the Virgin Mary. They call her the Suicide Virgin. Supposedly she watches over the souls of those who died here. It's a famous statue. A lot of people go and take flowers and things for her and pray for the souls of the dead, so they don't end up in limbo."

I raise my eyebrow at him. "You know, for an atheist you're pretty well versed on all things Catholic."

He shrugs. "In Colombia it can't be helped."

After another long pause he looks at me and shakes his head. "You know, you're full of surprises."

"Me?"

"You see anyone else out here? Yeah, you."

"'Surprising' is not the worst thing I've been called."

He laughs, a warm, rumbly laugh that I feel in my gut. The warmth spreads to my cheeks and I realize I'm blushing. I look away and the wind picks up, blowing my hair in my face. Juancho reaches out and takes a strand off my forehead and tucks it behind my ear.

His touch makes me jump, the intimacy of the gesture so foreign that I don't know what to do. I think I scowl because Juancho retracts his hand like he's afraid I'll bite. I want to say I'm sorry, that I don't mind, that I kind of liked it, that I kind of like him, but that would only complicate things.

He clears his throat and tries to talk his way out of the discomfort. "Like I said, full of surprises."

"Like what?"

Not fishing for a compliment.

"Like you being crazy talented," he says.

Here, fishy, fishy.

"Not talented enough," I say, the bitterness stinging my lips.

"Not getting into a school and not being talented are two very different things."

"Not when it comes to Juilliard."

"Yes when it comes to Juilliard. You're a bad fit, or you're not a good fit now or not yet. That's not the same as not being talented. That just means they have an idea in their heads, and the reality of you doesn't fit that idea."

I shake my head. "They have an idea of what talent sounds like, and I don't sound like that."

Juancho growls in mock frustration. At least, I think it's mock frustration because he's smiling.

"How can you be so beautiful and so hard on yourself?"

My mouth is open because I was going to say something but hearing him say I'm beautiful makes me forget what.

He seems to find this funny, and for a moment I think he is going to tease me, tell me how dumb I am to think he really meant it.

I scowl in anticipation, and he looks worried.

"Hey, I take it back," he says, and I look away.

Of course he does.

But he's not done. "I mean, I do think you're too hard on yourself, but I didn't mean to make you feel bad."

Relief flows through me, which immediately makes me feel stupid.

"Oh," I say.

"Oh?"

"I thought you meant to take back . . . the other thing you said."

He gives me a puzzled look and I turn my head as he works it out.

"No," he says slowly, "the other thing I said I very much do not take back. I think you're pretty, Yolima. I think you're very pretty. I've liked you since that day when we had lunch together and we talked about music and you told me about Miami and all the cool places you go there. I've been thinking about you all summer."

I remember that lunch. I was still hopeful, then, convinced that I was a few weeks away from having my talent confirmed with an acceptance letter. I was buoyant with optimism. Maybe that's why he had liked me.

If that's true, there's nothing left of the girl he liked, and everything else will soon be gone.

"I have to admit, though, I'm seeing a darker side of you today."

I slow-blink, daring him to say more.

118

"I'm just saying, this morbid curiosity about suicide . . . it's pretty dark for someone nicknamed Jolly," he says.

"Oh, God. Good old Jolly Fats," I say, gritting my teeth. "I hate being Jolly Fats."

He's taken aback but recovers in no time. "What, you hate being Jolly?"

I hate having to be, I hate being expected to be, I hate that it's become the only emotion I'm allowed to have, as though every deviation from total, manic joy is undesirable or makes me undesirable. Undeserving.

"I hate being fat," I mumble.

"Well, for one thing, you're not fat. You're curvy. You're a woman, and you look like one."

He stumbles a bit there, his voice catching at the end, and I feel the warmness coming back.

I smile. "I look like a woman? As opposed to . . . ?"

"As opposed to a stick figure, as opposed to an unrealistic cartoonishly Photoshopped cover girl. You are real, and I am real," he inches closer to me, so close I can smell his aftershave, I can feel the heat of his breath, I can look into his eyes and make out the little flecks of yellow in the rich dark chocolate brown. I feel a moment forming, something is there, something that requires me to lean in and close my eyes and maybe . . . but then he ruins it, he ruins everything because he says, "and whatever is going on in your head to make you think different? That is definitely not real."

I don't know what to say, and then I don't have to say anything because we hear a whistle above us. There's a guy standing there, wearing a crew t-shirt, so I know he works for Samir.

"Hey, primo!" he says, waving to Juancho. I know by now that all costeños call each other primo, even if they're not cousins. When I asked why, they said it was because we were one big happy family.

Juancho glances at me before looking up at the guy. "What up, Charlie?" he yells back.

"We got a problem. Get your butt up here and earn your paycheck," Charlie says.

We share a look, an unspoken promise to pick this up later, and head back to the building.

INSIDE, THE FIRST FLOOR IS MASSIVE CHAOS. It's been converted into a dance space with spooky decorations to mark the theme, more Goth than Halloween, all done up in black with fuchsia and silver accents. It's cool, funky, sophisticated, and has Dee and Nee written all over it.

Juancho and I are barely through the large double doors when Charlie pounces on us.

"We're screwed," he says.

"What happened?" Juancho says, taking off his jacket.

Anger and frustration are building up heat, so I take mine off too and start to wander away.

"There was a power surge and the computer we set up for the DJ got fried," says the other crewmember, a girl with multiple piercings and green hair, striding up to Juancho and Charlie.

"So? Use another one. Hell, she can use mine," Juancho says. He sees me make to leave and holds my gaze like he doesn't want us to be done.

And, I realize, neither do I.

I linger and hear the girl groan, "You think we're stupid? The thumb drive she had loaded with tonight's music was in the laptop. It got fried, too."

Juancho says nothing, looking from one to the other, waiting for the rest of the bad news.

"She could load another thumb drive, but she didn't bring her laptop. She'd have to go back to her studio," the girl says.

"She said she didn't bring it because she figured that this house would have faulty wiring and didn't want her computer to get fried," Charlie says with a snicker, "so, like, ironic, right?"

Juancho gives him a death stare and turns his attention to the girl. "How long?"

"From Soacha to downtown Bogotá and back? On a Saturday night? At least three hours."

Juancho looks at his watch and groans. "VIPs will be here in an hour and the party should be in full swing in two. Does Sammy know?" he asks, and both shake their heads.

Juancho looks at me, and I get chills because he smiles like he's hit the jackpot. "Alright, nobody say nothing for now." He turns to the girl again, hands her an envelope and says, "Here, get an Uber and go with the DJ, make sure she brings at least three damn thumb drives with the music and get back here as soon as you can. Tell the Uber to wait. You," he says to Charlie, "go get me the equipment from the car and set it up in the van."

He walks towards me, eyes glistening. "And you? You get to be the hero."

WE ARE IN THE BACK OF SAMIR'S VAN. THERE'S plenty of space and the AC is cranked up despite the chill outside, but it still feels stuffy. Juancho exchanged a few words with Charlie and sent him off to do something, so it's just the two of us now.

Juancho finishes hooking up stuff to his laptop and hands me what looks like an instrument case, but I can't tell what instrument is in there.

"Here. Take it," he says, all but chucking it at me.

"What the hell is this?" I say.

He doesn't answer me, turning instead to his laptop and clicking away. I don't want to care but I do, so I open the case.

Inside is a violin. An electric violin, to be exact, a gaudy metallic purple number that lacks the curves and warmth of my own.

"An electric violin?" I say, holding it out to him like it's a dirty diaper.

"You heard what happened. I have to come up with a way to entertain people while the DJ comes back with the music, right? Well, I happen to have a talented violinist right here."

"I can't play this, so . . ." I start to put the purple nightmare back in its case, but Juancho closes the lid with his foot.

"Listen, I might be just an entry-level assistant right now, but it's getting me closer to my dream, okay? I want to be in the music business, and that means I need contacts, which means I need to do well here so that Sammy can hook me up later, see? And you may not love this side of music, hell, from what I've seen you may not even love this side of your own family, but I'm hoping you care enough to help out."

I let what he said wash over me. Some of it stings, but I focus on the part about helping.

I could do this. Go out with a bang. What do I have to lose? I could make a fool of myself, but then my choice would make more sense. Then everyone would understand why I just couldn't go on being Jolly Fats anymore.

On the other hand, I could do well and go out on a high note, leave behind a legacy, let people see my potential before I make my exit from existence.

And my family would be grateful, right? At least they could see that I tried.

"What do you want me to do?"

AT FIRST THE ELECTRIC VIOLIN FEELS WEIRD, clunky and alien. It has an ergonomic chin rest and shoulder pad system and is pretty lightweight, but it sits in my hands all wrong. Also, the violin is passive, which means it only works when it's connected to the amplifier.

"It's a mute instrument," I whine. "That's just wrong."

"But it's perfect for this."

Juancho's idea is to lay a few tracks down now and then have me playing live on the stage. He says with the lights and me in a costume it'll look like part of the show, like it was all planned. He doesn't want to tell Samir, he says, because even though he's pretty sure this will work, he still wants to give my cousin full deniability just in case.

I make a mental note to tell Samir about this loyal streak.

The theme tonight is plancha music, so the older the song, the better. The idea is to spice the oldies up with some chords to make them more dance-friendly, but I'm not feeling it.

"Besides," Juancho says, smiling, "if we'd had your own instrument, we wouldn't be able to transfer the music to the computer so easily."

I roll my eyes but smile at the same time.

Truth is, he's been super nice, thanking me over and over, being patient as I fumble with the settings and complain about the tone and how I can't move around freely and that there's a slight lag between my movements and the sound. I'm enjoying his company, enjoying myself, more than I have in weeks.

Maybe my last day won't be such a waste after all.

BY THE TIME GUESTS START ARRIVING, WE'VE laid down some tracks we can work with and have worked out some basic chords that I can add to songs. I'm actually quite proud of some of the mixes, and we've managed to work out a system for integrating the beats with my playing so that the transitions are smooth, the tempo rising to a crescendo that will climax triumphantly with the DJ's return.

We hope.

Juancho says we're ready but I linger a moment. There's something I can't let go.

"What you said before," I start, "about me not loving this side of my family. That's not true, you know? I just never got to know them."

"Yet," he says.

"What?"

"You mean you haven't gotten to know them yet."

"Yet," I say, the word heavy on my tongue.

"There's a lot of power in that little word, Yolima. You haven't gotten to know the Fatamis yet; you haven't gotten into Juilliard yet." He smiles. "You haven't fallen madly in love with me yet."

I smile at that, and his smile gets wider.

"The power of yet? Sounds like the title of a cheesy self-help book," I say.

"Well, it's nice to have a backup plan in the cheesy book business in case this evening doesn't work out."

BUT IT DOES WORK OUT. IT'S SLOW GOING AT first but the electric violin and I have made a truce by the time I take the stage, and Juancho's confidence gives me the boost I need to get creative with my little touches. I interject sass into Daniela Romo, jazz me up some Maria Conchita, and by the time Emmanuel's *Toda la Vida* hits, I've invented and mastered the art of the Plancha vibrato, pulling double stops, shuffling and chopping my way through a dozen songs, and when the beat drops and the crowd swarms and swells, responding to me, I am mighty. Powerful. Alive.

I did that. I made them feel that. I made people feel something.

Then it's over. DJ Holocor comes in, I'm cheered off stage, and as far as anyone knows, all is as it was meant to be.

I'm two steps away from the stage, feeling happy, sweating, exhausted, when Sammy envelops me in a hug and drags me onto a couch where Juancho is sitting, beaming like the cat who found the cream.

"You two," he says, rustling Juancho's hair. "You almost gave me a heart attack."

Neither one of us says anything, so Sammy goes on. "I can't believe you pulled that off."

"We did good, boss?" Juancho says, and I can see his hero worship for Samir, I can tell that this really means a lot to him, beyond the entry-level job or whatever. He really likes my cousin, looks up to him, wants to please him.

And Samir is pleased. I can see that, too.

"I don't know what I like more, the smiles on my investors or the smile on my cousin," he says, winking at me.

Juancho shifts in his seat and we both look away. I don't know if Samir can tell something's going on and wants to drill me or if he really has something to say, but he asks Juancho to leave us alone for a moment.

Juancho's eyes linger, a promise to look for me later plainly written in his smile.

"That was really cool," Samir says.

"Thanks."

"You remind me a lot of your sister," he says, his voice soft and melancholy.

I snort. "Yeah, right. We get confused all the time."

He tilts his head. "I don't mean you look like her. You're your own kind of beautiful. I mean the way you play reminds me of the way she writes. Nene says we are part Wayuú, so we are all of us weavers. Addie weaves words, I weave people. You weave notes."

A note weaver. That's new. I like that.

I can't think of anything to say and so I start to leave but Samir grabs me gently by the wrist.

"She wanted this for you, you know. She wanted you to be free to discover yourself, to be yourself."

"Well, being myself means being the accident that followed the miracle, so . . ."

I mean to be funny, but the look Samir gives me is full of pain. It takes me off guard.

"Being a miracle carries a lot of expectations. Being the reason your parents got married and your mother had to leave her beloved Cartagena? All that weighs on Addie. She feels that she has to be perfect all the time."

"She is perfect," I say bitterly. "Effortlessly perfect, beautiful, smart, kind. All of it."

"She may be all those things, but it's not effortless. She is constantly afraid that she'll fail, that she'll let everybody down, that if she's not able to live up to their expectations, the weight of those expectations will fall on you. And she doesn't want that for you."

Samir loves Adira, it's there in his eyes. Looking back, I can see she loved him, too. And I understand why she couldn't return here, how being with him would've meant straying from the trajectory of perfection that had been laid out for her.

Honestly, I had never thought of Adira being anything but happy, basking in the light of my parents' attention. It had never occurred to me that all that attention came at such a price.

This time when I get up to leave, Samir lets me go. I wander outside, the bottle and its contents heavy, bouncing off my thigh with every step.

THE BALUSTRADE CALLS TO ME AND I WALK towards it, slowly. Deliberately.

Jolly Fats dies tonight. The decision has been made. It's time, it's long overdue.

I know what I have to do.

I place my hands on the flat and try to gauge how hard it will be to get on top. I could sit first, then turn, or maybe one leg up . . . ?

As I ponder the logistics of the deed, Juancho comes up behind me.

"Hey," he says, eyeing the gorge with unease. "Are you looking for me?"

"Not really," I say.

"Oh."

His shoulders slump. He nods and starts to leave, but I reach out and grab a hold of his jacket.

"Oh," he says, a breathy whisper.

His eyebrows ask a question and my smile provides the answer. He inches closer to me and instead of letting go of his hand I put my other hand on his arm and now his hands are on my waist and he is looking into my eyes.

"Are you okay?"

I nod.

The warmth of his hands spreads from my waist to the rest of my body and I start to sway to music we can't hear, and he sways with me and we stay this way until our foreheads touch.

When I don't pull away, he presses closer and we kiss, tenderly at first, but then I realize how much I like this, how much I like him, and I kiss him more deeply. He presses against me and I use his shoulders to prop myself up on the balustrade and now I'm almost as tall as he is. I wrap my legs around his waist and one of his hands holds me just above the knee while the other one works its way from my hips to my neck. He pulls gently on my hair and we separate so he can kiss my exposed neck.

I've kissed boys before, but this is different. He's not a boy, technically. He's eighteen, an adult, but there's more to it than that. The other kisses, the other boys, it felt like I was trying to

127

be someone else, something else. I kept sucking in my tummy, thinking of back fat, trying to stand on tiptoe to look taller, wishing my lips were thicker and my thighs were thinner. I don't feel that now. I feel like he likes every inch of me, and every inch of me likes him back.

This idea of inches makes me smile and soon I start to giggle. Juancho pulls away instantly.

"Oh, God, Yolima, are you drunk? Are you . . . are you high? Because I don't want to do this with you if you're not 100 percent you right now."

I smile at him, touch his face, run my fingers through his hair. "No, I'm all me right now. I can honestly say this is the most me I've felt in a while."

He lets out a big breath of relief. "Good, because Dee and Nee told me a while back about some pills . . ."

He lets the sentence hover, unfinished, and I shake my head. He seems to relax and leans in, ready to pick up where we left off, but I put my hand gently on his chest.

"About those pills, though," I start.

This time he takes a full step back and the place where he was feels cold and wrong.

"No, Yolima. I'm not into that."

I smile because this is so the perfect thing for him to say, but he misreads my smile and turns away.

I reach and manage to grab his hand. "Wait, Juancho. Hear me out. Please."

He hesitates but turns back. Instead of putting his hands on my waist, my hip, anywhere on me, he puts his palm on the balustrade and takes his other hand away from mine.

"About those pills, I have them. Here. But I don't want to take them," I rush to say. "I want to throw them away. I want to toss them, this whole bottle and everything in it, away. Will you help me?"

His eyes narrow. "You need help finding a trash can?"

I laugh. "No, I don't want to throw them in a trash can. I want to fling them into the gorge, far and away."

He takes a breath like he wants to say something, but he looks into my eyes and just stops. I don't know what he sees in there, whether it's how badly I want this or how serious I am or what, but he seems to sense that this is important. Maybe he understands the symbolism, knows that there's more to tossing the bottle into the gorge than just getting rid of something.

In any case, he nods.

I hold his hand tightly and stand on the balustrade in one fluid motion. Juancho clearly wasn't expecting this, and he freaks out a bit, but he doesn't pull me down. Instead, he grabs my calves and says, "I got you. Do what you need to do."

I want to kiss him so hard for that.

I take the bottle and undo the knot that secures it to my harem pants. It feels heavier than before, heavier than it should with just a suicide note and a few pills in it, but I guess it's got more than that in there. It's got years of frustration and resentment, entitlement and bitterness.

I take a deep, deep breath and toss the bottle as far as I can, over the edge, into the mist, into the gorge, away, away, away.

"Jolly Fats is dead!" I say, and I look at Juancho, who looks terrified. I yell louder, "Jolly Fats is dead!"

I laugh and fall into Juancho's outstretched arms and he places me gently on the floor and crushes me into his chest. I can hear his heart beating so hard I actually feel the thump through his shirt like a tiny slap on my cheek.

"Better?" he says, his voice a little strained.

"Way better," I say, melting into him.

We stay like that for a while and then he asks, "What now?"

I look up to see his face and think about that.

Maybe we kiss some more, go back to the party, and later I call my sister and we have a good cry; maybe we go upstairs and I make the same mistake my mother made; maybe I come back to Colombia after this summer and go to la Javeriana;

maybe Juancho and I become a famous DJ duo; maybe I get into Juilliard.

I don't know. But the power of yet and the mystery of maybe fill me with something new, something fresh and scary and possible and unknown and I feel there are choices to be made and I am not sure who is making those choices now but it sure as hell isn't Jolly Fats.

Because Jolly Fats is dead at last.

STUDY NIGHT AT THE MUSEUM
S.E. ANDERSON

"There's a mummy eating yogurt in the breakroom." I glance up from my half-finished homework. Nat's propping herself up in the doorframe, her face as white as a sheet. She looks as if she's just seen a ghost—which, if you're inclined to believe her, is exactly what's happened.

Well. Somewhat.

I stare at her across the dim light of the library, trying to think up a witty reply that will elevate my social status to *cool*. Something along the lines of: *Well, what else is it going to eat? Marty's tuna-sub reeks!* or *You see, this is why we both need coffee.*

When I open my mouth, all the words I could say stay stuck in my throat. Honestly, I'm hurt. I've had my fair share of hazing before, with how many times I've changed schools, but I really thought I was making strides in befriending Nat. Maybe she's planned this with her *real* friends? *Oh, I know, let's see if Kate is scared of ghosts. No, mummies!*

Do they know?

Still, I've never seen Nat so pale before. Her face is so drained she's gone practically monochromatic. Granted, I haven't known her long at all, but I doubt even a total stranger would miss the red flags.

"You okay there?" I ask.

She shakes her head, oh-so-slowly.

No. Definitely not okay there.

She must be a terrific actress, if this really is a prank.

I get up, cut my way to her in three strides, and help her to the nearest chair. I hit the main lights. For the first time, I'm glad the Natural History Museum has a cold, sterile library rather than the ornate wooden one I've always dreamed of.

The stark fluorescent beams chase away the shadows on Nat's face. Her lips are moving, but she's not saying anything. I thought I'd read enough about quivering lips in fiction to recognize it happening in real life, but this is so much worse. I'm still not sure exactly *what* has gone wrong. Something terrifying and terrible, but a mummy of all things? Impossible.

This can't be happening. There has to be a reasonable explanation for this. There's always a reasonable explanation.

I'll stick with prank. See how far this goes.

"Are you going into shock?" I ask. As if she'd know. As if either of us would know what to do if she was.

"D'you have any water?" She finally manages to say something, but her voice is so hoarse it cracks a little.

"Just tea. It's cold." I hand her my thermos, and she chugs it down in a single gulp. Too quickly. She chokes and coughs, sending spray over my arms.

"Easy," I say, wiping her saliva from my skin. Gross. "Have you eaten anything recently?"

Nat shakes her head. "I was hoping for something from the vending machine, but the mummy . . ." Her eyes go wide again.

I don't like this feeling in my chest, the rising heartbeat at the sight of her. She's so scared, her fear is catching. Which is why this absolutely cannot be real. This has to end now.

"I'm not falling for this." I drop myself back on my chair, and she looks up at me sharply.

"What are you talking about?" She's staring at me, *still* putting on the act. It's so convincing I'm starting to give in. I can't.

"Oh, come on, do I have to say it? I'm the new kid, it's Friday night . . . This is some elaborate prank."

Her face falls. I thought it was impossible for her to look any more haunted, but whoops, now she's left ghost-territory and looks outright corpse-like.

"Seriously?" Her word is a whisper. An earnest, pained whisper. I'm actually feeling sorry for her. "Kate. Please."

"Ok, fine." I roll my eyes. "Show me the mummy, then. But if your football buddies think they can get the drop on me . . ."

I expect her to try and convince me more, but instead she quietly slips off her chair and waits for me to take the lead. Which I do, grabbing my phone off the desk and clutching it tightly to my chest as I go. I won't be taken by surprise.

I don't know if this is a good plan or not. At the very least, I'm stretching my legs, even if it is just a hop and a skip down the hallway to the breakroom. I've been crouched for hours over that desk, reading through the old books and reference papers that Dr. Lauren Eagleman, the director of Egyptology, pulled out for us. I've literally been taking notes until my wrist feels sprained for the past ten days. I *need* this college credit. I can't have anyone put that in jeopardy.

I'm not supposed to be here or anywhere near this stinking town. My parents decided last month that their 'research' was more important than family and deposited me and my little brother Teagan with our grandparents before they caught a cargo ship to Antilles. I was supposed to be finishing my senior year with my friends, kicking butt at soccer and dominating the field. Instead, I'm forced to take every available AP class in a desperate attempt to look good for universities, now that I'm out of the running for a sports scholarship. Apparently, there's no room for me on my school's new team. I can't just come out of nowhere and squeeze myself into places where I don't belong.

The field isn't the only place that doesn't have room for me. I'm joining classes midway through the term, which means most projects have already started. My new AP English teacher runs a project every year partnering with different universities, sending her students to affiliated museums to give them real-world research experience and connections for potential summer jobs. Since I showed up late, I didn't get to choose where I was assigned, which is how I got paired with Nat, working in the back library of the Natural History Museum at 9 P.M., reading about scarab beetles for hours and hours, without a drop of coffee in sight.

Not the senior year I was dreaming of.

We're not even meant to stay this late. Nat's plan for our project is so overwhelming, she just *had* to ask for extra time on-site. Dr. Eagleman was thrilled—thrilled!—to give us access. It's not like we're running around the museum floor after hours though. We just stay in the staff areas. Marty, the security guard and the only other person here at this time, checks on us once an hour, so I am literally the only person inconvenienced by Nat.

And on Valentine's Day, too. Not that I had to cancel any plans, but having the option would have been nice. Maybe Nat planned this because she doesn't want to admit she's single on a night like this.

Thirty seconds later, we reach the breakroom. It was once an animal research lab, back before the biology department moved to a larger space on the university campus, so it has a big glass window in the door. While it sucks to feel like a fish in a bowl every time you take a snack break, knowing everyone can see you slacking off, the window does have its perks: especially right now, when it means I can see clearly into the breakroom.

To the mummy currently licking the last of the yogurt out of the cup.

Oddly enough, my first reaction is to be rather peeved, because that's *my* yogurt, and I was really looking forward to it. My second reaction is pure and utter panic.

It takes every ounce of courage I have not to take to my heels and run away.

Ancient linen wraps span the mummy's body head to toe, worn thin in some areas, where they hang off in tangled strips revealing skin that's wrinkly, coppery brown, like old leather. Its hands are bound tight like mitts, but it still manages to hold a spoon. Its black hair is long and surprisingly shimmery.

But it's the face that is truly traumatizing. In the movies, mummies' faces are always wrapped up so you can't see a thing. Only their mouths remain, so they can moan and groan and make generally terrifying sounds. But the being before me has a *face*. There's obvious mounds and indents where the features should be, gauges revealing muscle. There are two slits where the eyes are, like the mummy is squinting as it tries to clean its cup, because, let's be honest, it is clearly enjoying my strawberry Yoplait.

The mummy is *alive*. And, as far as I know, mummies aren't meant to be walking around museums—or walking around at all, for that matter. This is uncharted territory. Whatever brought it back from the dead screwed with the laws of nature.

"Shit," I say. It's all I can manage not to panic. My hands are trembling so much I can't keep my phone steady as I press it to the glass window. The mummy's in full view on my camera app, though my jittery fingers are making the image shaky. I start recording immediately.

"What are you doing?" Nat asks.

"Filming. No one's going to believe us otherwise."

I know from experience—well, my parents' experience— how much crap paranormal truthers get for their terrible video evidence. One thing Mom and Dad never seem to grasp is that recording your reaction to a ghost isn't the same kind of proof as actually getting the ghost itself. My phone is always on me; I have no excuse for letting this get away.

Nat and I stop beneath the window in silence as we watch my screen. The mummy laps up the dregs of my late-night snack with a tongue that shouldn't be there.

None of *it* should be there.

"What do we do?" Nat's voice is a harsh whisper.

"How should I know?"

"You're the one with muscles!"

I didn't think she'd noticed. The heat in my face is either from my terror or my blushing. "So, you want me to go in there and *beat up* the two-thousand-year-old mummy? That's your plan. A mummy which, I should mention, shouldn't be alive or eating anything?"

"Five thousand."

"What?"

"It's a *five*-thousand-year-old mummy." Nat's words tumble out so fast they're tripping over each other. "First Dynasty. Come on, you should know this! It's the only mummy in the whole museum."

"Well, how do we know it's the *same* mummy that's meant to be on display? Hmm?"

"What other mummy could it be?"

"And it's eating my yogurt."

"Further evidence Marty's tuna sub is inedible to everyone."

We don't have time for this. My arms are still shaking, holding my phone up at the window, and my back's beginning to ache from the hunkering down. I chance a discreet look through the window, and my heart skips a terrible beat. The breakroom is empty; the discarded yogurt cup on the table is the only evidence the creature was ever here. Oddly, this isn't reassuring.

What's worse than finding a mummy in your breakroom? Finding one—then losing it.

"Crap," I say. "The mummy's gone."

"What do you mean, it's gone?" asked Nat. "Hold on—what's that?"

A single bug scurries over the glass, almost as large as the palm of my hand. I'm instantly entranced by it—it's shimmery, somehow, like it's made from polished metal. The click of its feet on the glass is the only sound in the entire building as the two of us hold our breath. It shouldn't be here.

"Is that a beetle?" asks Nat.

"Scarab," I say. I've spent enough of my afternoons and evenings reading about them to recognize the buggers on sight, even if we're watching its underside. Not that I ever expected to see a real one. It's incredible, the way it moves, like jewelry in motion.

Nat shudders, close enough for me to feel it, and the bug marches out of view. If I hadn't just seen the mummy, I would have called it an omen. Now it just feels like postscript.

"It's—"

Neither of us has time to speak as we're interrupted by a massive thump. We both shriek as the door handle turns, as the weight that slams against us again makes it abundantly clear the mummy is *real*. It wasn't gone, just too short to see. There is a live mummy in the breakroom—and it's breaking out.

Nat and I hurl our full weight against the door. The mummy must be strong, because the two of us are straining to keep it closed. My muscles burn, dull from weeks of stagnancy. I stuff my phone into my pocket, but even with both hands, holding the door back feels impossible. The weight on the other side releases for a split second, then strikes again, full force.

"We can't let it out!" Nat shouts.

"Why? Let's just let it go back where it came from!"

"It's museum property. Who do you think they're going to blame for this?"

The glass window shatters. A linen-wrapped fist flies through, grasping at whatever it can. Nat and I cry out as sharp shards fly into our faces. The smell hits me like a fist: it's as if someone has condensed a musty old church into an essential oil and plugged it right into my nose. A wave of scarab beetles bursts through the jagged breach and spills out over the edge, hundreds of them shrouding the door until we can't see it anymore, overflowing onto the floor where they skitter over our shoes.

I can't see the mummy's face, but I can hear it: a garbled wail fills the hallway, anger and anguish all wrapped up in one.

I don't need to speak ancient Egyptian to know it wants out, and it's *pissed*.

The undead hand grabs a clump of Nat's hair and rips it back. She screams again, but this time it's a bloodcurdling sound, as if the mummy's tearing her very life from her. Without thinking, I grab its wrist and yank hard so its elbow catches on the broken glass edges of the window frame. The hand releases Nat's hair and the mummy growls, now fumbling blindly for me.

"Run!" I shout at Nat, before I take my own advice and dash down the corridor after her to the safety of the library.

"Tatakat!" the mummy moans. Words—it's saying actual *words*. It's smart, it's thinking, and it wants something. Not that I have any idea what that is. 'Tatakat' isn't in my vocabulary, but it feels ancient and raw.

I'm faster than Nat and reach the library first, turning back for her. The mummy's close at her heels, arms stiff as it reaches for her. It's worse than any movie I've ever seen, so much faster. Individual fingers are breaking free of the bandages, linen-wrapped bones extending, grabbing for Nat and—

I pull Nat inside the library and slam the door, locking us both in quickly.

"Oh God, oh God, oh God." Nat clasps her scalp with both hands, as if the dried-up fingers are still tangled in her hair and she's desperate to rip them out.

The mummy pounds on the door. I push back hard, but there's no need. It lets out a guttural moan and stops. Just keeps repeating that word—*tatakat*. It almost sounds like the creature is in pain. The words get softer and quieter, more and more distance between us and it—the mummy is walking away.

"Wh-wh-what the hell is that thing?" I stammer. I'm not ready to let go of the door yet. To believe we're safe here. "Do we call 911 for this? What do we even say?"

"A real, live, mummy," Nat says, her eyes shining with fear. Her voice is fast but hushed. "See? I told you this wasn't a prank." She could have been mean about it, but she says it simply, like a statement of fact. I suppose we're beyond petty squabbles now.

I retrieve my phone from my pocket, relieved not to have lost my only lifeline. I start dialing. Two numbers in, Nat grabs my wrist.

"No! They'll think we're crazy."

"What else are we going to do? We've got no weapons. We can't defend ourselves against a literal *monster*."

"Who says we have to fight it? Maybe it wants something."

"Like what? I mean, other than yogurt?"

The doorknob shakes, and the two of us shoot into the air. Some reflex kicks in, and I dive under a desk, dragging Nat down with me. There's a pause, a jiggling, and the doorknob turns all the way around. Nat's breath hitches. I throw a hand over her mouth as the door opens—

"Girls? Are you alright? Katherine? Natalie?"

I turn into a puddle of relief, exhaling so strongly I could have shot into the stratosphere. It's not the mummy—it's the night guard, Marty, on his hourly check-in.

Nat pushes my hands away and scrambles out from under the table. "Oh, thank God." She rushes toward him, stopping short of actually giving him a hug.

He lifts one of his eyebrows. "Should I even ask?"

"*Thereisamummyanditbrokethewindowtothebreakroom!*" Nat blurts out.

"A what in the where now?"

"We saw someone in the breakroom. Close the door!" I pull out my phone and load the video. "Well, some*thing*. . . Take a look."

Marty could well have told us this wasn't the time and gone back to his rounds, but he watches all the way through, his brows knitting tighter and tighter until I think they might stitch into one.

"It *attacked* us." Nat is on the verge of tears, her body shaking. "It shattered the breakroom window and is somewhere in the museum. We came back here to hide."

"I don't know who this hoodlum is, but he can't be allowed to break in and threaten you like this," Marty says, handing me back my phone.

Wait, he still doesn't believe the mummy is real? That it's just a costume? Then again, if I hadn't smelled the mummy for myself, I might have believed the same.

"You two stay here and lock the door. Don't move until I come back for you. You hear me?" Marty doesn't wait for us to respond—he's already through the door and running down the corridor again in the direction of the security room.

Nat doesn't hesitate, just shoves the library door shut again. *Click. Click.* She turns the key twice in the lock. I don't feel any safer, though. Not now I know mummies are real.

"Marty will find it." Nat reaches for her backpack—it's still on the floor, where she left it at the start of the night. She pulls the bag onto her lap as she takes a seat. She wraps her arms around it without opening a single zipper, clutching it close to her chest. "He has to."

I look again at my phone, at the thumbnail on my screen. At the mummy frozen in the pixels.

It's real. It's real. It's real.

"Kate . . . Are you okay?" asks Nat.

"Are you?"

We don't answer each other. So, instead, I sit back at my desk. My chair is still warm. My books are the same as before I ran off—everything is. But I'm not. I clench my fists to stop my hands from shaking. This must be what being in shock feels like.

Is this why I'm dying for a protein bar?

"Do you think they have any books on mummies in here?" Nat gestures to the sterile metal shelves.

"The kind that runs through museums and steals yogurt? Yeah, of course."

"You know what I mean."

"Then I seriously doubt it. And, also, I doubt Dr. Eagleman will appreciate emails about them ruining her Friday night."

S.E. ANDERSON

Nat glances down at her phone, exhaling sharply. "I don't even have any signal, anyway."

I check my own phone, and my heart drops. I don't have a single bar—and the WiFi isn't on, either. It makes no sense: I've always had signal here before.

My mother's pseudoscience technobabble floats into my head. *The dead can manipulate magnetic fields, Kate. It's why lights flicker when ghosts are around. It has nothing to do with haunted houses having old wiring—*

I can't believe I'm actually going to say this. "This is going to sound batshit crazy, but I think the mummy must be creating electromagnetic interference."

"What? How?"

"Ghosts do it. Mummies could too."

I bet Mom felt me speak from her bunk on the ship. Because there's no way in hell she didn't hear her only daughter—normally a huge skeptic—agree with one of her theories. Or maybe she's out on a hunt and will put the feeling down to ghost activity. In any case, the mere fact I acknowledged the undead at all must have seriously shifted the equilibrium of the planet.

Nat snorts. "Right, yes, because ghosts are such a reliable source of information."

"We should just, you know, go? We can just walk out of here."

"Marty said to wait for him here," says Nat. "And who knows? Maybe it's not actually a mummy, just a creep in a costume."

"All the more reason to get out of here."

"I'd rather listen to Marty. He's the expert."

An expert in what? How to handle monsters? I doubt they cover that in museum training.

"Okay, well," I say, "you're the one who knows the museum so well, so who was that mummy? Maybe we can figure out what it's doing walking around, if we know who it is? Or was?"

143

Nat smiles sheepishly. "Well, it has to be Queen Hathorhat." I search through my gray matter—nada. "Who?"

"You have to be kidding me," Nat says. "You've been here a month, and you haven't stepped inside the actual exhibit?"

"It's always been packed. I don't like crowds. Sue me."

Nat wakes up her phone and slides it across the desk to me. Her lockscreen is a sarcophagus. She truly is obsessed. "She's the only mummy on display in the entire museum. And a bit of a big deal." She pauses—as if waiting for me to say something along the lines of, *Oh, that Queen Hathorhat! We go way back!*—and when I don't, she continues, slightly more peeved than before. But peeved is better than traumatized.

"She was one of the last queens of the first Dynasty, having lived sometime in late 3000 BC-ish. The markings on her sarcophagus lead us to believe she might have been one of the wives of Horus Den himself. But what's truly remarkable is that she's clearly from the end of the dynasty, since her tomb only had a single human sacrifice. It might be the last one to have had sacrifices at all."

I was so ready to call her out on the use of 'us'—she's a high schooler, not an archaeologist—before I heard the end of her spiel. *"Human sacrifice?"*

"You know the ancient Egyptians were obsessed with the afterlife, right? Well, in the early tombs, archaeologists found skeletons in the chambers near the dead royals. Apparently, the first pharaohs were so concerned with their standing in death that they wanted to be sure they had their attendants waiting for them in the afterlife. Skeletons of young people—in their early twenties, from what we can tell—show that some were even entombed alive."

The museum suddenly feels much colder than it had just minutes before. "That's barbaric."

"Well, the practice was abandoned as the great Egyptian civilization rose. And Queen Hathorhat only had a single handmaid buried alongside her."

"Right. So, dead lady who loves some live burials is now up and walking the museum halls. Any idea why?" I run my fingertips across my scalp, trying to scratch up some good ideas.

"Beats me. Maybe someone cursed her before she died?" Nat suggests.

"And you believe in mummies being cursed?"

"I don't know what I believe in right now."

My throat feels too dry. "Well, in my experience, when someone rises from the dead, it's because they have unfinished business here on earth. Actually, that's for ghosts. Not so sure about where mummies fall."

"In your experience?"

A bone-chilling scream echoes through the museum, deep and masculine and beyond terrified. It's the same kind of scream Nat uttered as the mummy tugged at her hair—the *I'm going to die* scream.

Marty's in trouble—so much for being safe. I don't hesitate as I race for the door.

"What are you? Crazy?" says Nat as I fumble with the lock. "We have to stay here!"

"If Marty's in trouble, I'm not going to sit here and do nothing." I unlock the door and bolt into the hallway, both hoping for and dreading a second scream to direct me. I chase the first one to the ground floor, the one with the lobby and animals. While I haven't had the time to read the panels of the main exhibit, I do know my way around the museum. I race through the dark staff hallways and into the Egyptian exhibit hall.

I feel like I'm on a movie set. The fake torches are burning with *real* fire. In the flickering light, the walls of the museum are almost tomb-like, despite the stupid Papyrus font that adorns every sign. The torchlight flickers off the gold jewels and treasures in the glass cases all around. Banners hang around showing off the Valentine's Day events I sadly missed from earlier today: costume reenactments, romantic poetry readings,

STUDY NIGHT AT THE MUSEUM

biology-of-love seminars. There's a massive banner strung up in this gallery, showing hieroglyphs of a black-haired woman holding hands with a bird-headed being.

In the very center of the hall sits the ancient sarcophagus, the glass case which once held it having entirely shattered, forming a perfect circle around the raised plinth. Even in the low light, I can make out the central symbols: black-haired women, their palms pressed against each other, below the death portrait of the queen. They're leaning their heads together, so close they're almost touching, like they're sharing some ancient secret.

The mummy, however, is nowhere to be seen.

"Marty?" I shout.

No answer.

Maybe I shouldn't have shouted in the first place. I swear under my breath. It's not like I know what to do if I find either of them, but I can't let Marty get hurt while protecting me. It's just not right. Maybe if it comes down to it, I can kick our way to safety.

"Tatakat . . . tatakat . . ."

But the voice is too deep to be the mummy's. It can't be . . . It sounds like Marty.

My stomach drops like a stone. I whirl around, and there he is, just feet away, his eyes swirling with white, smoke filling his irises which seems to almost glow in the torchlight. He stands tall and painfully rigid, walking in a straight line through the exhibit floor.

"Tatakat . . . tatakat . . ." he says again. He seems to be looking for something, or someone.

Thankfully I don't think he's seen me, and I duck behind one of the decorative columns. Marty winds his way through the hall like a toy soldier, past my hiding place, repeating the same words over and over again. He's in some kind of trance, hypnotized by the only being who knows what the words he's saying actually are.

"Marty?"

I regret my call instantly. The impossible speed at which he spins around is disconcerting, and the look on his face . . . The smoky eyes really are glowing. His face is red, much too red to be caused by torchlight. His every feature radiates fury.

Well, shit, Marty's been possessed. Not only is the mummy strong for her age, but she's also got superpowers. This *so* isn't fair. Since when did death give you superpowers?

A shiver runs through me. This is serious. This is terrible. Marty was our strongest ally, our only ally, and the mummy's taken him as her pawn. Her—or whatever magic brought her back to life tonight.

I stand painfully still in the shadows, hoping the smoke in his eyes keeps him from seeing me in the dim light. Finally, Marty turns back away from me, returning to his march, and to his intoning. "Tatakat . . . tatakat . . ."

Whatever the mummy is looking for, she's so desperate to find it she's recruited a helper. Wonderful.

There has to be a way out of here for Nat and me, so we can go for help and then save Marty. I step out from behind the pillar and tiptoe down the hall in the opposite direction he just went, looping around the giftshop that's all locked up for the night. I keep to the shadows, which is easy in the low light, from the oversized columns to the large plasterboard walls of text that turn the exhibits into a maze. Everything is still, silent as the grave, so quiet I can hear my own heart pounding in my chest.

I reach the great glass doors of the museum's main atrium. I hesitate for a second—opening the door would set off an alarm. But that's exactly what I want: at least, then, cops would come and we'd have backup. I take a deep breath and push the bar—only the doors don't budge an inch. There's no movement, and no alarm.

We're trapped in here.

A thud echoes from an adjacent hall, like a small cardboard box tumbling to the ground. It's as loud as an explosion in the emptiness of the museum. I take a deep breath. As much as I want to go back to the Library, we won't get anywhere if I hide and wait. I have to follow that sound to the Hall of Animals.

Like most—if not all—natural history museums, there's a large collection of taxidermized animals on display. I've always avoided these kinds of exhibit halls; their beady, glass eyes are a terrible imitation of life and freak me out. I find the mummy with her linen-wrapped hands tight around the neck of a stuffed alligator, muttering something. She grunts as she shakes it up and down. The alligator says nothing. A crocodile lies overturned beside her.

"Life force." Nat's voice makes me almost jump out of my skin.

My head turns so quickly I swear I hear my neck crack. Nat's right behind me. If the mummy looks around, Nat's won't be hidden at all from its sight. Her face is slick with sweat, orange in the night lighting of the Hall.

"When did you get here?" I hiss.

"I got here first! I was looking for you. I couldn't let you run into danger by yourself! But instead I found her." She points dramatically at the mummy.

I slap her hand down, dragging her behind the stuffed caribou. Who knows just how much the mummy can see? She's not exactly following the laws of nature.

"I think she's trying to drain the life force of the alligator," Nat explains, "only she doesn't realize it's dead, too."

"How would you know this?"

"*The Mummy.*"

"Yes?"

"I mean, *The Mummy* franchise. I'm basing everything I know about her . . . condition from that. She's been asleep for a few thousand years, and she's hungry."

"The yogurt wasn't enough, then?" I ask, and she rolls her eyes again. She could be right—maybe *tatakat* is some kind of regional delicacy. I'm not convinced. "But you can't siphon life force out of people, can you? Life force isn't a thing! It's all paranormal hoopla!"

"She's a mummy. We have to suspend our disbelief and all that." Nat rolls her eyes.

"Right." I watch as the former queen moves to the next animal on display—a nice and sturdy antelope.

Hathorhat squeezes the antelope's neck, hisses, and then swipes at it, as if to toss it aside—only it doesn't move. Its feet are bolted to the floor. She lets out a howl of frustration.

Nat shudders. "What if—you don't think she did this to Marty, do you?"

"No, no, he's still alive—the mummy's just got him hypnotized."

"He's *what?*"

Instantly, the mummy whips her head around and lets out a bloodcurdling wail. Locusts spring out of thin air where she points—as if she summoned them herself. Like the wall of scarabs in the breakroom, there's an endless supply of the pests. They instantly fill the hall, swarming all around.

Nat and I grab for each other and run, the mummy roaring behind us.

The thunder of a thousand wings beats a frenzy in my ears until it drowns out Queen Hathorhat and everything else, until there's nothing but an endless ringing. There's so many of them, I could well be in a blizzard. I can't see what's in front of me. I can't hear anything around me. I clutch Nat's arm tighter and rush forward, in whatever direction is away from the mummy.

Nat shouts something I can barely hear.

"What?" I shout back.

"Kids! Playroom!" She tears off to the left, pulling me with her, practically wrenching my arm from its socket.

Something heavy slides over me—a curtain. It is the easy-to-push, thick kind of curtain that kids lead their parents through as they race for their favorite hands-on exhibits.

The locusts can't get through the wall of fabric. I fall to the floor in the children's hands-on learning center, my face crashing into the rough carpet, squashing a locust in the process.

I push myself up and roll over, breathing heavily. My heart is pounding so hard I can barely hear. My ears ring like a struck bell. Nat is panting too, sitting on one of the low stools in the dim, orange light.

I run my hand over my forehead, smearing the bug juices there. Sticky legs cling to my fingers. I shake them off, too tired for disgust.

"What . . . was . . . that?" Nat asks in between breaths.

"Locusts. The mummy can summon insects. Remember the scarabs?"

"Do I remember the—*are you kidding me*?"

I'm not thinking straight. I can't think straight. I finally manage to push myself up into a seat. The LEDs of the displays lighten the kids' learning center, which should have been off at this hour. I guess this is just more evidence of whatever electromagnetic mess is going on tonight.

"I'm really sorry I dragged you into this," Nat says.

"You didn't. It's not like you brought the mummy to life or anything."

"Yeah, but I'm the one who insisted we stay late, and I'm the one who . . ."

"Look. We don't have time to toss blame around," I say. "We need to find Marty. Who knows what she did to him."

I don't like the idea of losing track of Hathorhat, but Marty's our priority right now. So, we leave, tiptoeing out of the kids' learning center, through the staff exit, and toward the only place that will give us an advantage: the security room. Two Fridays ago, when we were staying late, Marty made sure we knew exactly how to get into it, in case anything happened. Though he probably hadn't thought a mummy would be the reason we'd need access.

Thankfully, it's not far. We take the stairs one flight up and then run along another dark corridor, using the flashlights from our phones to guide us through the staff areas. We reach the small white door, and Nat types in the pin code. Total disappointment awaits us inside: every screen is filled with either static or bug legs. The locusts have taken over most of the museum, landing all over the cameras, leaving the screens mostly black. Those that aren't black are fuzzy with static.

There's a radio next to the keyboard, and Nat picks it up and holds it to her mouth. "Marty? Are you there? Marty?" she asks. Nothing but static. "Are you there, Marty? Over!"

But it's no use—there's no answer.

"Nothing's working." I gesture at the cameras. Nat takes a seat, huffing.

"We need to try the cops," she says.

I join her—boy does it feel good to sink into a padded chair.

"I mean, they have to take us seriously now," she continues. "The museum is full of locusts! That's not something we could have done, right?"

"You're asking me if we could have filled the museum with a swarm of bugs for shits and giggles?"

"I'm sorry, I'm sorry. I'm tired. This whole thing is messed up."

"The mummy really does seem to be creating electromagnetic interference." I wave at the monitors. "That explains why the cameras are only capturing static and our phones don't work. Only the hardwired cameras are still running, and they must be the ones on the ground floor, where all the locusts are. That explains Marty's radio, too."

"What are you saying?"

"We can't call for help. We can't get out." I clench my fists to stop them trembling. "We have to deal with this on our own."

"Can't we break out at this point?" Nat shudders a full-body shudder that spreads to me. "Can they really blame us if we shatter a window?"

"But if we break out, so could the mummy, and who knows what she'll do?" I say. "She can hypnotize people, maybe suck the life force out of them . . . Oh, *and* rain down swarms of bugs. Look, I think we need to do the opposite: keep her inside until help arrives."

Whatever this mummy is looking for, she might very well have to cross the whole world to find it, and who knows the devastation she'll leave in her wake. I can't help but picture Teagan sobbing in Grandma's arms as the locusts fill the streets. I can't break out of here if it means putting my family at risk. Or anyone, for that matter.

"I'm supposed to be home by eleven," says Nat.

"Yeah, so am I. I'm also supposed to be spending my Friday night *not* fighting the undead, so yeah." I promised Teagan I was going to read him a bedtime story. He hates it when Mom and Dad go, and he won't sleep until I'm home with him. It's slowly hitting me that I might not make it back to him at all.

"So, what do we do?"

"Our guardians will check up on us, I hope." I lean my head forward, propping my chin up on my hands. Deep breaths. "Until then, we need to find Marty and break him out of that trance. Then we return the mummy to her eternal rest."

"But how do we do that?"

"I don't know, Nat. You're supposed to be the expert on ancient Egypt!"

"Just because I actually like this assignment doesn't make me an expert." She glares at me. "What did you mean, earlier? When you said 'in my experience'? Before we got cut off by Marty's scream?"

My blood runs cold. Shit. I didn't think she'd picked up on that. "I didn't mean anything."

"No, you sounded *really* confident," she says, "and you said something about ghosts. Are you into the paranormal? It's okay if you are! Honestly, it could help."

"I'm not *into* the paranormal." I let out a sigh. "Look, you can't tell anyone at school, okay? Every time people find out, I become the butt end of every ghost joke. It's even turned violent before. You know how high schoolers can be. I'm trying to make friends here. I'd rather this stays between us."

"That you believe in ghosts?"

"No—that *my parents* do. Did you ever hear of *Ghost Stalkers?*"

"How could I not?" She stifles a laugh. "It's one of the worst History Channel shows I've ever seen! It's so . . . hold on. Are your parents fans?"

"Worse—I'm Kate *Mercer.*"

It takes her a second. That, or her brain took a quick break. Her eyes grow wider and wider, and they just don't stop widening. "You're their *kid?*"

I nod. "So yeah, I grew up hearing a lot about ghosts. Not that a single one of my parents' 'stalks' ever found evidence of ghosts, though. But I know the drill. *I know* all the hocus-pocus bogus jargon about EM fields. *I know* about the unfinished business that keeps them here. And I know, without a doubt, that they're not real."

"But mummies are, apparently?"

"Yeah."

She turns to face the monitors. I shrink back into my chair. My parents' fascination—no, *obsession*—with ghosts is common knowledge. The massive *Ghost Stalkers* franchise keeps spawning spin-offs, and, with each one, they drop me and Teagan and every other responsibility in their lives in order to chase literal smoke. My grandparents are wonderful people, always picking up my parents' slack, but it's obviously not what they signed up for. *Ghost Stalkers: The Triangle* is what's currently costing them their retirement and me my future.

Nat leans towards me. "So, if this mummy *was* a vindictive ghost, what would you do?"

"I told you, I don't believe in that crap."

"Well, then, what would your parents do?"

I mull it over for a good minute. The bugs on the monitors shuffle around. The mummy could be anywhere. "Right. Well, it all comes down to unfinished business. The ghost usually wants revenge, or peace. They want to be heard in a way they couldn't when they were alive, but they can't now, because of their current undead state. So, it's up to the living to fulfill their last wishes and allow them to move on, to cross the threshold to the afterlife."

"That's . . . that's oddly poetic," says Nat. "So, what could Queen Hathorhat possibly want? My hair? She sure was grabby earlier."

"Honestly? She probably wants to be put back to rest in Egypt, where she belongs. But she keeps going on about *tatakat*, whatever that is."

"Then, why now?" Nat asks. "Why tonight? Queen Hathorhat's been studied across the world for decades. She's on loan from the British Museum, and I'm pretty sure we'd know if she was making a mess over there."

"Good point. But, then again, she's not a ghost—she's a mummy. They play by different rules."

"I know, I know," she says with a sigh. "Mummies are cursed."

"That's not what I was going to say." I want to laugh at the absurdity of our conversation, the way I laugh at all my parents' episodes and lectures, but it doesn't feel right. "Okay, fine. What do you know about mummies?"

"Well, all the mummy movies I've watched show their mummies as being some kind of . . . I don't know, bad guy? Like they did something terrible in life, which meant they were cursed in death."

"So, what did Queen Hathorhat do in her lifetime?"

"Not much that we have records of." Nat shrugs. "She was really young when she died. Our age. The only historical reference calls her a wife of a king, and that's one symbol on her sarcophagus. There's not much to go on."

"So, maybe she wants to do more with her afterlife?" My head is spinning. It's exhausting applying my parents' reasoning to reality. "What is this *tatakat* thing, anyway?"

"I don't know. But, if we want to break the curse, we need to know what caused it. Same for if we want to help her with her unfinished business, we need to know what that is, too. The problem is, we don't know anything about her, except what's painted on her tomb. *Tatakat*'s not enough to go on."

"Then let's go and find out."

"What?" Nat shakes her head so fast it makes me dizzy. "No, no. We can't go back down there."

"Do you have a better idea?"

"Actually, I might. We can't get in more trouble than we already are in, can we?"

NAT GRABS THE KEY FROM THE BOX INSIDE THE security desk, and I follow her through the hallways to Dr. Eagleman's office. She lets herself in and flicks on the lights. I blink out the dark.

"Right. What are we looking for?" I ask.

"Anything about Queen Hathorhat that didn't make it onto the displays, I s'pose," Nat says, as she plops herself down on the director's chair. "And maybe an ancient-Egyptian dictionary while we're at it."

Not having read the displays, I'm not as discerning as she is, and it feels so wrong to be rifling through the director's things. I try not to mess up the chaos of research data in their stacks around the office. Some reference books are left open, seemingly strewn haphazardly across the stacks. While Dr. Eagleman's office appears orderly in general, the closer I look, the more I realize the research really is all over the place. If there's any structure to be had here, I can't see it.

"Oh, what do you know? A book about death," says Nat, brandishing a glossy brown textbook.

"What does it say about the afterlife? Is there a section on the undead?"

She flips through the pages. "This might be helpful—there's a chapter about the soul. Or, at least, the different souls they believed people to have . . . Yeah, this is it. The ba is the personality, and the ka is the lifeforce. Collectively, they're known as the akh."

"And this is helpful how?"

"Just listen." Her eyes glaze over as she reads quickly before she glances back up at me. "So, it says here the ba is but one part of the soul, the one that is able to detach itself from the body and roam independently by means of astral travel—sound familiar?"

"Okay, this is borderline ghost territory. But where does the mummy come in?"

Despite my apprehension towards my parents' work, it feels oddly comforting to find familiar territory at this point. I cling to every drop of recognizable mumbo jumbo. Their rhetoric is there for me now in a way they never were.

Nat taps the page with her finger. "Well, apparently, it has something to do with the ka, the lifeforce?"

"The stuff our mummy was trying to zap from the dead gator down there?"

"Yeah, I think so. The ancient Egyptians believed if you didn't properly care for the corpse, the ka was able to leave the body and wander about. So, if you don't bury your mummy with food and drink, it will wake up and wander about at night in search of its own sustenance."

"So, we just have to feed the queen, and she'll go back to sleep? Maybe Marty's tuna sub can be useful after all—I mean, it's clearly not its first choice," I say, thinking of my yogurt, "but maybe the mummy's hungry enough it'll consider it? *Tatakat* could just mean 'hungry' or 'food.' Still doesn't explain why she's up in the first place, though."

"There's more. In order for the dead to achieve true immortality, the ka and the ba have to be reunited in the afterlife to form the akh. It says those that have not lived their lives according to maat—Egyptian religion and morality— would either be annihilated or would not pass into the afterlife, putting them at risk of joining the ranks of the undead."

"Okay, she screwed something up in her past life," I say. "So, on top of feeding her, we have to help her right a five-thousand-year-old wrong? That's basically what I was saying about ghosts and unfinished business. I guess there's a sliver of truth there, after all. And ghosts are said to rise when something related to said business has been disturbed, forcing them to act. We could look through the museum records and see if they, I don't know, damaged something that was important to her. Maybe an amulet."

"Wait. Apparently, in Egyptian magic, knowing an individual's true name—or ren—gives one power over them. According to the book, a name provides an individual with an identity. Without a name, they would cease to exist. To the Egyptians, this was the worst possible fate they could imagine. Therefore, they went to extreme lengths to safeguard their names. If one's name was erased on purpose, they might be erased from the afterlife as well."

"Did someone desecrate Hathorhat's name then? Like on her sarcophagus?" I think back to the way it had looked in the exhibit hall. The glass around it had shattered, but I don't remember the sarcophagus having been damaged. Then again, I didn't know what condition it was in in the first place.

"Let's hope not," Nat says and shivers. "We have to figure out how to make this right."

We spend the better part of an hour like this, poring over the pages and pages of photocopies strewn around the office. Most of Dr. Eagleman's work is probably on her computer, but we can't figure out her password. So, instead, we try to decipher the printouts—a bunch of ideas that don't make sense on their own, and we're missing the key ingredients to bring them together.

"It's the handmaid, isn't it?" says Nat, finally.

"Who?" My eyes are so tired they're starting to close, but her words jolt me awake. "What is?"

"All of Lauren's work," she continues. I don't voice the weirdness of her referring to the museum's director on a first-name basis. "She seems to be trying to look into the identity of the handmaid—*not* Hathorhat."

"Who's the handmaid again?"

"The skeleton that was found in the tomb with the queen."

"The human sacrifice?"

"Yeah. Lauren seems to be working on identifying the handmaid through forensic archaeology. They apparently went through a lengthy process to get the handmaid's skeleton and the rights to test it. She's had dental and bone analysis done and everything."

"What can forensics even tell anyone at this point? What it was like to be buried alive?"

"Or why she was chosen as the only one entombed with the queen, I think." Nat puts the papers back down on the desk and slides a photo over to me. "Here."

It's a black-and-white copy of a photo of the inside of the tomb, possibly when it was first opened. It shows the sarcophagus from the museum, but draped over it is a single skeleton, entirely intact. Bracelets loosely enclose its wrist bones. The skeleton is stretched over the sarcophagus, like the human-*freaking*-sacrifice just fell asleep resting their head on Hathorhat's death portrait.

"Wow," I say. "I can't imagine going like that."

"Buried alive?"

I nod. "And still clinging to my queen. What was going through the handmaid's head? Did she believe so much in her queen's power she just sat down and died?"

Nat shrugs. "There was no trauma found on the skeleton. No injuries, I mean. I bet dying in the dark, alone with a corpse, must have been terribly traumatic."

"Maybe she was drugged? I heard about religious leaders forcing their victims to drink stuff so they wouldn't panic and ruin ceremonies."

Nat seems surprised at my insight. Honestly, I am too.

"That's what Lauren was looking for in the teeth," she says, "but the lab didn't find anything. Imagine being a queen who commands that kind of respect and love that someone apparently willingly sacrifices themselves without any signs of a fight. I can't see myself dying for anyone."

We stare at the photo, and I ask myself if there is anyone I would be willing to die for. Maybe if my sacrifice meant something. Like if I had to give up my life to save Teagan—then the answer is yes, no questions asked. But other than that . . .

There's so much of history I'll never be able to understand. Maybe that's why my parents are so determined to find their ghosts: to be able to talk to someone tangible from a time and place so distant from us, it could almost be alien. Our world changes so fast, but people are always the same.

Queen Hathorhat returned from the dead for a reason. Whatever she's looking at is more important to her than death. What is she hanging on to?

Before I can say any of this to Nat, there's a sound: a low, gentle sound, like the rushing of the wind. And it's getting louder.

"What is that?" I ask. At first, I think the sound has to be waves, but it's getting louder and louder. As it grows, it sounds more like a storm.

"The locusts!" I shout, but I'm wrong because as I say the word, hundreds—if not thousands—of *rats* scurry past the door, in the corridor outside.

They're as big as cats, gray, and moving so fast I can't see any details—I'm thankful for that. I don't want to think of their tiny eyes and teeth. There are so many of them they cover the ground completely.

In an instant, they're all past the door, running down the hallway in the direction of the stairs. The sound dies away. They must have reached the exhibit halls.

Nat stands on the desk chair, breathing heavily. Somehow, she's paler than she was before. I don't wait for her to catch her breath. I dart for the hallway.

"No!" Nat calls after me. "I told you last time! Don't go running into danger!"

"We have to do something before the mummy does something worse!"

"Wait for me!" There's a thump as her feet hit the floor. She joins me, still out of breath. "Why are we running after the rats?"

First the scarabs, then the locusts, now the rats. I'm not too thrilled at the idea of seeing the mummy again, but if she escalates this all even further, who knows what she'll make happen. Maybe we'll get a plague of crocodiles. We rush down the stairs to the main lobby.

That's where we find our guard in shining armor, along with thousands of locusts. They carpet the welcome desk and every single bone of the dinosaur statue that dominates the atrium. The rats appear to have trampled quite a few as they scurried through, because there's a path of very dead locusts that weaves past where Marty sits, rubbing his head, before extending toward the doorway.

I can't help it—I snap a pic of the destruction. Call it shock or whatever. I mean, what's everyone going to believe if we make it out of here? I'm not getting blamed for this.

"What's the deal with all the bugs?" Marty asks. His eyes are back to normal, and he looks more dazed than entranced, glancing back and forth around the hall.

"Marty!" Nat rushes to him and helps him to his feet. "What happened to you?"

"The rats," he says, groggily. "At least . . . I think. It's all been very blurry. There was a rush, and then I woke up on the floor, rats all around me. There was . . . a voice in my head."

He rubs his scalp again, and I see sticky blood there. Could the rats have knocked him over and out of his trance?

"You've been whammied," says Nat, sounding all-knowing. "I saw it in a movie. Queen Hathorhat must have hypnotized you."

"Queen what?" he asks, and then, louder: "She did what now?"

"We've deduced that the mummy is Queen Hathorhat, the one on display in the Egyptian exhibit. And she hypnotized you. You were wandering around the museum, chanting in ancient Egyptian. It was creepy to say the least."

"We tried calling for help, but she's causing interference with the phone lines and Internet," I add. "The doors are bolted shut—you did that, right?—but we didn't want to break out, in case she got out too and caused chaos out there."

"You two make quite the pair of monster hunters," Marty says, then promptly vomits into a nearby trash can.

"Definitely whammied," Nat whispers my way. That, or he has a serious concussion and needs a hospital badly.

"Does *tatakat* mean anything to you?" I ask him, as gently as I can muster.

He shakes his head. "Should it?"

"You were chanting it earlier. It must mean something."

"I did what?" Marty shudders. "That's messed up. Have you found a way to kill it?"

"We're hoping to help *her* find peace, actually," I say. "Help Hathorhat resolve some old issues."

Marty's face is the wrong shade of pale. He's borderline green now.

"Right," he says. "Help the magical mummy queen. Anyone got a therapist on speed-dial?"

"Solving unfinished business works with ghosts," I mutter.

Marty shakes his head. "And if that doesn't work, how do we take it down?"

"Well, according to *The Mummy* franchise, the best way to capture a runaway mummy is to bring a cat, but we don't have one," says Nat. "So to break the curse, we either need to feed her, right the wrongs of her past, or—worst-case scenario—erase her name from her sarcophagus."

"Oh, curses!" Marty pinches the bridge of his nose. He still has a tinge of green in his cheeks. "*Of course* it's a curse. This can't be happening."

"Suppose for a minute, that it is," says Nat. "Do you have any idea what's different about tonight? What could have made her rise from the dead? Maybe that can point us toward the wrong we need to right."

"Hell, no!" he says. "I'm just the night guard. I come in, I do my rounds, I go home, I get some sleep. No one tells me anything. I don't know anything other than what's written in the exhibits."

Nat frowns, crossing her arms over her chest. Marty is our muscle, but he doesn't seem to be helping at all. Then again, it's hard to expect a lot from someone who has just had their brain taken over by magic.

"Then we need to investigate the sarcophagus itself," says Nat before I can further traumatize a grown man. "Maybe there's a clue there. If Hathorhat really was cursed, it would probably say somewhere."

Marty says nothing. He might be a foot taller than both of us, but he suddenly seems very small. He's not cut out for this—none of us are. We just have to get through this night.

"Wouldn't scholars have found something about a curse long ago, though?" I ask.

"Maybe it's something that only makes sense in context?"

"Context being she rose from the dead."

The three of us huddle together for safety and tiptoe our way through the locusts as silently as possible. Thankfully, they're not as thick as we move into Hathorhat's exhibit hall. Nat immediately makes a beeline for the sarcophagus and swipes away the locusts so she can examine the hieroglyphs painted there. I cast a glance over it, though the symbols make no sense to me.

The face painted at the top bears no resemblance to the linen-clad monstrosity that chased us, but Queen Hathorhat must have been quite beautiful in her day. Her long, black hair stands out a little like Darth Vader's helmet, framing a delicate face and small pouty lips. I wonder how much of it is accurate. I try to imagine her, as best I can: like Nat or me, but Hathorhat was also queen of an entire civilization at a younger age than Nat and I are now. I wonder how much we might have had in common.

So long as I can learn from her mistakes and not come back as a mummy myself.

"I think I found something," says Marty.

I'm surprised to hear his voice. I didn't think he'd be helping us hunt, not in his post-trance shock. I turn to see him pointing at a large banner on the wall. It doesn't have anything to do with the exhibit. Well, hardly anything. It's one of the big signs for the Valentine's Day event at the museum, listing all the shows they're hosting throughout the day.

"They did poetry readings in each of the halls," says Marty. "I was sad I missed it. My wife recorded a few for me to watch later, bless her."

"What does this have to do with Queen Hathorhat?" I ask.

"They read an Egyptian love poem, didn't they?" says Nat. "To keep with the theme?"

Marty nods. "I have it right here."

He pulls out his phone and the two of us squeeze in beside him, watching on the small screen, listening to Dr. Eagleman read off a tablet to a packed crowd. She's standing in front of a massive banner, the one with the hieroglyphs of the woman holding hands with a bird-headed being.

163

To hear your voice is pomegranate wine to me:

I draw life from hearing it.

Could I see you with every glance,

it would be better for me

than to eat or to drink.

"That's beautiful," says Nat.

The director continues, saying each verse first in the original Egyptian—I assume, since I don't understand it—then in English.

"I didn't realize there were poems back then," says Marty, "but apparently some of the oldest recorded texts are ancient love songs."

My parents' voices are screeching in my head: *Ghosts react powerfully to familiar things! If a song meant a lot to them in life, it can trigger them to awaken from dormancy, even hundreds of years later.*

My eyes widen. I can practically feel one of my parents' cameras turning on me, capturing my realization as I connect two impossible things.

"Could that be what happened?" I ask. "When Dr. Eagleman read the poem, she could have woken the mummy."

"Wait, what?" Nat scoffs. "How would an ancient love poem wake up a mummy? What does it have to do with curses?"

Ghosts react powerfully to familiar things. Familiar features. Familiar people.

I glance around the room. What would Queen Hathorhat have seen? What would she have recognized? My eyes fall on the banner of the hieroglyph. Of the woman with her pitch-black hair.

"She looks like you, Nat. That's it—that's why she was chasing you! She was trying to touch your hair!"

"She wants my *hair?*"

"Don't you see? The way she reached for your hair, Nat. This whole time, she's not been looking for a thing, but a *person*. It's love! It's always been about love!"

Marty snorts. "This isn't a Disney movie, Katherine."

"I know, but listen. When a ghost wanders the earth, it cries out for the thing that was most important to it in life. What if Tatakat is a name?"

"So, Tatakat is a *person*? The one who—"

Nat doesn't finish her sentence because there's a moan from one of the arcades: the queen has arrived.

Nat grabs my arm. Marty immediately draws his taser from his hip, stepping in front of us both.

The queen marches forward with an awkward, shuffling gait. She must have been drawn to the poem again, to her own tongue. She shouts something at us, something cold and impossible, and all at once, everything falls apart.

First, the fire in the torches grows bright. The locusts begin to swarm again, rising from their perches all around the exhibit hall. They rise and circle in the air above the sarcophagus, above their ambling mistress. Then, Marty's eyes glaze over. They go white and misty, and before I can react, he grabs Nat, who lets out one of her trademark screams. I freeze. I don't know if I should get any closer, caught between a mummy and a re-entranced Marty. I don't know what I can do. There's nothing *to* do. Nat's thrashing against his grip, but her punches have no effect on him. It's like he doesn't feel anything at all.

Marty brings Nat to Hathorhat. Nat's sobbing now, her tears running thick down her cheeks. I take a step forward, and both the queen and Marty turn to me at once—she hisses as he points his taser. I can't save her. I'm just one girl.

Hathorhat reaches for Nat the same way she did before. Nat closes her eyes as the mummy's bony fingers reach to touch her hair. There's a second where the entire museum is silent; then Hathorhat removes her hand, shouting a garbled order to Marty, something which sounds furious and final. He pulls Nat away, dragging her still kicking and screaming from the queen.

I was right—she was looking for someone. Someone who Nat definitely is not.

Hathorhat lets out an earth-shattering roar that drops me to my knees. Her bandages start to dissolve, turning into—is that sand? The air in the room starts to move, going from stillness to a gentle breeze to a storm in ten seconds flat. The air is scorching hot and sulphuric, making my nostrils curl. It whips the locusts into a frenzy as thousands of insects take flight at once. All I can hear is the roar of sand and wings.

In the heart of it all, Queen Hathorhat rises gently into the air, lifted by the otherworldly wind that spirals around her hands and feet. She calls the same word—no, name, it has to be a name—over and over again.

"Tatakat. Tatakat. Tatakat."

"Stop!" I shout at Hathorhat. "I understand now!" I struggle to get to my feet, to right the storm. I need to break free.

Her linen bandages are no more, the sand that consumed them now spiraling around her. Despite the wind, the torches still burn brightly. In the space where the bandages were, her skin is unblemished, a deep copper to match her face. The exhibit hall is unrecognizable, now the set of the next Indiana Jones movie. And, still, the mummy wails.

"Tatakat. Tatakat. Tatakat." Marty chants along with his queen.

Nat opens her mouth to scream as she struggles against his grasp, but the wind pulls the sounds right from her mouth. And then she's not screaming anymore—her eyes go smoky white and her tears stop as she joins in the slow chanting. Marty lets go of her, but she doesn't run. She's one of them now.

In her own words—she's been whammied.

"Hathorhat!" I shout. But the name does nothing. It doesn't give me the power over her I was promised.

Her eyes are riveted on me, and she lets out another banshee shriek.

I know what I have to do. I understand now—or I think I do. I could be naive, desperate. Probably both. But if love—on Valentine's Day—brought this mummy back to life, then I think I know who she's looking for.

I spin on my heels, making a mad dash for the shadows, a blind-side run outside her field of vision. I charge Marty—with his chanting, he doesn't see me at all. I grab his key ring from his belt and race for the exit.

I cut away from the wind and the sand and the bugs, and dive into the depths of the museum. I don't care about alarms or locusts anymore, it's too late for that. My legs are screaming, but I imagine I'm on the pitch, remember my coach telling me to focus on that all-too-distant goal. I dribble my way between the locusts. The rats are just training balls for me to kick. I evade them through the exhibit halls and staff hallways until I reach Dr. Eagleman's office.

Tatakat. Tatakat. Tatakat.

The word repeats in my head like a drum line. A constant beat, driving me forever forward.

I hope, beg, that what I'm looking for is stored beneath my feet.

There. On the results of the tooth analysis. A serial number. The unnamed handmaid has an identifier: 089762343. A number which should be in the collections catalogue.

I burst out of the office and sprint down the corridor once more. It can't be more than a few doors down. I have Marty's key ring, and I use his beeper to throw open the door to the storeroom, flicking on the lights as I go. My heart is racing. I can't hear the mummy's wails through this many floors and walls, but her words are still running in my head.

Tatakat. Tatakat. Tatakat.

I search for 089762343. I've only been here once, when one of Dr. Eagleman's colleagues showed me the ancient jewelry which isn't on display. I pass the overflow collection of taxidermized animals that don't fit upstairs, their beady eyes following me as I hunt for something much more valuable. After the roar of the storm above, the silence here is welcome but cold.

I find the drawer holding 089762343 and pull it open. As a high schooler, I probably shouldn't be anywhere near it, but tonight is an emergency. There, beneath me, is the unnamed handmaid of the tomb of Queen Hathorhat. The five-thousand-year-old bones of a woman who loved her queen so much she died by her side. A woman who must have cared about her so, so much. There's only one thing that would mean you'd die willingly like that: love.

This woman was not the queen's handmaid—she was the queen's *lover*. A woman so passionately in love with Hathorhat that neither could live without the other.

A love that history erased, because the evidence—which was so flipping obvious, carved and painted into the sarcophagus itself—didn't match what they thought they knew. A love so powerful it brought a mummy back to life, transcending time and space, surviving death itself—well, I sure hope it's that strong, because right now I'm staring a skeleton in the face, and if I'm wrong about any of this, I've just abandoned Nat and Marty to a five-thousand-year-old non-consensual treasure hunt.

"Uh, hey, wake up?" I say.

The skeleton remains dead.

It's not like I have any Egyptian love poems memorized, and I didn't think of bringing Marty's phone with me, so I'm screwed in that regard. I'm not serenading her back to life.

"Hey, lady. Your queen is up and making a mess of the museum. Do you think you could talk some sense into her? Please?"

Still nothing.

I fall to the floor, my back against the drawer. I gave up my one chance to help Nat and Marty for *this?* The desperate hope that love could save the day, if I just believed in it hard enough? That a mummy, of all things, could be defeated by wishful thinking.

I can't cry. Not here, not in this basement storage room, not while my only allies are at the mercy of a creature straight out of a movie. I've never felt so alone before.

"Did you feel alone?" I ask the skeleton. "When those tomb doors closed behind you, and your torch finally went out, did you have any regrets?"

The skeleton, of course, says nothing. Maybe I need to present it to Hathorhat and hope she'll understand what happened to her. But would that really make things right?

"You were her lover, right? You loved her so much, and she loved you in return. She's looking for you, you know." The only word the mummy can say is a name. "Tatakat," I say, "I name you."

With that, I release the power of her name, returning her ren to her.

First, a twitch of the pinky bones. Then a clenching of a fist. The skeleton begins to move on its own, pushing itself up, held together by the same magic that allows a five-thousand-year-old mummy to speak. I spring back. Who knows what a reanimated skeleton can actually do? Maybe she can summon spiders.

Her eyes—well, eye-*holes*—land on me. Waiting. She must be as confused as I am. Maybe even more so, to be awoken like this. To see me.

"Um, hello," I say. "Welcome back to the land of the living?"

The skeleton opens her mouth, then closes it again. Not a sound. *Of course.* She doesn't have vocal cords. Or lungs for that matter. She's lucky enough her bones move in unison, since the ligaments are long since gone. I don't even know if she can understand me.

"Hathorhat?" I say, and the skeleton springs to her feet with surprising agility. Now *that*, she understands. "Tatakat, we have to go to Hathorhat now."

I reach out my hand, hopefully, tentatively, and Tatakat reaches for it, grasps it. Her bones are surprisingly toasty, like stones warmed by the sun. I'm trembling as she holds on to me, bracing her weight to allow her to step delicately down from the box she's been stored in.

I realize she is trembling, too.

I lead her through the museum. Her bones rattle as she walks, and I think of nuts cracking with her every step. I want to tell her to rush, to run, to hurry to save the living. The halls howl with a distant wind, growing louder and louder as we approach Hathorhat. I can feel Tatakat's anticipation, the way her steps are restrained, like I'm holding her back from sprinting. I can't even imagine what's going through her head. How anything can even go through her head at all, seeing as how her skull cavity is empty.

The rushing wind becomes a deafening roar. When we finally reach the exhibit hall, it's worse than I could possibly have imagined.

The locusts and sand have stripped the walls bare. All the banners that hung there are now whipping around in the tornado that swings around the mummy's flying form. Her jet-black hair spreads around her like a halo of shadows. And in the storm are Marty and Nat, a good ten feet off the floor, holding the hands of the undead queen.

Along with a twister of giant rats.

"Hathorhat!" I shout. "Tatakat!"

She either doesn't hear me or doesn't understand me. The second her eyes—or the empty, black pits that once held them—land on me, she lets out a terrifying roar, a banshee screech that could rival any alarm. The locusts spill out of the tornado, spiraling right at my face. It's all I can do to fling my hands up, just in time for the locusts to bounce off my forearms. I scream—it feels as if they've taken all my skin with them.

In my panic, I've let go of Tatakat's skeletal hand. I don't know if the locusts have come for her, too, or even if they can

170

do anything to her at this point. I shout her name, but my voice is swallowed up by the winds.

There's a rush of small bodies at my feet, and I fall forward, barely throwing a hand in front of my face before slamming into the ground. The rats are returning to their queen, spilling out of the exhibit halls, trampling me as I lie helpless on the floor. Between the scurrying rats and swarms of bugs, the air is a cacophony of sound.

Locusts climb through my hair, and I can't help the sob that escapes my mouth as they push their way down the collar of my shirt. This is it; *this* is how I die. Eaten by plagues on the floor of a museum as a mummy wails above me. I want to believe it's all some bad dream, but I could never imagine anything so harrowing.

Then, all at once, the screeching stops.

The locusts stop their crawling. The rats freeze in their places. It sounds like even the wind has died down. I take a chance: I lift my head off the floor just a little, and, feeling no resistance, brush the bugs off my back. I'm too scared to do anything else.

The exhibit hall is eerily still. The swirling sandstorm hasn't abated—it's simply stopped. Right where it was. Warm torchlight flicks the walls, bare now and tomblike. Sand grains frozen in the air glow orange in the light. The sarcophagus's lid has landed upside down on the floor near the foot of the stairs, revealing the bare, featureless underside.

Time itself is holding its breath. Marty and Nat are still hovering in the air, but the queen is drifting slowly to the ground, the only thing moving in the entire museum.

I wriggle my fingers down to my pocket. Pull out my phone. Fumble for the camera. No way am I missing this.

Queen Hathorhat alights on the floor before Tatakat. They stand apart, a good ten feet or so, unmoving. For a second, I wonder if I misinterpreted the situation. If I jumped too quickly to conclusions and reunited bitter rivals instead. But, a second later, they're rushing to embrace, and my fear evaporates.

At once time starts up again. Sand falls from its perch as rats and locusts turn to dust. Marty and Nat drift gently to the floor, where they both collapse with a gentle thud. I should run to them, make sure they're okay, but I'm afraid to interrupt what's happening, to incur the mummy's wrath once again.

The queen and her handmaid seem oblivious to us, anyway. They hold each other tenderly, ancient hands running over what remains, face to face, cherishing as much as there is left for them to admire.

Blink, and we're no longer here. Blink, and we're in a hot and sunny world, where a beautiful gold-covered queen cups the face of a woman who rivals her beauty. The two share a passionate kiss so intense I feel like I need to avert my gaze. They radiate love the way the sun radiates heat.

We're in the great halls of a palace, the ceiling so high sunlight doesn't reach it, a cool jasmine-scented breeze drifting through and brushing long curtains in its wake. It's a gentle moment, until one of the drapes is ripped from its rod, a man dripping gold and shouting words I cannot understand destroying the beautiful moment.

A betrayal. A curse. It all happens so fast, and now the queen is lying on the stone floor, dead, as the woman she loved screams in agony.

The queen is embalmed, following the ancient rites, entombed in the city of the dead with the few belongings that were truly hers. As the great stone rolls into place to seal the tomb, the handmaid slips in, to the anguished cries of those outside.

No one saw it coming. No one dares defy the priests by attempting to remove the stone.

The handmaid is alone in the dark with the corpse of her love, and that's where she'll stay for five millennia. Soulmates with souls shattered, unable to move on to the next life. Until the day the stone is rolled away, and the queen is pried from her final resting place. Until today, when a love song in her own tongue reminds the queen what it means to be alive and in love. These moments play in front of my eyes as if I am actually there, as if they're my own memories. I blink, and I can still see the undead before me, but they don't look like a mummy and a skeleton anymore. I can see the women they once were, flesh and bone and beauty, clasping each other now, together again after death kept them apart for so long.

Before I can say a word, a gasp comes from all around—and, all at once, Hathorhat and Tatakat crumple to the floor. It's a quiet, unceremonial end, as if the life that had reanimated them simply stepped away, leaving their bodies empty husks once again. Deep in my heart, I hope it means that they moved on.

It's over.

I scramble to my feet, realizing I'm completely out of breath. The rats, the locusts, and everything the mummy brought to life are all now dust. She and Tatakat lie intertwined on the floor amidst the detritus of the storm, holding each other so tightly they're now a single entity.

Looking at them fills me with a sense of peace, despite the devastation. My breathing is even, and my heart is calm. After all this time, they are together again. Hopefully forever now.

Enough about the dead. I need to check on the living.

"Nat!" I cry out as I reach her. Marty's already pushing himself up, looking as dazed as when we found him earlier.

But Nat isn't moving. I drop to my knees, hand going to her wrist again, this time to check her pulse. It's there. Now I'm the one to sigh in relief.

She's alive. She's okay.

"Is . . ." Her eyes blink open, slowly, oh-so-slowly.

"They've moved on," I reply. "It's over."

None of us knows what to say. I help Nat to sit up, and I can't help it, I throw my arms around her in relief. She winces, and I retract immediately—but she pulls me back in, hugging me tighter despite her obvious pain.

"My phone's working again," says Marty. "I'll call Dr. Lauren. But what do we say happened? I'm *so* getting fired over this."

"No, you won't," I hold up my phone. "I got the whole thing."

"You did? You filmed the mummy?" Nat gasps.

"And you being a floaty, hypnotized mummy minion."

"I was not!"

We find ourselves laughing, the three of us together. I'm alive. They're alive. We made it through.

Of all the things my parents taught me, one thing stands out above the rest: video evidence is the most valuable proof there is of the supernatural.

They're going to be so mad when I go viral over this. Hathorhat and Tatakat's love is going to change the world. And Teagan is going to get the best bedtime story of all time.

THE BROLLACHAN
FIONA MCLAREN

ONE

Fog clung to the moor, obscuring Moira's jeans from the ankles down. How had she managed to get herself roped into this . . . again?

Wetness seeped through the hole in the sole of her boot, soaking her sock, and she frowned at the poor weather. Sneaking out after midnight to impress Lochlan over his dare to find the brollachan wasn't the best idea she'd ever had.

Her eyes drifted to her classmate, to his cute smile and the way his brown hair flopped over one eye. Warmth crept into her cheeks, and she looked away.

"How much longer?" whispered her younger sister, Catriona, from behind. She was hunched into her jacket, walking with Eirica, Moira's classmate.

Lochlan glanced over his shoulder. "Just beyond this field. The gate's not far ahead."

Moira nodded but stayed silent as their group of four traipsed on in the moonlight. The air bit so sharp it pierced her throat, and a shiver spidered down her neck. Images of dark spirits from the Highland myths wove through her thoughts—could there actually be some kind of supernatural creature out here?

An owl hooted and swooped past, making her jump. Damp grass slapped against her legs and mud squelched with every step. She wished it didn't, as enough wetness was seeping into her boot already, and the noise could attract attention. After all, out here on Munroe Moor, anything could be hiding in the dark, waiting to pounce on four wary teens sneaking out at night.

"I don't like being out here," whispered Eirica as she and Catriona caught up with Moira. "What if our parents realize we're gone?"

Moira frowned, biting the inside of her lip. "It'll be fine," she said, mustering as much courage into her words as she could.

"You're just scared of the brollachan, Eirica," teased Lochlan. He flicked a look at Moira, and her cheeks burned hotter.

Eirica snorted, and a clump of grass rustled as she pushed past it. "No, I'm not. It's not even real. I don't know why you believe in all this supernatural nonsense."

Lochlan winked and took a splashing step over a dank puddle. "Nothing to be nervous of then." A slash of moonlight cut across his face. "Besides, sixteen-year-olds aren't supposed to be scared of what their parents think."

Moira swallowed the lump in her throat. She'd be in more trouble than all of them if her parents found out she'd snuck out *and* brought Catriona with her. She rubbed at her forehead. Why had Lochlan talked about coming out here, when he knew her sister was listening? And why had she even agreed to let Catriona come?

She huffed. It had never been easy to say no to Catriona's pleading eyes. Especially after her sister had had such a tough piano lesson with Mrs. McAvoy today and was down in the dumps.

Moira glanced up and caught sight of a silhouette far out in the moor—hunchbacked and holding a staff. Her heart jumped, and she blinked. But then the image was gone, and a tree stood in its place. A shaky breath leaked out of her lungs. She was too tense, too on edge. There was no one there. She cracked her neck and trudged on.

Ten minutes later, they crested a rise, and she stopped.

"There." Moira pointed at the looming shape of the old hawthorn tree, leaning over the gate of a decrepit fence. "That's it, isn't it?" She wiped a damp strand of hair from her face. Her worries about her parents finding out gnawed at her stomach. She glanced at Catriona. "How long have we got?"

Her sister's shaky voice rose up. "It's just past midnight. So, maybe an hour and a half, at most." She hesitated, her lips pinched in. "It's kind of spooky out—"

"Plenty of time," piped up Lochlan.

Moira cast him a glance. He winked at her as he took long, loping steps, his lanky frame easily covering the ground.

The group stopped at the gate under the hawthorn tree. Its dark branches clawed at the patches of star-dashed sky. Villagers said the tree was the gate to the Otherworld, but that was just superstition. Moira gnawed her bottom lip. Ghosts and myths didn't exist. Did they?

"Catriona, you got the stuff?" Moira's shoulders bunched as she huddled into her jacket against the cold.

Catriona's gaze darted up. A brisk nod. She rustled in her pocket. Then she pulled out a flashlight, a scrap of paper, and a pen. She tugged at the end of her long, red braid. A surge of protectiveness bolted through Moira—her sister was so small, so naïve.

Moira was about to say something, to stop this before it started, when Catriona said, "Yeah. Here."

Moira stayed her tongue. She wouldn't embarrass her sister in front of everyone by insisting she go home.

"This is so cool." Lochlan ran a finger up the shadowy bark, the full moon lighting up his narrow face. "We're seriously going to do it, aren't we?"

Moira swallowed. "We did the last dare you set, didn't we?"

Eirica bobbed her head. "She's right. We spent the night in Hangman's Tower, remember?"

"Well," said Lochlan, rolling his eyes, "that's true. But that's nothing compared to looking for the brollachan."

An owl hooted, and Moira shuddered. Lochlan was all about dares, all of the time. Maybe it was because his father had left so long ago that he felt the need to compensate by being cocky and brave. Or maybe he was just made that way. Moira wrapped her arms tighter around herself. She knew he was a bad influence, but there was a tenderness under there that she thought only she could see. After all, he never did these things alone. He always invited her along.

"Okay," said Moira, taking the paper and pen. "Everyone, write your name on the paper." She pulled off her hat with her other hand. "Then tear it off and put it in the hat. We'll draw names at the end."

Catriona and Eirica nodded.

Lochlan ran a hand through his wavy hair. "Remember, whoever gets picked, there's no bailing out. You have to do one lap of the brollachan's field."

Moira frowned as she awkwardly scribbled down her name, put the paper in her hat, and passed the pen and paper over to Lochlan.

He clenched the pen between his teeth, his brow furrowing as though in thought.

"Lochlan," warned Moira.

He threw his hands up in the air. *"What?"*

Moira shivered and rubbed at her arms. "No putting anyone else's name in."

His wicked grin surfaced, and he held his hands in mock surrender. "Okay, you got me." He took his time in boldly writing out his name before waving it in front of them all and dunking it in the hat Moira still held. "There you go." He passed the pen and paper to Eirica. "Your turn."

The pen scratched paper, and then Eirica's name was in. Catriona took the pen and paper next, but then her hand froze.

"Cat?" Moira reached out a hand. "You sure you—"

"Mmh hmm." Catriona swallowed, and her slight frame wavered in the wind. She wrote her name quickly and put it in.

"There!" Lochlan grabbed the hat. "I'll choose."

"No. I'll do it." Moira snatched the hat back. "Knowing you, you'll cheat."

He laughed and rolled his eyes. Eirica giggled, too.

Moira went to laugh, but a shiver ran through her. She flicked a glance at the dark expanse of moor that lay behind the hawthorn tree. The fog had turned a sickly blue, hugging the ground. The shadows wavered, and the tree branches knocked together like the clacking of teeth. A dark picture of the brollachan—an entity of the old magic—slithered into her mind, a black, shapeless thing with burning red eyes.

"Brollachan, brollachan, where are you?" whispered Lochlan, echoing her thoughts. Though his tone was playful, she was sure it wavered. Perhaps he wasn't as brave as he made out.

Moira stuck her hand in the bag and yanked out the first piece of paper her fingers touched. It unfurled effortlessly. Cold swept over her. She stared at the name.

"So," said Eirica, "who is it?"

Her jaw worked, but the words didn't come out.

"Hello, earth to Moira?" said Lochlan.

She swallowed, her pulse hammering in her ears. "It's Catriona."

Catriona's eyes widened, and she shifted her weight from foot to foot.

"I'll go." Moira's words were out before she could stop them.

"Uh uh." Lochlan waved a finger. "Not the way it works."

"Come on, she's only thirteen." Eirica nudged Catriona in the ribs. "We only brought her along for a laugh. Let Moira go if she wants."

An uneasy silence fell on the group. The tree branches clacked.

"No, it's okay. I'll go," said Catriona, her pale eyes wide. "Honestly—"

"Moira. I said it's okay."

Though she said it, the tremble of her hands betrayed her. Moira stared at her, but Catriona wouldn't meet her gaze. She should never have let her sister come. This wasn't a place for little kids. What had she been thinking? Everyone else here had at least three years on Catriona.

"On you go then," said Lochlan with a bow to Catriona. "The brollachan awaits."

Without looking up, Catriona scrambled over the gate, her scarf snagging on a splinter. She tugged it off, and, before Moira had the chance to call her back, she vanished into the fog.

TWENTY MINUTES HAD PASSED AND NOTHING. Moira's palms slickened with sweat, and her neck grew damp and cold. Catriona should have been back by now. It would only have taken about ten minutes to skirt the fabled brollachan's field. Maybe she'd found the ground hard going. She shivered, bone cold. All this standing around and waiting sent ice into her fingers and toes.

"This isn't right. She's been too long." Moira went to climb over the gate, but Eirica grabbed her arm.

"Wait, don't. You don't know which direction she went. You'll just get lost and then that'll be two of you."

The visage of the malevolent Highland spirit swarmed into Moira's mind. A deformed floating creature of black mist and hunger, craving bodily form. She shuddered but not from the cold.

"No, I'm going. I'm not going to stand around and do nothing. What if she's fallen down somewhere?"

"She'll be back any minute. And if she isn't, we'll go and look together, okay?" Eirica's moon-like face glowed in the gloom.

"Yeah. She's going to be fine." Lochlan reached out as though to reassure her.

Moira whipped to face him. "She should never have gone. She's too young."

Lochlan huffed. "It's you who brought her here."

"Thanks to you."

"Hey, don't blame me. Everyone agreed. Besides, it's just a stupid story, anyway." He ran his hands through his hair. Too many times. He was nervous. "Look, she probably just—"

Crack.

They stalled, their gazes flicking to the thick, blue fogbank on the other side of the gate.

Eirica took a step back. "Wh . . . what was that?"

A small, dark figure stepped out of the gloom.

"Catriona!" Moira vaulted the gate and grabbed her sister into a hug. She reeled back. "My God, you're freezing."

Catriona stared at her, blank-eyed. A slow smile spread across her lips.

"Are you okay?" Moira reached out once more for her sister.

"Don't touch me." Catriona's voice came out barbed.

Moira's chest heaved. *What the heck?* She scrambled forward. "Catriona!"

Her sister stalked past her, climbed the fence, and strode by Nora and Lochlan, back toward their home.

"Catriona! Wait," called Moira, hurrying after her. She clambered back over the fence and sprinted past her friends. "Wait."

Catriona didn't look back, but Moira could swear she heard her laugh.

TWO

Moira didn't sleep. Shards of shadows spiked across her room, and she couldn't help replaying Catriona's laugh over and over in her head. And that smile. The more she visualized it, the less it seemed like a smile from sister to sister and more like one from predator to prey. She shivered. The old tales about the brollachan ran rampant in her mind—how it coveted the shapes of others due to its lack of form; how it needed to have its own body and would do anything to steal one, making its host wither away if it stayed inside it too long.

She scrubbed at her face. She needed to shake these thoughts off. It was nonsense, just superstition and myth. With a shudder, she pulled her covers up to her neck.

It stayed cold and dark. She did not sleep.

WHEN THE SUN BROKE THROUGH THE GRAY clouds in the morning, Moira rubbed the grit from her eyes. Her lungs felt as if last night's gloom had slithered inside, making every breath sluggish.

"You're being silly," she scolded herself as she pulled on jeans, a heavy-knit sweater, and her leather boots.

But was she?

She checked the clock—10 A.M. Ugh. She was late for breakfast. Stomach rumbling, she hurried downstairs.

The kitchen lay cold and empty. Strange.

"Mom? Dad?" She pushed by the scuffed table and chairs and peered from the kitchen to the living room. Empty. "Catriona? You around?"

The gloom in her lungs deepened when no one replied. Where was everyone? A quick once-over through the house—past the crooked family photos on the fireplace, down the too-narrow hallway, and through the stuffy dining room with its cabinet full of cat ornaments and candles on the table with dust stuck on top—revealed the house was entirely empty. Not even Tilly, their tortoiseshell, was anywhere to be seen.

Her mouth dried, and her neck prickled as though someone had just passed her by. The creak of a door screeched, and she jumped, her breath hitching.

"Mom?" She dashed to the kitchen, where she thought the sound had come from.

There, the back door swung back and forth, the push of a breeze lingering. Her pulse pounded in the hollow of her neck. On the table, a piece of paper fluttered. Moira swallowed; the weight in her lungs deepened. She crept forward.

She reached out and grabbed the paper quickly, as if it might burn her fingers. Her eyes scanned the page:

Town Hall. Come now. Urgent.

The world froze in Moira's mind for the briefest of seconds, everything suspended between a heartbeat and a breath.

Urgent?

She frowned. She didn't recognize the handwriting. It certainly wasn't her mom's or dad's writing, or Catriona's.

Moira's heart lurched, and she dropped the note onto the table. Someone had been in their house! Her mind whirred.

She dashed through the house once more, banging doors open as she went, checking each and every room for a second time. Her chest heaved, and her blood pounded by the time she got back to the kitchen. She was completely alone.

The words on the note stared up at her from the table. Why did someone want her to go to the town hall? A breath seeped slowly into her lungs. Only one way to find out.

She scrawled a quick message on a scrap of paper to let her parents know where she'd gone, should they return before she was back.

Now would be a great time for the island to be given cellphone reception, she thought as she slammed the pen down.

She grabbed her jacket from the peg, shut the door behind her, and jogged toward the village.

Everything about the day outside spoke of sharpness. The angle of the white sun's rays. The pinching cold of the breeze. The crunch of frozen grass beneath her boots. A raven squawked and dove in front of her, then yanked a worm from the ground. She jumped back.

The trek from her cottage to the village took half an hour. The raven had followed her from tree to tree—and was still there, watching her.

"Get! Go away," Moira shouted.

The bird cawed and kept close.

She ran through the cobbled streets. Thoughts circled like bats in her mind—who had left the note? What if something bad had happened? The note said it was urgent, after all. And why would Mom, Dad, and Catriona leave her alone in the house and not wake her up? Ice trickled down her throat, joining the damp in her lungs.

She picked up her pace. Houses whizzed by—soot-stained, gray-bricked terraces that could be seen in every village on any of the Scottish islands. Moira glanced to the side and stumbled as she caught sight of an old woman with a hunched back staring at her from an alleyway.

But when Moira righted herself, the old woman was gone. Her pulse thundered, and she ploughed on.

A few minutes later, Moira dashed around a corner . . . and smacked into someone's shoulder. Stumbling backward, she grabbed her nose and groaned. She looked up, and her eyes met Lochlan's.

"Moira! Did you hear what happened?" His voice came out strained.

She rubbed at her bruised nose. "I'm fine. Thanks for asking."

His narrow face pinched into a frown, and then his eyes widened. "Sorry. Are you alright? It's just . . . Didn't you hear?"

Moira dashed away the threatening tears and stood straighter. A murmur of voices drew her attention, and she peered around Lochlan. "What's going on?"

Dozens of villagers had gathered around the town hall, exchanging whispers.

"The police said there's been a murder." Lachlan's voice came out low, but his eyes shone bright and fevered. "They've been organizing interviews in the town hall. Not enough room in the station."

"What?"

"The police arrived at my door about seven this morning. Said everyone in the village was getting pulled in for questioning. I went in about half an hour ago. My mom just left. Hey, why didn't you come when your family did?"

"Who . . . who was murdered?" She could hardly believe she was asking the question. It didn't seem real. Murder. On her island? That couldn't be right. That was stuff for TV and books. There was never any crime on their island—

"It was Mrs. McAvoy," said Lochlan.

A dark stone lodged in Moira's throat. Mrs. McAvoy was Catriona's piano teacher. Catriona couldn't stand her.

Moira shivered, ice running down the back of her neck. "Wh . . . What happened?"

"I don't know." Lochlan fiddled with his eyebrow piercing. "They found her in the lane behind her house. Her skin had turned gray, and she was all withered away."

Moira gulped. "What makes them think she was murdered?"

Lochlan swallowed, his shoulders curling in. The words came out shakily, like he could barely stand to say them. "Her eyes were gouged out."

Moira's stomach plummeted. The weight in her lungs expanded and clogged her throat. That . . . No. There was no way . . .

Her eyes itched, and she shook her head. "Have . . . Have you seen Catriona? My parents?"

Lochlan motioned through the crowd to a makeshift stall where Headmaster Dailey had set up cups of coffee and tea to keep the crowd warm. Catriona stood beside him, pouring black liquid into the coffee cups. She looked up and caught Moira's eye. A smirk played on her lips. Moira blanched.

"Look, there's your mom and dad. They must be finished with their interview," said Lochlan.

Moira followed his gaze to her parents, who stood on the steps of the town hall, looking away from the rest of the villagers. An uneasy knot coiled into her chest. There was no way they wouldn't have woken her up to bring her here. And she still didn't know who'd left the note. A police officer? No, that didn't feel right. None of this made any sense.

Her dad bent to her mom's ear, his face strained and sallow as he whispered something.

"Sorry, I've got to go," Moira said to Lochlan and hurried off through the crowd.

She shouldered her way past two old biddies dressed in tweed coats and pillbox hats, gossiping about the grim news. Her mom looked up just as she got there.

"Mom? Dad? What's going on?"

"Moira! Thank God you're here. Where did you go this morning?" Her mom's voice was high-pitched and tight. She grabbed Moira into a hug, her arms shaking.

Moira pursed her lips. What did she mean, *where did she go?* "I was in bed all morning. I got up, and you were all gone. Why didn't you wake me? And who left that note?" She cast a look to the side, her eyes skimming over Catriona, but her sister didn't look up.

"No. You were out this morning. We looked everywhere for you. Your father even drove over to that Lochlan boy's house."

Moira's throat thickened. "Lochlan . . . H-h-he said something about a murder."

Her mom's cheeks paled, and she tugged her thick scarf tighter. She looked so small, bundled up so heavily. Just like Catriona. "The police called us first thing—"

"Everyone in the village," added her dad. "They called everyone in the village." He scrubbed at his stubble. He hadn't shaved that morning. "You'll need to go in and get interviewed. One of us will come with you. Catriona already did hers. Headmaster Dailey has her helping with hot drinks to keep her mind off things. She's too young to hear about all this."

Her mom placed a thin hand on Moira's shoulder. "I know this must be a shock, but I don't want you to worry. As soon as you've done your interview, we can go home."

Her dad tugged the collar of his stiff, gray coat into place. "And you're not in trouble for going out this morning without letting us know. Not today. Let's just get this over and done with." He took her arm and tugged her up the steps to the town hall.

"Wait, I didn't go out—" she tried again, but her dad silenced her with a warning glance.

THE INTERVIEW WAS QUICK AND FUNCTIONAL. Where had she spent last night? Had she been out in the early morning hours? Did she know Mrs. McAvoy? Had she seen anything suspicious?

Moira stared blankly throughout the entire thing. It was as if any answers she might have known had escaped her mind completely. She couldn't think if she'd seen anything when she'd snuck out last night, so she chose not to admit she'd crept up to the moors at all. It even took her a few minutes to remember who Mrs. McAvoy was, even though she'd known outside. By the end, it was as though tar filled her brain. What if her friends had admitted to going to the moor? Maybe the police would find holes in her story and think she had something to do with what happened. She went to open her mouth, to change what she'd said, but her dad was already hustling her out of the door, then down the steps of the town hall.

They joined Moira's mom and Catriona as they headed for the car.

"Don't worry, honey," her dad said as he bundled Moira into the car. "You did fine. It's a lot to take on board."

Catriona slid in beside her and buckled her seatbelt. She flicked a look at Moira, a dark smugness in her eyes.

"Where were you this morning?" asked Catriona, her tone light.

Moira groaned and rubbed her eyes. "I don't know why you all think I went out. Did no one bother to check my bedroom?" She scowled at Catriona and turned her attention to the window as they pulled out of the car park, leaving the crowd of villagers to gossip and complain in their wake. "Anyway, no one had even locked up when I left."

Her mom cleared her throat. "Listen, Moira. I understand you're upset about what's happened, and I'm not going to ask where you went this morning."

Moira opened her mouth.

"But," her mom continued, "I don't want to hear any more of this nonsense. You went out, and you lied about it. Let's just leave it alone with no more silly excuses."

Catriona nudged Moira's hand, and Moira flinched. Jesus, Catriona's skin was ice-cold. Moira glared at her sister, but Catriona just raised an eyebrow and smiled. Moira sniffed and looked back out the window. Something odd was going on, and she was going to have to find out what.

The car engine juddered and sputtered as if someone had put the wrong diesel in their beat-up Volvo. No one spoke. It wasn't until they got back home that Catriona piped up.

"Eirica's here."

Moira glanced out the grubby window. Eirica stood by their front door, parka huddled around her, hood pulled up to shield her pale face. As soon as the car stopped, Moira unbuckled her belt and raced outside. A gust of wind slapped her across the face, so hard it stung.

"Did you hear?" called Eirica over the weather.

"Yeah. What are you doing here? How come your parents let you out?"

Eirica's ruby lips pursed. "You told me to come. I got your note. Do you know how hard it was to sneak out with everything going on? You said it was important. So, what is it?"

"What? I didn't leave you a . . ." Moira's voice trailed off as the car door banged shut behind her. Catriona's hair fluttered in the wind as she walked by. She didn't glance Moira's way, but something in the way she carried herself stank of smugness. The tilt of her shoulders and the way she sauntered up the path seemed so . . . un-Catriona like.

Moira's flesh crawled, and she glanced back to Eirica. "Uh, there seems to be some kind of mix-up. I can't talk right now. I need to speak to Catriona."

Eirica huffed out a stream of foggy air and turned on her heel. "Thanks. Real nice. I trekked all the way over here just for you to tell me to go away. Fine." She stalked off before Moira could reply.

Moira watched her go and then looked back at her house. Catriona had disappeared inside, as had her parents. What the hell was going on?

Dashing across the icy path, she hid her face from the wind and scurried inside. The house was colder than usual. She wondered if the heating had conked out. Everything felt off-kilter, as if something fundamental had changed, and she was the only one who could see it. She hurried past the kitchen. The murmur of voices indicated her parents were inside it, so she headed upstairs, searching for Catriona.

191

Catriona's bedroom was at the end of the hallway, and Moira found her sitting at her desk with a sketchpad. A charcoal stick flew across its page. She didn't move when Moira entered the room.

"Catriona?"

The charcoal stick continued to race across the page.

"Are you okay? Do you know what's going on?"

Catriona's grip on the sketchbook tightened. She ditched the charcoal and picked up a red pencil. She scribbled faster but didn't say a word. Moira peered over her shoulder. A large, black entity filled the page, towering over the form of a little girl huddled in the lower-right corner. Red eyes blazed out from the creature's head.

"Catriona?"

Her sister whipped around in her chair, hissing.

Moira jumped back. "What the hell?"

Dark bags lingered under Catriona's eyes, and her hands were stained black. Moira swallowed, holding her sister's gaze. Catriona's eyes were blank, concave like a hollowed-out tree.

"It's all your fault." Catriona glared. "Yours and Eirica's and Lochlan's. None of this would have happened if it wasn't for you three. Mrs. McAvoy would have been fine if you'd just left things alone."

"What do you mean? Wait, you mean last night? But you're the one who asked to come with us." Moira reached out to grab her sister's shoulder, but Catriona shook her off. "Hey, you're scaring me. What's going on?"

The temperature in the room dropped, and Catriona turned back to her sketchpad, flipping it over and then picking up a fresh stick of charcoal. "Leave."

"But—"

"I said leave!"

The sheer venom in Catriona's voice forced Moira to back away. Shaking, she ran to her own bedroom and slammed the door shut. What was going on?

The previous night forced its way to the front of her mind. They'd sent Catriona to find the brollachan. Moira had thought it'd been fairytale nonsense . . . but . . . what if it wasn't? What if there really was a dark spirit who'd possessed her sister?

She scrubbed her hands over her face. She was being ridiculous. There were no such things as demons. But then, what about what had happened to Mrs. McAvoy?

Lochlan's words echoed in her mind: *Her skin had turned gray, and she was all withered away.*

Didn't the stories say that the brollachan killed people by making them wither away?

THREE

Moira paced the worn carpet. She stopped and stared out the window at the frosted fields outside. The white sun glared into her eyes. Stung, she spun away. She had to speak to someone. Perhaps she should use the landline to call Eirica? No. She'd left in such anger she'd no doubt refuse to answer the phone. That left Lochlan. Also, not a good idea. Her dad had no time for Lochlan's cocky behavior and bad influence, so he wouldn't let her phone him on the landline. Her hands tugged through her hair. She was by herself.

"Okay, okay," she mumbled as she paced once more. "What do I need?" To keep hold of her sanity, for one. She huffed out a breath. "Just go with it," she encouraged herself. What did she have to lose?

She paused, then hurried over to her laptop. Information. If she was going to entertain the ludicrous idea of dark magic, she needed to understand what she was tackling. She flipped open her laptop, booted it up, and opened a new tab. She typed 'brollachan' and waited for the search engine to spit out a response.

A Scottish mythical creature said to take the shape of what a person most fears.

A shapeless dark entity that craves a bodily form—one of the most feared creatures in Highland myth.

A fae mist that mostly haunts bogs and forests.

An entity that is ruled by the Cailleach, who appears as a black bird of death. The Cailleach is also known as the divine hag, Great Grandmother, and storm hag.

She clicked on each link, skimming for information. Black mist with red eyes—like Catriona's drawing? Victims dying with gray skin—just like Mrs. McAvoy.

Moira's mouth turned dry, and she could barely swallow.

She read the next line of the latest weblink: *A formless mass that pours into the host, trying to possess the body. Due to its chaotic nature, it only lasts in its host for a few days before the host body withers and dies. Then the brollachan must find a new host.*

The air sucked out of the room. All that was left was a heavy dampness, hanging in Moira's lungs, smothering her. She gasped, trying to find air. Her head spun. A few days? Wither and die? She tried to shake the thought away. Was that what had happened to Mrs. McAvoy? Had a dark spirit invaded Catriona and then possessed Mrs. McAvoy, draining all the life from her body?

Wait. That didn't make sense. If the brollachan was real, it would have had to have possessed Catriona, withered her away, and *then* jumped to the teacher. Besides, Moira and her friends had only snuck up to the moor last night. She wiped a hand across her sweating brow. And that didn't explain how Mrs. McAvoy's eyes had been gouged out, either.

Moira pulled back from the screen, her hands shaking. A tremor rippled through her stomach, and she leaned over and heaved into the wastebasket beside the desk. All that came up was bile. Her skin prickled, and her whole body trembled.

This was ridiculous . . . it had to be. It was a myth, after all. Not a fact. But the dark sketch, the sharp change in Cat's behavior, the murder . . .

Turning back to the laptop, she typed into the search engine once more. She needed as much information as she could get. Right or wrong, it was all she had to go on, and if Catriona was possessed, Moira needed an idea of how to get the brollochan out of her.

Her computer dinged and the answer spun up:

Expulsing a brollachan from a possessed individual is incredibly difficult to accomplish. An application of herbal medicine is required, though it's not clear whether the herbs themselves poison the brollachan or the ritual surrounding their administration drives it out. The necessary herbs are difficult to acquire, and it may be necessary for the practitioner to seek the assistance of other magical fae.

"'Other magical fae'?" Moira's words came out with an incredulous laugh. How was it possible she was sitting here thinking about magical fae and considering whether her sister was possessed?

The window rattled, and a loud caw made her jump. On the sill, a raven cocked its head at her.

"Go away." She waved her hands at it to shoo it away, but it didn't move. It just tilted its head the other way and cawed.

Moira shook her head. "I'm losing my mind."

She returned to the laptop and deepened her search.

HOURS PASSED. SHE MISSED LUNCH. DINNER. Her parents came and went. Yet Moira couldn't find anything that would help her, other than vague references to invoking other fae to help with a ritual involving some herbs that no source appeared to know the names of. She ran her fingers through her hair, then stretched out on her bed. The raven still watched her from the windowsill.

"Stop staring," she muttered.

It cawed.

"You're getting really annoying, you know."

It hopped closer. Something like intelligence glinted behind its eyes. She groaned. Great. Now she was talking to a bird.

It squawked again.

Moira quirked her eyebrow as she looked up. "Seriously?"

The bird watched her, turned, and flew away. A heavy sigh escaped Moira's lips. Rolling over, she buried her head under the covers.

ANOTHER HOUR PASSED, AND MOIRA couldn't stand not knowing what to do. She pulled on a fresh pair of jeans and a jumper, then wrapped a scarf around her neck. There was an old man in the village, Mr. Uist, who used to deliver eggs to their house, but he'd retired some years ago. He used to tell her all manner of ghost stories when she knocked on his door at Halloween as a kid. Maybe he had thoughts on the brollachan. It was a stretch, but she needed to do something.

Thundering downstairs, she ran into the living room. The TV buzzed in the corner, but no one was there. Strange. A quick check of the house revealed she was once more on her own. She glanced out of the window. No car in the drive. A pit of nerves writhed in her stomach. There was no way her parents would leave her alone again. What was going on?

She flicked a look at the clock. How was it four o'clock already? She could have sworn it wasn't past two.

She pursed her lips, her cheeks drawn taut. They must have just popped to the shops. Surely, they wouldn't be long. Grabbing a piece of paper, she scribbled a quick note to let them know she'd be back and hurried out the door.

The needling wind poked at her all the way from her house to Mr. Uist's farm. The crumbling, white building leaned over her at an uncomfortable angle. She knocked on the flaking, wooden door. Creaks and shuffling drifted from the other side, and then the door opened.

"Hello?" The old man squinted through a multitude of wrinkles, a flat cap angled over his brow. "Young Moira, is that you, lass?"

"Yes, Mr. Uist. I'm so glad you're in. I wanted to talk to you. I have some questions." The words poured out so fast she could barely keep them in.

"Calm down, lass. What's got your goat?" He pulled the door open wider. "Come and have a cup of tea, and you can tell me what's the matter."

A tight breath heaved out of her chest. Finally, she had someone to talk to.

FOUR

The old sofa creaked as Moira sat down. From its depths, a spring poked up, jabbing her in the back of the thigh. She shifted her weight.

Mr. Uist took off his flat cap and laid it on the coffee table. "So, what can I do you for, lass?"

Moira fiddled with the cuff of her jacket, squishing the black fabric between her fingers. Where on earth did she start? It wasn't like she could just blurt out that she thought a brollachan had possessed her sister.

Mr. Uist settled his mottled hands on his knees but kept quiet.

"You remember when I used to come around at Halloween?" Moira said eventually.

He nodded, his watery blue gaze not leaving hers. "Yup, me and Mrs. Uist used to make all you kids bags of candy, and we'd hide coins in there, too." His gaze turned glassy. "My Barbara used to love making up those bags and decorating the farm. Always said it felt like you kids were the ones we'd never managed to have ourselves."

Moira's gaze dipped. That was right. The Uists had had no children, yet he and his wife had always been so friendly to all the kids, whether it was Halloween, Easter, Christmas, or any fair in town.

"So, umm . . . You used to tell us folktales. Really old ones." She shifted in her seat again, and the loose spring poked her in the back of the thigh once more. "I was wondering if you remembered any of them?"

Mr. Uist scratched his balding head, then picked up a curved pipe and tamped down the end. "Long time ago, that was." He sighed. "It's a shame, you know. Kids stopped coming by years ago."

A knot formed in Moira's stomach. "Do you remember a story about the . . . the brollachan?"

His beady eyes lit up. "Ho! That's an ancient tale, that one."

Moira didn't say anything, just waited for him to continue.

He inhaled, his breath wheezing a little. "Nasty piece of work. Possesses people unawares. You can find it out in the moors, they say, right in the darkest part of night." He paused, lit his pipe, and then took a long drag. "Say, why do you want to know?"

Moira straightened, and her pulse jumped a beat. "Uh . . . it's . . . it's for a school project. We've to research Scottish myths." She tugged harder on the cuff of her jacket. "I picked the brollachan. I've managed to get most of the information, but I'm still trying to find out how they're defeated." She leaned forward, holding her breath.

Mr. Uist puffed out a long stream of foul smoke. "Hmm. Not a lot known about that, lassie. They're not something to be messed with, that's for sure."

The knot in Moira's stomach moved up to her throat, choking, strangling her. She could barely catch a breath. "So . . . you don't know anything that could help?"

"You seem a little spooked, lass. You haven't been messing with anything you shouldn't, have you?"

Moira shook her head, too quickly. Mr. Uist frowned. He took another drag on his pipe. A draft slipped through the living room, curling around the drab curtains and making them flutter.

At last, Mr. Uist blew out his smoke. "The old tales say there's a ritual to cast out the brollachan. Uses some special herbs. And you have to be right careful as, when it comes out the body, it can go into another if you're not quick enough."

"Do you know what the herbs are?" The words came out so quietly it was as though they'd barely escaped Moira's throat. *Please let him know what they are,* she thought desperately.

He clicked his tongue. "Nah, lass. They say only the fae know. The divine hag, too, I'd bet. But ain't read anything about it myself." He winked. "And trust me, I've read a lot. Love me some old myths, you know."

The grandfather clock in the corner of the living room ticked, and Moira shot a look at it. She rubbed at her temples, and a cold sweat came away on the tips of her fingers.

"How long does a brollachan stay inside someone? I mean, I heard it's a few days . . . but could they come out sooner? Do they always kill the body they're in?"

Mr. Uist set his pipe on the scratched coffee table. He licked his lips. "Supposed to be two or three days." His pale gaze met hers again. "But there was a story once about a young lass who had it in her for just one day."

Moira's eyebrow quirked. "Really?"

"Aye, but that's an old tale." He sighed. "Can't remember the rest. But I ain't ever heard of them leaving a person alive." With that, he climbed to his feet and bent over to pick his pipe back up. "I hope that helped. I gotta go into town to get some shopping now, before the shops close." He glanced at the grandfather clock. It was just after half past four. "I'm afraid I'm going to have to cut this short. I hope that gives you enough for your project."

"Project?"

His eyebrows furrowed. "Aye, for your school."

"Oh, yes, right. It is. It's great. Thank you so much." Moira rushed to her feet.

Mr. Uist took her elbow and guided her to the front door. As they passed the window, Moira glimpsed an old woman in a tattered shawl staring in at them.

"Who's that?" she asked, looking back to Mr. Uist.

He turned and looked out the window. "Who's who?"

When Moira turned back, the old lady was gone. She shook her head, the hairs on her neck prickling. "Nothing. Just thought I saw someone. Must have been my imagination."

They reached the doorway, and Mr. Uist patted her on the shoulder. "You take care now. And good luck at school."

She nodded, and, in the next moment, she found herself outside, with the door gently shut behind her.

She sighed and traipsed home, her heart heavy and her shoulders bowed. Her thoughts whirled, but one in particular pounded in a rhythm she couldn't ignore: Mr. Uist had said something about the brollachan not always staying in someone's body for as long as a few days. The muscles in her jaw clenched.

But the logic still didn't quite tie up. It explained how the creature could jump from one person to another so quickly, but not how Catriona could still be alive.

Her pulse increased at the thought that Catriona could die from this. The world spun, and she stumbled to her knees on the wet lane. Her breath came out in rasps. Everything was getting on top of her, and she wasn't getting any farther ahead in how to find out what was going on.

With a grunt of discomfort, she climbed to her feet and headed for home. What she needed was a few moments of rest, then she'd get back to it.

FIVE

"Moira! Moira! Where have you been?" Her mother's voice snapped Moira from the sleep she'd lapsed into. She shoved the pillow away and stared up at her mom's flushed face. "Mom?"

"When did you get home? I've been searching for you for over an hour."

"What are you talking about? I've been here." Sitting up, she scraped her hair back into a ponytail. Her laptop was on her desk. After she'd got back from Mr. Uist's, she'd done more research. "I went out earlier, but I left you a note."

Her mom scowled, her fine brows deepening into a vee. "Enough of this. There was no note, but there is something dangerous going on in the village, and it's not safe for you to go wandering about on your own."

"But I didn't—"

"We've been called back to go to the police station." Her mom straightened up, fiddling with the buttons of her blue cardigan. "There . . . Something's happened."

Moira blinked. Once. Twice. The silence in the room ballooned. Her mom sat on the bed and took her hand. Her pale fingers wrapped tighter than they should.

"I'm so sorry, honey. I don't know how to tell you this . . . " Her mom's voice trailed off, and she bit her lip.

"Mom? What is it? You're frightening me."

Her mom's throat bobbed. "There's been another murder . . . It's Eirica."

The room dissolved into static. Buzzing. Crackling in her ears. Words coming from her mom's mouth that didn't reach her. Her chest expanding so quickly it might burst. Her lungs filling up so much it might drown her. But she couldn't breathe out. Didn't want to breathe out. Because breathing brought the next moment, and . . . and . . .

"Honey, I'm here. Are you okay?"

Dizziness swamped Moira, and she yanked her hand from her mom's and held onto a handful of covers instead. She twisted the fabric until her fingers turned white.

"H . . . how? How did it happen?"

The dip between her mom's eyebrows deepened further. She bobbed her knee up and down. Moira twisted the covers so hard her hand hurt.

"It was the same as Mrs. McAvoy," her mom said at last.

Moira groaned and collapsed forward. Sobs heaved from her chest.

"I'm sorry, but we need to go to the police station. They sent an officer over to let us know, and I said we'd come down as soon as you were back. They're doing second interviews of anyone who knew both victims. That means your sister and you . . ." She rubbed Moira's shoulder in big, sweeping circles as Moira heaved in and out.

At last, Moira straightened into the unreal world that was somehow her life. "Catriona? Where is she?"

Her mom stood. "She's ready to go. I'll give you a minute to gather yourself, and we can all go together." She paused, her brown eyes crinkled at the sides. "I'm so sorry, baby. I wish I could make this easier."

Moira pushed her laptop shut and headed out with her mom. The last thing she wanted was time alone with thoughts of dark and unimaginable things.

THE DRIVE TO THE STATION SEEMED TO TAKE forever as their car wound its way through the dark lanes. Catriona hummed a tuneless tune under her breath and drew smiley faces on the foggy window of the car. When Moira went to point them out, Catriona swiped her hand over them, wiping them away. Black smudges curved down her sister's palm. Moira startled. Was that charcoal or something else? She fought to find her voice to ask, but Catriona's raised eyebrows rendered her mute.

"Are you sure you're ready for this?" her mom asked as they pulled up in front of the shabby station.

Moira nodded, and Catriona shrugged.

The wind screeched outside, and in the darkness, Moira spotted a raven wheeling in the currents, picked out by the moonlight. Its black wings looked even darker than the night.

Ravens.

She'd seen mentions of animals when she'd read about fae on one of her deep dives through the Internet. Different sites said the birds foretold both loss and ill omens, as well as linking the mortal world with the fae one. Moira swallowed. She'd need to look into that more later. She glanced at the bird one more time as she hurried inside.

Stuffy heat hit her face-on as they entered the brick station. Several plastic chairs were bolted to the wall, and a few pictures of inspirational quotes with images of salmon swimming upriver melded in with the beige walls.

She was surprised the station was still open at this time of night.

"Ah, Mrs. Holden. Thank you for coming." The desk sergeant stood, putting his mug down, and came out from behind his desk. He nodded to Moira and Catriona. "Girls. I'm sorry to have you down under . . . " His bushy mustache quivered. "I know she was your friend."

Catriona nodded. "Thank you." Her reply sounded false.

Moira simply nodded to the sergeant and followed as he led them to the back office. A door clicked open, and Lochlan walked out, ashen and drawn. Moira wanted to say something to him. Anything. But the sergeant led them onward, and she never had the chance.

TWO HOURS LATER, THE INTERVIEW CLOSED, and Moira brushed the dry, salty tracks from her cheeks. Eirica. Gone. Sucked dry, her skin gray. She shook her head, trying to rid the image from her mind. It was so unreal. And yet, here she was, leaving a police station as real and solid as Moira herself.

She climbed back into the car, along with her mom and sister. The heater sputtered. Then they trundled down the road and fresh tears swamped her once more. Catriona sat and rubbed her smudged hands together.

As soon as they were home, Moira raced upstairs. She sprinted into her room, grabbed her laptop, and sat down. Her cat, Tilly, jumped off the bed and sat on the floor. Moira opened up a search bar—she needed to find out how to call some kind of fae.

A tap sounded at the window. The raven—still here, in the dark. "What are you trying to tell me—?"

Her bedroom door banged open, and there stood Catriona. She leaned against the doorjamb, casually propped up as if she didn't have a care in the world. Tilly hissed and darted into the hall and away.

"What is it?" snapped Moira, sharper than she intended.

A coy smile tugged on her sister's lips.

Moira stood. "What the hell is wrong with you? What happened in the field the other night?"

"You really need to watch that temper of yours." Catriona's voice dripped as sweet as honeysuckle. She shrugged. "And you need to be very careful about where you go when other people aren't around. Haven't you heard there's a murderer on the loose?"

Moira stumbled back a step, and the backs of her legs hit her bed. "What are you talking about?" Her voice pitched higher. "Why does everyone keep saying I've been gone when I haven't?"

A red glint sparked in Catriona's eyes. "Oh, but you have."

Sweat trickled down Moira's forehead into her eyes, making them sting. She scrubbed it away. "I don't know what you're talking about. Everything about you is all . . . wrong. You came back different. And then those deaths started—"

A grim chuckle escaped Catriona's lips. "Oh no. You seem to be confused. That wasn't me."

The air turned to ice. A faint tapping sounded behind Moira, and Catriona scowled.

"The brollachan," Moira whispered. "It did something to you, didn't it?"

Another laugh. Brittle like glass. "Yes." Catriona's eyes narrowed. "But it wasn't hunting with me."

The thud in her chest made Moira startle. It was as if someone had punched her. "You're not saying it's going into *someone else* to kill people?"

Catriona smirked and looked Moira dead in the eye.

A cold sensation flooded Moira's chest. "Wait. What? Me? No. There's no way that's happening. I'd know if . . . if a dark spirit had come into my body—"

"But would you?" Catriona cocked her head. "I suppose you would if it stayed in you. But what if it just used you to hunt? Blocked out your memory and returned to somewhere safe later." Catriona tapped her temple. "Somewhere nearby. Innocent."

Moira's throat burned as she gasped. "You mean the brollachan is inside you, resting, but then it's jumping into my body to hunt? That's impossible." Blood rushed through her ears.

"Is it?" Cat twirled a loose strand of hair and rolled her eyes. "It's impossible because you read some old legend on the Internet? A fairytale passed down through generations, molded and distorted for people's own purposes?" Her voice deepened, a hiss weaving an undercurrent of anger. "You shouldn't believe everything you read."

Moira opened her mouth, but nothing came out.

"Thinking of calling for help?" Catriona smirked. "And what are you going to say? *A demon possessed my sister and is using me to hunt?* That you took me to the moor in the middle of the night and threw me to the wolves?"

The blood drained from Moira's face.

"Thought not." Catriona spun away and strode into the hall. Before she turned out of sight, she glanced back. "And if you want to stay safe, you better get rid of that damn bird."

Her eyes flared, and she left Moira shaking in her room.

Moira turned to the window, but the raven was gone.

SIX

Weak moonlight glinted across Moira's bedroom, spotlighting her on her floor where she sat cross-legged. Every bone screamed at her not to mess with dark magic, and yet she had to. She must do something to save Catriona. She had to try the only thing she could think of: an exorcism. It sounded ridiculous even to her own ears. But without a way to call on magical fae, she was out of other ideas.

She picked up a Celtic cross her grandmother had given her before she died and clutched it in her sweaty grasp. Her chest heaved, and she had to take long, slow breaths to calm down. This would work. It had to.

The fact she wasn't religious needled at Moira. She had no idea what she was doing. Everything she'd read up on pretty much said the same thing: holy water, cross, prayers—a snort came out of her nose—and, generally, some kind of priest and other people to help. She shifted uncomfortably on the itchy carpet. Well, she had to work with what she'd got.

She picked up the bottle of water from her desk and sprinkled some in a circle around her. She pressed the cross so tightly into her hand that it cut her.

She breathed out. "Spirit, whose nature is . . . " Dammit, what were the words? She cleared her throat. "Umm . . . whose nature is merciful and forgiving, accept my prayer that I, bound with sin, may be pardoned by your loving kindness."

She groaned. She sounded idiotic. The bottle shook in her grasp as she sprinkled more holy water around herself. The temperature in the room dipped. The shadow from the wardrobe seemed to waver.

"Depart, then, spirit," she continued. "Leave with all your deceits, for you are not—"

The door slammed open, and Moira jerked straight.

Catriona strode in, peering at the damp carpet. She tossed her braid over her shoulder and raised both eyebrows, stopping a few feet away. "Is that a . . . *cross*?"

Moira glanced at the top of the cross poking out of her fist. Her blood ran like ice water through her veins. She closed her eyes and began reciting the lines of her prayer again: "Spirit whose nature is merciful and forgiving—"

A sharp laugh cut her off, and her eyes flew open. Catriona's face was inches from her own. How had she got over here so quickly? Moira hadn't even heard her move.

"*Tsk, tsk, tsk,* Moira," said Catriona, crouching and leaning back onto her haunches. "Trying to get rid of something, were you?"

Moira gritted her teeth and rose to her feet so that she towered over Catriona. "Leave with all your deceits—"

Catriona leapt up and slapped her square across the cheek. "Stupid girl." Her eyes blazed like coals. "You think an exorcism will save you? Don't be ridiculous." Her eyes burned into Moira's. "You'll regret this."

Moira forced her voice to stay level. "We'll see about that."

A hiss rushed from Catriona's lips, and a black form whirled into the air. It towered over Moira, red eyes gleaming. Ice formed in the breath that left Moira's mouth. And, suddenly, everything was rushing toward her. Faster and faster. Until she was enshrouded in black and the unholiest fire raged within her.

Moira's eyes opened groggily. She was slumped on the floor, every bone aching. The memory of the brollachan hitting her with its full force flooded through her. *Shit.*

Then another thought assailed her: trying to exorcise the brollachan hadn't worked, and now she'd used her only option *and* she'd pissed off the brollachan at the same time. Pains gathered in her shoulders and neck, vying for place. Something bad was going to happen—and soon.

The first rays of dawn bled into the room. Her eyes were blurry and full of grit. Had she slept? She glanced down at her clothes. Hold on. She hadn't been wearing a hoodie last night. Her stomach dropped. *No. Oh please, no.* She scrambled through her memory of late last night, but there was a gaping blank. She assumed she'd fallen asleep, but oh God, what if the brollachan had possessed her and gone hunting again?

She leapt to her feet and barreled downstairs. Catriona sat alone at the kitchen table.

"What the hell did you do?" Moira shouted.

Catriona played with her spoon over a bowl of porridge. "Me? I didn't do anything. You, on the other hand . . ."

Moira paced the kitchen, hands flexing into fists. "Tell me what you've done. I swear to God—"

"I think you tried that already, didn't you?" Catriona smirked. "That was what the cross and holy water were all about, no?"

"Shut up!" screamed Moira. "Tell. Me. What. You. Did!"

Catriona got to her feet slowly and placed her hands flat on the table. Her dark gaze locked with Moira's. "Wagging tongues do talk, don't they?"

Moira paused, her thoughts spinning. Then her stomach sank. *Oh God no.*

She took off at a sprint.

MOIRA SKIDDED TO A STOP IN FRONT OF THE white farmhouse. Every atom in her body screamed at her to charge through the door. She slammed her fist against the wood.

"Mr. Uist! Mr. Uist! Are you in there?" She pounded harder. "Mr. Uist! Can you hear me?"

She glanced around the cobbled road and fields. A rusty tractor. An old fence. A battered old Beetle. Nothing stirred.

Dammit.

She looked at the door, her blood thrumming. She'd just have to go in. With a grunt, she pushed, and it swung open, unlocked. Moira gulped and stepped inside.

The hallway was eerily quiet. Motes of dust floated past the Uists' wedding photos in the poor light. The smell of burnt toast wafted in the air.

This is a bad idea, she told herself. *What am I doing?*

She took a steadying breath as she tiptoed along. She had to check. Just to be sure.

The carpet shushed beneath her shoes as she crossed into the kitchen, then the living room. She stumbled to a halt. Mr. Uist lay slumped on his couch, withered and gray. Tongue ripped out.

Wagging tongues do talk.

She threw up on the coffee table. Dizziness blurred her vision, and she stumbled to the counter, searching out the phone. Her hand trembled as she jabbed in the numbers. She couldn't breathe. Her pulse thundered. The room spun.

"999. What's your emergency?"

"He . . . Mr. Uist . . ." Bile burned up her throat. Nausea swamped her, and she crashed to the floor. "There's been a murder."

EIGHT

"Where were you this afternoon?" asked Moira's dad as they sat down for dinner.

Dinner? How did she get to dinner? Moira shook her head, trying to get the cobwebs away. Mr. Uist's withered face reared into her mind. His dead face, and the gaping hole where his tongue should be.

"Yeah," Catriona tilted her head. "Where were you?"

Moira bolted to her feet. "You!" Her voice came out more of a shriek than a shout as she stared at the ... *thing* in her sister. "You killed him! You murdered that poor old man!"

"Moira!" hissed her mom. "What on earth has gotten into you?"

"That old man! The one who used to deliver our eggs. Mr. Uist. He ... he ... died, and—"

Her father slammed his fist on the table. "Enough." He glared at her before releasing a heavy sigh. "Please tell me it wasn't you who prank-called the police today?"

"What?" Moira flashed a look at Catriona, who just grinned. "He's *dead*. That old man is—"

"Away to see relatives on the mainland. His cousin, Mrs. Campbell, phoned to confirm with the police," said her mom. "A lot of people got disturbed due to that hoax."

Moira's eyes stayed on Catriona who gave an innocent, who-me? expression.

"She ... She did something ..." Moira said, pointing at her sister.

"Moira. I think you need to go upstairs and lie down. The events in the village seem to be overwhelming you." Her dad looked to Catriona. "Take your sister upstairs and make sure she settles, okay?"

Catriona got to her feet and nodded solemnly. "Of course."

Moira went to shake her off, but Catriona tugged her by the elbow and whispered in her ear. "Shut up and keep walking."

Moira stumbled up the stairs after Catriona. "That old man did nothing to you."

Catriona smirked. "And I didn't do anything to him. In fact, everyone thinks he's still alive. People really are so trusting when a cousin they've never heard of phones up."

Moira's hand flew out, and she slapped Catriona across the face. "You're going to regret this."

Catriona shoved Moira into her room. "There's nothing you can do about it." She turned and walked out, leaving Moira on her own.

Moira's blood boiled. She had to do something. The exorcism might not have worked, but there had to be something else.

The caw of a bird sounded somewhere outside.

She looked up. The raven sat on the windowsill and stared in.

She frowned at it. She needed help. Was that what the raven was trying to do? Help her? The brollachan *had* been angry to see the bird yesterday . . .

She grabbed the laptop and tapped open her search history. She needed to read it again.

There.

She leaned forward. *The brollachan is an entity that is ruled by the Cailleach, who appears as a black bird of death. The Cailleach is also known as the divine hag, Great Grandmother, and storm hag.*

A black bird. A raven. Could it . . . could this bird be a fae?

Moira's heart pounded as she tapped wildly into the search engine, drawing up page after page of information. Her hand froze on an invocation for the Cailleach, the Great Ancient Grandmother. Could she help? Would she?

Excitement and terror buzzed in her veins. She couldn't sit and let more people die. She had to try something.

Outside, the raven cawed.

Four hours later, Moira's breath tightened in her chest as she crept across the landing to Catriona's bedroom. The door lay ajar. The air fuzzed with static. With another quiet step, she pushed the door open further. Catriona lay asleep on the bed. At least, Moira hoped she was asleep. Hopefully, the sleeping pill she'd slipped into her tea before bed had worked.

It *had* to have worked. The alternative didn't bear thinking about. Her shoulders tensed at the memory of Mr. Uist's withered corpse.

She adjusted the backpack on her shoulders—full of items she'd learned about online that were said to summon the Cailleach. She'd briefly considered tying herself up so that the brollachan couldn't take her possessed body anywhere, but soon realized it wouldn't work. No. This was her best—her only—option. And the last hour spent scouring the nearby area and the sea cliffs for what she needed for the exorcism would be put to good use.

Steeling herself, she snuck into her sister's bedroom. Icy chills ran over her skin. Catriona lay unmoving, red hair fanned around her, her breathing steady. She looked so . . . innocent.

Moira squared herself. No. Catriona was possessed by something dark, and it needed to be dealt with.

She grabbed the cloth from her bag and hovered it over Catriona's mouth. Then, as quickly as she could, she pressed it against her sister's lips to muffle a potential scream should she wake up.

Moira waited a few seconds. When Catriona didn't stir, she removed the cloth and hoisted her sister into both arms. This was going to be a long walk.

THE MOON SHONE BRIGHTLY, AND ITS BEAMS
sliced the midnight sky as Moira took the last few steps toward
the hawthorn tree. Sweat poured down the back of her neck,
and her arms and legs burned. As gently as she could, she
slumped Catriona against the old tree. Mud stained the hem of
Catriona's nightgown, and her red hair lay frazzled against her
face. Moira's stomach clenched. It was horrible to see her sister
like this. But this had to be done.

She pulled out the rope she'd stowed in her backpack.

Catriona still hadn't stirred by the time Moira had tied her
to the tree and firmly knotted the ropes. She laid out a circle of
stones on the damp ground. She'd remembered the sequence
of the stones for the ritual by heart.

"Please work, please work," Moira muttered as she paced
the circle.

Catriona stirred, and the rope shushed against the bark.
"Moira," she cried. "You have to let me go. You don't know
what you're doing." Tears tacked down her pale cheeks, and
her voice wobbled. "Please."

"Be quiet," Moira hissed, looking away quickly. Her heart
twisted.

It's not Catriona. It's the brollachan.

But, right now, it sounded just like her. Moira couldn't help
but look again at her sister, in the end.

Catriona shivered in the cold, her face so ashen she looked
ill. The ice of the day was gone, replaced by a heavy fog that
wrapped around her ankles.

Casting her gaze away, Moira picked up the items to create
her altar—plaid cloth, rocks collected from the nearby sea
cliffs, ale from her father's cabinet, and a shard of bone from
the skeleton of a mouse long dead. The latter had been
surprisingly easy to find—once a victim of their cat, no doubt.

Moira set everything within the circle she'd created. Then she gazed up through the branches of the hawthorn tree to the sky. Was she really going to do this? Was it going to work?

She stopped in the middle of the circle and lifted her hands into the air.

The words left her lips, shaking and terrified. "Hear me now, Cailleach Baere, Great Ancient Grandmother, Lady of the Deep Forest, Old Witch of the Roots and Cauldron. I, your child, pray that you come to me, that you look favorably upon this holy rite. Come into this grove and provide your blessing, please."

She moved across the circle, keeping her eyes from Catriona, who whimpered pitifully. Moira picked up one of the larger rocks and held it high above her head.

"I offer you precious stone, so that the Bones of the Earth may be freshly clothed anew." She placed the rock atop the altar. Then she picked up the flask and sprinkled the liquid over the stone. "I give you ale so that the Waters of Life may flow in abundance and the spirit may become flesh again."

Catriona's pitiful cry caught her ear, but Moira turned away. It wasn't really her sister, she reminded herself, despite the pang in her chest; it was the dark magic talking.

She moved to the mouse bone and held it high. "And I offer you bone so that the old and unnecessary may be rested."

The wind rose around her, rattling the trees. Moira swallowed. "Be welcome, Cailleach, and heed my call."

The wind fell, and a shiver coursed through the ether. It was like the earth was shrugging off a shroud, casting away a layer that hid what it normally didn't want other people to see.

In a blink, a cunning old woman appeared before Moira.

Moira's heart slammed against her ribs, and she stumbled back a step. The woman's river-cold eyes sparkled beneath craggy brows, and her spindly hand sat gnarled atop an ancient staff. Her fingers twisted like the roots of old trees around it. Moira gulped. It was her—the woman she'd thought she'd seen outside Mr. Uist's house, the woman who'd then disappeared.

217

"Why do you call upon the Great Grandmother?" The old woman's voice came out like the scatter of autumn leaves.

"I . . . I . . . "

"Speak, youngling, or I will send my wrath upon you. No one calls the Great Grandmother from her slumber without good reason."

"I saw your raven."

The Great Grandmother rubbed mottled fingers over the top of her staff. "Unusual. What troubles you?"

Moira rubbed a sweaty hand over her face and nodded to her sister, who cowered into the hawthorn tree. "It's my sister. There's a brollachan inside her. I need your help."

The Great Grandmother pursed her lips and made her way over to Catriona. Her steps were labored, and she leaned heavily on her staff all the way. Moira swallowed. What could one old woman do against an evil entity of old magic?

The Great Grandmother shot a look over her shoulder. "Do not let appearances deceive you." She turned to look at Catriona, without waiting for Moira to reply.

Catriona's eyes turned pleading. "Please, my sister—Moira—has gone crazy. She thinks I'm some kind of monster. You've got to hel—"

"Quiet, brollachan. Who do you mean to trick? I am older than you and rule these lands. Do not anger me."

Catriona's eyes blazed a fierce red before simmering. "Indeed, Lady of the Deep Forest. Forgive my insolence." The voice came out smooth and buttery.

Moira shuddered.

"But I question your appearance here," the brollachan in Catriona continued. "This is not an issue for one such as you. This is a mere tussle between fae and mortal."

"It's got my *sister*! It's *murdering* people!" shouted Moira, dashing forward. Her sweaty hair stuck to her forehead. "Look, we didn't know this would happen when we . . . We didn't know he would possess my sister. We were only trying to scare each other."

The Great Grandmother whirled, fire flaming in her eyes. "And why should I care for the follies of mortals?"

Moira stumbled to a halt. "I . . . I . . . It's killing people."

Silence bubbled in the dark space. The Great Grandmother straightened her crooked back. "If that is all you have to offer—"

"No!" Moira racked her mind, fought for the tiniest scrap of information that could help. "The raven was the reason I called you. It must have wanted you to help me." The information she'd read spun in her mind. "They represent life and death. The same power you wield over life and death." The heaviness in her lungs began to lighten. "And the brollachan is breaking those rules and the power you hold. It's not following its . . . " She scrambled for the right words. "The laws of its kind."

The old crone's brows dipped, and she took a step toward Moira. Her wrinkled skin creased further, as dented as the bark of the hawthorn tree.

"Don't listen to her. She lies," shouted the brollachan in Catriona's voice.

"Quiet," hissed the Great Grandmother. She turned to Moira and waved for her to continue.

"It's living inside my sister but moving to other people to kill them—"

"That is the nature of the brollachan, to change hosts—"

"But it's not, though," Moira insisted, and the crone scowled fiercely at her interruption. Moira pushed on. "It's taking over me to kill people, then returning to my sister." Great whooshes of breath heaved in and out of Moira's nose, and icy sweat ran down her back and neck.

She bent double, then fell.

She was in Mr. Uist's house. The light was dim. Grocery bags sat on the floor next to the sofa. An old '50s song played on a rattly radio, and Mr. Uist lay asleep on the sofa. She tiptoed forward.

219

A dark sensation filled her lungs, like billowing smoke, embers burning inside her. She jerked.

Black veins spidered over her skin. Claws grew like talons from her fingers, sharp and lethal.

Her gaze turned red as she leaned over Mr. Uist's sleeping form.

Then her hand arced up . . . and down across the old man's throat.

Moira bolted up. Colors swamped her vision.

"It's true," she cried, tears pouring down her cheeks. "It . . . It made me kill Mr. Uist . . ." Jagged breaths cut her throat and words failed her.

The Great Grandmother turned to the brollachan. "Is what the youngling says true?"

"You must understand, Lady of—"

"Do not bring your lies to me, fae mist." She swiped her staff in the air. Before her, a bowl appeared on the boggy ground.

Moira could barely focus, but the Great Grandmother glared at her. "Focus, child." She pointed at the bowl. Several herbs tied by string lay together. The Great Grandmother motioned for her to come closer, and Moira stumbled toward her.

"I cannot undo what has been done. The people who have passed to the other side will remain where they are."

Moira's body lurched. "But, Eirica, my friend. You have to bring her back—"

She held up a finger. "I will *not* bring people back from the dead. That is not the natural order of things. But I will release your sister of the brollachan. However, you must give me something in return."

Moira's mouth turned dry, and she tried to swallow. Her eyes went to Catriona. The image of Mr. Uist replayed in her mind. "Anything."

The Great Grandmother's eyes met hers. "For interfering with that which you should not, you must surrender one thing most precious to you."

The pressure in Moira's chest built. An owl hooted in the distance. "What's that?"

The old crone's face darkened. "A memory of my choosing. One that you hold dear." The wind swirled around her and lifted the hem of her cloak. "Well, child. What do you say?"

It was as though Moira's whole life spiraled through her mind all at once. Every happy moment she had ever had—her birthdays, her first horse-riding lesson, playing with Catriona on the moors, the family trip to Skye. Each of them and more tumbled through her.

"I will wait no longer," said the Great Grandmother.

Moira swallowed and stuck out her hand. "Deal."

The old woman took Moira's hand in her own and bowed her head. "And, so, it shall be done."

The pain that lanced through Moira's brain sent her toppling to her knees. It was as though part of her was yanked from her brain, squirming and fighting, trying hard not to be taken from her soul. And then it was gone, and she was left with a space of emptiness inside her head. One that she instinctively knew would never be filled with its original contents.

"Come," said the Great Grandmother. "It is time to rid your sister of the brollachan."

A mighty screech rent the air, escaping through Catriona's lips. The Great Grandmother ignored it, her fierce, dark eyes upon the bowl she had left on the ground.

Her eyes fixed on Moira. "This will be easy, but not without pain. It will change you both. You will remain marked for crossing paths with a fae you should never have sought." She lifted a craggy eyebrow in dark appraisal. "Do you agree to these terms?"

Moira swallowed and cast a glance to her sister shivering against the tree. Black veins now snaked up her throat and face as the brollachan raged inside of her.

"Yes," she whispered. "Anything to save my sister."

The Great Grandmother motioned for her to pick up the bowl of herbs. "So mote it be. Cast these herbs around your sister and follow my incantation. Do not fear the flames. They will harm neither you nor your sister."

Shaking, Moira took the herbs and tossed them around Catriona.

"You will be punished for this," shouted the brollachan. "I will hunt you down, Moira. Kill all you know and love—"

The Great Grandmother waved her hand. Flames rose instantly from the herbs, burning a circle around Catriona.

"Repeat after me, youngling. 'No evil things shall cause me fear. With this smoke, they flee from here.'"

Moira's voice rose, tremulous as a fledgling bird. "No evil things shall cause me fear. With this smoke, they flee from here."

Inside the flames and smoke, the brollachan shrieked. Moira's heart clenched.

"Brollachan, you are cast out, flee from the light back to the dark," boomed the Great Grandmother, her gray hair streaking back in the gathering wind.

Moira yelled the words along with her. Chanting, chanting, chanting. Smoke stung her eyes. Flames heated her cheeks. Yells and screams lifted into the air.

An intense pain lanced through Moira's arm, and the impact of it had her buckling to the ground. Pain, like fire, coursed over her skin. Her arm burned as though blisters popped. Tears welled in her eyes. Smoke clogged her throat.

And then it was gone.

She collapsed, heaving.

When she opened her eyes, the moor lay empty. No fire or smoke. No spells or fae. Just the lingering scent of burned hair.

"Moira? Help. What's going on? Why are we here? What's happening to me?"

Moira rushed to her feet, darting to where Catriona sat tied to the tree. Her eyes had cleared, and her skin was void of black veins. Her sister was back.

Relief flooded Moira's veins, and she hugged Catriona tightly before darting to the back of the tree and tearing off the bindings.

Catriona collapsed forward, and Moira rushed to scoop her up in her arms.

"I'm so sorry, Catriona."

Catriona sniffed, shaking. "What happened? One minute I was in the moor and I was freezing cold. And then I was here." She paused, looking up to meet Moira's eyes. "Why was I tied to a tree?"

Moira just shook her head and pulled her sister close.

"Hey, what's that on your arm?"

Moira glanced down to see a long, dark streak on the inside of her elbow, like a black tattoo. The same place she'd felt the burning pain. The Great Grandmother's words came back to her: *Take it. This will be easy, but not without pain. It will change you. You will remain marked for crossing paths with a fae you should never have sought.*

A shudder ran through Moira, and she pulled Catriona to her feet. "Don't worry about all this. I'll explain it later. Right now, we need to get you home."

She took Catriona by the hand and pulled her along through the fog.

BEHIND HER, SILENT AS THE GRAVE, A DARK mist wove along the ground, tendrils stretched out and searching . . .

SMOOTH THE DESCENT
EMILY COLIN

ONE

I woke, panting, from a nightmare of books aflame to see Genevieve Johannsen staring down at me, her lips pressed into a thin, suspicious line.

"What were you dreaming about, Miriam?" There was a note of accusation in her voice, undergirded by a hint of vicious curiosity. "Something you need to confess to the Priests?"

Genevieve had the cot next to mine in the girls' dormitory, and I'd known her since we were children in the Nursery. Still, we rarely spoke beyond necessities, and I wasn't inclined to confide in her about my dream—the one that violated every oath I'd sworn.

I was a scholar. It was my responsibility to tend the Commonwealth's store of books, to peruse their moral content for lessons that could help us better understand the thorny path that led to virtuousness and the slippery slope toward sin. Fire was a scholar's worst enemy, and I lived in fear that I'd somehow make a mistake that would lead to the Library's destruction. Apparently, that terror had bled into my dreams.

"Nothing," I told Genevieve, pushing my blankets back and sitting up. I couldn't control my subconscious—but there was no way I would admit to dreaming about the Library's destruction. To Genevieve, that would be one dangerous step away from the act itself.

"Really?" Her feathery blond eyebrows knitted, and her thin lips pursed tight. "Because you look quite guilty. Also, if you don't get up now, you'll be late for catechism."

In the Commonwealth of Ashes, we were not allowed to have friends—attachment was seen as the first step on the road toward chaos—but of course, there were people one felt an affinity for, and people one did not. I'd grown up in the Nursery with Genevieve and had never been able to stand her—though of course I couldn't admit such a thing aloud. She was quick to find fault, a natural Informer. I knew at the slightest whiff of wrongdoing, she would go running to the High Priests.

Here in the Commonwealth, citizens lived and died by the rules of the Seven Deadly Sins—pride, greed, lust, envy, gluttony, wrath, and sloth. Failure to protect the books for which I was responsible would be a slothful sin of the highest order. It was no wonder I had nightmares about destroying the Library; if I did, I'd surely find myself kneeling on the stones of Clockverk Square, a bellator's blade pressed to my throat and one of the Priests standing over me, carrying out the Executor's sentence of death.

The Executor ruled the Commonwealth; what he said was law. He commanded the blades of the Bellatorum Lucis—the warriors of light. These were the Commonwealth's enforcers, sworn to protect us from the corruption that stained our souls. All my life, I'd found them terrifying, not least because I'd witnessed their punishments in action. I was determined never to give them any reason to notice me—and not drawing a potential Informer's attention to me was the first step.

"I'm fine," I said, sliding off my cot and ignoring her judgmental sniff. I went about my business—taking my allotted three-minute shower, dressing in the green tunic that marked me as a scholar, filing into Clockverk Square for catechism under the watchful eyes of the crimson-robed Priests, eating breakfast with my fellow citizens—but all the while, I could feel her eyes on me, assessing, judging. As I left the dining hall, I trembled under the weight of the Priests' stares, half-expecting them to drag me away.

I was relieved when Genevieve and I went our separate ways—her to her work in the dairy, and me to the Library— but I couldn't shake the worry that she'd seen or heard something untoward. What if I'd talked in my sleep, and she'd heard me say something about setting the Library aflame? What would happen to me then?

I was still preoccupied by this an hour later, as I stood on a ladder, straining to reach the Library's highest shelf. Aric, the scholar assigned to work alongside me, was taller—but he was busy sorting through a box of moldering books, so the task fell to me.

I'd never fallen from one of the Library's ladders before. Half my focus was on my work; the other half was on Genevieve, which was the only explanation I had for what happened next. One moment I was reaching for *Paradise Lost*, and the next I was falling, the ladder going in one direction and my body in the other. I grabbed for the shelf to steady myself, missed, and crashed to the ground in a hail of books.

Dante's *Divine Comedy* struck me in the solar plexus, tumbling into my lap. I looked up, stunned—in time for a volume so massive it could only be *The History of the Commonwealth: A Compendium* to smack into my forehead. The world grayed and blurred at the edges, narrowing to a single, wavering point. And then, all at once, it went dark.

I WOKE TO SEE A MEDIC KNEELING OVER ME, no doubt summoned by Aric. The Commonwealth was relatively small—no more than 10,000 people—so the medic was familiar, though I'd never spoken with him before. His name, I recalled through the fog in my head, was Kennett Gundarson.

We were the same age. I'd been Chosen to be a scholar the same day he'd been Chosen to be a medic—almost a year earlier, when we'd both turned seventeen—but I'd never spoken to him. Why would I? In the Commonwealth, boys were an irrelevance. Our children were conceived in test tubes and carried by surrogates—then raised in the Nursery by Caretakers, with no knowledge of who their biological parents had been. We considered fellow citizens only in light of the services they could provide—a seamstress to sew our clothes; a butcher to slaughter our beasts; an Instruktor to teach our children—not in terms of what they meant to us on a personal level.

Friendship, as I've said, was forbidden. Romantic love—and of course, lust—was punishable by death or exile to the Borderlands that surrounded the Commonwealth, filled with brutal hordes bent on our destruction. Sometimes, the Priests would have the bellators deliver particularly egregious sinners to the Borderlands, sedating the Bastarour who roamed the forest that ringed the edge of the Commonwealth and the electric fence. On other occasions, the Priests released the sinners into the forest, where they were at the mercy of the Bastarour—genetically-modified beasts trained to rend their prey limb from limb. If, by some miracle, the sinners managed to evade the Bastarour, they'd come smack up against the fence, which would fry them where they stood.

We never got to see what happened to sinners who were exiled to the Borderlands or condemned to the forest; we just knew they never returned. By contrast, I'd witnessed a man and woman executed for fornication the year I turned fifteen.

They'd been beheaded side by side, holding hands in one last futile gesture of rebellion. The horror of it was with me still.

Just the same, as Kennett knelt over me, I couldn't help but notice how gentle his touch felt on my forehead, blotting away the blood. His eyes were as green as the pines in the woods that surrounded the City, and his hair as black as the night sky, just before the first stars came out.

I closed my eyes, horrified. Poetry belonged in the pages of the books I studied—to be analyzed for its moral content, not appreciated as an art form. It certainly had no place in my mind as I lay on the floor, looking up at Kennett. What if he noticed? What would he think of me then?

"Miriam," he said. "How do you feel?"

I must have been delirious from the blow. That was my only excuse. Because when I blinked and looked up at him, I didn't give him a sensible answer. *My head hurts, but I'll be fine,* I could have said. Or, *Thank you for your attention; I'm sorry to have required your services.*

But instead, I blurted, "'I did not die, and yet I lost life's breath.'" It was a line from The *Divine Comedy*, which had quite literally knocked the air out of my body.

The moment the words left my lips, I felt like a fool. Most citizens of the Commonwealth didn't read much; they learned their lessons at the hands of the Instruktors, and then went on to pursue whatever their Chosen career might be. Those selected as medics studied science and mathematics, not literature. I expected this one to dismiss my words as evidence of possible brain damage, and, dragging myself up to my elbows, prepared to explain myself.

But the boy with the gentle hands looked down at me, a small smile lifting his lips, and replied, "'There, pride, avarice, and envy are the tongues men know and heed, a Babel of despair.'"

He had quoted The *Divine Comedy* back to me. I stared up at him, stunned.

"You'll need stitches," he said. "Here." And, with a minimum of fuss, proceeded to numb my skin and sew my wound closed while I lay on the Library floor.

"Watch for signs of concussion," he said in a professional tone as I sat up. "Headache, dizziness, and nausea. One of the Caretakers should probably check on you each hour through the night. And also—wait. What are you doing?"

Though I was indeed dizzy, I'd gotten to my feet, The *Divine Comedy* in my hand, and was making my way back to the ladder. I wasn't badly injured, and there could be no excuse for leaving the books scattered on the floor. "Reshelving," I said as I stepped onto the bottom rung of the ladder.

Kennett was free to leave. But instead, he lingered, standing at the base of the ladder to hand me the books. His forwardness unnerved me. What if he'd noticed how I'd looked at him before, and his continued presence was a test of my virtuous behavior? What if—Architect forbid—he was an Informer?

I eyed him carefully, but there was nothing on his face but a resolve that matched my own. "If you're going to be so stubborn," he said, "then the least I can do is to stay here and keep an eye on you, in case you need further medical assistance."

I could've pointed out that Aric was perfectly able to pass the books to me, as well as to call for a medic again, should one be needed. But then Kennett would've gone away, and to my bewilderment, I didn't want him to leave.

"You like to read?" I said despite myself as he slipped a copy of Machiavelli's *The Prince* into my hand, careful not to let our fingers touch. I'd often felt that curiosity should be the eighth Deadly Sin—certainly it was mine.

"I do. Though I don't have much time for it. I come here on Idle Day sometimes."

Aric, who had gone back to sorting through the box of volumes that had fallen victim to moisture, snorted. "You do," he confirmed. "And you don't always put the books back where you ought to, either."

To my amusement, Kennett flushed and ducked his head. "When I was here reading last week, I lost track of time and was almost late for evening catechism. I didn't get a chance to finish the book and shoved it back on the shelf haphazardly." He bit his lip. "I'm truly sorry. It won't happen again."

My curiosity got the better of me. "What were you reading?"

There was only one book left on the floor; he bent to lift it, smiling up into my eyes. Something about that smile made me feel as if he'd pushed me off a cliff and then stood there, watching me plummet. How could a simple lift of his lips make me so dizzy? Surely it had to be the blow to my head.

"Milton's *Areopagitica*," he said, pressing the volume in question into my hand. "'For books are not absolutely dead things, but do contain a potency of life in them to be as active as that soul was whose progeny they are.'"

I took the book from him, momentarily speechless. If my soul possessed a language of romance—not that such things were allowed here—he had just spoken it.

"You read philosophy?" I said, finding my voice. I glanced down at Aric, who—thank the Architect—was still focused on his box of books. The last thing I needed was for him to look up and realize I was behaving in such a peculiar fashion. All it would take was one misplaced glance, a single word spoken out of turn, and I could find myself face-to-face with the Bellatorum's Lead Interrogator.

The Library was my life; I was just one of twenty-three scholars chosen to safeguard our history and the knowledge our citizens needed to carry out their work—a coveted position. I'd never wanted to be anything else. The careers that the Executor Chose for us were a lifetime assignment; should we sin badly enough to lose our appointments, we were relegated to a life amongst the natural-born, carrying out the

Commonwealth's most menial duties. If I lost my position, I would have nothing . . . and that was *after* I'd endured whatever punishments the Priests had in mind.

The Priests' punishments were creative in the extreme—the only art form permitted in the Commonwealth, where creativity for its own sake was seen as the first step down the road to dissolution. Covet your neighbor's promotion to supervisor? Labor from sunup to sundown alongside the natural-born, your body caked in mud, so everyone who sees you knows you're as base and low as the earth from which our ancestors crawled. Show pride in your work as a carpenter? Wind up chained in the Commonwealth's dungeons while a bellator smashes your fingers with a hammer—the tool of your trade. I could only imagine what punishments they'd devise for me. Maybe somehow they could make me forget all the knowledge I'd ever gained?

Fear flashed through my body for the second time that morning—but Aric merely grunted, hefting the box of books in his arms and winding his way back into the stacks, toward the restricted section of the Library. I watched him go, then turned my attention back to Kennett, who shrugged.

"I prefer to read books about science—or medicine. If I'm to be a medic, I want to be the best one I can be—to truly help people," he said. "But I've read all the science and medical books the general section of the Library has to offer, and so I figured I might as well keep going and work my way through the other tomes. Though I'll be honest—they don't come as easily to me as the rest."

Despite my anxiety, a strange thrill moved through me. Kennett Gundarson wasn't prolonging his time in the Library because he was an Informer, bound to report to the Priests. He was still here because he loved books, like I did—because he wanted to *learn*.

I understood hungering for knowledge, feeling as if what you wanted to know was just out of reach. Even as a scholar, the information I was allowed to access came in bits and pieces, based on what the Priests and then the Senior Scholars believed was appropriate for my experience and rank. It was the same for any occupation in the Commonwealth—we were allowed just enough information to perform our tasks well, and no more. Anything else could lead to undue pride in one's work and envy of others' prowess.

Still, when I read the classic volumes that comprised the bulk of the Library's holdings, I found myself taking more from them than I knew I was meant to. Turning the pages, I often thought not of the frailty of the human soul, but of the fantastical quests that the characters took—adventures of a kind I would never get to experience. As a scholar, I was not meant to imagine, but rather to analyze—but sometimes I couldn't help myself. I found myself craving to know what the volumes in the restricted stacks held, even though I wouldn't be allowed to access them until I was a senior scholar. I wondered if the restricted books would broaden my world, giving me insight into what lay beyond the Commonwealth's electric fence. We'd always been told the Borderlands contained no more than ruins through which hordes of vicious sinners prowled, searching for victims—but I harbored a sinful desire to see for myself . . . and, barring that, to *know*.

This curiosity was a terrible flaw, one I did my best to hide. But it was part of me, nonetheless—and I saw the echo of it in Kennett Gundarson's eyes.

This was no good. I needed him to leave, now. I needed to never see him again. I needed—

"You need to come back in a week for me to check on those stitches," he said. "Ask for me at the Infirmary." There was that smile again.

I wanted to demur, but on what grounds? "Fine," I said and gave him a curt nod.

Gathering up his medical kit, Kennett nodded at Aric, who'd reemerged from the stacks, and left the Library. I turned to slide *Areopagitica* back into place, appalled. What was happening to me?

I knew one thing—I shouldn't go to the Infirmary to see Kennett, not even if I ripped out all of my stitches and was gushing blood. Being in his presence somehow brought out the worst in me.

I had to go, though; to do otherwise would be to arouse suspicion, since Kennett had doubtless entered medical orders into his log under my name. If my supervisors followed up— after all, I'd been injured in the course of my duties as a scholar—and I'd failed to obey Kennett's instructions, the senior scholars would want to know why. They might interview me, and Aric too—he'd been present when Kennett stitched my forehead. And under such pressure, who knew what my fellow librarian might say?

So I would go to see Kennett—but I would be on my guard. For as I clung to the ladder with one hand and reached up, finally managing to retrieve *Paradise Lost* with the other, I knew in my heart how easy it would be to fall.

TWO

B y the time I went to the Infirmary, I'd convinced myself the events of the previous week had been an aberration—the unfortunate result of head trauma. I'd even brought Kennett a small token of appreciation—a copy of *Areopagitica*, checked out for him with my scholar's privileges, so he could take his time perusing it and not have to cram all of his reading into Idle Day.

The side benefit of this was that should I choose to spend my Idle Days in the Library, Kennett wouldn't be there. He could read the book on his own and return it via the drop slot when he was finished. I wouldn't have to risk running into him and dealing with the bewildering feelings he evoked in me—unless, of course, I fell off the ladder again.

I hadn't seen Kennett since the previous week—but I'd dreamed about him, terrible nightmares in which Aric had dumped his box of books onto the wooden floor of the Library and gone racing to the Priests to tell them I'd engaged in inappropriate banter with the medic who'd come to stitch my wound. I dreamed of the bellators dragging me down to the dungeons, of sitting filthy and starving in a cell as I waited to hear what my punishment would be. And then I woke to see Genevieve asleep next to me, her body turned to face mine as if waiting to blink her eyes open and catch me in the act of subconscious sedition.

The Priests encouraged us to confess our sins—to Inform on ourselves—but I hadn't felt the need to do such a thing. They were only dreams, after all; my behavior toward Kennett hadn't crossed any lines. Still, to say it hadn't been a restful week was an understatement.

The Infirmary was crowded with patients and medics, the hum of complaints and diagnoses filling the air. It smelled of antiseptics and bleach, an astringent scent that stung my lungs when I inhaled. I had to wait to see Kennett and spent the time sitting in an uncomfortable molded chair, paging through Plato's *The Republic*—which I'd read many times before, but always had something new to offer.

I actually found myself looking forward to seeing Kennett in this simple, controlled environment. It was an excellent opportunity for me to perceive him as a fellow citizen, not as some kind of absurd composite of leaves and sky who shared my thirst for knowledge. I would laugh at myself, banish my nightmares, and be more careful on the upper rungs of the Library's ladders forevermore.

But when they called my number and sent me back to his station, I was disturbed to find that those clear green eyes of his, blazing with intelligence, were as distracting as they'd been before—as was the wide smile with which he greeted me. I settled onto the wooden examination table, wishing I was somewhere—anywhere—else.

"So," Kennett said, oblivious to my discomfort. "How goes it? Any more painful literary encounters?"

I shook my head. "No, thanks for asking." Rummaging in my bag, I pulled out *Areopagitica*. "I checked it out for you with my privileges," I said, my tone as neutral as I could manage. This wasn't forbidden; a scholar could do such a thing for a citizen, as long as we kept careful track of our lending history and ensured the books were returned in a timely fashion. "So you can actually finish it."

Kennett glanced down at the book. His arched eyebrows rose, those green eyes widening. "You climbed that ladder again—against medic's orders—to bring me *Areopagitica*?"

I narrowed my own eyes at him. "It's my job," I said stiffly. "You expressed curiosity about this book; as a scholar, it's my responsibility to provide intellectual resources to fellow citizens as appropriate. Rather than criticizing me for fulfilling my duties, you might thank me."

That infuriating grin widened—as if he found me amusing. "Thank you, Miriam," he said, taking the book from me. I felt his fingers brush mine—accidentally, of course—and had to suppress the shiver that radiated out from the place where we'd touched.

Kennett set the book on the counter behind him and moved in to examine my stitches. He brushed my hair back from my face, his touch light but sure. "These look fine. They'll dissolve on their own in another week or so."

His eyes were still fixed on me, with more intensity than seemed warranted. I fidgeted on the table, glad I was only here for my head injury and not a physical exam; if I'd come for the latter, he would surely be able to hear my heart pounding. "What is it?" I said, my voice harsher than I intended. "Why are you staring at me that way?"

He took a step back, dropping his gaze. "I apologize. I was actually wondering if you might be willing to tutor me. As I've told you, I find the philosophical books I've read difficult to interpret—but I've found there's an element to healing beyond the merely scientific. If I had a more nuanced understanding of the working of my patients' minds, then perhaps I'd be better at my job."

"You want me to tutor you?" By the Architect, of course he did. It was true that information was given to all of us on a utilitarian basis—piecemeal, based on what we needed to do our jobs. It made me think better of Kennett, somehow, that he was interested in seeking more—but did he have to seek it with me?

"There are twenty-three scholars available for such a task," I said, hoping I sounded dispassionate rather than desperate. "Why me?"

He gave a one-shouldered shrug. "I don't know any other scholars personally. When you brought me *Areopagitica*, I thought you might be willing, since you have such great commitment to your work. But if it isn't possible, I understand."

This was not how our encounter was supposed to go. I'd been trying to get rid of him by handing him the book, not encouraging him to seek me out. But if I refused, how would that look?

"Alright," I told him, getting down from the table. I tried not to look directly at him; what if my expression gave my peculiar feelings away? "Meet me at the Library on Idle Day at one o'clock sharp. We'll start with *The Odyssey*."

THREE

On Idle Day, I secured my favorite table in the Library—near the front windows, where the waning autumn sunlight found its way inside—and pulled a copy of *The Odyssey* off the shelf in preparation for my discussion with Kennett.

The book had always been one of my favorites, because of Odysseus's epic quest. I'd always identified more with Odysseus than Penelope—I was enthralled by the battles he fought with mythical creatures and gods, his shipwreck and narrow escapes. I loved how Odysseus used his mind rather than brute strength to find his way out of difficult situations, and fantasized that if I were ever in such trouble, I would do the same.

Of course, I wasn't supposed to imagine myself having adventures like Odysseus, but rather to consider the sins that had inspired Homer to compose such a poem—the wrath that led to the Trojan War; the lust that caused Calypso to trap Odysseus on her island; the greed of the men who opened the bag containing Odysseus's treasure; the gluttony that spurred the men to feast on the cattle of the Sungod Helios despite dire warnings not to do so. Still, I couldn't help but imagine myself in Odysseus' shoes—and I contented myself with the thought that if I never spoke of this to anyone, then surely my imaginings did no harm.

The sunlight struck Kennett's face as he walked toward me, his hair gleaming blue-black and his eyes lighter than usual—fresh-cut grass rather than pine needles . . . and *why was I still thinking of him this way?* Heaving a sigh, I got to my feet and greeted him in a whisper, heedful of Senior Scholar Joseph seated two tables over. The senior scholar was in conversation with Aric, who never failed to seize an opportunity to claw his way upward in the ranks.

Aric's groveling attitude aggravated me. We were meant to earn our positions on merit alone, not by jockeying for advantage. I wouldn't stoop to his level—but when I considered the idea of him getting promoted while I spent my days reshelving books, I had to suppress a verboten twinge of envy.

No wonder Aric had known Kennett hadn't restored *Areopagitica* to its rightful place. He must live in here, taking every opportunity to cozy up to the senior scholars. I myself usually chose to spend my lone free day outside when the weather was fine—and sometimes even when it wasn't—preferring the fresh air, however cold or damp, to the confines of the room where I spent six days a week.

I loved my library, but sometimes I needed to escape.

Through Kennett's eyes, though, I saw the Library as it had the first time I'd set foot in it—a magical box filled with books, whose pages, once cracked, could transport me to the corners of the universe I would never be privileged to see.

Sitting down on the chair next to me, he gave me a bright smile. "Alright," he said in a stage whisper. "Where do we start?"

"With Telemachus," I said briskly, opening *The Odyssey* to its first page and doing my best to ignore how my pulse quickened at his proximity. He wanted a tutor; that was what he would get, my vulnerability to sinning be damned. "As you may recall, the goddess Athena appears to him in disguise . . ."

This was the beginning of our conversation, which would continue on every Idle Day for the next two months and beyond. *The Odyssey* is a lengthy tome, after all, and there were many thorny moral questions to discuss. We studied one book each week, gradually making our way through the epic poem. Kennett hung on my every word, listening to my analysis of the text and posing questions of his own. I came to live for Idle Days, for our conversations and the questions he provoked in me. My mind felt as if it were coming alive bit by bit, and despite my initial reluctance at tutoring him, I hoarded textual interpretations in between our meetings, eager to share my opinions with him and ask his own.

I worried about this, even though none of it was strictly forbidden. Was it wrong to look forward to our conversations this way? Nothing we talked about was inappropriate; anyone else in the Library could overhear anything we said, and frequently did. Still, I found myself as captivated by him as I'd been the first time we met. Once, eager to underline our respective points with backup from the text, we'd reached for the book at the same time, and our hands had brushed. In the instant before Kennett drew back, whispering apologies, I was swept by the same all-consuming shiver that had rippled through me when I'd handed him *Areopagitica*.

What might such a thing mean? Did he feel it too? If so, he gave no sign.

Whatever it meant, it couldn't be good. I had to hide it from him—and anyone else—at all costs.

Over the weeks that we'd studied together, I'd sometimes felt as if his gaze lingered on me longer than necessary—but surely it was my imagination? There was no way he saw me as anything other than a scholar and a tutor, which was as it should be. I was the sinner, the one who stupidly—and sinfully—wanted more. I'd prayed to the Architect for this desire to go, but it wouldn't leave me. Every time I saw him, it was worse—and my nightmares of imprisonment had returned, even more virulent than before.

All I'd ever wanted was to be good at my job. Now here he was, destroying everything. And yet, at the thought of our sessions together ending, a sick feeling curdled my stomach.

The fall passed this way, dying slowly into winter. On the eighth week of our Idle Day tutoring sessions, we'd just finished discussing Calypso's sinful behavior toward Odysseus when Kennett glanced up at me.

"Do you want to take a walk?" he said.

"A what?" I gaped at him. In the two months we'd met to study, we'd never once left the confines of the Library.

"A walk, Miri." He raised an eyebrow. "As a medical professional, I'm recommending it. We've spent an awful lot of time sitting. And, you know, cardiovascular activity is important for overall health."

It occurred to me that he was teasing me—not a typical occurrence in the Commonwealth. "Very funny," I said, my voice dry. "And what did you call me?"

He had the good grace to blush, ducking his head as he'd done that first day in the Library when Aric had given him a hard time about misshelving books. "Miri?" he said, making it a question.

My name was Miriam. No one had ever called me anything else. Nicknames weren't illicit in the Commonwealth—just pointless. But I found I liked the sound of 'Miri' in Kennett's mouth—like I was someone else with him, a braver, freer version of myself. A girl who might actually go on a quest, like Odysseus.

"I'm sorry," he said, pushing his chair back from the table as if he thought I might ask him to leave. "Did I offend you? I think of you that way sometimes—like a sort of shorthand—"

"I'm not offended," I told him, doing my best to suppress the frisson of excitement that swept through me at the idea that he thought of me when we weren't together. Maybe someday soon I'd get over this, like the bout of influenza I'd had last autumn. Until then, I'd have to pretend it didn't exist. "And yes, fine. We can continue our discussion outside. But first, reshelve *The Odyssey*. Properly, of course."

"So bossy," he said, giving me that impossible smile of his. But he did as I said.

I found myself watching him as he lifted the book from the table and strolled to the shelves, stretching to put *The Odyssey* back where it belonged—and dropped my eyes, horrified, a hot blush heating my cheeks. I had no business noticing the lean, long line of his back as he slid the book into place, or the way his dark hair fell into his eyes and he brushed it back again. This could only end in disaster.

As he made his way back to our table, I stood hurriedly, my eyes on the ground. He stopped in front of me, clearing his throat. "Your face is all red, Miri," he said, pitching his voice low so as not to disturb the smattering of other citizens in the Library. "Are you feeling alright? Do you have a fever?"

He lifted his hand, as if to press it to my forehead, and I leapt backward, nearly tripping over my chair. "I'm fine. It's just hot in here. Can we go?"

"Of course," he said, dropping his hand to his side—but I caught the hint of puzzlement in his eyes. "After you."

I strode toward the door, more embarrassed than ever. What had he made of my peculiar behavior? With any luck, he'd think I hadn't wanted for *him* to touch my forehead because it was improper—not because I nursed a secret, sinful desire to feel his fingers on my skin.

Outside, the frigid air cooled my burning cheeks; it was December, a week before the celebration of the Architect's Arrival that marked the turn of the new year. This ceremony constituted the Commonwealth's only festivities. Everyone would gather in Clockverk Square and the surrounding streets, even the Executor and the Priests. There would be a bonfire, and spiced hot chocolate, and chanting. It was the one time of year all of us came together for celebration.

Kennett led the way through the Square, which was crowded with people enjoying the fresh air during Idle Day. We passed Genevieve, who glared at us both. It was her default expression; still, I felt a twinge of uneasiness at the sight.

I reassured myself for the thousandth time that Kennett and I were doing nothing wrong. We were simply a tutor and a student, taking a walk during which we would discuss the finer points of *The Odyssey*. Still, I couldn't shake the suspicion there was something amiss—something Kennett wasn't telling me.

Otherwise, why choose to leave the Library now, after two months of studying inside?

Kennett leading the way, we stepped off the cobblestones of the Square and onto the path that led to the outskirts of the City and the vineyards, where the Priests grew the grapes for our ceremonial wine. That warning sense flared again, stronger this time.

"Where are we going?" I asked Kennett, my skepticism clear in my voice.

"For a walk." He spun to face me, lifting his hands—the picture of innocence. "I'm not spiriting you away to the Borderlands, Miri, I promise—just going for a stroll. How do you expect to exercise if you won't venture off the streets of the City?"

He set a brisk pace, and I struggled to keep up, ignoring his ridiculous comment about the Borderlands. Though gluttony was a sin and we ate no more than our allotted rations each day, poring over books day in and day out hadn't done much for my physical condition. I was sufficiently winded that, as we went up one hill and down another, I didn't waste my breath on conversation—at least, not until we came to a stop in the vineyards.

I looked around at the bare arbors and the skeletal remnants of the vines. "You want to talk about *The Odyssey* here?"

A shifty look crossed his face, and the alarm bells inside me clanged at a fever pitch.

"Or—you don't want to talk about *The Odyssey* at all." I fisted my hands on my hips. "What are we really doing here, Kennett?"

He looked left, then right, as if assuring himself that we were alone. "I have a question to ask you, Miri," he said, lowering his voice. "And before you say no—hear me out."

"A question you couldn't ask me in the Library?" To the nine hells and back again with this mess. I knew I should turn around and walk right back the way we'd come, but curiosity held me in place. What could Kennett possibly have to ask me that was so important, he needed to keep the conversation a secret?

He scuffed his regulation brown leather shoes in the dirt, his voice pitched just above a whisper. Even though we were alone in the vineyard, one never knew who might be listening. "You know how much being a good medic matters to me. I do the most I can for my patients, but I know there must be more. I can feel it. There's so much I don't know." Raising his head, he met my eyes. "I get so frustrated sometimes, Miri. It's not a matter of pride. I just . . . I want to be able to heal them, and it troubles me so much when I can't. It's my calling, the way being a scholar is yours."

He was sincere—I could feel it. Still, I didn't understand why he was telling me this. "Your concern for your patients is admirable, Kennett. But what does any of this have to do with me?"

His gaze held mine, and I fought not to look away. "I know the Library has a restricted section. There have to be more medical books in there—there must be."

"You want me to get you into the *restricted stacks*?" My voice squeaked. "I don't have a key. I'd have to get one from a senior scholar. And even then, you'd need permission from the Priests to enter. I'd have to fill out the paperwork—"

"You misunderstand. I don't want a single book, like you get with a formal request. I want to see all of them, so I can decide for myself what I need to learn." There was a quiet insistence to his voice I'd never heard before. "People's *lives* are at stake, and information's given to us in dribs and drabs—just enough to do our jobs. I'm a good medic, but I could be so much better. I just need to know more."

I backed away from him, shaking my head. "I can't, Kennett. No matter how noble your cause. If we got caught, I'd lose my job."

"We won't get caught." His voice was honeyed, convincing. "I've thought about this a lot. We can go during the celebration

245

on the eve of the Architect's Arrival. It's dark, and the streets will be crowded. No one will notice we're missing."

It would be the best chance we'd have—but still, how could I justify taking such a risk? I shook my head again, feeling vaguely regretful when I saw the disappointment in his eyes—but not regretful enough to change my mind. "I'm sorry, Kennett. I can't."

But he didn't give up. "I have a young patient—Annalise—in my care who's sick with a fever she can't shake. I've tried everything, but she's getting worse and worse. What if there's something in those stacks that could save her life?"

I froze, my foot catching on a root that protruded from the soil and almost dumping me onto the ground. Kennett caught me by the arm, then let go, as if the act had scorched his fingertips. "Please, Miri," he said, his eyes fixed on mine. "There's no time for the paperwork. And I can't just let her die."

I didn't know what to do. On the one hand, doing as he asked would be violating the letter of my oath—and though I didn't know what the punishment would be, I was sure it would be swift . . . and terrible. That was one of the worst parts of the Priests' punishments—how, each time, they devised them to fit the sinner and the sin, unerringly coming up with what would devastate you the most. No two punishments were the same—and somehow, not knowing what to expect made it all the more terrifying.

It made me quake to think of facing the consequences of violating the oath I'd sworn on Choosing Day, when I'd sworn to uphold the duties of a Commonwealth scholar. On the other hand, my life was dedicated to the pursuit of knowledge. If I refused Kennett now, was my oath just empty words?

Giving Kennett access to the stacks would be upholding the spirit of my promise, if not the letter—wouldn't it? If there was knowledge in the restricted section that could save the life of a child, how could I stand in his way?

It was sinful to care for this child, as I suspected Kennett might. But perhaps his feelings went no further than a medic's sworn duty. And I imagined he could no sooner let a patient die if he had the power to save them than I could willfully set the Library's books aflame—no matter what my nightmares held.

In all the books we'd been reading together, the hero took a risk and made a difference. What if this was my chance?

Kennett stood still, those clear green eyes scanning my face. "Please, Miri," he said again. "Please help me."

I drew a deep breath. And then I leapt. "Alright," I told him. "I will."

FOUR

This was how we found ourselves alone in the Library, while the celebration carried on outside. It was pitch black—we didn't dare turn on a light and risk discovery. The only windows were at the front of the building, nowhere near the shelving units, since sunlight could damage the books—but that was danger enough.

It was a terrible risk—but I told myself this was my quest, the only one I would ever have. And it was for the sake of knowledge, which couldn't be a terrible thing. All Kennett wanted was to be the best medic he could, to save a child's life. The Priests would never let him explore the restricted section on his own. As a scholar, I was performing the ultimate service. And then there was the rest of it—my own insatiable curiosity to know what these hidden stacks held.

"Miri?" he said from beside me, his voice a breath. "I can't see anything."

I couldn't, either. But I didn't need to. I knew the Library the way I thought I'd known my own heart, before I'd tumbled from the ladder and woken to see Kennett kneeling over me. I knew its scent of ink and paper, the peculiar stillness that always seemed to hover in the air.

"Here," I said, reaching out in the darkness. It wasn't a sin if it had a purpose, was it? Not if he needed me to find his way?

My fingers brushed his, and he jerked backward in surprise. "You want me to take your hand?" There was a curious note in his voice—not the revulsion I'd feared, but something unfamiliar I couldn't interpret.

"How else will you know where to go?" I whispered, my voice brisk. "Otherwise you'll wind up blundering into shelves and knocking things over. You'll make a bunch of noise, and where will we be then?"

Slowly, without another word, he slid his fingers between my own. He must've been keeping his hands in his pockets; his touch was warm, enveloping the iciness of my skin. A strange, electric current seemed to prickle between us, but I didn't pull away.

"You're freezing, Miri." Ever the medic, he rubbed my fingers, trying to warm me. If he felt any hint of that odd current, he gave no sign.

"It's cold outside," I said, doing my best to keep my voice steady. "Come on."

Our fingers linked, I led him to the back of the stacks, moving between the shelves by memory. We reached the door that led to the restricted section, and I fumbled in my pocket for the key I'd stolen. I'd never done such a thing before, never stepped outside the rules that governed all our lives. I felt terrified—but also excited, as if I was part of something larger than myself . . . as if my life had finally begun.

It was a challenge to make the key fit in the dark, but finally I succeeded. The door swung open with a creak that made me wince, and then we were inside.

Kennett shut it behind us and turned the lock, plunging us into blackness. Then he pulled his hand from mine. I heard him fumbling in his coat pocket a moment before I heard the scritch of a match, and the wavering light of a candle pierced the darkness of the stacks.

I sucked in a breath, horrified. It was as if my nightmares had come to life. "You brought *fire* into the Library? Are you crazy?"

"How else are we going to see?" he hissed back. "It's not like we can turn on a light. I couldn't do it out there because of the windows. But in here, there are none."

He had a point. Still, I couldn't help but imagine all of these precious books going up in flames—all of that knowledge lost forever. "Be careful," I warned, and beside me, I heard the ghost of a laugh.

"I think it's a little too late for that."

Kennett had a way of making me smile in the most troubling of circumstances. I couldn't decide if it was one of his best qualities or a dire flaw.

By the light of Kennett's candle, we made our way down the aisles one by one, holding the flame close enough to the spines to see their titles. I thrilled at what the candlelight revealed— books about art and dreams and music. A whole world at my fingertips, if I was brave enough to read. And before we left, I swore to myself, I would.

Kennett rounded the next corner—and then stopped so short, I ran into his back. "Look, Miri." He sounded awed. "Here they are. And there's so *many*."

He held the candle higher so I could see, moving it along the shelves. He was right—these were all medical books. Studies of human anatomy and physiology, disease processes, the mind itself. We had taken a risk—and thus far, at least, it had paid off.

"Hold this, would you?" He thrust the candle at me and grabbed the first book at hand. Opening it, he gave a low growl of frustration. "By the Sins. I can't see a thing."

"Here," I said, stepping close to him and holding the candle over the page. He smelled of winter and the spiced chocolate he'd drunk in the Square, before we'd made our escape. Those baffling feelings of wanting to touch him, to brush that dark hair back from his eyes, surged through me. And yet I didn't back away.

I told myself he needed the candle to see—which was the truth. But the deeper truth, the one I was reluctant to acknowledge even to myself, was that if this was the only chance I'd get to be this close to Kennett, I didn't want to give it up.

"This is incredible," he said, turning the pages. "I suspected—but I had no idea—" He glanced up from the book, his eyes bright. "Thank you, Miri. Thank you for risking so much to bring me here. I'll find something here to help Annalise. I know I will."

"You're welcome," I told him, striving to keep my voice dispassionate—though the fervent gratitude in his voice moved me. "I suppose in a way, this could be considered an extension of my duty."

Kennett bit his lip. "Don't do that, Miri. Please."

His statement confused me. "Don't do what?"

"It's just the two of us here. Don't hide behind your job. Admit it—you're curious, like I am. You're driven by what drives me—to *know*."

I felt as if he'd stripped me of my skin. How had he seen so much? What if all of this had been a trick, to root out my deepest vulnerabilities?

"I'm supposed to want to know." My voice shook.

He was silent for a moment, during which the candle flickered and went out. But he didn't light it again. Instead, there was a slight current of air between us. Then, gently, carefully, his palm came to rest against my face. "Don't be frightened. I'm not threatening you. I'm trying to say—you don't see yourself clearly. You're more than just a scholar. You're brilliant. And brave." He sucked in a breath. "And beautiful." The last word was a rasp, torn from his throat.

I stood still, mesmerized by the feel of his palm against my skin, the words that had just left his lips. Was I dreaming? Surely this couldn't be real.

Then Kennett snatched his hand away. I felt a sudden coldness where it had been, and stupidly wanted it back again. "By the Architect, Miri," he said, sounding as stunned as I felt, "I'm sorry. I shouldn't have done that—I don't know what—"

He stammered on, apologizing, assuring me such a thing would never happen again—but I was only half-listening. Yes, such a touch was a sin—and I was a sinner for wanting it. But if I was truly brave, as he'd said, as I'd always wanted to be—if this was the only qusest I would ever have—then perhaps I owed it to myself to experience it to its fullest. After all, when would I ever get another chance?

"Miri." Kennett sounded desperate. "Please, say you'll forgive me. If you need to confess this to the Priests, I understand. What you must think of me . . ." He sank to his knees, as if his legs had given out. "By the Sins, I don't want to think about you like this. I know how incredibly wrong it is." His voice was a gravelly scrape. "I told myself it was only about the books, the knowledge I needed to help my patients. But I knew better. And now . . ."

My mind whirled, snatching possibilities out of the air and then discarding them. I thought about the two of us, alone here; the enormity of the sin that might lie before us—and to my shock, found the notion didn't trouble me nearly as much as it should. I wanted this one night, this miracle of an evening, with Kennett and these mysterious, strange books. No one would know; no one would find out. It would be our secret.

I was tired of living in terror. This one night, I wanted to be brave. I wanted to take what I craved—what was freely given— without worrying about the consequences.

"We should go," Kennett said, sounding more miserable than ever.

I found my voice. "But your books—"

"To the nine hells with the books," he said fiercely, rising to his feet—but I stood with him, threading my fingers through his to make him stay.

This was a moment I would never have again. I wouldn't let my fears make me give it up. Kennett had as much to lose as I did; he would never betray me.

"'I have been and still am a seeker,'" I told him, my voice a whisper, "'but I have ceased to question stars and books; I have begun to listen to the teaching my blood whispers to me.'" It was a quote from Herman Hesse's *Damian*.

Kennett froze, his fingers stilling in mine. I swore I could feel his pulse stop. Then it resumed again, this time at a frantic pace. "What are you saying, Miri?"

252

"I don't want to leave." My voice shook, but it came. "And if you've sinned, then so have I—because I've thought about you, too."

The book fell to the floor. One hand still in mine, he braced himself on the shelf behind me with the other, as if to keep from falling. We stood for a long minute, listening to each other breathe. And finally he whispered, his words stones that tumbled into the dark, "'Smooth the descent, and easy is the way.'"

He didn't say the first line of the verse, from Virgil's *Aeneid*, but he didn't have to. I knew it well: *The gates of hell are open night and day.*

There in the blackness of the Library, the spines of the books pressing against my own and Kennett's chocolate-scented breath warm on my skin, I felt a certainty that had nothing to do with the things we had been taught—the sanctity of virtue and the boorishness of sin. I lifted my hands to his face, feeling the roughness of his stubble rasp against my palms—then slid them lower, learning his body the way I'd learned the words of so many books . . . with utmost attention to detail and a singular focus that committed them to memory.

His breath caught in his throat as my fingertips traced the abacus of his ribs. "Miri, what are you doing?"

I had no idea. But I did know that being here, with him, like this, was exactly what I wanted, despite the risk.

"'The more a thing is perfect,'" I quoted Dante, my hands drifting across the flat plane of his stomach, hearing him gasp into the dark, "'the more it feels pleasure and pain.'"

He pressed his face to mine, and only then did I realize he was crying. "I'm not perfect, Miri. A perfect boy wouldn't want you like this. Wouldn't risk your life. I'm selfish. How can you not see that?" His voice turned bitter, like he had a mouthful of ash and was spitting it out with every word.

I shook my head, and felt his fingers tangle in my hair, his grip desperate, as if he feared that at any moment, I would be ripped away. "These past two months have been the best of my life, Kennett. I don't want to lose that—or you. We can go back to how it was; no one has to know. Let us have this—just for tonight."

He exhaled, a slow, broken breath—the sound of surrender. "This is a doomed venture, Miri. I know it. And yet—all I want is to be here, with you, in the dark. I know—I *know*—it's a grievous sin. And yet, I can't bring myself to care."

I realized then that the death grip he had on my hair had little to do with thinking I would vanish. He'd wrapped his fingers in my hair to keep from touching me—because he didn't trust himself.

But I trusted him. I knew he would never hurt me—would sacrifice himself before he let me come to harm—and not just because he'd sworn an oath to heal. I wasn't sure how I'd come by this conviction; it was bone-deep, nothing like the intellectual knowledge I'd gleaned from my books. But it was strong, and true, and real.

"I'm sorry, Miri." He lowered his face to my shoulder. His tears wet my skin. "I promised to do no harm, and look what I'm doing to you."

His grief tore at me, as if something was ripping loose, deep in my chest. I felt it go—the last mooring that tethered me to who I'd been, fraying and finally giving way. I was a tiny boat, adrift in the unfathomable sea of myself. And what I was comprised of, it turned out, was a bottomless pit of rage—not at Kennett, but for him.

I didn't care if wrath was forbidden in the Commonwealth. I wanted to get my hands on a bellator's sverd and skewer everyone who had ever made the boy in my arms despise himself this way.

"Kennett," I said, struggling to keep my voice level, "I've spent my life inside books. I've read of love and hate, of civilizations that have crumbled to dust because of men's wickedness. I know what evil looks like, and you're not it."

He lifted his head from my shoulder. I couldn't see him, but I didn't have to. I knew every line of his face, every expression that coursed through those deep green eyes. "You're so certain." His voice was a whisper; his fingertips skimmed my cheek, drifting over my skin.

I lifted my hand to wipe away his tears. "You can believe me," I said, willing him to listen. "For I am a scholar, and we do not lie."

Kennett's hands were still in my hair. Slowly, carefully, he closed the tiny distance between us. I felt the length of his body against mine, felt him tremble. He lowered his head, his lips ghosting over my temple, my eyelids, my cheeks. "Miri, be sure." His voice was a breath in the darkness. "There is no going back from this."

But I didn't want to go back. I wanted only to go forward, with him—no matter how short our path.

His lips were a centimeter from mine. And yet still he held back, waiting.

Like every child growing up in the Commonwealth, Kenneth and I had watched vids from before the Fall, showing us the ramifications of the Deadly Sins. We'd seen the perils of dating, a sinful practice which often ended in a lustful kiss and the mysterious *more* that was punishable by death. And in the pages of the books we'd studied together, we'd read of characters sinning. We were meant to study such things, to learn how easy it was to commit acts of sin and how important it was to cling to our virtues, since a single choice could strip them away.

I had, as I told Kennett, lived my life in those books, rarely looking up. There had been so little worth fixing my eyes on. But he was different. Even invisible in the darkness of the Library, he shone—the brightest, most beautiful thing I had ever seen. He was the candle that illuminated the endless gloom of my days—a tedium I had mistaken for comfort and safety. And I knew I would rather live a week by the light of that flame than be condemned to a lifetime of the dark.

I stood on my toes and touched my lips to his, tasting chocolate and the salt of his tears. "I am absolutely sure."

He didn't ask again. Instead he kissed me back, his hands leaving my hair at last, roving over my body with a reverence that made me wonder if he wanted to memorize me, too. He lifted me, and I felt the spines of the books bite into my back as our clothes fell away. It seemed fitting that they were our witnesses—filled with words, but mute. They would never betray our secrets.

I had been wrong to think he was a candle. He was a fire, blazing bright—and I threw myself into it, wanting only to be consumed. Together, we burned.

What we were doing was forbidden. We had no map, no instruction manual. None of my books could show us the way. But we found it, somehow, together.

After, in the stolen minutes we had left to ourselves, he held me close. I half-expected words of love; but it was both too soon and too late to speak of such things. Instead, his palm still flat against my heart and our bodies slick with sweat, Kennett whispered into my hair, "Alea iacta est." Latin, for *the die is cast*—the words Julius Caesar had uttered when he crossed the Rubicon.

That was the first time. But it wouldn't be the last.

FIVE

I would never regret loving Kennett. But I had no illusions about what would happen if anyone found out there was more between us than Idle Day study sessions and lively debates about the finer points of ancient philosophy.

I'd thought what happened between us would only occur once—but I'd known nothing of such things. Instead of quenching the thirst I felt for him, our sin had only made me want him more—and he felt the same.

In public, we ignored each other—not overly difficult, since other than mealtimes and ceremonies, we were rarely in the same room. We stole our time together, snatching it from the jaws of our daily lives under the ever-vigilant eyes of the Priests and the Informers. Never again did we risk the confines of the Library—though the information he'd found that night had indeed saved Annalise's life. Instead, we met in the woods despite the cold, in the vineyards, in the shadows of the trees that edged the rocks of Black Falls.

I knew what Kennett and I were doing was beyond wrong. But I craved him, the way I'd only craved knowledge before. When I wasn't with him, I longed to hear his voice, to feel his touch on my skin.

I told myself we were already damned. The Architect had judged us from the moment we committed our sins—maybe even from the first second sinning had crossed our minds. Kennett was right; there was no going back. And what choice did we have? It wasn't as if we could leave. Even if we were willing to take our chances with the hordes in the Borderlands, the only way out was through the forest, where the Bastarour roamed—which was no way out at all. We were stuck here, chained to our fate—and although both of us knew we inched closer to discovery with every clandestine meeting, we couldn't seem to stop.

The first time I missed my monthly courses, I figured it was a fluke. After all, I wasn't always regular. By the second time, though, I began to worry. The food in the dining hall smelled peculiar to me; in the three minutes allotted to me to shower each day, my body felt different to me somehow, more rounded. Very quietly, I began to panic.

I said nothing to Kennett, hoping I was mistaken. But the next time we were together, he cupped one of my breasts in his hand, his touch not that of a lover but of the medic who had stitched up my forehead that very first day. "Miri," he said, and in his voice I heard both an extraordinary joy and a foreboding horror.

I burst into tears, which was as much answer as he needed. He held me to him, stroking my back, trying to soothe me. But both of us knew the truth: by giving life to the child that now grew within my body, we had signed our own death warrants.

"We'll hide it," Kennett said when we drew apart. "As long as we can."

It was February. I knew from watching the surrogates who bore our children that the process took approximately nine months. As a medic, Kennett knew this even better than I— though only midwives delivered the Commonwealth's babies, so male medics would not be exposed to the impurity of the process. "But it'll be the summer," I said, wiping the tears from my eyes.

I didn't have to say more. All of our clothes were standardized, to prevent the sin of taking pride in our appearance. The uniforms librarians wore in the summer months were modest but light. I knew what the surrogates looked like when they were bearing heavily. There was no way I could hide a full-term pregnancy.

"We'll figure something out. I promise." He took my hand in his. Despite his efforts to stay strong for me, his green eyes were filled with tears. "By the Architect, Miri, I am so very sorry."

"Will you stop apologizing? This is *not* your fault," I told him. "We made our choices together. And I would rather die alongside you than live in a world where you didn't exist."

"You're not going to die." He pulled me to him again, his voice rough. "We have a little time," he said against my hair. "We're smart, the two of us. You're the most brilliant person I know. We'll think of something."

He stroked my hair as I tried to imagine what that might be. I wracked my mind, as I had every moment since I'd suspected I was pregnant, but could think of no solution.

And then I felt Kennett suck in a breath, as if something had occurred to him.

"What?" I asked him, but he shook his head, his arms still tight around me.

"Tell me." I pulled back, looking up into his face.

"There are herbs," he said, sounding hesitant. "It would be dangerous—but I could get them for you . . . if that's what you want."

Herbs—to get rid of the child, he meant. I knew I should consider this. My life would be forfeit anyhow, if we were found out; what was a little danger? But before my conscious mind could make a decision, my mouth spoke for me. "If I pay for this with my life, then so be it. But the child is innocent. I'll not condemn it, too."

I drew a deep breath, then said the rest of it: "Don't worry. I won't betray you, Kennett."

His eyebrows drew down, as if in puzzlement. "What do you—"

"If they find me out, I will never speak your name," I said, tugging my shirt to rights. "I don't care what they do to me."

Kennett's jaw dropped. "By the Architect, Miri, do you think I care about any of that? All I care about is *you*. And if you think I would let you go through this sin-infested mess alone, then you are insane." He folded his arms across his chest, staring me down. "You are *not* to protect me from this, Miri, do you understand? We started this together, and we will finish it the same way—no matter how we end. Promise me."

I knew I could be stubborn—and normally, Kennett was the one to give. He was far more likely to compromise in most scenarios . . . but apparently, not this one. His eyes fixed on mine, refusing to let me drop my gaze. And finally I said, the words emerging on a sigh, "I promise."

His arms came around me again—but then one of his hands dropped to my stomach, his palm curving around the baby growing within. "In another world," he said, sounding immeasurably sad, "this would be cause for celebration. I wish that was the world in which we lived."

I laced my fingers through his, holding our baby together, and for a moment, imagined that world—where I could bear Kennett's child and watch it grow, where we could be a family, together. "I know," I said, leaning against him, listening to the steady beat of his heart. "I wish so, too."

MY EIGHTEENTH BIRTHDAY CAME AND WENT. We didn't celebrate such things in the Commonwealth, other than a means of marking the time. I personally measured the months in smaller increments, based on the changes in my body, the way my stomach grew. I felt as if I were a ticking clock, the hands moving ever closer toward an inevitable end.

Soon, I felt the child stirring within me. At night I would lie with my hand pressed to my belly, marveling at the jab of a knee or an elbow. Kennett smuggled me some of the special vitamins meant for the surrogates, and I took them daily, wanting to give our child every advantage.

I named our child Lucien, which meant 'bringing light' in Latin. I'd always thought of Kennett as the flame that lit my darkness, and I resolved to think of our baby the same way. If I managed to carry him to term, he—I had decided it was a boy, for no other reason than a feeling I had—would be relegated to being one of the natural-born, fated to do menial tasks. But at least he would be alive.

I hated the idea of leaving Lucien, but what choice did I have? Our best-case scenario was that somehow Kennett and I would escape detection until he was born, and we'd be able to smuggle him into the Nursery among the other newborns, his parents unknown. I'd never heard of doing such a thing, but it seemed the only path open to us. Even that seemed a dicey proposition—surely the Executor would demand the midwives check each woman of childbearing age for signs of a recent birth, and then it would be all over for us.

It made me furious to think of Lucien subjected to the indignities of the natural-born. I imagined a little boy with Kennett's beautiful eyes and my olive skin, my thirst for knowledge and Kennett's gentle heart, forced to scrub toilets and dig ditches for his entire life, and felt a forbidden wave of wrath break over me.

All along, I'd thought my worst sin was the overt pride I took in my work. How wrong I'd been.

Was this the only way people lived, in all the world? Was there no other way?

The months passed, and the clock of myself ticked. Kennett and I hardly dared to meet, terrified to draw any unnecessary attention to ourselves. The last thing I wanted was to give anyone a reason for their glances to linger on me.

But as my belly grew, I could feel time slipping away, like sands through an hourglass. One night, as I climbed into bed, Genevieve said, her voice laden with suspicion, "You've put on quite a bit of weight, haven't you, Miriam?"

My heart pounded unevenly, but I lifted my chin. "I don't know what you mean," I told her. "Perhaps you should visit the medics and have your eyesight checked."

"My eyesight is fine." She slid beneath the blankets of her cot, her gaze fixed on my midsection, as if she could see through my coverlet and the fabric of my shift to what lay beneath. And I knew then that our time had run out.

When Kennett and I met again, in the vineyards at dusk the following evening, I told him what Genevieve had said. He ran a hand through his dark hair, his face grim. In the fading light, his broad shoulders blocking out the last bit of the sun as it sank below the line of the arbors and beneath the horizon, he looked like a boy made of light and shadows—as if I had conjured him from the deepest desires of my heart. But when I blinked, he was still there—flesh and blood, pain clear in the depths of his sea-glass eyes.

"Miriam," he said, "no matter what happens, remember I love you."

Despite all we'd been through, we'd never spoken these words to each other before. Perhaps it was ridiculous, given that I was bearing Kennett's child—but there were few words more forbidden to utter. It was as if Kennett had been saving them up for me like some kind of treasure, a precious gem for me to carry next to my heart.

"I love you, too," I told him, and watched his face light with joy.

He lifted a calloused hand to cup my chin and bent his head, his mouth finding mine. The kiss was bittersweet, flavored with the tears I hadn't known were streaking my cheeks and the unmistakable taste of goodbye.

We were standing that way when they found us—Priest Traasen, in his blood-red robes that swept the ground as he walked, and the two bellators that accompanied him, clad all in black and studded with weapons. I recognized one of them by his bright red hair—Kilían Bryndísarson, who I knew had had the cot next to Kennett when they were both seventh-formers, before the Choosing. The other one was Efraím Stinar, five years into his training and already one of the Thirty, the Bellatorum's elite corps whose services were reserved for the most egregious of infractions. Next to them was Genevieve, her pug-nosed face set in a vicious mask of vindication.

"You see," she said to the Priest, pointing at me—specifically, at my belly, which there was no longer any point in trying to hide. "I told the truth."

The Priest's eyes swept over us, contempt clear in every line of his face. Then his voice rang out through the vineyards, righteous and resonant. "Miriam Larsen. Kennett Gundarson. I find you guilty of the sins of lust and fornication. You will be sentenced to execution in Clockverk Square. As you have sinned, so will you die—together."

I felt a tremor run through Kennett and into me. Still, he squared his shoulders, and I straightened my spine. We had agreed to meet this fate with dignity. I had just a single question—the only one that really mattered.

"What about the child?"

The Priest drew himself up, regarding me with disgust. "You will be confined to the hospital until the child is born, and your fellow sinner held in the dungeons, to contemplate the fate that awaits you both. Then your bastard spawn will join the ranks of the natural-born, and the two of you will face the bellators' blades."

His lip curled, as if the air surrounding myself and Kennett had gone rancid. "Bellators, remove the boy from my sight. I'll escort the girl to the hospital myself. She's no threat to me."

The bellators strode forward, their faces expressionless. They crushed fallen grapes as they went, the tart, sweet scent of happier times filling the air. Neither of them drew their weapons; they didn't have to. There was nowhere for us to run.

I clung to Kennett—for what did it matter now?—and felt his arms tighten around me. He'd worried they were a cage—but they were a cradle, a place of refuge. They had always felt that way to me.

He held me close, the child alive and moving between us. The person we had made, together—the physical manifestation of our love and our sins.

"I am a medic." His voice was a shattered whisper. "But I have no idea how to heal a broken heart."

Those were the last words he said to me, before they took him away.

SIX

The pain of childbirth was nothing compared to the ache in my heart—from losing Kennett, and from the knowledge that I would soon lose my son.

I saw my Lucien only once, just after he was born—when the midwife pulled him from my body and took him to the scale in the corner of my hospital room to be weighed. I wasn't meant to see him, but I struggled to my elbows nonetheless and strained to look. Hungrily, I drank him in: the olive skin and high cheekbones so like my own, the shock of black hair and lucent green eyes that marked him as Kennett's. He was beautiful, perfect. Mine, if only for that moment.

When he started to wail, the need to comfort him was visceral. I hated the clinical way the midwife prodded and poked him. I wanted to tear her hands from him, to hold him close. But I knew better than to move.

"Can I hold him?" I said, my voice cracked from screaming. "Just once?"

The midwife glared at me in silence, swaddling Lucien in a blanket. She swept my baby up, still wailing, and took him away without a word.

I knew I would never be allowed to see him again. Still, that didn't stop me from pleading when Efraím Stinar entered my room hours later, doing the bellators' regular sweep to ensure I hadn't leapt out the window—which, in my current state, was a laughable proposition.

"Please," I said, hating how pitiful I sounded. "Please let me see him one more time."

Bellator Stinar paused, his hand on the doorknob. "I couldn't do that even if I wanted to—which I most certainly do not."

Something about the gleeful tone of his voice alarmed me. "What do you mean?"

"Your bastard son is dead." He bared his teeth at me in a snarl. "And tomorrow at sunrise, you will be too—by my hand."

I felt my heart thud to a stop—not at his casual mention of my execution, which was hardly a surprise, but at what he'd said about my beautiful Lucien. I'd heard my baby cry—loud and healthy, if gut-wrenching, like Kennett had told me he would. What could have happened to him?

"How?" I choked out the word.

Bellator Stinar took pleasure in my misery; I could see it in the expression of satisfaction that lit his eyes. "That's none of your concern, girl," he said. "But perhaps the Architect sensed the evil in his soul and snuffed it out before your bastard could bring a blight upon the world." That malicious shark's grin lifting his lips, he turned his back on me.

I thought of the single, shining moment when I'd been allowed to see Lucien. When those wide, green eyes had looked into mine, I hadn't seen corruption. I'd seen pure, perfect innocence.

I refused to believe the Architect had taken Lucien because of my sins. Perhaps something invisible in his body had been broken. I wished more than anything that I could ask Kennett if such a thing were possible, but of course I could not. I was marooned with my grief, which was so monstrous, it threatened to devour me whole.

In the Commonwealth, we didn't cry often, save in the case of children who'd skinned a knee or broken an arm. Crying implied that you'd lost something that mattered to you, and we were never allowed to possess anything worth having. But as the door shut behind Efraím Stinar with a click, leaving me in darkness, I felt the first hot tear trickle down my cheek. And alone in the dark, I wept for the loss of my child—and for everything that might have been.

"GET UP." THE VOICE WAS HARSH—AND vaguely familiar.

I blinked and opened my eyes, which felt swollen from crying. Through the thin white curtains, I could see that it was still pitch-black outside. Surely it wasn't time yet. "Who's there?" I asked, my voice hoarse.

"Bellator Bryndísarson."

So it was time, after all. With difficulty, I struggled upward. The place between my legs ached and throbbed. "Alright," I said, my voice dull. Lucien was dead, and soon Kennett and I would be too. All that remained was to see it through. "I won't fight you."

"You'd better not." There was an odd hint in his voice—was it *amusement*? "I've come to help you escape."

Obviously I was still asleep—or perhaps hallucinating. Could enough grief and terror do that to a person? I fell back down on the bed with a thump, shutting my eyes again.

"Get up." A large, strong hand shook me by the shoulder. "We don't have much time."

Even my hallucinations were demanding. I opened my eyes again, squinting into the darkness of my room. Sure enough, Kilían Bryndísarson was crouching by my bedside, his hair a flash of copper in the shadows and a blade in the hand that wasn't gripping my shoulder. "Is this some kind of trick?"

He tugged me to a sitting position, and I had to bite my lip to suppress a hiss of pain. "Kennett said you wouldn't trust me—although what you think you've got to lose, I can't imagine—so he made me memorize something for you." Hooking a hand beneath my elbow, he pulled me to my feet. "'But to return, and view the cheerful skies, In this the task and mighty labor lies.'"

My heart, which had been lodged behind my ribs like a lump of ice ever since Bellator Stinar told me Lucien was dead, gave a painful thump. That night in the Library, before we'd kissed for the first time, Kennett had whispered a line from the

Aeneid to me: *Smooth the descent, and easy is the way.* This was the second half of the quote—about how hard it was to find your way back from Hell.

Hard—but not impossible.

"Do you believe me now?" He gave my upper arm a shake. "I mean you no harm. Quite the contrary. But we've got to go."

Setting my feet, I looked up into his shadowed eyes. "Why would you help us?"

A pained expression flickered across Kilían's face before it returned to its usual inscrutability. "Because if we were allowed such things, Kennett would be my friend." His lips flattened into a grim line. "Now, move."

Outside my hospital room, the two bellators assigned to guard me sat, slumped and unconscious, in the chairs that flanked my door. "What did you do to them?"

"You can thank Kennett. There are unanticipated advantages to having a medic's knowledge of drugs and herbs." He stared dispassionately down at his fellow warriors. "They went to sleep like babes in the nursery. And Kennett swore that when they woke up, they'd have no memory of anything beyond the moment they took their places for their shift."

I had a moment of fierce pride in Kennett, and allowed myself the privilege—after all, we were well beyond the point where such things mattered. "What a pity," I said, my tone short, and saw Kilían's eyes widen.

"You'll have to move fast," he said, looking me up and down. "Can you do that?"

"I can do anything I need to do," I told him, and it was the truth. If this was our one chance, I wouldn't waste it.

Kilían didn't ask again. Silently, he led me down a back stairwell, then out into the dark and toward Marketour Square. We ducked into an alleyway, and he paused at a metal door set into the concrete, pulled a keyring from his belt, and undid the lock. The door swung open, revealing a steep staircase that led into blackness.

The thought of forcing my weakened body down those stairs was overwhelming. But waiting for me at the bottom was Kennett and—somehow—freedom, so I made myself step through the trapdoor and onto the steps. They were metallic and slippery with moisture, and I hung onto the railing with all of my strength, imagining that I was climbing down a ladder in the Library. I had done that a hundred times; this would be no different. I wasn't descending into the pit of Hell. This was just a staircase, and it would have a bottom. All I had to do was keep climbing down.

The door clattered shut above me, and then the steps creaked as they took Kilían's weight. Oddly, his presence reassured me. I took a renewed grip on the railing and willed myself to climb faster. And finally I took one last step and felt not metal under my feet but the firm grit of concrete.

I stood to the side, and then Kilían was on the ground beside me, unclipping something from his belt. A moment later, the thin glow of a flashlight pierced the dark.

"Come on," he said, and turned without another word, heading into the gloom beyond the weak beam of his light.

We walked through what had to be some kind of tunnel system for what felt like forever. The damp air clogged my lungs, and I felt the blood dripping between my legs, which trembled with the effort of holding me upright—but I refused to slow us down, even when it meant I had to hold onto the wall to keep from falling.

Kilían cleared his throat. "Are you alright?" His voice was gruff, as if he was unaccustomed to asking such things. Most likely he was; bellators dealt in death and pain, not comfort.

"I'm fine." I kept my voice clipped, so as not to reveal the extent of my exhaustion. "Keep going."

A low, grudging chuckle emerged from the dark. "Kennett said you were tough. Alright; I'll take you at your word. It's not too much longer now."

He hadn't lied. In a few minutes, the tunnel narrowed, then dead-ended at a door. Kilían pulled the keyring off his belt again and fit one into the lock, which swung wide with a groan, revealing a small room filled with—of all things—books.

But for once, I hardly had eyes for them. Because in the middle of the room, one eye blackened and a deep purple bruise on his cheek, was—

"Kennett!" I threw my arms around him, and felt his come tight around me in return, holding me close. He smelled of dirt and blood and hunger—but the thump of his heart beneath my ear was as strong and steady as it had always been.

He set me away from him and laid a palm against my cheek, gazing down at me with wonder, as if he could hardly believe I was real—and a deep, abiding sadness. "Miri, I heard about the baby. I'm so sorry."

"There you go, apologizing again." I sniffed, trying to hold back the tears.

"I wish I could've been there." His eyes shone, glassy with tears of his own. "Maybe I could have saved him."

"It's not your—"

Kilían cleared his throat. "About the infant—I have reason to believe Bellator Stinar might be mistaken."

My eyes grew wide, and I felt my pulse quicken, threatening to choke me. Into the fissure that had cracked my heart ever since I'd heard those horrible words—*Your bastard son is dead*—flowed a thin river of hope. "What are you saying?"

The bellator met my eyes. "Efraím told you what he knew to be true," he said, his voice expressionless. "But I have reason to believe otherwise."

"Our baby is *alive?*" I was torn between wanting to leap for joy and claw his face to ribbons for not telling me sooner. "By the nine hells, what are we doing down here, then? We have to go back. Kennett, we have to find him, take him with us—"

But Kilían was shaking his head. "There's no way. I don't know where they've taken the child, and tracking him down would take more time than we have." He shifted his weight, and the weapons on his belt clinked against each other. "The

270

sun will be rising in an hour, and you need to be well clear of here by then."

"To the Sins with the sun! You got Kennett out, and me too. Surely we can rescue Lucien. I'm not leaving him behind." My voice broke. "I can't. Kennett, tell him."

"Miri." Kennett took my hand, and when I looked up at him, the tears had overflowed, streaking his cheeks. "This is wonderful news. But Kilían's right—how are we supposed to find him in time? If we go back, we'll all die—together."

I lunged for the door, heedless of the way my abused body protested. "You leave, then. I have to go back—I have to find him—"

My hand closed on the knob, and then Kennett's arms were around me, restraining me.

"I'm sorry, Miri. I really am. But his best chance at life—and ours—is for us to go."

I kicked and struggled, but Kennett held me fast. "I'm so sorry," he said again and again, but for once I didn't tell him to apologize. I hated both him and Kilían with a bright, fiery intensity that threatened to tear me apart. All I could think of was my Lucien, lost and crying, subjected to who knew what fate, as Kennett and I abandoned him to save our own skins.

"Let me go!" I said, fighting against Kennett's grip, but he wouldn't loosen it.

"I can't, Miri." Tears choked his voice. "I wish I could. Seeing you this way—leaving him behind—it kills me. If I thought we had the slightest chance, I'd go back for him in a heartbeat."

"So you're not even going to try?" I struggled harder.

His voice broke. "Please don't hate me. I can't lose you, too."

I wanted to ask if he didn't care about losing Lucien—if I was all that mattered to him—but I knew the answer. Of course he cared. I knew him too well to suspect anything else. He was stopping me from going back because he'd brought himself to accept what I couldn't bear to—that our only chance at salvation was to leave our son behind.

Misery churned in my stomach. It surged upward, into my chest, my throat—and then I was sobbing, harsh, animal noises that tore themselves from my body. My grief was so great, it seemed to inhabit me—like an invasive force I was helpless to resist.

At last I wore myself out and collapsed, limp, against Kennett's chest. The anger was gone, replaced with a weary sadness . . . lit by a gleaming hint of joy. Lucien was alive—but I would never see him again.

Kennett stroked my hair. "It's the right choice," he said, sounding as exhausted as I felt. "The only one."

"It might be the only choice." I forced the words out. "But that doesn't mean it's right."

"Miriam." Kilían had never said my name before; it sounded unfamiliar coming from his lips, stilted. "I'll look after the infant."

"What?" I lifted my head, eyeing him incredulously. Bellators didn't look after anyone but themselves.

"You have my word. I'll do all I can to make sure he comes to no harm."

I stared at him, looking for a twitch or a sidelong glance that would indicate he was lying. But his eyes were steady, clear and blue, with nothing in their depths save sincerity.

It was a peculiar promise, from a suspect source. But it was all I had.

I drew myself up and stepped back from Kennett. "Swear it, on your honor as a bellator." My voice was hoarse from sobbing, but the words came clearly, laden with conviction.

Kilían held my gaze. When he spoke, his tone was solemn, his face grave. "On my honor as a bellator and the strength of my sverd, I do so swear."

Next to me, I heard Kennett suck in a surprised breath. A bellator could swear no higher oath. They valued nothing more than their honor and their sverds—the razor-sharp blades they wore strapped to their backs. It would have to be good enough.

"Alright," I said, lifting my chin. "Alright, I'll go."

Kilían inclined his head, as if acknowledging what had passed between us. Then he turned to Kennett. "You remember what I told you?"

Taking my hand, Kennett nodded. "Go through the tunnels beyond there." He pointed to a small door I hadn't noticed before, set in the opposite wall of the room. "Follow the sketches of the wolf's face; they'll lead us where we need to go. We'll come out on the other side of the electric fence. Someone will meet us there and help us get away."

"That's it." Kilían nodded. "And remember, they'll ask you for proof that you've come from the Brotherhood. When they say, 'Speak of the wolf, and he will come,' you'll reply—"

"A wolf does not bite a wolf." Kennett's voice was clear and sure.

The Brotherhood? It had to be some kind of resistance movement. Which could only mean one thing: Kilían Bryndísarson, loyal bellator, was a traitor to the Commonwealth. He'd brought the two of us to a hidden room full of books—which I wished desperately I could explore; their content had to be incendiary for them to be concealed this way—and was facilitating our escape, for no other reason than that he considered Kennett to be his friend.

Then again, Kennett could lead a person to take incredible risks. Who knew that better than myself?

"I have to get back," Kilían said, his voice rough—not from indifference, but as if it concealed some deep, forbidden emotion. "May the blessings of the Architect be with you both. Stand strong."

"Thank you, Kilían. For our lives. And for your promise to our son." Kennett's voice was as rough as his. And then, to my amazement, he let go of my hand and embraced the bellator, heedless of the deadly weapons that hung from his hips.

Shock spread across Kilían's face—followed by a grief so profound it mirrored my own, and a strange, aching hunger. Then his face went blank. Slowly, he lifted his arms and returned Kennett's embrace. "Don't waste it," he said, his voice a croak—and then he disengaged himself, slipped through the door to the tunnels, and vanished back the way we'd come.

Kennett and I stared at each other—for once, wordless. And then I crossed to the small door that led to the unknown and yanked it open. Together, we stepped through, taking our first steps on the road toward freedom.

But as the door that led to the tunnels thudded shut behind us, as Kennett pulled a flashlight from his pocket and shone the beam on the moldering walls, looking for the face of the wolf, I couldn't help but look back. And I swore an oath of my own.

Somehow, someway, someday—I would come back for our son. I didn't care how long it took, or what I had to sacrifice. I would see my Lucien again.

"Miri." Kennett's voice was a whisper. "Look."

I followed the beam of the flashlight. There, on the uneven wall of the tunnel, was the sketch of the wolf, just as Kilían had promised. Beyond it was darkness—but at the end, if the bellator could be believed, someone was waiting to welcome us. We just had to be brave enough to find them.

I had always wanted to know what lay beyond the Commonwealth's boundaries—though I had never intended to find out this way, at such a terrible cost. At long last, I had my quest—at the expense of a broken heart.

But I made up my mind that whatever happened, my story would not be a tragedy. It couldn't be—because I had the boy I loved by my side, and a promise I'd sworn to keep.

With one last glance at the world that had raised and tricked and trapped me—the one that still held Lucien prisoner—I plucked the flashlight from Kennett's hand and led the way toward the light.

OF MARSHMALLOWS AND MONSTERS

KARISSA LAUREL

The New Horizons Juvenile Rehabilitation Home looked like any old three-story Victorian built in the previous century. A little worn and dilapidated, it needed a fresh coat of yellow paint, new shutters, new shingles, or maybe just a fateful lightning strike. One good spark to burn the whole thing down. Then Astrid McLean wouldn't have to be there—not that she could think of any better place to be. *At least it'll keep me dry on rainy nights.* She eyed a suspicious brown stain on the entryway ceiling and detected the slight odor of mildew in the air. *Or maybe not.*

Astrid's social worker and the assistant DA had shown her the New Horizons website. They had reviewed its mission statement about teaming troubled teens with wounded animals, many of them dangerous, in hopes of rehabilitating both into functioning members of human and wildlife society. It seemed a legally tenuous situation at best—putting defenseless minors into a perilous situation had to violate some kind of child labor law—but it also seemed better than going to adult jail, which had been her only other option. Maybe an angry coyote would eat her, but even that sounded preferable to being shivved to death on a cold prison floor.

On the morning of her first day as a new resident, Astrid stood at the threshold between the entryway and a large, open living room. A group of six or seven new faces stared at her—some guarded, some hostile, none familiar. She gritted her teeth and kept her chin raised. *Show no sign of weakness.* Kids who lived in places like this smelled fear the same way any animal, human or not, did. She'd give them no reason to think she was an easy target.

"Astrid?" Martin Jackson, the group home's founding father, or whatever you wanted to call him, gestured at the crowd. "Meet the family. Family? Say hi to Astrid."

A tall, lean white boy with pale skin and a shock of unruly black hair bounced on his toes. "Hi Astrid!" He was cute in a goth kind of way, but Astrid had caught a whiff of mockery; his greeting was too animated to be sincere.

She dismissed him and studied the other faces, noting a pair of Black girls standing hip to hip, one in braids, one with natural curls framing her face in a dark corona. Both wore carefully guarded expressions, giving away nothing. The one with braids waved halfheartedly. "Kanesha."

Her companion didn't even bother with a wave. "Jasmine."

Astrid's gaze landed next on a brown girl, possibly Hispanic, with high cheekbones and long ebony hair. With earbuds peeking from her ears, the girl bobbed her head to the rhythm of her music and ignored Astrid. Beside her, smiling, stood a short, round Black boy who looked too young to have ever caused the kind of trouble required to end up in a place like New Horizons. He pointed to himself once he'd caught Astrid's attention. "I'm Reggie. I'll be your mentor for the rehab stuff."

Astrid quickly re-evaluated, noting the world-weariness in Reggie's gaze as well as the thick bandage on his forearm. He looked no older than fourteen or fifteen, but his eyes said he was at least a hundred, and he had seen some things—some things that had bitten and scratched, apparently. Trepidation swirled coldly in Astrid's stomach.

Before she could appraise the remaining kids in the group, Martin was tugging the backpack from her shoulder. "Let me take this. I'll show you to your room."

She clutched her bag's strap. "I got it."

His serene brown gaze held her hazel one for a heartbeat. Then he nodded and motioned toward a staircase before them. "Your room is upstairs. You'll share with Carmen and Henrietta."

"It's *Henry!*" someone shouted. Following the voice to its source, Astrid spotted a young person of ambiguous ethnicity and gender standing in the rear of the group. Shaved to the scalp on both sides, their chestnut ringlets curled into a floppy mohawk. Henry rolled their eyes. "And the top bunk's mine."

"I apologize, Henry." Martin motioned at the stairs again. "Astrid, let's go. It's going to be a busy day, so you'll want to get settled and then meet us downstairs. Classes start in half an hour."

"Online, right?" Astrid followed Martin to a second-floor bedroom with hardwood floors and a faded rug. Someone had hung a picture of Dream from *The Sandman* comic on one wall. "I've never done online school before."

"It's got its pros and cons." Martin motioned to a bare mattress on the bottom bunk of a bed adjacent to a recessed dormer window. Someone had turned the space into a reading nook. Pillows, paperbacks, and comic books littered the floor. On the bed, a stack of folded linens balanced on top of a bare pillow. "Yours is on the bottom. Henry's is on top. If you want to change places, you'll have to take it up with them." He pointed at a door that Astrid had assumed was a closet. "Bathroom's in there. You're lucky this room has its own. Everyone else has to share the one in the hallway."

Martin backed through the doorway into the hall. "You've got time to make the bed if you want. Or, if you just want to sit and, you know, catch your breath or whatever, you can do that too." He raised his index finger and furrowed his brow.

"Just don't be late. You get *one* tardy. After that, there are consequences."

When the sound of his retreating footsteps had faded, Astrid plopped on her bunk, dropped her bag to the floor between her feet, and exhaled. She felt like she'd been holding that breath all morning, from the moment her social worker had signed off on the paperwork, escorted Astrid to her car, and driven her across town to this ancient old house, in this ancient old neighborhood on the edge of the city.

They may as well have driven to the other side of the universe. And now she was an alien on a strange planet. She quieted her breathing and closed her eyes, trying to claim some inner control or calm she wasn't sure existed.

A sudden yelp outside her window interrupted her attempt at meditation. She jumped to her feet and raced to the window that peered over an expansive backyard. A tall metal fence lined the perimeter, and strings of barbed wire adorned the top. Wooden sheds—like huge dog houses—huddled together in the rear of the yard. *The kennels . . .*

Astrid liked the idea of helping animals in theory but lacked real-world experience, except for a classroom guinea pig in kindergarten, and that hardly counted. While in lock-up, before she'd signed her probation agreement, she'd heard rumors about New Horizons, jokes about rehabilitating mythical beasts like sasquatches and chupacabras. She didn't need to believe them to be afraid—wolf teeth and bear claws were real enough to scare her. The thought of failing, of losing this second chance, terrified her even more. She'd stick her head straight into the jaws of a grizzly bear if it meant she could have a normal, jail-free life someday. *But hopefully they'll start me out with a nice cuddly raccoon instead.*

Another yelp broke the quiet. It turned into a long echoing howl. If she were alone in a tent in the woods in the middle of the night, the howl might've sent chills down her spine, but from here the animalistic cry sounded sad and a little lonely.

She squinted, focusing on the shed in the farthest, darkest corner of the yard where a copse of oaks and maples blocked the sunlight. A shadow shifted, something bulky and dusky appearing and disappearing in a blink.

Behind her, someone cleared their throat.

Astrid squealed and spun to face her intruder. "Don't sneak up on me like that!"

Henry frowned. "I wasn't trying to sneak up on you. It's my room too."

Astrid scowled as she retreated from the window and returned to the bunk assigned to her. She rifled through the linens, found a fitted bottom sheet, and shook it out. "Are you the one who likes *The Sandman*?"

Henry glanced at the gaunt, pale man in ebony robes and solid black eyes, staring at them from the poster on the wall. "Miles hung it up there." They shrugged. "None of us cared enough to take it down."

"Miles?" Astrid tugged the bottom sheet over the last corner and reached for the top sheet now crumpled on the floor.

"The kid who waved at you like an idiot?"

"The one who kind of looks like the Dream Lord."

Henry rolled their eyes. "Don't tell him that. He'll gloat for *days*." They shuffled to the reading nook, dropped onto one of the overstuffed pillows, and picked up a tattered graphic novel, a copy of something called *Nimona*.

Astrid unfolded a faded blue quilt, draped it over her bed, and stretched out. On the underside of the bunk above her, someone had used a permanent marker to write, MALLORY WAS HERE.

"Who's Mallory?" Astrid asked.

"She's none of your business." Henry's tone was cold and final.

While their reply only piqued Astrid's curiosity further, she didn't feel like starting a confrontation over it. Not on her first day. She closed her eyes and had just drifted to sleep when her bed shook. She jerked awake with a gasp.

"School's starting." Henry tapped the chunky watch on their wrist. With a bright, cheery, Mary Poppins voice filled with sarcasm, they said, "Don't be late."

Dragging herself to her feet, Astrid stretched and yawned. She tugged her scrunchie loose, ran her fingers through her straggling brown hair, and wound it up in a messy knot again. She shuffled downstairs, following the sound of voices coming from the opposite direction of the front living room. *The people who built this place probably called it a parlor or a salon, something fancy like that.* She imagined women dressed like characters from an Austen book sitting on stiff chairs, sipping tea from delicate white cups. Snorting, she dismissed the image as she stepped into a bright, sunny room.

On three sides, floor-to-ceiling windows let in a torrent of cheery sunshine. Astrid frowned. She hadn't had enough sleep or coffee to cope with this much sunlight. The tiny cup of gas station brew that her social worker had bought her on the trip from the assistant DA's office to New Horizons had barely scratched the surface of her caffeine dependency. *God, I hope Martin doesn't have anything against caffeine.* Some of these places were known to discourage even the most harmless of addictions, which would be . . . unfortunate.

"Astrid?" Martin pointed toward an empty computer terminal in the corner of the room. "That's your spot. Go ahead and log in." On the opposite side of the terminal sat Miles, the Morpheus wannabe. Around the room she spotted six other terminals exactly like theirs. Cords and plugs snaked across the carpet. She stepped carefully, trying not to trip. *This has got to be a fire hazard.*

She sat in a creaky wooden chair and faced the computer screen that prompted her to enter her login credentials.

"Your username is Astrid05," Martin said. "Follow the prompts to create your password. When you've done that, Miles can tell you what to do next." Martin turned his attention to the whole of the room. "I'll see you all in the dining room at lunchtime."

Glancing up, Astrid met Miles's kohl-rimmed gaze. He batted his black lashes and grinned like the Cheshire Cat. Bracing his elbows on his desk, he rested his chin on his knuckles. "So . . . what are you in for?"

"Don't answer him," Henry said. "Ignore him like the rest of us."

Miles rolled his eyes. "Juvenile records are sealed, or else I would've already looked you up. Whatever it is, it had to be pretty nasty for you to end up here. Martin only takes last-chance cases, you know."

Astrid arched an eyebrow. She did know. The assistant DA had told her as much.

"So, what was it? Sex, drugs, theft . . . *murder?*"

Gritting her teeth, Astrid ignored Miles and typed in her username. She followed the prompts to create her password and school account. "Now what?" she muttered, not expecting Miles to be particularly helpful.

"One fact," he said, raising a single bony finger. "Give me one clue about what evil thing you did, and I'll tell you what to do next."

Astrid shook her head. She wasn't a sucker, and she wouldn't let Miles hijack her morning with stupid games. She scanned her school app's dashboard, clicked around, followed some links, and stumbled onto several tutorial videos. She tugged a pair of old earbuds from her pocket and watched the videos. She wouldn't confess it to the others, but she *liked* school and had been good at it before she'd screwed up everything. This online thing wouldn't be the same, but she'd give it her best. Going to college might be the only way she'd ever get her life back on track.

After the tutorials, she'd figured out enough to find her online classes and course lists. She started on the tasks in her eleventh-grade ELA agenda, her favorite subject, and had fallen so deep into concentration that the hours passed unnoted. Only when the others shut down their computers, stretched, and shuffled out of the room did she realize it was lunchtime.

"It's meatball sub day," Miles said, inhaling deeply. He clasped his hands over his heart and gazed at the ceiling with a look of faux adoration on his face. "Oh, joy!"

Following his lead, Astrid also inhaled and scented garlic, basil, and tomato sauce wafting through the air. Despite her distaste for meat, her stomach growled. *Maybe I can just make a cheese and marinara sandwich or something.* Hanging back, she watched Miles plod out of the room, then followed, keeping several feet between them. He seemed to like poking and prodding. So far it had only been mental, but she didn't plan on giving him the chance to make it physical.

As if reading her mind, he glanced over his shoulder and winked. "I won't bite, but I can't say the same about everyone, or *everything*, else around here."

BRIGHT LIGHTS CAREENED TOWARD ASTRID. A racing engine roared. Tires screeched. A harsh blow struck, throwing her across the hard ground. Her scream sounded like an animal's high-pitched cry. Pain lanced her hip and she landed hard on her shoulder. Her vision blurred, yet those headlights still burned, exposing her soft, vulnerable belly.

Shadowed figures knelt. Hands reached. Voices chattered unintelligible words. They lifted her, carrying her into darkness, into nothingness . . .

Astrid awoke with a start, her whole body convulsing as if shocked by an electrical current. Breathing hard, she stared into the darkness above her bed and tried to remember the details of her dream, but they faded quickly, leaving her awake and unsettled. She thumbed on her phone to check the time, and the screen's illumination revealed Mallory's name again, scribbled in bold black Sharpie, demanding not to be forgotten.

Maybe Mallory and Henry had simply been enemies and that explained why Henry hadn't wanted to talk about her. Maybe she'd finished the New Horizons program and moved on to a bigger, better world just as Astrid hoped to do someday.

An uneasiness in the back of Astrid's mind wouldn't let her dismiss Mallory so easily, though. Despite the warmth of the room, Astrid shivered.

She turned over and scratched her wrist, trying to remove the constant itch of phantom handcuffs, of the shackles that usually haunted her dreams. That, and all the blood. She had never expected there to be so much blood. She had never expected murder and mayhem. It was supposed to be a simple burglary.

Simple. Ha!

A forlorn howl ghosted into her room from the backyard. In the bunk above, Henry grumbled and rolled over. The whole bed wobbled. Astrid held her breath, waiting for it to fall and crush her. Put her out of her misery. But she wasn't that lucky.

Sighing, she sat up. Previous experience had taught her she wouldn't be going back to sleep anytime soon, and her stomach rumbled, reminding her of the slim vegetarian pickings at supper. *Should probably say something to Martin about that.* She shoved her feet into her beat-up, secondhand Chucks and tiptoed across the room.

"Where are you going?" Henry whispered. Carmen, their third roommate, snuffled loudly but didn't wake up.

"I'm hungry. I'm going to look for a snack."

"You'll regret it if Martin catches you out of bed."

"Are you going to tell him?"

Henry rolled over, giving Astrid their back. "Just don't say I didn't warn you."

Creeping, she made her way to the first floor, keeping her ears attuned for the sounds of Martin on the prowl. She skulked through the shadows until she reached the kitchen. After rifling through the pantry, she uncovered a half-empty bag of marshmallows. She hadn't eaten a marshmallow in years, but she'd loved them as a child. She unknotted the bag and inhaled. They smelled of everything good she'd once had and lost: sweetness, innocence, childhood, and family. She plucked one from the bag and sank her teeth into the soft, puffy cloud of vanilla and sugar. Her eyelids fluttered closed and she sighed.

Aroooo-oooooh!

That same sad howl she'd been hearing since her arrival interrupted her moment of childish ecstasy. She'd expected to be introduced to the animals after her school day had ended, but when she'd asked, both Reggie and Martin had told her she'd have to wait. But she'd never been particularly good at waiting. Popping another marshmallow into her mouth, she followed the howl's echoes toward the rear of the house.

Her path dead-ended in a utility room with a washer and dryer and a door leading to the backyard. *Just a quick look,* she told herself. *To see if it's a wolf or a coyote or . . . something else? What else could possibly howl like that?*

Astrid eyed the exit and searched for signs of an alarm system. Instead she found a bolt lock that required a key. She clicked her tongue and cursed under her breath. *"Damn."* Not so long ago, a lock like that would've never thwarted her, but those days were behind her now. She was trying not to be that girl anymore.

"What's the matter?"

A shriek rose in Astrid's throat, but she choked it back as she spun around and found Reggie grinning at her in the darkness.

"Looking for this?" He held a flashlight in one hand and a key pinched between his finger and thumb in the other.

"What are you doing here?"

"Heard Ozzie singing and heard you sneaking out of your room. You really shouldn't go outside alone. It's better if we check on Ozzie together."

"Ozzie?"

Reggie pointed at the back door. "Short for Ozark Howler. Ever heard of them?"

Astrid's eyes narrowed in skepticism. Was Reggie messing with her? "Is it, like, a type of wolf or something?"

"*Something* is right." Reggie shrugged. "Why don't we go find out?"

Eyes wide and round, she blinked at him. Her earlier bravado drained away, and words of protest hung in her suddenly-dry throat. "Martin said I would have to wait a while, get adjusted to the house and the other kids and the rules first."

As if sensing her distress, Reggie smiled, revealing dimples in his round cheeks. He raised a hand like a policeman stopping traffic. "Hey, don't freak out. All we're going to do is get acquainted. Cool?"

Astrid swallowed. She grimaced. "Wh-what does that mean, exactly?"

"It'll be safe, I promise. You'll meet Ozzie, and she'll meet you. We can hang out together for a little while."

"H-hang out? With a . . ." She lowered her voice to a whisper. "What exactly?"

Reggie unlocked the back door. He flipped on his flashlight and made a *follow me* gesture. "You'll see."

Dread hardening in her stomach like concrete, she followed Reggie down rickety wooden steps descending into a backyard that was mostly patches of weeds growing like small islands in a sea of bare dirt. "I can't believe this is legal," she mumbled. "Letting kids go around dangerous wild animals."

"They're more misunderstood than monster." Reggie flashed a grin over his shoulder and waggled his eyebrows. "Kind of like us."

"I don't eat people, though."

"Neither does Ozzie." Reggie gestured toward the collection of ramshackle sheds. "Most wild animals won't attack humans unless provoked."

"'Provoked' can mean a bunch of different things, though."

He nodded as if acceding to her point. "Listen to me, do what I tell you, and you'll be safe."

"Is that what you told Mallory?"

Reggie froze mid-step. He kept his face forward, toward the kennels. "What do you know about Mallory?"

"Nothing. It was just a guess."

Reggie faced her and crossed his arms over his chest. "How'd you know her name?"

"She scribbled it on her bunk. I found it when I was making my bed. Henry wouldn't say anything about her. Obviously, I was curious." Already, Astrid's throat was tired. This was more talking than she'd done in days.

"Mallory's . . . *gone*." His expression darkened. "This place, it's not for everyone."

As they crept closer, Astrid wondered if this place might not be for her, either. The trees and darkness had concealed another layer of fencing surrounding each kennel, separating one from another. Chitters and yips and sounds of animals shifting and moving suggested plenty of residents occupied the kennels, but darkness concealed their identities. She could've been standing mere yards from unicorns and hippogriffs for all she knew. *And it's also possible I read way too much Harry Potter in middle school.*

Or maybe not.

From the kennel Reggie was approaching, there peered a pair of eyes that glowed an eerie, unnatural blue. Sure, animal eyes could do strange things in the flash of a camera or in headlights, but she'd never seen any creature whose gaze shone with an ethereal light, as if from some otherworldly source.

Reggie paused at the kennel gate and motioned for Astrid to come closer.

"N-no thanks," she whispered. "I'm okay right here."

He sank to his knees at the fence and whistled a note that was deep and quiet. A low, menacing growl rolled through the air, vibrating in Astrid's chest. She nearly ran. Nearly sprinted for her bedroom upstairs to pack her things and escape before Martin knew she was missing.

As if sensing her fears, Reggie took her hand and squeezed it. "It's okay." He pointed his flashlight at a dark shape emerging from its kennel. "Look."

It was hard to see clearly at first, as if the shadows clung to it, camouflaging it. But as she stared, she made out a bulky form with the body of a black bear or a panther, or the strange lovechild of those two creatures combined. Short, shiny black fur covered it from its boxy snub nose to the ends of its claw-tipped paws. *Claws or small scythes?* A pair of horns—one broken off and one curled like a ram's—crowned its head. Sniffing the ground, it hobbled closer, revealing a bad limp.

Astrid retreated several feet. "Th-that's not a wolf." And yet she felt like she'd seen it somewhere before. In her dreams perhaps? But how was that even possible?

"No," Reggie said. "It's an Ozark Howler. I told you."

"What the *hell* is an Ozark Howler?" She waved her hands frantically as if the gesture might dispel her fear and confusion.

"Shhh." Reggie pressed a finger to his lips. "Everyone in the house will hear you. We're not supposed to be outside after lights-out."

"Then why are you here?" she whispered harshly.

"I'm trying to make sure you don't do something stupid and get yourself hurt."

"Did you do something stupid?" She pointed at Reggie's bandaged arm.

"Yes." He chuckled. "I got between a hungry raccoon and his afternoon snack."

"What else lives here? No phoenixes or giant spiders?"

"It's pretty mundane. A fox cub, a few raccoons, an opossum . . ." He laughed again. "This isn't a menagerie from *Fantastic Beasts*, Astrid."

She pointed at his bandaged arm. "Yeah, but you also said this wasn't dangerous."

"Everything's dangerous if you don't know what you're doing. But this isn't my first rodeo, as they say." Reggie motioned for Astrid to step closer to him. "We don't know much about Ozark Howlers. Creatures like her, cryptids, are rare, and the information about them is mostly rumor and speculation. Most people don't even think they really exist, and Martin likes it that way. Keeps everyone safer, us included."

Reluctantly Astrid moved forward, curiosity temporarily overruling her fear. "Why's it limping like that?"

"Hit by a car and left to die out on Highway 42 not far from here. Some good Samaritan spotted her and called animal control."

Why does that explanation ring a bell? The hairs on the back of Astrid's neck rose. *Feels like I've heard a story like that somewhere recently.*

"It's kind of a well-known secret in the animal rehab community that Martin takes on the . . . *special* cases. He has to keep it on the down-low though. We all do. If the wrong people find out, it could cause problems for Martin." Reggie cut his gaze, looking at her from the corner of his eyes. "For *all* of us. They could shut this place down. Then where would we go? To jail? And what would happen to these animals? It's your secret now, too, Astrid. I hope we can trust you with it."

The howler limped closer, and its disturbing blue gaze seemed to focus on the bag of marshmallows Astrid was still clutching like a safety blanket. She'd forgotten about her snack in the excitement of discovering the existence of this strange and unusual animal.

The howler licked its lips.

"I think . . ." She shifted the marshmallow bag. The howler's gaze followed. "I think it's hungry."

"Well, then give her one," Reggie said.

"Are you sure?"

He shrugged. "Can't hurt."

Astrid opened her bag. The creature's nostrils flared, and it sniffed, scenting the air. She pulled out a marshmallow. The howler leaned forward, its eyes widening, ears pricking, muscles vibrating with excitement.

Astrid bit her lip and tossed the marshmallow. It struck a fence link, bounced off, and landed on the ground at Reggie's feet.

Easing onto its rear haunches, the howler gave the marshmallow a longing look and whimpered. Reggie chuckled, picked up the treat, and chucked it through a fence link. It landed at the creature's paws. The howler's long, pink tongue lashed out, swiping the confection from the ground in a blink.

"Monsters like marshmallows?" A nervous giggle escaped Astrid.

"Don't *you* like marshmallows?"

"You calling me a monster?" she countered.

"It's why we're all here, isn't it? A second chance to atone for the horrible things we've done?"

"Who says 'atone'?" Astrid narrowed her eyes at her companion. "How old are you, anyway?"

He chuckled, stood, and dusted off the knees of his jeans. "If you were brave enough, I'd tell you to hold your knuckles close and let Ozzie smell you."

"Brave? Yes. Stupid? Not so much."

Reggie pushed his knuckles against the fence links. The howler snarled and flashed its fangs. Astrid flinched and swallowed a shriek. Reggie, however, remained calm. He held out his hand. "Give me another marshmallow."

She obliged.

He held the treat between the fence links. Slowly, warily, the beast approached, black nose twitching, sniffing, huffing and puffing. Finding his offering acceptable, it swiped its huge pink tongue over his fingers, snatching the treat.

Astrid's whole face puckered. "*Ew.*"

"It's not so bad." Reggie poked several fingers through the links and scratched the creature's chin. It closed its eyes and sighed.

"What do you need me for?" She blinked, stunned at the monster's seeming gentility. "It looks like you've totally tamed it."

"Oh yeah?" Reggie raised an eyebrow. "Why don't you open this gate and see how tame she is."

Astrid scowled. Going all weak-kneed over a couple of scritch-scrotches wouldn't fool her into trusting the howler. Tigers at the zoo were cute too, but that didn't mean she wanted to climb into their cages and rub their bellies. This creature didn't have wicked claws and sharp teeth for no reason.

Reggie's next comment reinforced her conclusions. "Does a wild animal have to be actively trying to attack you for you to be afraid of it? If you caged a wolf, you would respect its potential violence, even if it was behaving docilely. Same rule goes for Ozzie."

"So, what exactly are we supposed to be doing with it?"

"Not an it. Ozzie's a *she*."

"What are we supposed to be doing with her, then?"

"First, we earn her trust. Then, we try to rehabilitate her."

"What does 'rehabilitate' mean, exactly, in these circumstances?" she asked.

"Save their lives first. Heal their injuries. Return them to the wild if we can."

"And if we can't?"

Reggie's face shuttered, his bemused expression disappearing. "What do you *think* happens? It's not like they can get adopted as pets."

"Maybe we can ask Carole Baskin to take her." She snickered.

"Who?"

"*Tiger King?*"

Reggie stared blankly at her.

292

"Never mind." Astrid tried swallowing the dry lump that had suddenly risen in her throat. "So, all I've got to do with this thing is convince her not to eat me, bandage her up, then throw her back into the woods?"

"Easier said than done." Reggie held out the back-door key, urging Astrid to take it. He was trusting her.

If she accepted the key—and his trust—that would create some kind of unspoken contract. She'd have to keep New Horizons' secrets. She'd have to protect Ozzie, too.

Astrid exhaled a sigh as she took the key from his hand. "Probably the understatement of the century."

OZZIE'S HOWLS AWAKENED ASTRID AGAIN ON her second night at New Horizons. Rubbing her eyes, she left her bed and crossed to the dormer window peering over the backyard.

"Ozzie sounds so sad." Henry's voice sounded drowsy and thick.

"You've met her?"

"Not officially." The bed creaked as Henry sat up. "But I've spotted her a couple times when I checked on my fox cub. And Reggie told me about Ozzie. Told me he'd introduced her to you already."

The howler cried out again.

"Am I just supposed to ignore her?" Astrid asked. "Should I pretend I don't hear her?"

"Martin doesn't know you've seen her?" Henry climbed down from the bed and joined Astrid at the window.

"I don't think so."

"Then, yeah, you keep pretending. Hopefully Martin will make introductions soon. Meanwhile, let Reggie take care of her."

Astrid considered Henry's advice. Maybe there was wisdom in it, but caring for this howler was the only thing she could think of that would show her commitment to New Horizons and to leaving her past behind.

Carefully, noiselessly, she put on her sneakers and snuck outside. Perhaps she should've woken Reggie and asked him to go with her, but she wasn't planning to unlock Ozzie's kennel or get too close. *Nothing dangerous,* she promised herself.

Something chittered at her, probably the demanding raccoon that had clawed Reggie's arm. Or maybe it was another mystical cryptid, but how likely was it that they'd be sheltering two such rare creatures at the same time?

She sank to her knees at the kennel fence. Ozzie's blue eyes glowed from the murky depths of her house, but the creature made no effort to approach, despite Astrid's diplomatic marshmallow efforts. At least she'd stopped howling like she was singing a sad country song.

"Don't feel bad," she told the howler. "I can relate. To *all* of it." She tossed another marshmallow, aiming for the black hole between Ozzie's glowing blue eyes. The marshmallow must have landed close, because she heard a slurping noise and several satisfied lip smacks. "It sucks being trapped somewhere you don't want to be."

As the night wore on, she tossed out most of the remaining marshmallows. Sleeplessness haunted her the same as it had in the two months since her arrest. Because of what she'd done, a man and his wife were doomed to sleep six feet underground for eternity. It was only fair that, in return, Astrid should never sleep again.

Despite believing that, Astrid must have dozed. How else could she explain the strange vision, the same dream from several nights before that was part nightmare, part surreal drama of Ozzie and bright headlights and pain? Images, mostly shadows, of human hands and figures kneeling, lifting Ozzie, carrying her away from the side of the road near the shoulder of a dense forest.

Astrid rubbed her eyes, trying to rid herself of the upsetting vision. The night sky had lightened to a bruised purple, warning of the approach of dawn, and she unfolded her stiff limbs.

Groaning, she stood. Sitting on the ground for several hours was hard on a body, even one that was only sixteen years old. She limped toward the house, shaking out her stiff joints. After locking the door behind her, she tiptoed back to her room, encountering no one along the way.

"Is Ozzie okay?" Henry asked in a sleep-roughened voice.

"What does okay look like for a monster?" Astrid slid off her shoes and plopped onto her bed. "But she seems calmer, so I guess that's a good thing."

"*Smmf puhh,*" Henry mumbled. Moments later, they were softly snoring again.

That was too easy, Astrid thought as she stretched out. *Security cameras probably caught me. Martin will probably bust me and kick me out tomorrow.* But then she was asleep and free, for just a few blessed minutes, from her doubts and fears.

ALTHOUGH SHE HAD MANAGED TO AVOID detection on her return to the house the previous two nights, she wasn't so lucky on her third try. On the top step outside the back door, wrapped in the shadows of pre-dawn gloom, sat Miles, the Lord of Dreams. He wore black jeans and a ripped white t-shirt. His black hair jutted from his head in unruly cowlicks that some dumb girl would be eager to smooth. Astrid, however, was not that girl.

His lips split into a smarmy grin as she approached. She tried to step around him, but he sprawled and blocked the entrance.

"Quit playing, Miles."

He clicked his tongue and pouted. "You'll have to be nicer than that. Say please."

Astrid clenched her teeth and balled her fists.

"Or, if that's too civilized for you, since you seem to prefer the company of wild animals over the rest of us . . ." He pointed a meaningful look toward the kennels. "I'll make a deal with you. I'll let you inside and keep my lips zipped about your nighttime rendezvous if you'll tell me one little secret about yourself. Just one."

"And if I don't?" She narrowed her eyes at him.

"I lock you out and wake up Martin."

She scowled.

He held her gaze, the smug grin still posed on his lips. He was almost pretty, with long black lashes and full lips. But Astrid had learned an expensive lesson about letting pretty boys think they could have their way. "Please," she said with as flat and dull of a voice as she could manage.

"Please what?"

"Please move aside and let me in."

"Oh, no," he wagged his finger, "it's too late for pleasantries. I want the secret. I want to know why you're here."

"Why do you care?"

He rolled his dark eyes and raked his fingers through his hair. "I *don't* care. But the only way to get through this life is with a little leverage."

"I'll show you leverage." As fast as a cobra striking a lizard, Astrid attacked. Her fingers squeezed the flesh between Miles's legs and her other hand gripped his long, smooth throat. He gasped and tried to pull away, but she gripped him harder, until he exhaled a silent groan. If she had told him her secret, what she'd done to wind up in this place, he wouldn't have let his guard down around her. "People are dead because of what I did," she said. "Compared to that, the fate of your balls means nothing to me. So, move aside." She shoved. He scooted, but hostility blazed in his eyes. "And don't screw with me again."

Astrid marched into the house, heart thumping in time with her hurried footsteps. *What kind of place is this? What kind of home is Martin running? I can sneak out every night and Miles can harass me without consequence?* New Horizons was turning out to be similar to some of the foster homes she'd lived in before she'd met Christopher, her ex- . . . whatever he was. She'd been so desperate to get away from her broken home, to have some control, to have someone give a damn about her.

It had all been a lie, of course.

She shouldn't be surprised if this place turned out to be another lie, too.

ASTRID RAISED HER GUARD, EXPECTING Miles's retribution to be waiting for her around every corner. No way could she pull a move like that and get away with it—surely he'd want revenge. So, she stayed inside at night and only visited Ozzie in the daylight hours. Reggie had vouched for her, and Martin had given his reluctant permission on the condition that Astrid never tend to Ozzie without someone at her side. Reggie didn't look like he'd be worth much in a fight, but at least he could be a witness if Miles tried to retaliate.

"What's the matter?" Reggie asked her on the one-week anniversary of her arrival. It was hot, and they sat outside Ozzie's kennel sweating and taking turns trying to entice the howler to leave her bed, but the creature seemed listless. The glow in her blue eyes had dimmed. "You've been like a ghost around here."

"What do you mean?"

"So quiet, clinging to the shadows like you hope no one notices you. You weren't like that the first few days. Something happened."

Astrid squinted at him. "You sure are observant, Sherlock."

"It's my job. I'm supposed to be your mentor."

"If you're so experienced, then tell me what the heck is up with this thing." She pointed at Ozzie. "She's not getting better."

"It happens sometimes. Something inside them is so broken they can't, or won't, recover."

"Should we call a vet? Is there someone Martin trusts?"

"Someone has already come and evaluated her. Other than some broken bones that will take a while to heal, nothing's technically wrong with her."

So, it was a case of a wounded spirit. Those sorts of things could easily turn fatal—Astrid knew this from experience. She still wasn't certain if she'd survive her own case of mangled heart and crushed hopes. "What can we do?"

Reggie shrugged. "Keep trying, I guess. Give her a reason to live."

"What reason?"

"If I knew, I would've already done it."

"I had a dream about her that first night." Astrid rehashed her vision of seeing Ozzie get hit by a car and then of her being rescued and brought to New Horizons. "It was so vivid."

"Don't be so sure it was a dream." Reggie tapped his temple, then pushed himself to his feet. "We don't know much about creatures like Ozzie. I asked Martin, and he's never had a howler here before. Maybe they're as mundane as any animal in the forest. But, then again, maybe they're not."

"How many different cryptids are out there?"

"I don't know if anyone could ever accurately count creatures that are so rare and secretive. How do we know how many are real like Ozzie or are just myths like most people believe?" He rolled a shoulder. "Martin's not much of a scientist. Mostly he's just very . . . sympathetic. But he's been doing this for a dozen years and probably has a better answer than I do. You should ask *him*."

Reggie strode away, heading for the house, leaving Astrid to wrestle with her confusion. He liked being cryptic, as if he'd taken all his cues about how to be a mentor from shifu stereotypes in B-grade Kung Fu movies. Christopher had loved those movies, and the memory of watching them together made her shiver with nausea. *Wonder if the guards let him watch them in the maximum-security wing.*

She hoped not. She hoped they let him rot.

EACH NIGHT FOR THE PAST WEEK, OZZIE HAD howled and cried, pouring her heartache out to the moon, but tonight the howler had remained oddly silent. Disturbingly so.

Despite her troubling encounter with Miles, Reggie's warnings, and the rules that forbade her to approach the kennels after sunset, she found herself sneaking out to check on Ozzie just before midnight. She might have given up her criminal ways, but she doubted she'd ever be good at following conventional rules, even the ones that were meant to keep her safe.

Something's wrong, Astrid thought as she crept into the silent backyard. A part of her dreaded discovering the poor creature had died. She might have feared Ozzie's teeth and claws, but she didn't wish suffering on the beast. The howler was an innocent being, and a close encounter with the world of men had stolen that innocence away. The same way Christopher had stolen hers.

Who are you kidding? He didn't steal anything. You gave it to him, freely and willingly. Facing up to the horrors of what she and Christopher had done together would never be easy, but she'd never atone if she couldn't be honest with herself.

She plucked marshmallows from a fresh bag and tossed them into the dark opening of Ozzie's house. One blue eye peeled open, its blue glow barely bright enough to pierce the shadows.

"If I didn't know better," Astrid said, "I'd think you had a broken heart." She popped a marshmallow into her own mouth and chewed. "I mean, can a wild animal even have feelings like that? What kind of thing would have to happen to make you give up on life?"

Astrid sank to the ground and folded her legs in front of her. The moon had shrunk to a sliver, a thin fingernail pairing, casting no discernible glow on the backyard. Light pollution from the surrounding city masked the stars, turning the sky muddy. "I'm sure Reggie told you already . . ." Astrid didn't allow herself to consider the silliness of talking to the howler as if it understood her. "Once you get better, we'll take you back to the woods. It won't be like this forever."

If Astrid had really expected Ozzie to answer, she would've been disappointed.

She chucked another marshmallow over the fence. Ozzie's other eye opened. The sound of the monster—*no, I should stop thinking of her that way. She's dangerous, sure. Could rip me limb from limb with those claws and fangs if she wanted. But she's given me no reason to call her a monster. She's only trying to survive, just like me*—the sound of *Ozzie*'s snuffling out the treat gave Astrid a splinter of hope. She kept up her inane chatter, telling Ozzie what it had been like when she was little, in the few peaceful years she'd known before her dad had left and her mom's string of boyfriends had gone from bad to worse, until CPS had intervened. She'd met Christopher in one of her foster homes, and he'd promised her independence, freedom, and love.

Well, at least one of those things had turned out to be false. Maybe all three.

Again, she must have dozed off, because she awoke near dawn with more vivid visions. She'd dreamed of a tiny ball of black fuzz with huge floppy ears, big blue eyes, and sharp teeth that promised mayhem one day but for now only served to gnaw sticks and crunch bugs. She envisioned that little furball nuzzling in search of warm milk. She felt a sensation of comfort, and hope, and . . . love?

"A puppy?" Astrid rubbed her eyes, clearing her vision, and met Ozzie's dim gaze. "Or, cub, or . . . what do you call a baby howler anyway?"

Ozzie slowly blinked and let out a beleaguered sigh.

"You're a momma?"

Ozzie blinked again.

"Am I losing my mind, talking to an animal and thinking it's sending me visions?" But she thought of her first night at New Horizons and the dream that had seemed like a vague memory of Ozzie's accident. And she'd experienced that vision once more since then—the first time she'd dozed off at the kennel.

Is Ozzie . . . telepathic? Does 'cryptid' mean something more than just being extraordinarily rare and incredibly strange?

Disquiet swirled in her stomach. Accepting that a creature like Ozzie actually existed had been hard enough. Believing it had some kind of paranormal ability . . . that it could communicate with her in her dreams? That required her to suspend disbelief beyond all reason.

Receiving no other response from her cryptid companion, Astrid packed up her marshmallows and headed for the house as dawn broke across the backyard. She made it only a few steps before she spotted a familiar figure waiting on the steps.

Her stomach churned and her feet turned leaden as she trudged forward.

Martin's downturned lips and narrowed eyes looked dour. Disappointed, maybe. But . . . not angry, necessarily. How had he found her? Bad luck, or had Miles ratted her out?

Martin folded his arms across his broad chest. "Want to tell me what's going on?"

"I'm *rehabilitating*." Astrid gestured toward the kennels.

His nostrils flared. "In the middle of the night? After curfew?"

All out of excuses, Astrid merely shrugged.

He held out his hand. "Key."

She pressed the cold metal into his palm.

"Where'd you get this?"

Although Christopher would've disagreed, Astrid wasn't a snitch. "I found it."

"Reggie give it to you?"

She shook her head. "I stole it from him. He doesn't know he's missing it."

Martin harrumphed, clearly not believing her. "Get inside." He motioned toward the door. "Classes start in a couple hours. Maybe you can get some sleep between now and then."

Unlikely. Having expected anger and vitriol, her shoulders were tense. A hot throbbing sensation pulsed at the base of her skull. Any moment, Martin could let loose with hard words or brutal fists. But a violent outburst never came. Instead he stopped at the base of the stairs and watched her climb to the second floor.

"We'll talk about consequences and punishment this afternoon in my office," he said. "For now, you're confined to your room, the classroom, or dining room. Don't leave the house, understand?"

Astrid paused at the landing, gathered her courage, and looked down at Martin. His face was carefully masked, and if he was angry, he'd hidden it well. She didn't know what to make of his composure. It was . . . unusual, in her experience. So, she pricked him, a test to reveal whether his calmness was real or merely a façade. *Better to know a person's true nature sooner than later.* "Who was Mallory?"

Martin froze, posture tensing into a rigid statue. "Why do you ask?"

"Her name is scribbled on my bunk. She's like a ghost around here. No one will talk about her."

Martin inhaled, then let out his breath until his shoulders slumped. "She was a lot like you, fierce, brave, impulsive. Heart too big for her own good. She pushed the boundaries. Broke some rules." He motioned toward the backyard. "In a place like this, rule-breaking—going out at night, approaching the animals alone, not telling anyone where you're going—can be lethal. The rules are there for a reason, to protect both you *and* the animals. What you did tonight . . . you could've wound up just like Mallory."

A lump rose in Astrid's throat. She swallowed. "She's . . . dead?"

Martin jerked his chin in affirmation. "It was a wampus cat. One of the first cryptids we'd had in more than a year. It tore her throat out." His hands went to his neck, fingers curled like claws. "She bled to death before anyone found her, but we told the authorities it was a mountain lion that happened to be rehabilitating here at the same time. We had to euthanize the wampus cat and hide the body before anyone could find it."

His voice went rough, like he'd swallowed sandpaper. "The county made us kill the mountain lion. It was innocent. So was Mallory. They both died for my mistakes." Taking a shuddering, grief-filled breath, he scraped his fingers across his scalp, leaving furrows in the short black curls. "They almost shut us down, talked about sending the kids to prison, killing the rest of the animals we were housing."

He looked up and held Astrid's gaze. Tears swam in his eyes. "I could lock you all down, monitor everything like a C.O. at the state pen. But I won't risk creating evidence that could be used against us, and you all need trust and latitude if you're going to overcome your pasts. This place is not supposed to be just another prison."

Shoulders slumping, Martin let his hands drop to his sides. "You can Google the official story about what happened to Mallory. Maybe you should. Learn something from it—she would've wanted that. Would've wanted her death—and her life—to be remembered. She wouldn't want you to make her same mistakes."

With that, he turned and strode away.

"HEARD YOU GOT BUSTED LAST NIGHT," MILES said as soon as Astrid took her seat at her computer terminal.

"No thanks to you."

He frowned. "What did I have to do with it?"

"You ratted me out."

He leaned back in his seat, smirking, and tented his fingers under his chin. "Snitches get stitches, don't you know? And I'm way too pretty for scars."

Astrid ignored him. She didn't believe him and didn't want to waste time arguing about it. Instead she logged into her computer, opened her search engine, and typed in Mallory's name along with "New Horizons," "mountain lion," and "mauling." *Why didn't I try looking her up sooner?*

"You think you're the only one who noticed Ozzie was unusually quiet last night?" Miles waited for a reply, but Astrid continued ignoring him. She read a few lines from an article on Mallory, and that was more than she needed to know. The girl's death had been gruesome and painful.

Miles huffed and leaned closer. "I'm sure Martin noticed too and went to check. It was just a matter of time before he busted you, anyway. Especially after what happened to . . ." He glanced away, then pretended to find something on his computer screen intensely interesting.

"After what happened to Mallory?" Astrid twisted her monitor around, so it partially faced Miles. She motioned to the screen and the search results listed there. "Martin told me about it. Told me to Google it, too."

He shrugged, feigning indifference, but his little speech hadn't sounded so indifferent. No, he'd sounded like he'd cared. But about who? Mallory? Astrid? Or was it all an act? More manipulation? Astrid shook her head, spun her monitor to the correct position, and tuned out Miles. He returned the favor.

As the morning progressed, Astrid lost herself in her schoolwork, but a memory of the howler cub in her dream swam through the back of her mind. Over and over it surfaced in her thoughts until she could no longer ignore it. Letting out an irritated sigh, she opened her web browser again. She couldn't focus on her schoolwork until she got the dream out of her head, and she couldn't do that until she gave it the attention her subconscious demanded. So, she Googled again, searching for information about Ozark Howler procreation habits.

The information she uncovered was limited and likely speculation, but it was all she had to go on. According to a site supposedly dedicated to sharing scientific facts about cryptids, Ozark Howlers rarely reproduced. Mothers were lucky to give birth to one baby in their lifetime. They formed tight bonds with their offspring and nurtured them well into adulthood.

Astrid followed more and more links, and fell down more rabbit holes, until she stumbled onto a local message board for cryptid hunters in her area.

Howler Cub Recovered from Woods Near Hwy 42

Her heart stopped. *That's near where Reggie said they'd found Ozzie!* She scrolled, reading faster and faster. Responses varied from disbelief to wonder to offers to purchase the cub from the original poster. Feverishly Astrid read each word, searching for clues and details about the creature's current whereabouts. She found the exact address in a post by someone who claimed to not only have the howler cub but was setting up an auction at his house to sell the baby to the highest bidder the very next afternoon.

Astrid's heart slammed into her throat and throbbed hotly. If the cub was real, and if it belonged to Ozzie, that left her almost no time to work out a solution that was anything other than desperate and mostly illegal. She'd sworn off a life of crime, but this wasn't about proving her independence while trying to earn the love of some god-awful, narcissistic boy. When her motives were selfless, exceptions could be made, couldn't they?

You've got to do something, McLean. And you better do it fast.

She read the cryptid hunter's post over and over, confirming details, talking herself into the beginnings of a plan.

This is probably a bad idea, she thought as she shut down her computer for lunch break. *I should listen to Martin. Stay in the house, keep myself out of trouble . . .*

She was still telling herself the same thing later that night as she packed her bookbag with a few necessities before cracking the window in her bedroom and stepping out onto the back-porch roof. She hated to think of Martin catching her sneaking out again. The consequences of a second violation would likely be something more detrimental to her future than damaging Martin's trust and being made to clean the kennels without any help for the next two weeks.

Keeping low, she toddled to a section where the gutter had fallen away. Gritty shingles rasped beneath her sneakers as she skootched to the edge. She lowered herself, took a deep breath, then twisted, easing her legs over the side of the roof. For a moment, as she dangled, she second-guessed herself and regretted her decision, but before she could clamber back up, her balance shifted. Gravity grabbed hold and yanked her down.

Oof! She landed on both feet, but her knees gave out from the force of her fall. She crumpled to her rear, rolled feet over head, and sprawled, catching her breath. "Ugh."

Once her heart had recovered from the shock of her unexpected circus stunts, she stood and checked herself for injuries. Her ankles and knees weren't happy, but she hadn't broken or sprained anything, and her backpack had taken the brunt of her fall. Brushing dry grass and dirt from her clothes, she studied the house's dark windows and peered into the shadows, searching for witnesses to her clumsy escape.

"*Boo,*" said a quiet voice.

Astrid's spine tried to claw its way free as she slapped a hand over her mouth, muffling the screech escaping from her throat.

A flashlight clicked on, illuminating Miles's face into a ghastly rictus. "Busted."

"You asshole." Astrid clutched at her chest as if trying to catch her racing heart. At this rate, she'd have a stroke before she ever made it off the property.

"You don't have a very high opinion of me, do you?" Miles jogged down the porch steps and joined her in the backyard, careful to keep enough distance to prevent her from easily reaching his nuts again. He had obviously learned not to underestimate her. The realization made her smile.

"What are you doing here?" she whispered harshly.

"Going with you."

"Who says I'm going anywhere?"

"Why the hell else would you be creeping out of your room the way you did in the middle of the night?" He pointed at the strap over her shoulder. "And you don't need a backpack if you're going to just hang out here in the backyard."

"Maybe I wanted to bring Ozzie a lot of marshmallows."

"Contrary to your assumption, McLean, I am not an idiot."

"So, just an asshole then. Got it."

"But not a stupid asshole." He grinned.

Astrid glowered. She hated when guys tried to be charming. Readjusting her backpack straps, she marched to Ozzie's kennel.

Miles followed. "Take me with you or I tell Martin."

She stopped and spun to face him. "I knew you were a snitch."

"I'm not." His flashlight illuminated his frown. "I'm just manipulative."

"You told on me before. That's how Martin busted me for being out here last night."

"I didn't tell on you. You were completely capable of getting caught on your own. In fact, you probably wound up at New Horizons because you suck at being sneaky."

She jabbed a sharp finger at Miles's chest. "I wound up here because I told the truth."

He grabbed her finger before she could poke him again. "Well, that was dumb. Who tells the truth?"

She yanked her finger free and knelt in front of Ozzie's kennel. "I don't know if you can understand me, but I'm going looking for your baby. I think I know where it is. Try not to die before I get back, okay?"

A pair of dim blue eyes appeared in the kennel's shadows. Ozzie whimpered, but it was so quiet Astrid wondered if she'd imagined it.

"A baby?" Miles asked, following Astrid as she stalked across the yard, heading for the gate to the front yard and the main road beyond.

"I think that's why she's so lifeless—she's heartbroken, and I don't think she's going to last much longer. I've got to try this. I don't know what else to do. I did some research online this afternoon—there're rumors that some backwoods idiot cryptid hunter found a howler cub near the site of Ozzie's accident. He's going to sell it in an auction tomorrow afternoon. I've got to get to it first."

"Who the hell wants a cryptid cub?"

"Same people who pay ridiculous money for tiger cubs I guess?" Astrid shrugged. "People like to own rare and unusual things. And they'll pay a lot for the privilege."

"Where do you think the cub is?"

"The guy swears he has it in a cage in his garage." *Why am I telling him all this? Maybe it's in case that cryptidiot catches me trying to break in and shoots me. At least someone will know where to start looking for my body. If anyone cares.*

"How are you going to get there?"

Astrid gave him a thumbs-up and a wink.

"Hitchhiking?" He sneered. "I mean, if you wanted to get yourself killed, there are faster ways . . ."

"I called Uber, idiot." She didn't have much money, but she got a few bucks from her mom every now and then. Maybe it was her mom's way of assuaging her guilt for abandoning her daughter. What else did she have to spend it on? "My ride should be here any second."

Miles said nothing but continued to trudge behind her as they approached the road.

"Why do you care anyway?" Astrid asked. "Ozzie's *my* responsibility."

"This is the least boring thing that has happened around here in months. There's no way you're leaving me behind."

"If we get caught, they'll kick you out, too."

At the end of the driveway, Miles turned off his flashlight and motioned for Astrid to follow him into the deeper gloom beneath a nearby maple. "They won't just kick me out. They'll send me to jail. You too, I bet. So why risk it?"

Astrid shrugged. Maybe it had to do with wanting to preserve something's innocence, even if she couldn't preserve her own. Maybe it was about getting justice for those who couldn't get it for themselves. Maybe she wanted to see a mother who actually gave a damn be reunited with her kid. Or maybe she was just bored like Miles was. "What did you do to wind up here?" she asked instead.

"Oh no." His shadow shook its head. "You don't get to ask me that unless you're willing to answer in return."

"Fair enough." A flicker of headlights announced the arrival of her car and driver. "Wave your flashlight so he knows where we are."

Miles obliged and a little white Prius pulled up to their hiding spot. "You call for a ride?" the driver asked as Astrid and Miles piled into the backseat.

"Yup." Astrid clutched her backpack against her chest.

"Buckle up." The driver, a young white guy with a bowl-shaped haircut, tapped his screen. "This looks like a bumpy ride. Priuses aren't really made for off-roading, you know?"

"What do you mean?" Astrid asked.

"The address you gave me is at the end of a long gravel road." He turned in his seat to face them and narrowed his eyes. "This place . . ." He gestured toward the house. "It's some kind of halfway house for, like, troubled teens, right?"

Astrid said nothing. Miles shifted nervously in his seat.

"Are you two doing something . . . ?" The driver waggled his hand in a vague gesture.

"What?" Astrid asked.

"Illegal?"

Her throat went dry. "No, we're, um, buying something from a craigslist ad."

"This late at night? And I'm supposed to believe a couple of teen felons?" He arched an eyebrow.

Astrid reached for the door handle. "Look, if you don't want to—"

"I didn't say I didn't want to. But there's a *fee* for taking on added risks."

"You're extorting us?" Miles asked. He sounded slightly impressed.

"Why should I risk my neck without compensation?"

"I don't have much money." Astrid patted her backpack. "Took most of what I had just to cover the cost of this ride."

"Most?" The driver blinked slowly. "But not all."

"We don't have to do this." Miles squeezed her shoulder.

It was tempting to give up, to not give this asshole her last dollar, to tell herself it was probably an impossible task anyway, doomed to fail. But then she'd have to face herself in the mirror tomorrow morning, and that chore was already hard enough without adding this defeat to the list of reasons to hate herself. She exhaled a noisy sigh. "Yeah, we do."

She rifled through her bag, found the small stash of cash she had secreted in an inner pocket, and showed it to the driver. "But if I give you this, you have to wait for us and drive us back here when we're done."

The driver hesitated, but he greedily eyed the cash. "Yeah, whatever. I guess."

"I feel so reassured," she said, deadpan, but he swiped the bills from her fingers before she could change her mind.

Silently, the car accelerated away from New Horizons, and Astrid released a breath of relief. They'd gotten away. *But that was the easy part.*

Retrieving the howler pup and returning to New Horizons without getting caught would be the hard part.

As if reading her mind, Miles turned serious and lowered his voice. "You think Martin won't notice a new creature in the kennels that wasn't there yesterday?"

"I'll burn that bridge when I cross it," she said.

"I don't think that's how that saying goes."

"It does if you're me."

When they were still several hundred yards away from their destination, Astrid asked the driver to stop and let them out. "Turn your headlights off," she said. "If we're not back in fifteen minutes, you can leave without us." Honestly, she thought they'd be lucky if he didn't leave the second they were out of sight.

"You're making this up as you go, aren't you?" Miles asked as they crept along the dark road, continuing until a pair of illuminated windows set way back from the road revealed the location of Astrid's target.

"Why do you say that?" Astrid glanced at him from the corner of her eye before focusing again on their destination. Gravel shifted and crunched beneath her feet, and the air smelled like rotting leaves. Cicadas and tree frogs screamed like an orchestra of screeching violins.

"Do you even have a plan?"

"Break in, grab the cub. Get out without getting caught."

"Not much of a plan."

She gestured at the Prius behind them. "You can wait in the car if you don't like it."

"Didn't say I didn't like it." He sounded uncharacteristically appreciative.

Astrid eyed him suspiciously. "Why are you being so decent all of a sudden?"

He shrugged. "It's just for the short-term, until we see this through. Don't worry, I'll be back to my regular assholery tomorrow."

They both fell silent as they approached the house. A single utility pole in the backyard supported a bright light that illuminated a small one-story ranch with a sagging front porch and a detached garage. Astrid's heart leaped. If the guy who'd posted on the forum had been telling the truth, he was supposedly keeping the cub in that outbuilding—and she preferred breaking into garages over breaking into homes any day.

Strike that. She preferred not breaking into anything at all, but for the sake of Ozzie's wellbeing, she'd fall back on old, bad habits just this once.

Just this once. That's how Christopher had talked her into breaking into their first house together. But of course there had been more than one. She was certain the words inscribed on the first steppingstone on the path to damnation were, "Just this once."

"Put this over your face." Astrid withdrew a t-shirt from her bookbag and passed it to Miles. She tugged out a scarf and draped it over her head, leaving only her eyes visible.

"A t-shirt?" He eyed the pink fabric.

"I didn't know I was going to have a last-minute sidekick."

Miles grunted and yanked the shirt over his head, drawing the collar just below his eyes and leaving the rest to cover his nose and mouth.

They tiptoed through the backyard without detection and stopped at the outbuilding. A padlock and chain around the door handles slowed the execution of Astrid's plan but didn't derail it. She'd come prepared with the makeshift tools she'd purloined from New Horizons' kitchen and from Martin's office during their "talk" earlier that afternoon.

"How do you know how to pick a lock?" Miles asked.

"You think I wound up at New Horizons for picking daisies?"

"That's the first hint you've given me about what you did. Does that mean we're friends now?"

Astrid ignored him as she worked her homemade tools into the padlock. *Wish I'd stumbled on a pair of bolt cutters in Martin's office instead.* She pointed to her bookbag. "There's a baggie with some lunch meat in there. Get it out, will you?"

"You need a snack?" Miles rooted through her bag.

"It's not for me."

"You think something's going to attack us?"

"Maybe. Or something might just decide to quietly chew on some roast beef rather than alerting the people in the house to our presence." Astrid had brought the meat in case there were dogs guarding the yard, but they'd lucked out on that count.

Miles withdrew the bag of roast beef and held it up like a prize. "You have *a lot* more of a plan that you'd led me to believe."

"Haven't you learned by now not to underestimate me?" She gave a meaningful look at his crotch.

It was too dark to tell, but she suspected Miles was blushing.

The padlock clicked and fell open. Smiling, Astrid loosened the chains. "Still got it."

"Takes more than a B and E conviction to wind up at New Horizons."

She was getting weary of his prodding, and maybe that's why she gave in. "Then how 'bout accessory to murder?"

"Really?" His surprise was genuine.

"Pleaded down from being an accomplice."

Miles's silence felt like a blanket of ice on her shoulders, but she didn't care what he was thinking. There were more urgent matters to deal with. She tugged on the outbuilding doors and the smell of wild animal, urine, feces, blood, and unwashed fur smashed into her like a sledgehammer. She gagged.

"Ugh, it smells like death." Miles sounded like he was pinching his nose. Astrid shifted her flashlight beam and found he was, in fact, squeezing his nostrils shut.

She inhaled a deep breath, held it, and stepped inside.

Something whimpered at her feet. Astrid's flashlight illuminated a cage on the floor. Behind the bars, the creature from her dream stared at her with blue eyes that were dull like Ozzie's, full of heartbreak and despair.

Astrid snapped her fingers at Miles. "Marshmallows. Hurry."

"What about the roast beef?"

"Roast beef was for any hypothetical guard dog situations. Howlers prefer marshmallows. Trust me."

He dug through the backpack again, pulled out a plastic bag, and tossed it to her. She shook out several marshmallows and tossed them into the cage. The tiny howler, with black fur that had lost its sheen and little nubs showing where its horns would grow in, sniffed at her offering. A tiny tongue poked out and swiped up the treats.

"Let's get it and go, okay?" Miles glanced uneasily over his shoulder. "We've been lucky for way too long, and our luck's going to run out any minute."

Astrid clenched her flashlight in her teeth and put her tools to work on the smaller padlock at the door of the cub's cage. Her hands shook a little, slowing her down. Miles's panicked breathing on her neck didn't help either, but she managed to open the lock. She spat out her flashlight. "There's a blanket in the backpack."

"Already got it." He shoved the bundle of fleece at her.

Astrid swung open the door. "C'mon baby. Let's go see your momma."

The cub cringed back and quivered. Astrid sucked a tooth. "Sorry, but we don't have time for proper introductions. You don't have to trust me, but please don't eat me." She grabbed the fleece blanket and tossed it over the cowering cub like a net.

It whimpered, a sharp, sad sound. Astrid leaned in, swaddled the blanket tightly around the cub to limit its ability to scratch or bite, and swiped the bundle into her arms. "Alright, let's get out of—"

"Hey! What do you two think you're doing?" In the doorway stood a mountain of a man, bearded and in flannel pajamas and unlaced boots. "You think you can just steal from me?"

Before Astrid could overcome her shock, Miles was shoving her shoulder and whispering in her ear. "Go. I'll distract him."

"What are you going to—"

"Go, I said!" He shoved her again.

She stumbled toward the door and the huge man standing in her way. He lunged for her. Something swished past her head. The object struck the huge man in his forehead. He grunted and tumbled back, clutching his face. Astrid clutched the howler cub tighter to her chest. Thankfully it was cooperating—too afraid or too weak to fight her, she didn't know—and she ran through the yard, her gaze trained ahead, searching the dark for signs of the Prius's taillights and hoping the driver hadn't abandoned her the way she'd just abandoned Miles.

That thought brought her to a stop at the edge of the woods beyond the house's front yard. She turned back, searching for Miles, and spotted him swinging a shovel at the mountainous man's head. The man dodged, but Miles adjusted his trajectory mid-swing and took his opponent out at his knees. The huge man fell so hard, Astrid expected to feel an earthquake.

"Come on!" If they could outrun their pursuer, they could reach the car and make their getaway without the need for more violence. The thought of bloodshed made her want to throw up. *Puke later. Run now.*

Miles dropped his shovel and ran.

Hoping he would catch up—he was longer-legged and wasn't toting a twenty-pound howler cub, after all—Astrid raced ahead. When she reached the gravel road, she searched for the Prius, but didn't see it. Her heart sank, but she kept running. Footsteps pounded behind her, crunching on gravel as Miles caught up. She hoped it was Miles, anyway. She thought it unlikely the huge man from the house could run that fast.

"H-how did you learn . . ." she panted, "to fight . . . like that?"

"Abusive stepdad," he said. "Let me take the cub. It must be heavy."

"No . . ." Astrid's lungs were on fire. She wasn't much into cardio training. *Maybe I should take up jogging if I'm going to be all vigilante like this, though.* "I got it. But . . . where's the car?"

Miles searched the road ahead of them. "There." He pointed. "He's there."

"Oh, thank God." Astrid slowed her pace. She had to, or she would've passed out. "I was afraid he'd left us."

When they reached the back door, Miles opened it for her. Astrid fell into the backseat, careful not to drop the baby howler. Miles squeezed in beside her. She shifted over, making room for him.

"Go," Miles ordered. "Go quick."

The driver put the pedal to the metal, or so Astrid assumed. It was hard to tell with electric cars. But they picked up speed and zoomed down the gravel road, bumping and jarring but making a steady getaway.

Miles craned his neck, glancing out the back window. "I don't see him," he whispered.

Astrid sighed and let her head fall back against the headrest. Against her chest, the baby howler was snoring.

WITH AN HOUR OR SO REMAINING BEFORE sunrise, Astrid was relieved to see no lights on in the New Horizons house when their driver dropped them off at the driveway. No police cruisers with flashing lights were waiting to take them to the county jail for parole violations.

Astrid readjusted the weight of the cub in her arms as she and Miles skulked through the dark, tiptoeing toward the backyard. "So, you're a ninja with a shovel, huh?" she whispered.

"You either spend the rest of your life taking a beating or you learn to fight back. Sometimes you can take it too far. You're not the only one with a homicide on your record."

Astrid swallowed past the sudden tightness in her throat. "Your stepdad?"

"Self-defense. I did it while he was asleep, so technically it was murder. But in the end, it was always going to be him or me. I decided it wasn't going to be me."

"Technically, I didn't kill anyone," she said. Miles's confession, his moment of vulnerability, was contagious, it seemed. "But I was there when my boyfriend did. We thought the house we were breaking into was empty. We were wrong. I ran. He did too, but not before he killed them. I didn't even know he had a gun. He came out of the house covered in their blood." So much blood. "First chance I got, when I could get away from him, I went to the police and confessed and turned him in." Her throat burned with tears and guilt and shame and bile. "It's . . . it's the only reason I got a second chance."

"Damn," Miles said on a quiet breath.

"You have leverage on me now."

"We have leverage on each other." They stepped through the gate into the backyard. "But I promise not to use it."

"Does that make us friends?" She giggled nervously. It was either that or cry. She didn't want to cry in front of Miles, though. He hadn't earned her tears yet.

"I told you I'll go back to being an asshole again tomorrow." He laughed coldly. "Nothing's changed."

Everything's changed, Astrid thought, but she didn't say it aloud because at that moment she spotted two figures waiting at Ozzie's kennel. "Shit."

"Wait." Miles squeezed her shoulder. "Look who it is."

Astrid narrowed her eyes and looked harder. She realized she had terrible night vision. And she might be a bit myopic. *Maybe I need glasses?* "Reggie? . . . and Henry?"

"What are you two doing here?" Miles asked once they'd closed the remaining distance. He kept his voice low, almost a whisper.

"We could ask the same of you." Though Henry was also careful to keep quiet, worry was clear in their tone. "Where have you been?" They focused on Astrid. "Martin did a bed check. I had to lie and say you were in the bathroom. With the lights off. Because you had a headache and cramps."

"Thanks. Sorry you had to lie for me." Astrid readjusted the weight of her bundle. Her arm muscles were burning.

"I didn't *have* to. I just didn't want to see you kicked out so soon after getting here. It was nice having someone to talk to. Carmen's not much of a conversational roommate if you hadn't noticed."

"Whatcha got there?" His curiosity piqued, Reggie pointed at Astrid's bundle.

As if it knew it had everyone's attention, the howler cub whimpered. The blanket fell away, and its fuzzy black head popped out.

Reggie gasped. "How . . . ?"

"It's a long story." Astrid stepped around him and approached Ozzie's gate. "Can you open this for me?"

"I don't have the keys. After he busted you, Martin said he wanted to 'hold onto them for a while.'"

Astrid sighed and rolled her eyes. She shoved the cub into Reggie's arms. He took it by reflex, stuttering a few half-hearted objections before falling silent. Flexing her fingers, she shoved her open hand at Miles. "Tools please."

He rooted through the bookbag and found her lock picks, then held the flashlight while she worked.

The commotion outside her kennel caught Ozzie's attention. She awoke and limped into the little patch of dirt between her house and the gate in her fence. Catching its mother's scent, the cub wriggled in Reggie's arms and whimpered again.

"*Shhh*, baby," he said, glancing nervously toward the house. "You're going to give us all away."

The lock clicked. Astrid pushed the gate open and stood aside.

But instead of releasing the cub as she'd expected, Reggie pushed the wriggling baby into Astrid's arms. "You took the risks, didn't you? You should get the reward."

Astrid glanced at Miles as she snugged the cub close to her chest. He'd taken risks, too, and had saved her from a potentially terrible fate. She owed him big-time for that. But the cub heist and cryptid family reunion had been her plan. He'd only invited himself along because he was bored, not because he had an emotional investment in the outcome like she did. Was a guy like Miles even capable of emotional investments? Or was he simply a darker and broodier version of Christopher?

Miles quirked a questioning eyebrow at her. Realizing she'd been staring, Astrid blinked and focused on the squirming cub. Ozzie prowled closer, her blue-eyed gaze intent on the bundle in Astrid's arms. Holding her breath, she loosened the blanket and crouched.

The tiny howler leaped from her arms and zoomed to Ozzie's side. Mother and cub reunited in a blur of blue eyes, black fur, and happy whimpers and squeaks. Ozzie paused in her excitement long enough to swipe her long, wet tongue across Astrid's cheek. It seemed like an expression of genuine, if slobbery, gratitude.

Tears burned in her throat, but she swallowed them back. It would take more than one wet cryptid kiss to make her to cry in front of an audience, even if this audience was a group of kids who would probably understand everything she was feeling.

Amazement and wonder showed in Reggie's wide eyes as he watched Ozzie and her cub nuzzling each other. "How'd you know?"

Astrid tapped her temple. "I kept an open mind, I guess you could say."

"But how'd you find the cub?"

"I'll tell you all about it." She closed Ozzie's gate and set the lock in place. "*Tomorrow.* For now, I think we should get back inside before Martin finds us."

"How are we going to explain the sudden appearance of a new cryptid in Ozzie's kennel?" Henry asked as the group started toward the darkened house.

We? Astrid inspected the word as though someone had offered her a rare gem.

She'd never been part of a team before—the foster care system wasn't exactly known for promoting loyalty, and her relationship with Christopher had been more dysfunctional codependency than partnership. But now her heart was opening to the idea of belonging to something bigger than herself. "We" could mean something good for a change.

Realizing Henry was still waiting for her answer, Astrid cleared her throat. "They're mysterious creatures by nature, right? No one fully understands them and what kinds of abilities they have. How do we know Ozzie didn't send out telepathic messages that her cub used to find her?"

"You think Martin will buy that?" Henry asked.

"I think he's smart enough to know he can't prove otherwise," Reggie said, accepting Astrid's explanation. For now. "You have to give him some credit. He's not actually looking for reasons to kick us out. Give him a chance and you'll see."

How did a kid with so much compassion and wisdom end up in a place like this? Astrid wanted to know what Reggie's criminal offense had been, but she didn't dare ask. Unlike Miles, she respected other people's boundaries.

She didn't know if Reggie's claims about Martin were true or not, but she didn't find Martin waiting for them at the back door or inside the house. She and the others made it back to their hallway without getting caught. And whether that meant Martin didn't know, or didn't want to know, what they'd been up to, she didn't really care.

She caught Miles's shoulder and squeezed. "Uh, thanks, I guess," she said when he turned to face her. "Probably couldn't have done it without you."

"*Definitely* couldn't have done it without me." He shook his head, and a dark lock of hair fell over his eye. Astrid absolutely did not want to smooth it back into place.

Instead she offered him her hand. He bit his bottom lip and studied her fingers. His hesitation reminded her of her own uncertainty the night Reggie had offered the back-door key, as though he knew she was offering more than a simple handshake and was trying to decide whether he wanted to accept it.

Finally, his lips curled up at the corners and he took her hand. They shook, and he held her fingers a beat longer than necessary.

"Here's to us being *not* friends," Astrid said, biting back a smile.

"Not-friends." He winked. "Got it."

Ignoring the warm feeling blooming in her chest, she retreated into her room. Henry had already climbed into the top bunk. "Thanks again for covering for me."

They yawned. "Play D&D with me and Kanesha and Jasmine tomorrow, and we'll call it even."

"I don't know how to play."

"I'll teach you."

Astrid figured that was fair and crawled into bed. Maybe she'd like *Dungeons and Dragons.* Maybe there were a lot of things out there she'd like if she gave them a chance, including Miles.

Lying back, she stared into the darkness under Henry's bunk, focusing on the place where she knew Mallory's name was inscribed. She rolled over and searched the floor until her hand found her backpack. After digging out her flashlight, she turned it on, then unearthed a black permanent marker from the bag's front pocket. When she uncapped it, the ink's pungent scent tingled in her nose.

Astrid was here, too, she scribbled on the bed frame next to Mallory's inscription.

And maybe, if I'm lucky, I'll get to stay.

Astrid turned out her light, pulled up her covers, and rolled over. Faster than she had in years, she fell asleep.

She dreamed of blue eyes, black fur, and warm snuggles.

She dreamed of comfort and warmth . . . and hope.

INSIDE THE NIGHT

MADELINE DYER

ier

nd

on,

or

fter

to

Local Schoolgirl Found Dead in Suicide

BLACKTHORNE—The body of eighteen-year-old Maliah Swan was found in Blackthorne Woods in the early hours of yesterday morning, below the west tower of Blackthorne Castle. Mr. Reynolds, head-teacher at Blackthorne Community College—England's highest-achieving school for those aged 11-18 years—said Maliah was a promising student who had her sights set on Oxford University. Her loss will be sorely felt by all who knew her.

ONE

In the darkest corner of the darkest town, a small boy stands with his hands raised up to the sky. Allie watches him from her window, her cigarette smoldering in her fingers. She knows she shouldn't be able to see him, not when it's so dark, but the Power has done strange things to her eyes. She only has to hone in on something—*someone*—in the darkness, and her vision gets brighter, sharper, clearer. Allie almost wishes it wouldn't. It would be easier not to watch the transformations taking place. But she is transfixed, as always.

Allie takes a puff of her cigarette. The smoke hits the back of her throat, gritty, raw. She's still not used to it. But Riko suggested it would help calm her anxiety.

No one should do anything that Riko says, especially not Allie. He's an O'Donovan. She doesn't even know how she can look at Riko so calmly each day and not want to kill him. But she does look at him calmly, and she takes his advice. Three days ago, she took the cigarette pack he offered her, too.

Allie mused over that gift for a long time, and she still thinks about it now, as she tries to work out whether the cigarettes are a peace offering. Or maybe even a message that says, 'I believe you.' Riko might feel guilty about what Kyle did to her, about how the whole town treated her. And if he does, maybe that means not all the O'Donovans are bad.

Or maybe she's thinking too deeply about all of this. What Kyle did happened four months ago, after all, and with everything that's now happening with the stonifications, she's sure Riko's not giving it any thought. At any rate, she supposes he's right: smoking does calm her anxiety. Because she's not shaking with fear and constantly thinking about Ellie as she watches the small boy in the street. Sweat isn't running down her spine in torrents, sticking her shirt to her back. She's just .

. . there. Watching it all, a picture of calmness. Even though she's not really feeling it. What's happening can't sink into her now, because the cigarettes have provided a barrier. A numbness. Or maybe it's the alcohol that did that. She's not really sure.

When her mind is numb, she can't think about that night, the night it all started. And when she doesn't think about that night, it's like it never actually happened. Like Kyle never held her down on the scratchy carpet that smelt of cat piss while he mocked her, called her *baby*. The haze of the nicotine and alcohol rewrites the past, and Allie likes that. She should be in charge of her own story.

The boy's trying to move his arms—she can see the concentration on his face. He's not a screamer, and she's glad. Those are always the worst to watch. By now, he's probably too far gone. He'll no longer know his name, no longer know where he is. All he'll know is that he must lift his hands to the sky. Because that's what all of them do, the Night Worshippers. His fingers are offerings to whatever being is up there, the Power that is getting stronger and stronger. The Power that appeared eighteen nights ago.

Sometimes, Allie thinks she must be immune, that she won't ever succumb to the Power—not the way the majority of the town's other residents have. She'll never become a statue— she's convinced of it, at times. Because the Power's given her night vision instead. And it wouldn't do that if it was just going to claim her anyway, would it?

But no one knows.

Allie, her best friend Aion, Riko, and the others in their team appear to be the only survivors in Blackthorne. There aren't many people left alive in England now—most fled after the second night and most who stayed became Worshippers. Of the survivors—or the stupid remainers, depending on who you ask—Allie is the only one with a power. Not that she's told anyone.

So maybe others have the powers too. The best-kept secrets, because everyone's looking for someone to blame. The witch-hunts started after the third night—roving gangs of men and women who kill anyone they think could be behind the stonifications. There are still angry mobs out there, even if many of the hunters have been stonified.

The witch-hunts may not be happening near her town anymore—the last reports she heard were that the hunters were going north—but she's not stupid. Tell someone she has a gift? She'd be the next poor sod hunted down—and she wouldn't put it past Riko not to kill her himself. He's an O'Donovan, even if he does seem a bit nicer than Kyle and the others. He—or whichever hunter came after her—would think she deserved it, that somehow, this was all stemming from her, just because she's got a power and everyone calls the thing in the sky *the Power*. People invariably see patterns and connections where there aren't any.

That's what Riko's always saying, anyhow. He's the leader of Allie's team.

Only a few days in or so, after it became obvious that the Power that had taken over the night wasn't going away, the teams started to spring up across the country. The police and the army and the scientists weren't doing a great deal. The government was running daily conferences and live press announcements of their proposed actions—until the prime minister himself turned to stone on camera, with the whole country watching. Allie laughed darkly when that happened—it was the PM's own fault for doing the live update at night. He should've known better.

The stonification's only happening in England and Wales—so far. Twitter's full of Americans laughing about it. Only last week, a group of New Zealand teenagers made a video where they pretended to have caught the 'stone disease' too. They just wanted to go viral as the first case of stonification outside of the UK—but it was clear by their laughter that they didn't really believe it. Allie doesn't understand why other countries aren't helping them.

In Blackthorne, Riko was the one to gather up all the survivors. When he found Allie, he went white. Very white. Like he'd seen a ghost.

"What?" Allie said defensively. She wasn't pleased to see him—an O'Donovan. Sure, he'd not been directly involved in the bullying, in trying to discredit her worth to the whole town, but he was still part of that family.

"I thought you were dead?" He swiped at his head before shaking it hard. "I'm sure you were. You . . ." His face paled. "No . . . that's not . . . that can't be right," he said, his eyes on her. "Is the Power affecting anyone else's memory?"

Allie didn't know what he was talking about—and everyone else looked at him like he'd lost his mind. A moment later, he dropped the subject, and didn't bring it up again—but his eyes lingered on her for the rest of the night, heavy with suspicion and lit with a hint of fear. Sometimes she catches him looking at her that way still.

It makes her furious. By rights, Allie should be suspicious of *him*.

She finishes her cigarette, trying not to think of what her parents would say if they saw her drinking and smoking, as she watches the boy's final moments. As always, his hands are the last to turn to stone. The boy's fingers twitch twice, then no more.

The night air is cold through her open window. It is still outside. Silent. Until she hears voices.

Three men in their twenties, all drunk and loud, are staggering toward the boy. They see him, thanks to the flashlights on their phones, and they're laughing and shouting in a foreign language, until their flashlights flicker out.

Tourists, Allie thinks, darkly. Blackthorne still gets a lot of them now. Before, holidaymakers would come to see Blackthorne Castle—the oldest semi-ruined castle in Devon, infused with mythology and stories. But now everywhere in Blackthorne is a destination because people want to see the town where the stonifications started. Tour companies charge boatfuls of curious tourists extortionate amounts to cross the English Channel to see the "Land of the Petrified."

There are so many national and international visitors to Devon and elsewhere now, all wanting to visit the stone people. Tourists aren't affected, so long as they leave by nightfall. At night, anyone in the area is fair game.

A lot of the tour companies even supply their clients with booze; it's no wonder half of the tourists never leave, not when they're too inebriated to remember that they need to leave before night falls. Or maybe some are just cocky and think it won't affect them. That because they're not from England they'll be safe—but they never are. It doesn't matter where you're from, it just matters where you are when night arrives. Allie can't imagine what sort of person would set up tours and sell people tickets to see this, knowing their clients will be in danger if they don't get back to the boat in time.

And Allie's town isn't anywhere near the sea.

"Damn it," one of the men mutters, shaking his phone. But the phone is dead.

All their phones are dead now. It's what happens at night. Cellphones die—sooner, if you're outside. The indoor ones will splutter out by midnight too. Come the next morning, they're all fine, though, because that's when the Power's sleeping.

Silence falls.

And they know what's coming. Everyone knows.

Allie's kidneys hurt a little more than usual as she watches them. She didn't think she'd enjoy watching this—but she does, in a dark, weird kind of way. Something that she'd never admit. She knows men like these—the type who think they own everything, who think they're entitled to girls, who think they're the bee's knees.

Allie wouldn't say she's a violent person; she's only wished death upon three people, and one of them she didn't even really mean it. But she finds she likes watching these men as they run from the darkest corner of the darkest town, because she knows what's coming.

And so do they.

It's almost funny, that they think they can escape it.

Because no one can.

No one outruns the curse once they've offered themselves to the night.

TWO

"All across England we have reports of more of these *stonification* incidents," the reporter on the 10 o'clock news says. He's a good-looking man, but he looks scared now. Worried. He's speaking from France though. He'll be safe there. The Power's only in England. For now—because Allie is sure that one day, it'll spread. She's not sure why she thinks that, she just sort of feels it—and so far, she's been right about how it progressed, starting off only in her town, radiating outward, reaching the nearest city, then swallowing the county, before pockets across the whole of England started succumbing to it.

"The curse has already decimated the epicenter of its origin," the reporter continues.

Decimated the epicenter of its origin. Allie snorts. She's still alive, and her town's classed within the epicenter location. And she's not the only one. There are seven others on her team.

If they survive the night. She swallows hard. She doesn't like being alone in the evenings now—wrapped up in duvets, flinching at the slightest creak of a floorboard. The days are okay—because that's when she sees the rest of her team. When Riko allocates them all jobs and when they pretend like they're making progress fighting the Power in the sky.

In the day, Allie can pretend she's stronger than she is. But at night, she only has her cigarettes and booze, pilfered from the now-almost-empty supermarket shelves, and the TV for a distraction until the signal disappears. The welcome, numbing haze isn't enough to stop her feeling scared then. At night, Allie wishes someone in her household was still alive, so she'd have company.

She taps her foot as she watches the rest of the news on her phone. Then her alarm blares. Time for her meds.

After she's taken her cefalexin and methenamine hippurate, and forced down an apple because the cefalexin is always easier on her gut if she takes it with food, she checks the websites that log all the incidences of whatever it is that's happening to everyone here. The transformation has got various names: stonification, becoming stoned (that's her favorite), possession by the beast, petrification, succumbing to the curse, becoming a Night Worshipper. No one really knows what to call it.

If you'd told her this would happen a year ago, Allie would have laughed at you and asked what you'd taken. Not now though. Not when she's seen what the Power—as everyone is calling it, after the sky got darker that first night and a sonic boom went off—did to Ellie, her older sister. Graham, Blackthorne's greengrocer, found Ellie after her possession, on the morning of day two. She'd been one of the victims of the first night, along with seven-hundred-odd other residents.

Allie looks toward the cupboard under the stairs, where Ellie now lives. It hadn't been easy getting her in there. The statues are heavy, and most people leave them wherever they are when they get cursed now. It was only after that first night that people desperately tried to bring their loved ones back into their homes.

Allie and her father hadn't spoken about it—moving Ellie wasn't a decision they'd come to together over a cup of coffee. It had been a split-second decision, after Graham had phoned them to say he'd found Ellie, and yes, he was afraid it had happened to her too. *Terribly sorry*, he'd said when Allie and her father had reached Regent Street.

It had been strange, looking at Ellie like that. She didn't look like Allie's sister anymore—not when her eyes were gray. When all of her was gray and solid. Stone. A statue wearing clothes.

Her dad had sworn a lot when they were moving her, and Ellie's arm had banged against the inside of the front door, chipping three of her fingers and causing a crack to spread around her wrist. Allie often wonders what her mother would say if she saw the careless way her daughter had been brought back into the house. Maybe she'd wish that she'd taken Ellie and Allie with her two years ago when she'd fled to France to escape Allie's dad's alcoholism. Instead, she'd only taken Sarah, Allie's oldest sister.

Allie doesn't know why her mum left the two of them behind. She tries to pretend she doesn't think about why her mum hasn't been in contact now, either. The woman's probably eating cheeses and croissants and whatever else the French eat, watching all the drama unfold in Blackthorne and thinking that both Allie and Ellie are dead. Gone. Stoned. That's why her mum hasn't come for her—because she thinks she's too late. That's what Allie tells herself in the small moments where she wonders.

Now, Allie's coat is draped over Ellie's arm. Hides the damage to her wrist. Plus, it's convenient because her sister makes a good coat rack. And her dad isn't here now to tell her to *show more respect*. He's outside. Forever stuck looking up at the gutters. She'd told him not to leave the house. Not when it was starting to get dark. But he'd insisted on day five. Always thought he knew best on everything.

Allie looks at the clock. Sunrise isn't until 7:25 tomorrow. Nine and a half hours to go. She stares around the room, at the peeling paint, sick of the four walls. It should be easy to stay inside at night, knowing what can happen if you don't. But it isn't.

Every night, the Power turns people into Night Worshippers. The first ones it gets are always those who are not in their own homes. Whether they're in the streets or fields or in other people's houses, the Power gets them. It's as if being inside your own house provides some kind of protective ward.

But now the Power must be getting hungrier—or stronger—because it's started summoning people from their homes. The first time this happened, Allie got hysterical—insisting it didn't matter if the other members of their team stuck to their own houses at night, demanding for someone to stay with her—but Aion calmed her down. Told her it made sense for them to return to their own houses at night in case the wards still offered some protection. Allie trusts Aion, and she agreed. So now she stays in her house in the middle of town, and everyone else stays in their houses, and she hopes that the Power's not feeling greedy.

Allie's arms and legs itch and feel fizzy. Too much pent-up energy. She wants to run and run. She used to love running at night, with Aion. The two of them would jog on the moors, practicing for their cross-country competitions.

But that was before Allie got her kidney problems. Now, some days, she can hardly move because of the pain.

And, in any case, nightly runs have stopped now.

Everything's stopped.

People stay inside at night. People try to flee the country in the day, or, if they're remainers like Allie, they gather food from the shops with broken windows. They meet in houses as they try to come up with plans to beat the Power, to save the already stoned, to make life go back the way it was.

Allie misses school. Misses the days when her only worries were getting Mr. Richards's homework done in time, and whether or not Carly and the other popular girls were going to pick on her that day, and whether her father would be drunk when he eventually got home. She even misses all the endless doctors and hospital appointments. Her illness feels even more scary now it's not being monitored.

ALLIE WANTED TO BE AN ARTIST, BEFORE ALL this started. When she was often bedbound due to pain, she'd doodle in her sketchbooks. She was fascinated with Greek mythology—Medusa, most of all—and she drew her all the time.

A year ago, when she was sixteen, Allie's art class started studying Greek myths too. Allie was delighted. Drawing these figures was what she was good at.

Ms. Symons, the art teacher, assigned each student what she called a 'character'—one of the gods or goddesses, deities, Titans, giants, or mortals. Allie was disappointed to get Penelope rather than Medusa, but nonetheless, she sat next to Aion and tried to stay out of the firing line of Carly and her gang, who loved to throw paint at anyone who wasn't wearing the latest designer clothes.

"Oh, it's hardly made your outfit worse," Carly would say with a snigger, after she'd just pelted a red blob of acrylic at some poor kid's hoodie.

Carly mocked everyone—but for some reason, she hated Allie most of all. She made fun of Allie's father's drinking and her mother's desertion, getting the whole of her gang to join in. It had been humiliating, and even though Allie wasn't violent by nature, in that instant she wanted Carly to die. She didn't want to *kill* her—not like how she'd later want to stab Kyle— just for something bad to happen to her. Like for her to fall down a well. Or go missing.

Just something.

There was only one person that Carly and her gang never touched: Kyle O'Donovan. He was the most popular boy in their year. The best-looking—many of the girls agreed upon that. And he was an O'Donovan—the town's most influential family. Most people in Blackthorne practically worshipped them.

Allie and Aion often sat behind Kyle in art class, as if proximity to him could protect them, like an invisible forcefield. That was, until Carly got wise to their game and had one of her minions summon Kyle to the supply cupboard, under the promise of making out with him. Then Carly flicked black ink all over Aion and Allie, laughing.

Covered in ink, Allie stood up, anger fueling her as she stared across at Carly with her perfect hair and perfect skin—

never a pimple in sight—and perfect clothes. A burning desire rose in her to inflict hurt and rage, to make Carly pay.

But *of course* she didn't do anything because Allie was meek then, scared of Carly and the other kids from old money. Instead, she looked down, right at Kyle's artwork. To Allie's disgust, he'd been assigned Medusa. He'd drawn her severed head in copper tones—and it was this sheen that had caught her attention, as if Medusa herself had called Allie's name. The snakes of her hair almost seemed alive. Little snakes with little thoughts and feelings.

Fury filled her. That wasn't Kyle's original work—that was hers! Allie had drawn that exact portrait last year—the same style, image, and media. The old art teacher had dished out so much praise when Allie'd turned it in as her homework response to the prompt of 'beauty.' Everyone had seen it, including Kyle—he'd always been in her classes, right from when they were little children at the primary school. He'd even admired her work, saying the snakes were cool—the nicest thing he'd ever said to Allie. Everyone knew he was obsessed with snakes. Even had a pet one.

But now he'd copied her, and Allie was shaking with anger.

Leaving the copying aside, what had Ms. Symons been thinking, giving Medusa to someone like Kyle? The Gorgon should've been assigned to Allie, not him. Or to any of the girls, apart from Carly and her gang.

When Ms. Symons assigned Medusa to Kyle, she'd told the class Medusa was a symbol of female empowerment, but Allie knew the truth: Medusa might be strong, but she was also a victim. She'd been raped by Poseidon and became pregnant with Pegasus and Chrysaor. But was Poseidon punished? Of course not! It was Medusa who was punished. Athena transformed her beautiful hair into snakes and gave her the curse of turning anyone she looked at to stone. And then, if that wasn't bad enough, poor Medusa was beheaded by Perseus, an arrogant and entitled man who'd held onto her head, using it and her petrifying gaze as a weapon.

Kyle wouldn't understand Medusa's trauma. He'd just think her powers were cool and awesome and keep her silent, an image on his page. If Allie'd had Medusa for this project, she would've found a way to give the woman a voice. To show the world what evil had been done to her. And she certainly wouldn't have copied another student's work.

Allie complained to Aion about Kyle's copying and the teacher's poor job of assigning the figures. She'd told him that Ms. Symons should've assigned Aion the Greek god of eternity, who he was named after, instead of the Moirai—the Fates who control the life thread. And the teacher should've realized that Kyle had copied Allie's work—her drawing of Medusa was up in the art block for a whole month last year. Ms. Symons really was stupid. She couldn't see what—or who—was right in front of her eyes.

But Aion didn't seem to care, which annoyed her. Of all people, her best friend—who was named after a god—should've understood.

Allie thinks of that class a lot now, mostly because of Kyle's drawing of Medusa. How he didn't quite manage to copy the finesse of it, how his lines were cruder, more careless, creating a version of Medusa that was close to her own, but not quite. Kyle's drawing haunts her, probably because of Riko.

Kyle was a victim of the first night and in tribute to him, Riko tattooed the snakes from the picture of Medusa onto his own arms, depicting Kyle's copy of Allie's artistry like a bad version of the telephone game. She bets Riko doesn't even know that she was the original artist of that picture, and now he obliviously sports her marks.

When Allie asked him about his tattoos, all Riko talked about was that his brother had been obsessed with Medusa—as if a monster like Kyle O'Donovan cared about a woman preyed upon, victimized, and weaponized! Kyle hadn't been obsessed with the real Medusa, the one that Allie understood and felt connected to. He'd just been preoccupied with snakes because he'd thought they were cool—and because of what they represented: power over others.

That was one of the last things he said to Allie in that room that smelled of cat piss. Some stupid joke about how Allie wasn't powerful at all. How she was just a woman.

Allie's thoughts darken, and she tries to push the memories away. Tries to shove them in a box, somewhere in the depths of her mind, where they can't spill out and taunt her.

She won their war, the one between her and Kyle. Because she's still alive, and not turned to stone. But she can't help but feel like she's forgotten something huge.

Something important.

THREE

"We have to do something," Allie says, glancing at the rest of the team. It is the next morning, finally. She swallows several times, but her throat feels thick, like the pills she took are stuck in it even though she knows they're not.

"We need to find out the cause," Riko says, resting his beefy forearms on Allie's kitchen table. The team always meets at Allie's house because her house is centrally located.

Allie stares at Riko's muscles—elaborate designs of serpents swirl around his upper arms, while lizards with huge, protruding fangs adorn his forearms—and she feels bad because she can't stop. She should be repulsed by him. No matter if he gives her cigarettes and advice, the O'Donovans cannot be trusted. They are bad people. But Riko is Allie's leader because he is the strongest person in their team and for some reason that made the others vote for him. Not that strength stops you becoming stoned.

"The cause is the Power," Aion mutters, rolling his eyes.

Riko ignores him. "We need more information on that sonic boom." He points at Dan, the thirty-one-year-old firefighter. "That's your job for today."

Riko likes bossing people about—even someone ten years or more his senior. That's the problem with the O'Donovans. That, and they're not used to being told no.

He doles out more jobs. Vera and Oliver, the two eldest members of their team—both in their early eighties—are to go to the library and continue looking through the archives. Helen, the sixty-six-year-old music teacher, is to loot more food from the supermarkets. Kiersten and Gabe, a nurse and a physiotherapist, are to try more 'reviving techniques' on the statues.

Riko is still certain that the transformation is reversible. Maybe he just wants to believe that because Kyle, his parents, and his bossy old uncle are no more than decorative pieces on his lawn, around the town, in their beds, now.

He saves the two of them for last. "And Allie and Aion, search through social media."

It's always social media for them. As if they'll magically find that someone has cured the Night Worshippers and decided to tweet the remedy rather than report it on the news.

"What will you be doing?" Aion asks Riko dryly.

"What I always do," he barks back, his hand on the knife in his belt. Allie's noticed he always has that on him now. "Trying to find more survivors."

When he says this, the snakes on Riko's arms seem to hiss. They make Allie shudder.

"HOW ARE YOU DOING?" KIERSTEN PAUSES on her way out, asking Allie the question she always dreads. "Any more pain?"

Allie shrugs. The pain's about the same.

At least she's still got her meds. It was just luck that the doctor prescribed her new supply before the Power arrived in the sky. Allie has got six weeks of the pills left, and she thinks surely by the time she needs a refill, the world will have righted itself again.

They'll have found a way to reverse the stonifications of all the doctors and nurses and pharmacists. And then she'll definitely get better. Or better than she is now, anyway.

"How's the frequency?" Kiersten asks.

Shame clouds Allie's face, and she looks across at Aion. She knows he's listening, and she hates talking about this with anyone, let alone with him in earshot. He may be her best friend, but some things are just embarrassing.

Allie's kidney problems started as a UTI that just wouldn't go. She'd take the three-to-five days of antibiotics her doctor prescribed, and she'd improve while she was on them. But as soon as she stopped, the UTI symptoms would return. Then the UTI got into her kidneys, and treatment wasn't prompt. Back-to-back dipstick tests showed blood in her urine, and the infection had scarred her kidneys. Her blood tests began to show impaired renal function and doctors talked of the possibility of chronic kidney disease. Her blood pressure got higher, and scans revealed kidney stones. And still she had the UTI symptoms and kidney infection symptoms. It was a constant ebb and flow of them.

Finally, Allie saw a specialist who diagnosed her with an embedded infection that had got under the biofilm of her urinary tract system, scarring her bladder and kidneys. She'd been started on high-dose antibiotics and an antibacterial, and told she'd be on them for nine months at least. Meanwhile, her renal function would be monitored and she was to have regular tests done, counting her numbers of white blood cells and epithelial cells in her urine.

That's definitely not something she wants to talk to Kiersten about in front of Aion and the others who are still making their way out of her house, so Allie just whispers, "It's getting a bit better," even though it's not.

"I WILL SAVE YOU, ELLIE," ALLIE WHISPERS, looking toward the cupboard under the stairs where her sister is stashed. She and Aion are on the sofa, and she is supposed to be scrolling through Twitter feeds and Facebook pages.

But her mind is on Ellie.

Sorry, she wants to say, because she didn't make sure her sister was back home before dark and the last words she'd said to Ellie weren't kind ones. Ellie had been complaining about how Allie's 'story' was affecting her, how her friends had dropped her too and she'd been given a warning at work. But it wasn't a story—it was the truth.

Allie wants to scream it from the rooftops, make everyone hear her—the voice they tried to silence. Because no one believed her when she spoke up about what Kyle had done. Everyone turned against her.

Kyle's parents shunned her, spread lies about her being unstable and ill. Kyle and Carly made her life hell at school. *Slag* was written on her locker, no matter how many times she and the cleaners scrubbed it off. And her father, who worked for Kyle's uncle, nearly lost his job, because the O'Donovans are—were?—so deeply embedded in the fabric of the town. They owned Blackthorne, and they punished her for trying to tarnish their family name. She had to keep quiet and ignore everything, promising herself that as soon as she graduated, she'd get a place at a university far from Blackthorne where no one knew her.

Allie wants to shout now, shout anything. Make the world hear her, make everyone know that she has power, even if they've been stonified. Maybe there's a part of them that can still hear, and she needs them to know that she can't be walked all over. That's why she's still here, isn't it? Why the Power's not turned her into a Night Worshipper? Why she's one of the few people in Blackthorne who can still think and speak and act.

But she can't start thinking like that again, believing that people will listen to her. Because they won't—not when there's still an O'Donovan in this town. Even if Riko was out of the picture, she knows how strong the O'Donovan web is. Allie can't put herself through that torment again. It's a miracle the team is talking to her as it is—Kiersten and Dan were both friends with other O'Donovans.

She'd been suspicious of Riko when she'd realized she'd be in his team, thinking he'd continue the bullying. But he didn't.

He never mentioned it, just watched her strangely for the first few days, then gave her and Aion the menial jobs, like checking social media.

She and Aion make notes, gathering more and more of the theories various people have come up with. There's still a group going strong who reckon it's a sign of Hell coming to earth. Others think it's something to do with 4G. There's a small outcrop of people who are studying calcification and crystals too, convinced it's linked. Allie doesn't pay much attention to that.

"Do you think it is something supernatural?" she asks Aion as they make a quick lunch. She thinks of her night vision and wonders again if Aion has a power. Or if it's just her. She nearly told him once, a couple of days after it all started—but then the witch-hunters came to her street. They lit a house on fire, shouting that the flames would kill the 'witches' among them who were responsible for the stonifications. She and Aion and her father rushed out, as did all the other neighbors who still remained in town, and dowsed the flames with water for hours. Eventually the hunters left, and luckily the sky gave up rain, helped smother the blaze.

And so Allie kept her mouth shut about her power, after all. Sometimes, it feels like she's never allowed to speak in Blackthorne.

"It's ridiculous, people turning to stone," is all Aion says as he shrugs and pushes back his red hair. Allie has always liked his hair. It's the same shade as hers—and it's what bonded the two of them together, back on their first day of primary school.

The truth is, no one knows what is actually going on. And Allie thinks it's pointless, all this research that Riko has their team doing. As if they're going to be the ones to discover the cause of the night worshipping curse and therefore the cure.

ALLIE SAYS SHE'LL WALK AION HOME. SHE always does this after their meetings—there's just something comforting about walking through the decimated town with her best friend—and Aion still doesn't know that she never returns straight to her own house after.

She doesn't know why she goes to the O'Donovans' house. She just does. Something draws her over there, and she can't explain it. It's that feeling again—the one that makes her think she's forgotten something huge, something important.

As she picks her way over to the posher part of town, the part where the houses stand individually with huge driveways and iron gates, Allie keeps an eye on the sky. Sundown isn't for an hour yet. She and Aion worked a little later than normal, and with the nights drawing in earlier and earlier, she'll only have half an hour at the property before she should head back.

A grand sign welcomes her to Meadowview Road. Allie's pace quickens.

There. She sees the house.

Kyle is at the edge of the lawn, and he looks like a guard dog. He's crouching down a little, like he's about to pick a rose or something from the flowerbeds.

Allie looks toward the house. There are no lights on inside it. Riko isn't back. He's still out, looking for more survivors, like he does all the time. They never find any more though.

The air is cold—there may even be a frost tonight—and Allie picks her way to her favorite spot in the shrubbery right behind Kyle's statue, shrouded in shadow. Once, Riko was standing by the kitchen window when she was here, and she held her breath when he looked right in her direction. It had still been light and he could've come outside, demanded to know what she was doing, but he didn't. She breathed a sigh of relief when he didn't see her.

Allie doesn't know why she's drawn here almost every day. Why she stares at the statue of the boy she hates. Maybe she's lured here by her subconscious. Because she wants revenge on Kyle for what he did.

The Power's already had its revenge—but it doesn't feel like enough.

She shifts her weight from foot to foot, then looks down. Scattered pebbles lie in front of her feet. She bends to pick one up and feels the weight of it in her hand. It feels good. Allie closes her eyes and imagines herself throwing it at Kyle's statue. Throwing it at his head so hard a crack will appear around his neck and his head will fall off. His skull and face will shatter into a thousand pieces that can never be put back together.

Allie has this urge to behead Kyle every time she's here, but she never acts on it. She relishes in her imaginings of destroying him just as he destroyed her. And if she does, it will be over. Her revenge will be done, gone.

No. She's got to think of a better way to make him pay.

FOUR

The woman has pale skin and pale hair. Her forehead is high and domed, and her eyes are slightly too far apart. She is wearing a long white dress that billows around her hips and legs and clings to the curves of her breasts and the narrowness of her waist, covering her up while showing her womanly form.

Allie stares at the painting on her kitchen wall. It's hers—a painting of Penelope, Odysseus's wife in Homer's *The Odyssey*, from that same art class where Kyle had drawn Medusa. She read the book twice that term, trying to find inspiration, but instead she found herself getting annoyed at how Penelope's whole life revolved around being loyal and faithful to her absent husband. She wanted Penelope to do something of her own accord, something exciting beyond deceiving and tricking the suitors who came looking for her. Even then, she was still no more than 'the faithful wife.'

When Carly saw Allie's painting, she told everyone that Allie must be gay as well as inbred—lumping the two together, as if homosexuality was a crime. Not that Allie particularly minded the inbred accusation either—that just meant she was like Medusa, for Medusa's parents Phorcys and Ceto were siblings. But Carly had said it to be an insult, which cemented Allie's desire for something terrible to happen to her. Something that would make Carly feel weak and helpless and like she didn't matter at all.

Or maybe even something worse. Something that would remove Carly from Allie's life altogether.

Allie stares at her painting of Penelope a lot in the evenings, after she's had a few drinks and a few cigarettes. When the world's becoming a little more hazy around her, when her heartbeat is sluggish. She wonders, as she stares at Penelope's form, if it would be easier if she *was* a lesbian because then people wouldn't keep making jokes when they hear rumors that she's asexual—likening her to a plant because that's the only other time they've really heard the word *asexual*, thanks to biology class. Sometimes Allie wonders if she actually is a lesbian even though she's asexual. A website she saw said you can be both.

Allie reaches for her third can of lager. Maybe she's addicted now. An alcoholic. The thought's almost funny, and she laughs, in spite of herself. Her laugh is throaty and low, and it doesn't sound like her. But then again, Allie rarely sounds like herself now. Rarely even looks like herself.

She layers dark makeup around her eyes, and she doesn't take it off to sleep. Her pillow smudges it, making bigger circles appear around her eyes—though maybe those are partly real. There's something comforting about putting makeup on after she's stolen it from the supermarket—though is it stealing, if no one's there to take money now?—as if the act of applying it makes her stronger. Makes her into a different person. Someone who is strong enough to cope with all this, someone who drinks and smokes, someone who can survive the curse, someone who isn't afraid of telling others she's probably asexual and maybe she likes women too. Or maybe she doesn't.

She thinks of Aion.

She likes him—emotionally and intellectually, and yes, he has a nice body. And she appreciates Riko's muscular arms, even though she hates herself for it. So, shouldn't that mean she should feel something else? She doesn't know, and she's too embarrassed to tell anyone.

The clock strikes seven. Allie sighs. It's going to be a long night. Maybe she should get a cat or something. An animal to keep her company at night. Or a dog. Dogs won't want to leave the house at night like a cat might.

Yes, she should get a dog. There are plenty of them roaming the streets now. There used to be a rescue center in town, especially for dogs, but the owners were cursed to stone that first night, and then someone opened the dogs' pens. Let them out. Now, they run free.

Her legs have that jittery feeling in them again, so she gets up to stretch them. The movement makes her bladder spasm and her kidneys hurt. Allie heads to the bathroom and relieves herself, wincing as her bladder pain gets stronger. She stares at the crystals on the shelf above the sink. They almost make her want to laugh.

She and Aion ordered the crystals especially from Greece, maybe six weeks ago, for a summoning spell. She's not sure of the timing—nothing is in order in her head anymore—but she knows they ordered the crystals before the stonifications started. Before the Power appeared in the sky. Before the sonic boom.

They'd been reading loads of blogs on summoning gods and convinced themselves they'd be able to summon Medusa. Allie had always believed in magic and mythology as a child, convinced there was a dimension of the world that wasn't visible to her. And she wanted to make Kyle feel pain and fear when he realized Medusa was real. She wanted Kyle to hurt just as he'd hurt her.

Allie was never quite sure whether Aion really believed that a goddess could be summoned. Not like how she did. Maybe he thought her obsession with Medusa was a reaction to the trauma she'd been through, and was just trying to support her. Of course he knew what Kyle had done to her—even if they never talked about it properly because Allie told him she didn't want to.

He knew. Everyone in Blackthorne did. But now, no one speaks of it at all.

Still, whether he believed or not, Aion agreed to summon Medusa in the end, after Allie told him that they could enact revenge on Kyle, the O'Donovans, and even Carly and her gang—everyone who made Aion's life a misery because he'd dared to be friends with Allie. Not to mention get revenge on Kyle for what he'd done to her.

But she and Aion never actually got a chance to try out the spell. It was bizarre—there they'd been, talking of summoning Medusa, and now there was a Medusa-esque power in the sky, turning people to stone. A power that got Kyle pretty quickly. Aion whooped when he heard the news.

Allie swallows hard, dismissing the memory. After washing her hands and then taking more of her medications, she heads downstairs. She grabs a book from the shelf, settles down and—

Something thuds above her head, and Allie freezes, looks up. She watches as a crack appears in the ceiling. Her heart pounds as it spreads across, getting bigger and bigger. A grating sound fills her ears, then the ground's shaking.

Rushing sounds wrap around her, and mugs fly off her draining board.

Run!

The house shakes. Dust fills the air, and the air's gritty, sharp fragments diving down her throat.

The painting of Penelope clatters to her feet.

Get out!

Allie pants, and the room spins. And she's in the lounge now. The front door's ahead of her—but no! She can't go outside.

She mustn't go outside! She—

A beam crashes down. Allie screams. Wood splinters, and stone—so much stone. And a stone hand—her sister's—on the carpet in front of her.

Another beam falls. Something hits the back of her head, and Allie grunts as she falls forward. Her vision goes dark for a moment, but then she's scrambling about. Is it the Power doing this, wanting more victims, hungry when its prey are caging themselves away? Something else? Is there more that can hide inside the night than what she's already seen?

Her hands close on chunks of plasterboard, and she clings to them as if they can save her. She's on her knees, debris pressing through her jeans, painful and sharp.

The ground rumbles, and above her is a creaking sound. She jolts and looks up. The ceiling above—where her bedroom is—is bowing. A high-pitched pop, and then a loud hissing sound, fills the air.

Allie smells gas.

Her lungs ache. She looks toward the front door. There's a pathway clear through the debris to it. Her heart pounds.

No! Don't go outside! It's dark!

If she stays here, she's going to be crushed and suffocated.

Allie surges forward, dragging herself to the front porch, and yanks open the door.

FIVE

The darkness has teeth, and the night is trying to eat Allie. Huge welts form on her bare hands and arms, and the darkness is burning her, tearing her skin to shreds. Something wet and slick slides down her arms, and she screams as needles of pain drive into her face.

She blinks frantically, trying to see, but she is panicking, breathing too fast, and she can't stop gulping. Her throat is closing up, and the air feels too thick, too heavy. It's weighing her down and the ground shakes. She falls to her knees on the concrete slabs, drags a hand down the side of her face, leaving a wet trail.

Behind her, her house is falling in at one end. No longer a protective sanctuary. The Power is tearing it apart, and Allie's sure the whole structure's going to come down soon. She concentrates and hones in on the rest of the street; her vision gets brighter, clearer, sharper, and she sees the other buildings crumbling at a much faster rate than her own home.

There is nowhere indoors that is safe.

She looks up at the sky. She cannot see the Power there. But she can feel it. It is greedy. It is taking and taking, and it's not going to stop.

Allie forces herself to her feet and runs. The ground shakes again, and the trees at the end of the road move toward her, swaying. She ducks as a branch flies past her. Her lungs ache and burn and her head spins. She's got to find the others.

Gabe's house is closest, so she heads for Manor Close, the posh part of the town where the physiotherapist lives. She runs and the ground is still moving, and the sky breaks, a booming sound echoing around her, bouncing off the fallen homes.

A dog barks, and Allie sees it, a Labrador cowering by a house that's partly fallen down, only propped up precariously by one pillar. Allie falters a little—should she try and calm the dog? See if it's okay?

But something booms from the sky, and rain soaks her suddenly, blinding her. Her body stutters and ice-cold winds wrap around her. Allie tries to catch sight of the Labrador again, but the water's swirling in the road now, and everything's shaking, and she can't see.

She's got to find the others.

Allie's head pounds as she runs. A fence post flies past, barely missing her. As she races forward, she can't help but imagine it spearing her body, puncturing her lungs. Coldness lassoes her heart.

Broken statues—broken Night Worshippers—are everywhere. A stone head rolls toward her. The person's still smiling. Allie gulps. She doesn't recognize the face. It's not one of her team.

"Mulberry Close . . . Cranmore . . ." She mutters the names of the streets as she passes them. Some have their signs still rooted in the tarmac, some don't, but it doesn't matter. Allie memorized the layout of the town long ago.

At last, just when Allie thinks her heart is going to explode, she reaches Manor Close. It's no different to the estates she's passed: full of wreckage, trees and bricks and stones everywhere. It's just a pile of rubble. Red bricks and chunks of cement and broken window frames. The wind picks up and howls, and the sound of it makes the hairs on the backs of Allie's arms stand on end.

"Gabe!" Allie shouts, her heart pounding as she looks at what should've been number one Manor Close. Nausea twists inside her as the wind whips the name from her mouth. She claps a hand to the base of her throat, which stings, as if nature literally snatched something from her throat when it took away her scream.

The rain gets colder, harder, bouncing off the debris. Water runs down the ground, like a river, sweeping away wooden planks and plastic containers. A teddy bear floats by, and Allie hears a laugh. An evil one.

She whips her head around, heart pounding. No one is in sight. She looks up at the sky. Is it the Power? The Power is laughing?

The sound is too close to be the Power. But who else can it be? She is alone. And terrified.

Oh, God. She's going to die.

They're all going to die. This is *it*.

Allie screams her frustration, and it surprises her, the guttural sound that rips from her soul. How animalistic it feels. She's been reduced to nothing but a creature who screams sounds that aren't words, that have no shape other than terror.

A hand sticks out from the rubble by her feet. It looks rubbery and gray. It's stone, not flesh.

The hand is cold. Doesn't move when she touches it.

Allie's heart leaps, and she falls to her knees, bashing her shin on a lump of rock as she moves the rubble from the person's arm, from the person's body.

Then she screams.

It's Gabe, and his face has been smashed in. His skull has broken, and she can see the rough, cracked edges of it. And the brain beneath, mashed up, spilling out beneath his jaw.

Her stomach lurches.

The Power in the sky laughs even harder. It has a female voice. It sounds exactly like Allie, and Allie pretends it doesn't.

Local Suicide Victim Was Pregnant

BLACKTHORNE—The postmortem carried out on the recently-deceased Maliah Swan has revealed the eighteen-year-old schoolgirl was pregnant at the time of her death. The identity of the father of Swan's baby is currently unknown, but there is speculation that the pregnancy was the cause of Swan's decision to end her life.

SIX

"Allie!"

The cry is raw, a knife piercing her insides, and Allie jolts, looks up. She's been running for what seems like hours. She doesn't know how she's still moving, and she can't recognize any of the town now. It's all rubble and broken Night Worshippers and the odd fleeing shadow of a dog, the hiss of a cat.

Two figures hurtle toward her. Her heart jumps. Aion and Riko. People. Relief hugs her and she nearly misses her footing, only manages to right herself at the last moment. A shard of pain squeezes through her ankle.

Allie pants hard as Aion and Riko reach her. Aion wraps her in a hug. He smells of blood, rusty and tangy. His head is bleeding and she feels his blood pressing against her face, sticky and hot.

"Alright?" Riko looks her up and down and grabs the knife from his belt—ha, as if that can save him from the Power. Then Allie realizes he's holding the knife against her, as if she's the threat.

"What are you doing?" Aion stares at Riko. "That's Allie! She's not the threat here! We have to stick together."

"I'm not going to hurt you," she mutters, as much as she wants to get revenge on the O'Donovans.

Riko grunts, doesn't look convinced, but he turns the knife away. Allie likes that he is scared of her.

Something howls in the distance. It doesn't sound like a dog.

"Have you seen anyone else?" Riko demands. Light glints off the knife's blade, but Allie can't tell where it's coming from.

"Gabe's dead," she says.

"So's Oliver," Aion grunts.

Ice-cold needles of rain drive down. Allie gasps as they burn her skin. She lifts her arms, trying to protect her face.

"No! Don't!" Aion grabs her hands, pulling them back down.

It takes Allie a moment to realize she'd mimicked a Night Worshipper. Her face stings and she tries to hunker down. The three of them crouch low, together. There's a rushing sound in Allie's ears.

"The castle!" Aion shouts, pointing. "It's the only place still standing!"

Allie looks ahead. The skyline is lit up by the eerie color of the sky—a vibrant purple—and Allie can see the buildings falling as the storm wraps around them, all of them except for the castle. It looks exactly the same, and the storm's angry fingers are leaving it alone.

Blackthorne Castle has been half in ruins for a good few hundred years, but the west side of the castle has been intact for centuries. A few years ago, a historian made a documentary about Blackthorne and it was closed to the public while filming took place. Allie watched that documentary when it aired six months later. The producers and historian had been up at the top of the west tower—the only part that's not open to the public as Health and Safety officers deemed it too dangerous. But it didn't look dangerous in the documentary. The historian, whatever his name was, was lounging about, leaning against the walls. There were no safety ropes anywhere. It was probably just deemed unsafe because of the height. The west tower stretches up for six stories, considerably higher than the main part of the castle that's been crumbling down in slow motion.

"We can't go there!" Riko bellows over the chaos of the storm.

"What?" Allie screams, staring at him.

"We can't!" he yells. There's something in his eyes that doesn't look quite right. "You haven't heard the stories?"

"The stories?" Allie shakes her head. What the hell is he on about? *Of course* they've got to go to the castle—it's the only place the Power isn't ripping apart and they can't stay out here.

"Ghost stories?" Aion frowns at Riko. "You're scared of ghosts?"

Ghosts. Allie wants to laugh.

"No, I just don't like that place." Riko folds his arms, looking defensive as he glances over at Allie quickly before looking away from her.

He doesn't want to go to the castle? Allie frowns. Why? Instinctively, she feels like that is something she should know—but she can't remember. It's that feeling again, that she's forgotten something huge, something really important. But looking at Riko now, the way he's breathing hard and staring anywhere but at her, makes her sure that Riko does remember something, knows something she doesn't.

I thought you were dead. Is the Power affecting anyone else's memory?

The howl rises again, closer now, and her skin prickles.

Allie turns to ask Aion if he feels like he's forgotten something too—suddenly overcome with the urge to discuss it—but a dog hurtles through the air, a black streak of fur and teeth, almost hitting them, and once again she's silenced.

"We have to go now!" She grabs Aion's hand. It is surprisingly warm, and she clings to him, suddenly realizing how cold she is. Her own hands are like blocks of ice.

"No, we can't!"

Allie ignores Riko. They'd be stupid not to go.

Allie and Aion hunker down as much as they can as they run. The storm sends daggers of semi-frozen water at them, cutting Allie's face. She feels something thicker than water sliding down the side of her face and tastes rust at the corner of her mouth. Her feet slip on the sodden grass and in the pools of mud and blood several times, but Aion catches her.

Twice, Allie twists her head and looks behind her, trying to see Riko. Because he must be coming with them, right? But the night's too dark and moody, and even when lightning flashes— burning an imprint of her zoomed-in surroundings into her retinas—she can see no other life in the area. Even the dogs and cats have gone. It's just her and Aion, panting, clinging to each other as they run.

They jump over broken statues, and Allie tries not to look at their faces. Mrs. Mack from the bakery. The boy who used to deliver the newspapers, before the Power came. A local farmer. The postmaster.

She tries not to think about Ellie, in the cupboard under the stairs. She wonders if that part of her house is still standing, if somehow the house has managed to protect her sister, even as the Power has ripped down the walls. She thinks of her painting of Penelope, and she imagines it whipping through the vicious air.

"There!" Allie shouts, pointing ahead. Blackthorne Castle. The air around it is completely still.

When Allie steps into the calm pocket of air, into the sanctuary of the castle, something happens inside her head. It's a crawling sensation, like her brain is slowly rotating in her skull, twisting round. Her vision jars and blurs. She sees Aion, the way his dark eyes get lighter—because everything's getting lighter. And she feels terror—terror, remembered. She hears angry male voices—Riko's and Kyle's? She feels hands on her arms, shoving her forward. She shouts—but it's just a choking sound, and the stone wall of the inside of the west tower is in front of her. Just a glimpse, before there's bright light, shining as if through a window. The sky. Trees.

A scream.

Then she can see and hear and feel nothing, because there is nothing there. The world disappears, and there's fire in her veins.

Her last thought is that it doesn't matter if she burns up. The castle will protect her—she doesn't know how she knows it, but she does. Because the castle remembers her, and this memory is a promise.

"*Y*ou really think you can win against me?" Kyle is laughing. "Don't you know who I am?"

Allie is not laughing. She's scared, her heart is pounding. She stares around the castle tower—her sanctuary. Until he followed her.

She shifts, trying to get Kyle to move away from the wall. She doesn't want him to see the drawings there—her designs, her reclamation of her work. Kyle would recognize them from the drawing he plagiarized from her, and then he'd see it as a confrontation, she's sure. Or he'd claim she'd copied him. Or worse—that she admired him, and maybe he'd want to draw on her wall too. And she can't have that. This is her place. Kyle is an intruder.

"What do you want?" she snarls. "Another go?"

"I want you to stop with all these lies," Kyle says.

Her notebooks are spread out on the floor, and Kyle mustn't see them— she mustn't give him more ammunition to hate her, not when she's trying to plan revenge. And where the hell is Aion? He was supposed to be there to help her. They'd planned this carefully, and it had to be now—today was the summer solstice. The date that all the books said was perfect for the summoning.

"I'm not lying," she bites out through gritted teeth.

"But you are." His laugh gets darker, deeper, more sinister. "That's what my family thinks. That's what everyone thinks. And face it, you can't prove anything happened. It's your word against mine."

Allie swallows hard. "Oh, I can prove it."

Kyle takes a step toward her. "No. You won't be able to. Oh, it's a shame it's come to this," he says. "Such a shame."

EIGHT

"*Allie . . .*" a voice whispers. "*Maliah . . .*"

Allie doesn't hear the voice at first. Not properly—she knows it's there, but the words it speaks—her name—don't mean anything to her. She doesn't know where she is. She is . . . somewhere and nowhere and everywhere.

But then she realizes she has a body, because she is hurting. There is pain, everywhere, and she is gasping, trying to breathe the air that's too thick, and the voice won't stop saying her name.

"*Maliah . . . Maliah . . . Maliah!*"

It's a female voice, a woman. She sounds scared.

Allie opens her eyes.

At first, she can't see anything. The world is too bright, too white around her. She blinks and blinks, but then darker shapes appear, and she sees the woman leaning over her. Brown skin and dark hair.

"Allie, oh, thank God," Kiersten whispers, and then she is hugging Allie to her chest and Allie can barely breathe.

Allie doesn't like being touched, but she pulls away from Kiersten after allowing the woman to hug her a bit. She blinks slowly and looks around. Rough stone walls and a dirt floor. They're in the castle, and the air's all strange. It's like something's humming—like the air is full of a pulsing, unseen energy.

"Aion!" She sees him sitting a few feet away, his back to the stone wall. His head is in his hands, but he looks up at Allie when she shouts his name.

A smile flicks across his face.

Allie tries to stand up, and Kiersten helps her. She looks around. It's daylight.

"What . . . what's happened?" She looks up at the sky—it's just visible through a gap in the wall, up near the ceiling. She can see a beautiful blue color. "Is it just us three?"

Kiersten shakes her head. "Helen and Dan are just outside. We can't go far."

"What?"

Allie pushes her way toward the window. She looks out and her heart thumps. Helen and Dan are both standing a few feet away. The air is still and calm around them, but it is like the castle's in a dome of sorts, something to protect it. Because beyond Helen and Dan, the air is dark and the storm is still going. Chunks of wood and debris fly through the air in swirling patterns. Rain is battering down and the clouds are dark, furious, angry.

"How is this . . ." Allie trails off as she turns to look at Kiersten. The nurse looks tired. Exhausted. Huge circles hang under her eyes.

"We don't know," Kiersten says.

"The castle's protecting us," Aion says.

Is the protection the energy she can detect, that humming?

Aion pulls himself up slowly, grimacing. The cut on his head looks deep, nasty. He joins Allie by the window, nods at her. "Riko didn't follow us."

Riko.

It was his hands on her upper arms. His scream. His touch. And Kyle's. The threats, the tower, the window, the fall.

They were both here. With her. Before. According to that . . . whatever it was, before she passed out. A fragment of a vision, a memory? Could it have been real?

Allie swallows hard and looks outside. There are no signs of anyone. She looks around again, taking note of everyone not here. Everyone who they know is dead or will be dead. Riko. Gabe. Vera. Oliver.

"We're trapped in here?" she asks, feeling a sense of relief despite herself. She couldn't protect her sister, but insisting she and Aion come here was a good idea. At least she's kept him safe.

Kiersten nods. "Seem to be. Dan tried to get out, but it's some sort of forcefield. Burnt his arm badly."

Allie nods like she understands, like all of this makes sense, but it doesn't. "How can the castle be safe from all . . . this?"

"We don't know," Aion says.

Allie nods again. "I'm going to look around."

The others don't stop her and no one volunteers to go with her, not even Aion, so Allie walks into the west tower. A year ago, she photographed it with Aion for a project—that was the first time they'd been to the castle, even though they'd lived in the town all their lives. But it was nearly always a monetized tourist attraction.

She and Aion sneaked through the barriers late one evening. She remembers running her hands over the cold, sand blocks, the callouses on her skin catching on the rough textures.

It looks the same, and it reminds her of all the time and she and Aion spent secretly in the castle thereafter. It was their special place, for just the two of them, until their space was violated.

They grab her, knocking her notebooks and crystals flying, and she screams. She's kicking and punching, trying to hurt them, but they lift her up easily, lift her toward the window.

"No!" she screams. "Please, I'll do anything!"

But neither brother's listening. Each has a steely, glazed-over look in their eyes, and she screams and begs. She shoves back, but they're stronger. Of course they're stronger. They're male and big and tall. Rugby players. They haul her up to the open window-space. No glass left. Just an empty square in the stone.

"Please!" Tears run down her face and her fingers scrape against the rough stone. She tries to get a hold on the stone, but she can't. "Please, please!"

They shove her out and Allie falls.

Allie gasps at the . . . memory. It doesn't make sense—doesn't link up with anything before or after. It's just there, floating untethered. Like it has no rightful place in her mind.

She shakes her head. She didn't fall from the tower. She'd have had injuries. She'd have remembered that—and surely Aion would've mentioned it. If he'd been late to meet her at the tower, when they were planning on summoning Medusa, and he'd found her lying on the ground outside, he'd definitely have said something. No, this is just her imagination trying to trick her.

She climbs the tower to the second floor, touching the stones that curve around the wall of the spiral staircase, as if the mere act of touch can ground her. She breathes deeply, and looks closer at the stone.

It's the same as the statues. It looks . . . the same? And it feels the same too—Allie feels connected to both.

But don't all rocks look the same? She shakes away that question and pushes through the doorway onto the second floor. The floor looks solid enough for the most part. Wood. She tests it cautiously at first, she doesn't want two broken legs on top of all this, but it holds.

The energy, that hum, is getting stronger.

She makes her way around the circular room slowly. The air is damp, musty, and she wrinkles her nose. Her lungs do a hitching, panicking thing, and suddenly she wants a cigarette. But of course she hasn't got any with her. Her pack of cigarettes was on her kitchen table.

Tears come to her eyes, and she knows it is silly to cry over cigarettes when the world is ending—because it must be—but she can't help it. She lets the tears fall, lets them blur her vision until she can't see the walls with the coppery serpent designs and—

She jolts.

Serpents? The serpents she drew, way before Kyle stole her art.

Allie drags the back of her hand across her eyes, wiping away her tears. She leans in closer. The wall's a foot away, and she stares at the tower walls, at the designs etched on them. Some of them are carvings, some are painted on.

She expects something to happen when she touches the crude drawings with her fingers, tracing their shapes, but nothing does.

"Allie? You in here?"

Aion's voice makes her jump. She hadn't heard him approach.

She turns to see him entering the room. His arms are stretched out in front of him, like he's feeling his way. Or like he's a zombie.

"Yeah," she says.

Aion moves toward her uncertainly, and Allie grabs his hand. He flinches a little.

"What?" she says, self-conscious.

"Your skin feels weird. Too cold and like rubber."

"Oh." She doesn't know what to say to that, so she pulls him forward. "Look at the snakes," she says, looking back at the wall in front of her. She knows they're important—because they're connected to *the before*.

"What?" Aion squints. "I can't see a thing."

Allie realizes there is no window—no window in the tower.

So she can't have been thrown from it?

She frowns.

"Allie, can you see in the dark?" Aion asks.

She jolts. She must've been using her vision power. And that realization makes her feel weird, like she's working with the Power in the sky that's taken away everything she's ever known. That's killed her sister and father, her friends, her teachers. Her life as she knew it.

"Wait a sec," he says, and then he's pulling out his phone. He flicks the flashlight on, and then raises his eyebrows as he sees the serpents.

"I can't remember it all, Aion," she says. "I mean, I know I drew these here, but . . ." Her words are fast, tumbling out of her. Allie knows this is important, suddenly she's surer of that than she's been about anything before.

"That's not your drawing. That's Kyle's. They're the same as Riko's tattoos," Aion says, sounding confused. "Kyle's been here—to our place?"

Kyle's drawings? What? Allie frowns. No, they were her drawings first. And she drew these ones! But then as she tries to remember drawing them, the memory disappears. It's just gone. It doesn't make sense.

"Something's not right," she says, and although her memory of drawing the serpents has gone, the rest of it hasn't—it's just like one piece of the jigsaw has been removed and the other pieces rearranged to seamlessly fill its place. Because everything else is still there. Kyle and Riko, throwing her from the window.

Only the window's not there.

Allie's mind spins, and she feels sick now thinking about Riko. What if that part of her memory is real? And somehow the window got filled in? What if they did both hurt her—and that's why Riko didn't want her to go back to the tower, in case it triggered her memory . . . and why he didn't come, himself?

No . . . it can't be. Can it?

"Hey, what's going on?" Kiersten calls up. "You two okay?"

"Come up here," Allie shouts back. Her voice wavers. Everything seems too dangerous, too uncertain now, like the past is being rewritten around them, and she wants to keep what remains of their group together, as if she can protect them.

"We've found something," Aion shouts back.

Their steps on the stone stairs echo and pound through Allie's skull as she waits for the rest of their team to enter the room. The wooden floor creaks threateningly. Dan has a flashlight with him, a big industrial thing, and Helen looks delighted when she sees the drawings, calls them cave art.

"It's the same as Riko's tattoos, right?" Aion says.

When they nod, Aion's explaining about Kyle. Well, not everything—he doesn't talk about what Kyle did to Allie, or how the whole town tried to ostracize Allie because of it. It's almost like by not mentioning it, Aion is rewriting history so it didn't happen.

But it *did* happen, Allie knows that. She claws at her face, listening to Aion drone on about how Kyle was obsessed with snakes, drawing them everywhere, using the style he copied from her Medusa painting.

"The energy's stronger in this room," Allie says. "It's just . . . vibrating with it."

"Energy?" Dan frowns.

"Can't you feel it?" she asks. "And Riko didn't want Aion and me coming here. Even though it's the only safe place. He chose not to come with us."

She's sure she's right—this must be because he remembers what happened—what he and Kyle did. Whatever's happened to all their memories since the Power came, his is less affected. The first moment he saw that she was in his team, he'd said she thought she was dead. Then he'd looked doubtful, hadn't he? And asked if anyone else's memory was affected.

And now her memory is healing. The energy in the castle has to be what's causing her to remember.

But there's no window in the west tower. So how can her memories be real?

"I can't feel any energy," Helen says. "But I don't like it, all the same. And those snake drawings are creepy. Let's go back downstairs." She moves toward the doorway, but then something flashes. Light, in the room.

Helen screams, and Allie turns, heart pounding.

Power floods through the doorway in waves, and the snakes on the walls are moving. Allie lets out a scream.

Roaring sounds fill the air. And then the energy is growing, increasing. Allie can feel it. It's swamping her, swamping them all.

The energy takes on a visual form. It's a woman's face. A heart-shaped face, large eyes, and snakes for hair. It's just her face, her head. Like she's been beheaded. Like the fallen statues Allie saw as she ran through the town on her way here.

"What the fuck?" Dan makes a choking sound, and Allie's head whips toward him. He can see the energy too? Even though none of them could feel it?

"It's Medusa!" Aion breathes. "Don't look at her!"

Allie's body jolts. Pain flickers around her kidneys as she stares at the woman. She does look like Medusa. And Allie is looking at her, but she's not turning to stone. So this can't be the Gorgon . . . only Allie knows deep in her heart that it is.

"Oh my God," she whispers. "What if Kyle and Riko summoned Medusa somehow?"

Could it be possible? Kyle *was* studying Medusa, and he was drawing the snakes, and then Riko had the snakes on his arms too. And he didn't want to come here . . .

Everyone stares at the woman's head, even though Aion said to look away. It's suspended a foot in front of the doorway. About twice the size of an actual human head. The snakes writhe and wriggle. Her face looks hard, like it's made of red rock.

But as Allie watches, cracks appear. They run from the corners of the woman's eyes, down her cheeks, like teardrops, until they get to her mouth. The rock around her lips crumbles as Allie watches.

"We warned you this could happen," the woman whispers, and her words are coldness and ice and anger. *"There were never any guarantees."*

A high-power wave of energy blasts out from the disembodied head. It slows, shimmering in the air, turning everything golden.

Allie screams, and Aion grabs her hand, pulling her to him. Kiersten flies across the room as the wave hits her.

Then the wave hits Helen and Dan. It doesn't throw them like it did Kiersten. It wraps around them.

They're petrified in an instant, and the rock mask of Medusa falls—discarded, because Medusa no longer holds onto it. Medusa is free now, and Allie watches as she rejoins the Power in the sky.

For a second, Allie sees the truth: the Power isn't one amorphous entity—it consists of several Gorgons and their energies, all staring down at her. And she's staring back, her chest feeling light and fluttery and her throat too thick, trying to take it all in, before the images are whisked away, and it's just the Power again.

NINE

"So, you think Riko and Kyle summoned Medusa, and now she's destroying the world?" Aion frowns, then nudges Dan's arm with his foot. Completely solid. "Do you realize how crazy this sounds? That's just Greek mythology. This is ridiculous."

"Um, but we had that plan to summon Medusa?" Allie says. Aion never said it was ridiculous then.

Aion's frown deepens. "What?" He shakes his head, disbelief written all over his face. "What are you on about?"

"You've forgotten?" She stares at him, a twisting sensation in her chest. "We talked about this right after the first stonifications happened! You know, how weird a coincidence it was that we were trying to summon her, and we didn't do it—but now people are being turned into stone."

He gives her an odd look. "Why would we want to summon Medusa?"

"For revenge on Kyle!" Her voice rises and she's aware of the look Kiersten's giving her—like she's mad.

Aion frowns more deeply still. "Revenge on Kyle? What for?"

What for?

Allie's gut twists. He doesn't remember? She swallows hard and stares down at the stone forms of Dan and Helen. Her head pounds.

Kiersten clears her throat. "Never mind that right now. There has to be a way to stop this."

Allie wonders if Kiersten remembers what the O'Donovans did to her, if she remembers how Allie had tried to expose that family for what they were. She wants to ask. But how can she, when both of them are looking at her like she's lost her mind?

"Wouldn't it be Riko and Kyle stopping it? Reversing it? If they're the ones that started it?" Aion says, going along with Kiersten.

Allie turns away. She doesn't want to see the statues' open eyes. "And they're both probably dead." She imagines Riko lying somewhere, stone head smashed in just like Gabe's was.

Her gut squeezes. Now that she's remembered the truth, she hopes Riko is as dead and stone-cold as Kyle. As all the O'Donovans.

But is it really true? There's no window in the tower, after all. And Aion and Kiersten don't remember a thing.

Maybe she's going mad after all.

She makes her way to the doorway—all that remains of Medusa is a crumbly red mess on the floorboards—and looks out the window on the stairwell. The storm is still raging, shredding everything beyond their bubble. She doubts anything could survive out there.

Allie's skin prickles. She's staring at the red dust on the floor, the remains of Medusa's mask. She wants to run her hands through it, let it pour from between her fingers, but she doesn't know why. And it would look weird, so she doesn't do it.

"Can you get a phone signal?" Kiersten is asking Aion when Allie returns to the room. "We should try phoning someone. Someone could rescue us. The army, maybe. They've got helicopters."

"They wouldn't get through the storm. And why would they even come for us now? We all chose to stay in Blackthorne."

"But they need to know we're alive," Kiersten says.

"No signal." Aion shrugs. "So that's that idea out the window."

"Then we have to look for somewhere with signal," Kiersten says.

"Go out *there*?" Are you mad?" Aion's face reddens. He shakes his head at Kiersten. "No. We're not leaving here."

"But we can't survive in here. We've got no food," Kiersten says. "No water." She glances at Allie. "Have you got any of your meds with you?"

Allie shakes her head.

"We've got to go back out there." Kiersten looks determined.

Allie makes a noncommittal noise. In her head, Medusa's words echo: *We warned you this could happen. There were never any guarantees.*

Who had the Gorgon been talking to? And what had they done?

"We could look for Riko too," Allie offers. "In case he's still alive."

They do need to find Riko—if he summoned Medusa, he's got to know how to reverse it. But more than that, she wants to demand the truth from him.

She wants to know what happened to her, and she thinks he is the key.

"The storm can't be everywhere. Maybe we can run for it," Kiersten says. "Get out of this town."

THE O'DONOVANS' HOUSE IS A MESS. IT DOESN'T even look like a house—none of the houses do. But this one seems more of a mess, and Allie is pleased about that.

She stares at the ripped curtains that peek out from the pile of wood and bricks. Plastic rubbish litters the area, swirling round and round in the icy wind. Twice, a garbage bag hits her in the face.

But Allie finds something, a book. A notebook, bound in red leather. It's the only thing that appears to be intact, and it's just sitting on the ground. The storm isn't touching it, just like the storm isn't touching the castle.

She picks up the book. It's heavier than she expected. Her fingers are icy, cramping up, and she nearly drops it. Her breaths almost still completely as she opens it and stares at the drawings and notes and annotations on summoning Gorgons. Something about them is familiar. Too familiar. It makes her stomach twist.

"Look at these drawings." She shows the book to Aion and Kiersten. "Medusa, Stheno, and Euryale," she says, reading the neat scrawl. It's not like how she remembers Kyle's writing, and it's not Riko's either, but it is familiar, though she can't place it. "The three Gorgon sisters," Allie breathes.

Allie thinks of her own sisters. Ellie was a year older than Allie, and Sarah three years older than Ellie. As much as Allie wanted to be close to Sarah, she wasn't. Not like she was with Ellie. And for some reason that makes her feel bad now. She didn't take the chance when she had it. Not properly with either of her sisters—just look at the argument she'd had with Ellie the last time she'd seen her. And now both of her sisters are gone, and Allie is sure she's never going to see either of them again. Not alive.

"He's summoned *three* of them?" Aion looks aghast. "This just gets better and better. All this time he's been telling us to find the cause, and it was him?"

"Wait." Kiersten holds up her hands. "Why would he summon Medusa and her sisters? It makes no sense."

"Aion told you," Allie says. "Kyle was obsessed with snakes. And power. He and Riko must've summoned Medusa together. It all fits."

Aion grabs the book from her. "Maybe there's something in here about reversing it."

The three of them search and search but there's nothing in the notebook about reversal and they can't find any more notebooks. The night has destroyed whatever else there was.

"Blood offerings?" Allie suggests after a while. "Whenever a sacrifice is needed in films, it's always blood. People cut their palms, don't they?"

That will bring Medusa back, at the least, won't it? And Allie wants to speak to Medusa again. She feels a connection to her.

Medusa is strong. Her position as the Power has proved she's her own weapon, and no one controls her. Allie wants to help Medusa and she wants Medusa to help her.

Aion nods. "Okay. I've got a knife."

The three of them cut their palms in turn. When it's Allie's turn, her skin seems to be tougher than the others' and her blood is strange, all thick and congealed, in clots. Kiersten looks horrified as she sees it, but she doesn't say anything, because they're trying to do a sacrifice, so they all just wait with their blood dripping.

Nothing happens.

"Maybe it needs to be in the castle—maybe in front of Medusa, or what remains of her. Or in front of all three sisters if all three have been involved in this?" Allie shudders.

"Or maybe it needs to be Riko's blood," Aion mutters. "Maybe we can't stop this."

Kiersten frowns. "Riko donated blood—he was always going on about how wonderful he was because of that. Lording it over those who didn't or couldn't."

"So, there'll be some of his blood somewhere?"

"At the hospital," Kiersten says. "We can take a look. Then do all the blood sacrifices together, back at the castle."

"Sounds like a plan," Aion says.

Allie doesn't say anything.

THE THREE OF THEM BREAK INTO THE hospital. Not that it's breaking in. They just walk in. No one to stop them.

Kiersten knows where they're going, so Allie and Aion follow. They get the blood and Kiersten finds some antibiotics for Allie. Not the right ones though. But Allie barely notices this or considers the implications for her kidneys. She's too preoccupied by the sight and smell of the hospital rooms. The places where the doctors should be, where they were when they talked her through her decision to have an abortion.

She'd never realized there were so many abortion methods. She thought she'd just book into a clinic and that would be it. But the doctors wanted to talk and talk and talk. She didn't want counseling. She just wanted it to be over with. The longer it went on, the longer she waited, the more people would find out.

And they did find out. Her father spitting furious words at her, not believing her when she tried to tell him what had happened, saying it was all her fault. Kyle calling her a slag, laughing, until he realized she was serious when she said she would go to the police, that she'd tell everyone, that she could prove it all. And then he saw only one option, and of course he had the perfect family to help him.

Allie had no one. Not really—because although Ellie had tried to comfort her in secret at first, she couldn't stand up to the O'Donovans publicly, not if she didn't want to lose her job at the factory. Even the bloody factory was owned by them. And one of them must've said something to Ellie, because next thing Allie knew, her sister was telling her to be quiet about her 'story.'

The O'Donovans even took her sister from her.

Lost in memories and miserable, she slips on something wet on the hospital floor, surges forward and—

She falls from the tower, screaming. She tries to turn, mid-air. Above her, leaning out the window of the west tower, the faces of Kyle and Riko O'Donovan are the last things she sees before her body slams into the ground. A moment of pain—thick, excruciating, suffocating pain—and then nothing.

Allie jolts back to the present, breathing hard.

"You okay?" Kiersten asks her.

Allie nods.

But she's not. Not in the slightest.

Kyle and Riko . . . They killed her. Only—she's alive.

TEN

Her head pounds. None of this makes sense. She doesn't know what to think. And she feels . . . nothing. She's just empty.

On autopilot, she and Aion follow Kiersten out of the hospital and back toward the tower, passing her house on the way. She stops when she sees it—the only house on the street that is still partly standing. Everyone else's has been flattened.

Where her father's statue once stood is only wreckage. But she doesn't care about him. Not after the hateful words he spewed at her when she needed a parent most. When she was traumatized and scared and alone and had gone to him for help—only to be shunned.

She just looks for her sister—because suddenly rescuing Ellie is the most important thing. She's got to make sure her sister's okay. She has to.

Aion tries to stop her, but Allie ignores him. She steps over broken timbers and shards of glass and wires—so many wires, green and red, with exposed ends—and steps inside the ruin of her house. It reminds her of Blackthorne Castle, how part of that is in ruins but part is standing. Her house is the same.

Allie reaches the cupboard under the stairs—jagged plasterboard and peeling paint and broken wood. But the cupboard is still there. *Ellie* is still there.

She drags her sister behind her, out of the wreckage of their half-surviving home. It's difficult, and her kidneys are hurting, and she's lightheaded. Hell, it's not even fair that her kidneys still hurt her. Isn't that supposed to stop when you die?

Then she reminds herself that this isn't Hell. This is real. Somehow, she's still alive. So she survived the fall?

But she didn't. She's sure of it.

She plows on, dragging Ellie. Neither Aion nor Kiersten offer to help her.

But she doesn't need them. She will protect her sister.

THEY TRY WITH RIKO'S BLOOD FIRST, USING the flashlight on Aion's phone. They drip the blood onto the floor of the west tower room. Allie finds herself wishing it was Kyle's blood they had as well. She wants to see both of them on the floor, weak and pathetic.

She'd have liked to see Kyle's transformation into stone. See the look of sheer terror on his face. She'd have reveled in it.

Still, his brother is the next best thing, and Allie is not careful with his blood.

"What's up with you?" Aion asks her, glancing at her strangely.

Allie realizes she's frozen to the spot. She's staring at the place where the window had been—that crude space she remembers, with no glass. She blinks and heat flushes through her and she sees herself being forced through there Riko and Kyle. Thrown from the window—by her murderers.

Murderers.

"Allie?" Aion's voice gets louder.

Allie shakes her head. "When did it happen?" she murmurs, and she's counting on her fingers, trying to work it out.

Kiersten stands behind Aion, looking confused.

Allie keeps counting. "A month ago . . . ?" Was that when she . . . died?

"What? Just before the stonifications started?" Aion says. "What are you talking about?"

Allie points at where the window should be. Shivers work through her body. "I . . ."

"Come on, just make a circle with the blood," Kiersten says, and Allie realizes she is holding Riko's blood still. It's in a transfusion bag, but she can't shake the way it feels like his actual blood is touching her.

Her *murderer* is in her hands.

"Make a circle with it," Kiersten says again.

Allie makes a circle with it while her gut churns.

"Or a star?"

She makes a very wonky star with it, and she gets some of it on her hands. She doesn't like that. Doesn't like the thought that one of the O'Donovan brothers is still touching her.

"Maybe it needs our blood too—as we're the ones trying to reverse it?" Aion says.

Allie doesn't wince as the blade slices open her palm. She barely even feels the pain. She can't think of anything but her murder—because she was murdered. She is sure.

Nothing happens. Maybe they're not doing it right. Maybe they need to say the magic words.

A snort rises in Allie's throat. This isn't a fairytale where magic words will save them all.

This isn't a fairytale at all.

"Try dripping the blood onto the notebook," Kiersten suggests.

"Or onto Medusa." Allie indicates the crumbled remains. She doesn't like looking at the small pile of rubble just off-center of the doorway. They need to bring her back here, talk to her, find a way to stop the stonifications, help each other.

The light from Aion's phone dims and flickers as they drip the blood on Medusa's old mask. Allie grits her teeth. Will this do it? Will this be enough?

"Please," she whispers, and her voice is strange. It's pleading and it's begging and it's desperate, because she's tired now. So tired suddenly. "I need to know what happened." And Medusa will tell her, won't she?

Her kidneys are hurting more, enough for her to cry, and it's not fair that she's still got their pain when all this is going on, when . . .

A loud thud fills the room. Allie jumps, turns.

The tower shakes. It's falling. The storm's gotten into the bubble. It's not safe.

Cold air whips around her.

"Run!"

They all scurry, and Allie tries to grab Ellie, tries to bring her with them, but her sister's hand breaks off in hers. She runs, holding onto Ellie's fingers, clenching them close to her chest and—

The wall of the castle blows out. Power erupts from the sky, and someone's howling.

No, *Euryale* is howling. Allie doesn't know how she knows it's her—the second oldest of the Gorgon sisters—but she does.

And Allie can't breathe. Her lungs are on fire, and she trips, falls—only she doesn't fall. Something catches her, the air catches her, the sky catches her, and she is up there and down here at once. Her soul is in two, three, four pieces. No, more. She is everywhere, and she looks over the town of Blackthorne, looks over the whole of Devon, of England, as she searches for people. Because man needs to pay. Man *has* to pay. That was the deal.

The deal? Allie blanches. But it's there in her mind—a foggy scene where the gods were there, around her, and she was broken, flying free and desperate.

"It's you . . ." Aion's voice wobbles, and he points at Allie, and she's back on the ground again. She's outside the tower, and her breaths aren't right, and she can't remember getting there. She doesn't know what is happening, and it scares her more than anything—more even than being in the tower room with Kyle and Riko.

Riko. The man she invited into her house. Her team's leader. Allie turns—in her human body—and throws up sour, stringy bile. She wipes it from her mouth, tries to flick away the long stringy pieces of it that stick to her fingers.

Kiersten is shrieking, and Allie wishes she wouldn't.

And Allie looks up and realizes that the face in the sky *is* her face. She is looking in a mirror, and it is her up there. What the hell?

"You're Medusa!"

Somewhere to her right, Aion's voice is full of disbelief, and Allie is staring at herself in the sky. Just her head. Beheaded. Her snakes are angry.

She's really dead.

Fury fills her and she turns, heading down from the tower, for the O'Donovans' property. Her muscles ache and burn, but the ache is good. It's pain. It means something is going to happen.

"Allie!" Aion shouts after her. "Allie, what's going on?"

But Allie doesn't answer—because power is flooding through her. Power that connects her to herself in the sky, to Medusa. She is Medusa. And she remembers.

ELEVEN

"*M*aliah? Maliah, you need to wake up."

A twisting sensation pulls through Allie as she opens her eyes. At first, she can't see anything. There's just darkness, and she's not sure she even is awake. Is alive—because she remembers plummeting from the tower window, remembers the fall, remembers the crack through her spine, the pain in her legs, and arms—and then nothing more.

"*Maliah, you need to see us.*"

The words twist inside Allie, awakening her senses. She feels small twigs digging into her back and something cold and hard beneath her left hand. The back of her head feels wet and sticky. Slowly the darkness lifts, moving at the corners first, like there's a square blanket over her and just the corners are being lifted.

But then the whole blanket disappears, and her vision is pixelated. A dark mass over her, moving, squirming, as the pixelation clears.

Medusa's severed head hangs above her. Just the head—stopping right below her jaw. No neck. Allie can see the vertebrae of Medusa's spine, the one anchoring onto the skull. Tissue and sinews hang down.

Allie screams—but only a squeak comes out. She tries to sit up, but she cannot move.

Her body . . .

Her eyes widen—or at least she thinks they do. She sees the tower above her, behind Medusa's head. The window looks even higher. Riko and Kyle are long gone.

"*I am here as requested,*" *Medusa says.* "*Now that the final piece of the summoning has been completed.*"

Requested? The final piece?

Allie frowns. Then she remembers her notebooks, the incantations, the spells she was trying to do in the tower—because she wanted revenge on Kyle. Only then he turned up. He laughed at her, called her names, and then his brother arrived. She abandoned the spell . . . and it needed the final bit to be cast still.

Someone must've done it.

A strange feeling brushes over her soul. She looks back up at the window, and sees a face. Aion. He's crying.

"He completed the summoning for you," Medusa whispers.

"What? Can he see me?" Allie nearly chokes. She doesn't want her best friend to see her like this.

"You are not really here, Maliah. They removed your body two weeks ago."

"My body? They all think I'm dead."

"You are. And the papers printed what the O'Donovans paid them to—or at least they did at first. Now, what do you want most of all right now?" Medusa whispers. "I want to help you. I recognize myself in your soul, and we never turn our back on a sister."

As she speaks, Medusa's snakes radiate out from her head, like a peacock's tail. And behind Medusa, Allie sees the Gorgons. Two of them. Monstrous women with snakes for hair.

"Stheno and Euryale," Allie breathes.

The three Gorgon sisters smile.

"We have contacts, we can get you whatever you want, Maliah, but you have to say it now. Time is running out."

Allie looks up at the beautiful creatures. "I want to go back. I want all of this to have never happened. Aion can't think I'm dead!"

"Cronus and the Fates owe us," Euryale says. "They can rewrite the timestream and correct the life thread."

"Cronus?" Medusa says. "The god of time? No. He is destructive. We need Aion, the god of eternity."

Aion? Allie thinks of her best friend.

"Aion does not owe us," Euryale says. "And seeking him out would alert others of what we are trying to do—they'd stop us."

Medusa's eyes fix onto Allie. "Very well. We can try, but Cronus craves chaos. We cannot guarantee time and life will resume as you know it."

Hope surges within Allie. She just has to be alive again—she can't have let the O'Donovans win. "That's fine!" It wasn't like life as she'd known it had been so great, anyway.

"Is there anything else you want?" Medusa asks.
"Revenge," Allie says. "I want revenge."
"Then this shall be revenge," Medusa says, and Allie feels no more.

TWELVE

The ground beneath her feet rumbles with every step Allie takes, and the sky cracks. A bolt of lightning shoots down and grabs a sliver of the horizon. Hissing sounds fill the air.

But with every step she takes, she gets stronger, more and more power flowing through her veins. The power of Medusa, who she's merged with. The power of Cronus, the god of time, who must've bent the timestream for her. The power of the Fates who brought her back.

The sign for Meadowview Road is lying down, broken clean in two. Adrenaline pounds through her as she makes her way to number thirty-one.

There. She sees Riko.

He is frozen to the spot, just outside the front door—the frame is still standing, and the door's hanging off its hinges slightly. With a smile, she realizes he's reaching for the door handle. A task he never completed.

Good. Look at how much *she* never completed.

She doesn't need him—not for answers, not as her leader. She knows what happened now, and who's to blame.

And she will make them pay.

Kyle's still by the flowerbed, but Allie runs at Riko's statue first. She slams his stone body into the doorframe, shattering his right arm.

She doesn't know if the stonified bodies can feel pain, but even if they can, it doesn't matter. Riko hasn't suffered nearly enough.

She grabs him, hauling him up, struggling under his weight, then shoves him back down. He doesn't break.

Allie lets out a guttural scream, her fury unleashing more and more power. Above her, the sky crackles, and she looks up—sees her face up there. The snakes on her head whip about in the sky, getting bigger and bigger, elongating until they're reaching down to the earth, down to Allie.

She doesn't know how she does it, but she controls the snakes, directs them to slither under Riko's broad shoulders, under his waist, his legs. The snakes lift him up.

"Higher!" Allie hisses, watching as the statue gets smaller and smaller above her, until he's small enough and got the farthest to fall. "Now!" she screams.

The snakes throw Riko down.

He lands in the rubble, shattering, throwing dust and grit against Allie's seeping eyeballs, but she doesn't blink. She doesn't do anything. She just watches the cracks as they run across his body.

And when the dust has settled and the snakes have returned to the sky, she turns her attention to Kyle.

"It's your turn, *baby*," she whispers, making her way toward him. And it's not fair that he's made of stone, because she wants him to flinch. She wishes he'd been able to see what she just did to Riko. She wants him to feel fear.

She wants revenge.

Allie grabs a handful of gravel. It's laced with broken pieces of glass and they stab her fingers, but she doesn't feel the pain, just stares at the streams of crimson from her hand, how they run in rivulets over the pebbles. It doesn't look right. Then she shakes her head, shakes all that away, and focuses on the one thing she's always wanted to do since Kyle hurt her.

With the power of Medusa flowing into her, Allie flings the gravel at Kyle's statue. She flings the gravel harder and harder, scraping more of it off the ground. *There.* She chips Kyle's eye. Satisfaction fills her, and it swells inside her, pulses to get out, to expand.

And Allie lets it, lets it drive her.

She looks toward the pile of rubble that is the house. Her eyes fall on a broken bit of wood. Within seconds, it's in her hands. Feels a good weight.

She strikes Kyle's body over and over again.

"Allie! What are you doing?"

It's Aion's voice. He grabs her, and Allie shouts at him, tries to push him away, but he doesn't back off.

"No!" she screams, whirling around with her weapon.

Aion's eyes widen. He's breathing hard, panting. There's a new cut on his face. A snake of red weaving down his right cheek. Crimson on white.

"What are you doing? Allie—what the hell is going on?"

She tries to turn back to Kyle's shattered body, but Aion gets in the way. Annoyance fills her. Does he think she won't hit him?

Then she startles—where did that thought come from? That wasn't her . . . that was . . . She looks up at the sky. Was it one of them? A Gorgon putting her thoughts inside Allie?

She'd never hurt Aion. He's her friend—her only one.

But she has work to do.

"Get away, I need to finish this." Her voice is a hiss.

"It was you?" He stares at her. "You summoned Medusa?"

"No! You did—*you* finished the summoning," Allie says. "You don't remember, but it's true."

Aion's eyes widen. "But how . . . You're her. You're Medusa. How is this possible? Why don't I remember?" Confusion and anger battle to win his face. "Allie! Why aren't you speaking? Answer me!"

Her heart beats heavier, and she looks up at the sky. The Medusa face—*her* face—is watching. She sees herself blink up there, and then just for a moment, she is up there too. Her soul in that body, and she's looking down. Down at the hundreds and thousands of towns and cities in England that she's taken out her revenge on.

This is what her enhanced night vision is good for. To see the havoc she's wreaked.

To see her revenge. To see how it spread beyond the men she meant it for.

"Allie?" It's Kiersten's voice.

Allie snaps back into her body—the rotting corpse—and jolts toward Kiersten, in shock. Power floods from her hand and fires out toward the older woman. It hits Kiersten in the chest, and Kiersten makes a small noise of surprise. Then her hands turn gray. Stone. Allie watches as the stone spreads.

"What the hell?" Aion's voice shakes. He is looking at Allie—pure fear on his face now. He backs away slowly, his hands held up. "Why are you doing this? Kiersten's our friend."

"I didn't mean to," Allie whispers, horrified. "It was an accident."

She looks down at her hands, ashamed—and then her skin begins to change. It's forming welts, and then it's splitting, and her flesh—rotten and swollen—is bursting out from under the skin. She is a monster, just as Athena made Medusa into a monster all those years ago, punishing her for the crime Poseidon had committed against her.

Allie looks at her body, her rotting carcass. At her face in the sky. Then back at her friend. He's staring at her, revulsion on his face—and she can't blame him. He takes a step back, then another one and another one. Trying to get as far away from her as possible.

Allie starts to reach out to him, and he retreats even further.

"No! I'm your friend! You're not doing that to me! I'm your only friend, Allie."

She's still reaching for him, and she realizes what he thinks. That she'd hurt him. And it reminds her of the thought she had earlier—that she *could* hurt him. But, no, he's her best friend. He was there for her—even if he doesn't remember everything. They have to stick together.

"Aion, I . . ." Her words get stuck in her throat. She feels strange. With Kyle and Riko dead—one smashed now by her hand, the other cracked and chipped—she expected to feel better. Freer. But she doesn't. Because she thinks of everyone else. She looks around. She can see the other statues on Meadowview Road. So many people.

Her family. Her own sister. Her father. Her chest hitches. She's responsible for all of this.

"Why, Allie?" Aion demands.

Her fingers start to shake, but she doesn't want to look at them, not when she can feel her skin is still splitting. "I wanted revenge," she says. Her words twist in front of her, ethereal ovals and oblongs that flip over and over.

"On what?" Aion cries.

"On the world, on everything." She shrugs out of desperation; she doesn't know which words to use. "On Kyle. On Riko. And on everyone who didn't believe me."

"Didn't believe you? About what?"

"What Kyle did. I wanted to make everyone pay," she says, and she has. "I wanted everyone to feel how I felt. And this is it . . . This is what death looks like, what it feels like." She lifts her arms, gesturing around them at everyone turned to stone.

"What did he do? Wait. You're *dead?*"

"Slain by the boy who took what he wanted from me and didn't want to face the consequences." She is remarkably calm. "They shoved me out of the tower. Kyle and Riko. The west tower in the castle. It used to have a window—before all of this. I don't know why that's gone . . . But Riko and Kyle made it look like suicide."

"Suicide? No, you're not dead." Aion starts to laugh, but then he stops, staring at her body. She doesn't need to see herself to know she is grotesque now, changed beyond recognition.

"I am dead. You read the articles, Aion," she says, and she keeps her voice soft. Everyone read the articles. She remembers that now—because leaving this world hadn't been immediate. She'd hovered in between, before the Gorgons found her. And she'd seen the newspaper reports, learned how her memory had been defamed.

"But you're here . . . And you're her!" Aion points at the Medusa head—the *Allie* head—in the sky. "And you've been doing this . . . I thought it was Riko?"

"No. It was me. The notebook was mine—the one we planned the summonings in. Kyle took it." And she's looking at him carefully. Because he completed the spell in the west tower room—he must've learned the spell by heart. He finished the summoning for Medusa. "You don't remember, do you?"

Aion's face is blank. He's just shaking his head. "You did this? The stonifications . . . my *family*."

She shrugs again. "I needed people to pay. He raped me, Aion. Kyle raped me, and my father didn't believe me. The town didn't."

Aion takes a step back. "Kyle did what?" His face darkens and there's fire in his eyes.

Allie looks down. She can't say the words again.

"Allie, I . . ." He runs his hands though his hair. "Allie, this is . . . I'm so sorry. Why didn't you tell me?"

"I did . . . before. But everyone's forgetting—and it's because of the deal I made. Because the O'Donovans killed me, and I wanted it all to be undone. So I made the deal—and you finished the summoning."

Aion takes several deep breaths. "They killed you?" He swears under his breath. His hands are shaking as he clenches them into fists. "Allie . . . this . . ." He struggles to find the words. "You should've told me," he says. "What they did. I would've believed you. Of course I would've."

"You did—the first time I told you." She tries to smile, but it doesn't work. Her face feels too rigid. "You believed me then— you were the only one who did."

"Then why didn't you just tell me this time?"

Allie lets out a shaky breath. She's now not sure exactly at what point she realized that Aion had forgotten too. Her memories are all jumbled, turned inside out. "It doesn't matter now. What matters is justice has been served." She casts her eyes over the remains of Kyle and Riko.

Then she looks at the other statues. Collateral damage.

"It's all my fault," she whispers. "Everyone . . . all the stonifications. It's because of me." She gulps.

Aion breathes out a long breath, very slowly. "Can you undo it?"
Allie feels cold. So cold. "I don't know."

"You can," a voice whispers, and Allie looks up. There are two more beings in the sky. Euryale and Stheno. Her sisters. She feels a pull to them, and she's in between them, in the sky as well. "You just have to want to. Put it right, Allie, and then you can leave with us."

"Leave?" Allie's heart pounds. At least, she thinks it does. Is she imagining it? Can her heart be beating inside her rotted body if she's been dead for months? She turns to Aion, panic rising in her chest. She can't leave! Where will she go?

"You have to," Euryale says, "else this curse will strike every human."

"But you said I could come back!" Nausea swirls in her.

They said she could come back, and she said she wanted revenge—and she's got it. She smashed Kyle and Riko to pieces. And everyone else who didn't believe her . . . they're statues too. Only it's spread too far, beyond her town, and she can feel it's still growing.

She should go now—shouldn't she? Before she hurts anyone else?

"We did," Stheno says. "But we warned you about Cronus—he's too destructive. He's messed up the timestream, he let that storm loose, and he made people forget the wrong things. He combined his desire for destruction with our powers and that of the Fates, and embodied it all in you—in Medusa's frame. The energy of the world is unstable now, and time cannot hold you here much longer. Come on, Allie. Say goodbye."

THIRTEEN

Tears stream down Allie's face, but her face must have split into raw wounds because the salt of her tears stings, corroding her flesh away.

Aion recoils from her.

"I'm so sorry," she whispers. "I didn't know this would happen." She looks back up at the sky. For a second, she sees Ellie's face in Euryale's and Sarah's in Stheno's. But then her sisters are gone, and she feels their loss as if they've just been snatched from her.

The pain of the loss gets bigger and bigger, and suddenly she's connected to every surviving person in the country who's lost family and friends. Because of her. She tries to disconnect from it, the all-consuming feeling of loss, and she concentrates on the sky, takes over Medusa's viewpoint. But looking down, Allie sees it all. Her vision zooms in one statue, and then another, and another, and another . . . So many, and she's seeing each in close-up snapshots: the frozen tears on a child's face as she took away his life; two elderly women sitting on a park bench; a mother trying to comfort her baby, both frozen. More and more and more images fill Allie's mind, until she screams, breaks the connection.

Shaking, trembling next to Aion, Allie feels sick. She pulls in huge gulping breaths and looks into the sky. "How do I reverse it?"

"You come up here, and you embrace us," Stheno says. "You have to leave that body behind. We didn't think it would get out of hand this badly, but it has. The Fates say you're too strong, you're tangling the life thread, and Cronus knew there would be this much destruction—because that's what he loves, that's what he always gets. That'll be why he said he'd help us. You can't trust men."

Allie's gaze crosses to Aion. No, she *can* trust him. She's always been able to trust him.

"Say goodbye and join us. Join us fully. We will welcome you to our ranks and we need our sister back."

"Medusa?" Allie says.

Euryale nods and points at the beheaded Medusa-Allie in the sky. "You are inhabiting her body, forcing her out. We have to right the order of the world."

"And do it quickly," Stheno says. "It is nighttime now and all across the country you're still claiming more victims. And while you can return some of them to life, not all will survive."

Allie nods and gulps. "I'm so sorry, Aion," she says. "I didn't mean for this to happen."

At last, he looks up at her. His face has never looked so angry. She assumes he's furious with her—as he should be—but then he speaks, and she understands.

"If Riko or Kyle somehow wake up from all this, I'll kill them," he says. "They don't deserve life."

Allie nods. "Thank you." She takes a shaky breath as more of her face burns away. "Can you find Ellie? Can you be with her when she wakes up, so she won't be scared?"

Aion nods. There are tears in his eyes.

"Please, go now," Allie whispers.

For a second, she doesn't think Aion's going to leave. That he's going to insist on staying with Allie until she's gone. But then he nods again, the slightest of movements, and turns away.

With a crumbling heart, Allie looks up at the sky, where the ghosts of her new Gorgon sisters float—and more and more of them are appearing, more Gorgons. It's not just Euryale and Stheno behind the Medusa mask. It's a whole sisterhood to welcome her, the transformed souls of countless girls wronged by man.

Allie feels her body lifting up—no, her soul, her essence, because she's looking down too and her rotting carcass collapses onto the rubble.

She knows where to go.

A thousand ethereal lights radiate from her body, and she's still rising, still embracing her destiny, her fate—and with every inch she rises, the lighter she gets, and on earth, one by one, a statue wakes.

She takes one last look back, and her eyes zoom in on Aion's figure as he runs to the west tower of Blackthorne Castle. It seems to take him both forever and no time at all before he is inside, racing up to the tower room where Ellie is. Aion gets there just as Ellie wakes, and if Allie still had a heart, it would be pounding or hitching or catching or something, as she watches life infuse the statue as light floods the room.

Light.

The window—it's back. The tower's returning to normal. The world is returning to normal.

Ellie's fingers move at first, and Aion's shouting in excitement, shouting Ellie's name, reaching out for her. He touches her remaining hand and sees her arm becoming flesh again, then her shoulder, her neck, her face. Allie smiles.

Then she is weightless in the sky, turning, spinning, following the dazzling light that leads to the sisterhood.

"Welcome," the Gorgons say. "We've got you, Maliah. You're one of us now, and we never let our sisters down."

INVISIBLE DEMONS
RISHI MOHAN

BEFORE

The amount of time Dad spends around hospitals, you'd think he's either a doctor or, well, my dad.

My small hand trembles in his as he pulls me off his horse. We're in front of a garbage-filled sewer that winds next to the Hospital de la Ciudad de México. No doubt the result of one of Dad's friends' work.

"Are they ready yet?" Dad asks my half-brother. I've never met him before. He has a name but I don't bother remembering it.

"I've been keeping them prepared for you," Brother says, as a scream of pain comes from behind him. The voice fractures the air into a million shards of glass.

Dad enters the sewer tunnel, gesturing for me to follow. I want to hesitate but demons never show vulnerabilities, so I keep my chin up and walk in confidently.

"You're finally ready to see this part of my job," Dad explains. "I'm proud of you, Isabella."

I flush at his approval, feeling a bit of pride that I'm finally old enough that he trusts me on his missions.

At the end of the tunnel, we enter a sickroom in the hospital's basement. This is my least favorite part. Sick people. Kind of inconvenient, given my dad's line of work.

There's a little girl around my age asleep on the bed. She probably has posters of Taylor Swift on her walls at home, an opinion on which One Direction band member is the most crush-worthy, and tons of friends at her school. Unlike me. Homeschooling sucks sometimes.

Her mom is holding her hands and sobbing as the girl coughs on the bed. I can see the germs from each cough spreading in the air. Humans are so weird with how they don't seem to care in the least bit about cleanliness.

"Please, God, don't let her die," her mom cries.

Uh-oh. Dad hates it when they pray. His wings start to glow a fierce red. Not that anyone in the room can see it, since Dad pulled us all the way into the ethereal dimension.

The girl starts to cough more, and the machine she's attached to beeps erratically. Her arms quake, as if trying to ward off the evil that surrounds her. Then the monitor goes silent. No heartbeat, no Taylor Swift songs, no friends.

I'm sure that the woman is about to scream: her mouth is opening wide, throat clenching up. Dad pushes me towards her. "Your turn."

"I don't want to do anything!" I say. "She's just lost her daughter. Isn't that enough?"

The woman lets out a bloodcurdling wail and Brother shoves me away. "We should put her out of her suffering." He places one hand on the mother's head. She grasps the left side of her chest and falls to the floor, a heap of gray clothes.

The room around me is now filled with death. I feel sick, vomit rising in my stomach. Thank goodness demons have strong control, or I'd be throwing up the enchiladas con carne Dad bought me for lunch.

A nurse runs in. Dad laughs to my right, a dark, deep chuckle that resounds through the room and the nurse screams in fright.

Dad grabs my arm and pulls us back outside. "Isabella, next time it will be your turn. Don't hesitate again," he says. I can see his disappointment in the harsh lines on his narrow face and I feel disappointed in myself too. I should be a better daughter. But my heart still stutters over what I just saw.

He places his hand on my shoulder. "What have you learned today?"

"How to kill people that way?" I ask. My voice doesn't quaver. Demons don't care. Don't care. Don't.

396

Dad doesn't reply, and I make another guess. "We don't have to stop at one death?"

Brother laughs coldly behind me. "We don't have to stop ever." I shiver a bit from his dead voice.

Dad nods. "We're demons, Isabella. We don't do love. We don't do kindness or service or community. What we do is fear."

PART ONE

I'm not allowed to have my wings out at school. Something about needing to blend in with the humans, half of whom don't believe in demons and the other half believe in the wrong sort. Dad says they're too dumb to pick up on the clues—really, the chem club actually thought I made it halfway across the city in LA traffic in ten minutes?—and they're too blind to see the literal rays of energy that glow off my body. I'm less anti-human than most demons, but I'm not going to lie. It's pretty frustrating that humans can't even see the ethereal dimension.

And other times, it's pretty frustrating that they see things at all. Like, they probably wouldn't miss the thick, dark feathers sprouting from my back as I sit in a huddle on the roof of my high school. It's a safe act of defiance, letting them pop out into reality and the human visual range. The students can't get up here, and Dad's halfway across the world, busy trying to make sure Bill Gates doesn't eradicate polio.

"Really, Isabella?" A voice resounds like a deep bell across the concrete. "The wings again? It doesn't look as edgy as you think it does, you know. It's just reckless."

Guess I should clarify. *Human* students can't get up here. Ethereals find it very easy.

"Shut up, Callum." I turn my head all the way around, without moving my body. Like an owl. My glare is piercing, but I smile at him. Even though he's an angel, and I'm a demon, and it's against every canonical law, that boy makes me smile.

Cal and I have been friends since the first day of ninth grade. I set the lab on fire, Cal got detention for it, and now it's been three years of classes and pranks like tricking school bullies into confessing on camera. It's always Cal and Izzy, Izzy and Cal. Somewhere along the way, I fell a very tiny little bit in love with him. Even though Dad also says demons can't fall in love.

"What if someone sees you?" Callum points a finger at a tall office suite at least seven blocks away. "Anyone could look out a window, you know."

"Human eyes aren't that good. If they notice anything, they'll think it's a late Halloween costume. And my wings were born to be free."

"Keep them in. Don't make me have to make you." Callum frowns and advances on me, his crystalline-white wings blown out behind him in the ethereal dimension. I see his long curls laced with gold, his glowing skin. To human eyes, he's a brown-haired mop top with glasses, wearing torn jeans, no wings. Which is a good thing, since humans aren't supposed to know we exist.

"It's cooler this way." I reach a hand out to glide across my right wing. "They're so obsidian . . . and pretty, don't you think?" I drop my voice to a velvet lilt.

He blushes like the sun. "You—you know I think you're beautiful, Izzy."

I freeze, my mouth falling open, cheeks turning flushed. It's been ages of me casually touching his arm, and dropping hints about his looks, and dressing up way more than anyone legally should for school. This is the first time he's called me beautiful.

He smiles. "And I can see them even if they're only in the ether, so there's no need to make them visible unless you *want* humans to figure us out."

Well . . . that sounds more like him. I sigh and let a glow wash over me, my wings fading into the ethereal.

"Fine. But you shouldn't threaten to use your magic on me." I stand up, facing him. "I'll jump off the roof if you try that again."

"Come on, Izzy. I'm just trying to help. If your dad caught you . . . if *my dad caught you.*" There it is, the fear in his eyes and trembling in his lips.

"You're a coward, Cal. And, if they caught us both up here, you and me," I point between us, "you think the wings are what they're going to care about?"

The Capulets were angels and the Montagues were demons. Look what happened to them. Angels and demons are never supposed to mix. Never.

He groans and stumbles to the edge of the roof, crumpling down next to me. "I don't want to do this anymore." At first, his words are so soft I barely hear him, but he repeats them. "I really don't want to do any of this anymore."

Dad says demons can't have hearts, but it's moments like this when I know he's wrong. There's ice in my chest. "You want to stop being friends?"

"I . . . didn't say that," Cal says and his eyes bore into mine. The light dapples on his high cheekbones and caresses his hair. "It's just. Come on, I know you hate lies. You can't like hiding any more than I do. You're upset about your wings, for Christ's sake. What about hiding your hopes, dreams, aspirations, and best friend?"

"You're not my best friend," I say automatically, a smile touching my lips.

"Liar." He sticks his tongue out at me, but his eyes are pale, the way they always are when something is really bothering him. "I'm just done with all this, you know? I want to be a normal teenager with normal parents. Plural. Not have some dad who's got a dozen other kids around the world and who cares more about if my wings are out than what my name is."

"At least your dad only has a dozen kids." I sigh as my thick black hair frisks in the wind. I have over two hundred siblings. Something about how demons are worse—better?—at certain temptations. But all Ethereal kids have pretty much the same story: large empty homes where we grew up with nannies and tutors and seeing our parent once every few months. A lot of the time we don't know who our human parent is, or they took off the minute they realized that we were half-Ethereal. Like my mother.

"Well, my point stands. I want to be seen with you. I want to hang out . . . and stuff. Not just at school when they aren't watching. I want to text you every night without being terrified your dad or mine is checking our damn phones."

"We—can't do that." I flex my fingers, feeling the gold rings on them twist and grate against my skin. "That doesn't mean we can't stay friends, Cal. We've done it for *years*. Nothing needs to change." *Even though I want it to, sometimes . . .*

"Maybe I want things to change," he says. I blink up at him and he's looking out at the school fields, squinting at the students milling around. "Maybe I don't want to be *just* friends anymore." He turns to face me, letting his wings out.

I release mine, too, until they're both billowing out behind us like art. My heart is thudding . . . surely, he doesn't mean what I think he does, does he? After all this time?

His eyes search mine and then fall to my lips.

I lean up and kiss him hesitantly. His lips part and his tongue brushes mine. The power of a thousand stolen glances from the past three years floods through me.

His arms wrap around me, and I feel his wings beating against mine. We levitate a full four feet off the edge before coming to our senses. His smile is blinding when I pull away.

"Yeah, obviously, idiot," I answer the question he never asked. "I didn't think I'd succeed at tempting you." I mean it teasingly, but the words choke me. I open my mouth to explain that of course I haven't been using love curses or spells or anything else on him—nothing except my natural demonic charm—but he cuts me off.

"I've *always* been tempted, Isabella." He puts an arm around my waist and pulls me against his body.

I shudder. "Yeah?"

He tucks a strand of my hair behind my ear. He's done it a thousand times in the past three years. Maybe he's been flirting with me this whole time. "Dinner and a movie Friday night or is that too cliché?" he asks.

"How about tonight?" I play with his curls.

He doesn't say yes, but his mouth is on mine again.

I LOVE TALKING ABOUT CALLUM AND ME, BUT here is quite possibly how I *should* have started this story. My name is Isabella Lance and I am the daughter of the demon Patrick Lance. Yeah, he's a demon demon. You know the winged creatures who spend their lives torturing humanity on behalf of hell? One of those. One of the most powerful, too.

I used to follow Dad around the world, homeschooled by some gnarly tutor who loved grabbing my ass, until he inexplicably caught Ebola and died. Hey, I'm Dad's daughter, after all. When Dad found out, I got screamed at, whipped, and put in a human school in LA. Dad went back to killing people.

Cal is Callum Gabriel, otherwise known as Cal, son of the Archangel Gabriel. Yeah, that Archangel Gabriel. It doesn't get worse.

He used to be homeschooled by some gnarly tutor who loved grabbing *his* ass, until that dude inexplicably got killed by a stray rocket in the Middle East. A Gabriel-inspired move if I'd ever seen one, but Cal got screamed at, whipped, and put in a human school in LA. Gabriel went back to killing people. And that was that.

We were both warned to never let anyone at the school know who we really were. On pain of death. And Dad told me that with his horns full and his horse rearing, so he meant it.

Then we both broke the rules that first day when we stumbled into each other in the hall and saw each other in the ether.

"Oh my God, you're an angel!" Callum said in the squeaky fourteen-year-old voice he luckily grew out of.

"Demon, technically," I muttered. Three years later and our parents still don't know we even attend the same school, let alone that we're friends.

Which means being seen together in public—going to La Villa, one of the busiest restaurants in LA, and flying out to Universal Cinema later—are both very, very bad ideas. But my dad's overseas, and I'm a demon. I do bad.

What's Cal's excuse?

"I'VE WANTED TO DO THIS FOR WAY TOO LONG," Cal says, his hand in mine, as we use dangerous amounts of magic to appear in an empty corner of a *Bohemian Rhapsody* screening. Our stomachs are full of spaghetti and garlic bread. "And I wanted to do it right."

"Hey, did you know Rami Malek won the Oscar for this movie?" I whisper in his ear, letting my lips graze his cheek. "It's been winning awards all year. It's supposed to be good."

I cuddle into my seat and Cal puts his arm around me. I figure we'll probably be making out the whole time, but surprisingly, Callum seems riveted by the film. So, I watch too.

It *is* good. But it's also sad. Really fucking sad.

It's about Freddie Mercury, the lead singer of an old band in the '70s. He's secretly gay, he gets AIDS, and he dies. That's basically the point of it. When the credits roll, Cal's eyes are laced with tears. He's a crier.

"It's not a good idea to cry in front of the girl on the first date." I elbow him, trying to lighten the mood.

He gives me a watery glare. "Let's just get out of here."

It's silent on the walk back and eventually we settle on some random benches and people-watch. It's these little moments I'm grateful to be an Ethereal. I listen to the patter of feet and a grizzled homeless man singing *Sugar* by Maroon Five. Cal runs over to give the man his jacket to keep warm, before we continue walking hand-in-hand.

I'm still thinking about the movie, and I guess Cal is too. Because when he finally breaks the silence, it's to say, "You know your dad was behind AIDS, right?" He says it carefully. They say not to talk politics, religion, or your parents' work with friends. This is all three. "I heard it on the Angel Song radio."

"We don't know that for sure. And don't quote Angel Song to me." I shove his arm off my shoulders. "They lie about demons, and you know I hate being lied to. Why are we even talking about this?"

"You know that YouTube video I showed you the other day?" Cal continues. He never gets hints. If I want him to shut up, I have to tell him to shut up. "Those kids were dying of malaria. That's on your dad too. Does it really not bother you? Does none of this bother you?"

I snarl at him and draw out my staff in the ether. I want to zap him with some lightning. This is a completely inappropriate line of conversation. For a first date or ever.

"Cal—" I warn.

"Izzy." He turns, and his eyes blaze into mine. "It's starting to bother me."

"Why?" I shake my head at him. "It's none of our business. It's the humans' problem. We're teenagers. Go donate some of your infinite money if you're feeling bad about it."

"You don't feel bad? I mean, we *still* don't have a cure for AIDS. People were homophobic for generations because of it. It affects minorities and—"

"So what, Cal?" I say. I'm not heartless, but AIDS isn't my problem, and it isn't worth ruining my first date with Callum Gabriel. "Come on, like the Archangel hasn't been a nightmare for gays and minorities too."

Callum's eyes darken. Literally. The blue becomes midnight black and that only happens when he's really, really angry. I back off from him on the bench.

"I wasn't comparing our parents," he growls. "My dad doesn't care about AIDS as much as he should. But he isn't as bad as yours."

"I'm not so certain." I tense every muscle in my body.

"I'm just saying, it's like Ms. Wheeler said in government class. We're old enough to start doing things about things. Even humans try to make a difference. We have no excuse."

I throw up my arms in aggravation. I guess there won't be a goodnight kiss tonight. "So, what in God's name *do* you want to do?"

Cal's lip curls. "I didn't say it has to be in God's name—"

I'm not in the mood for jokes. "I'm serious." I don't know what he's talking about. Little gestures, like pranking school bullies or giving a coat to a homeless man, are one thing. But neither of us can take on our parents. Neither of us can even try. We're invisible to them.

Cal stands up and glows a little. A couple point at him. I hope they think it's just a trick of the light. "We could destroy the Talisman."

My chest feels laced with live wires. I tune into the ether, just to make sure no one heard him, to triple check my dad and his demon pals are halfway across the world and the closest demon of any type is at least a hundred miles away.

"That's blasphemy," I whisper. Or treason. Or so far above our pay grade that it has to be someone else's problem.

"Just think about it," Cal says. "AIDS, a Talisman thing. Depression, a Talisman thing."

I can't believe we're having this discussion. "Why do we have to get involved? *Seriously*, Cal? We are living happy, peaceful lives and you want us to take on a demon. And not just any demon, either. My *father*." I grow my heels into five-inch platforms until I'm looking down at him. "The angels have been trying to destroy the Talisman since Eden, with no success. And you think we can take it on? We don't even know where it is!"

"Look," Cal says, trying to reason with me. "If we keep dating, we're going to be found out, threatened, punished, worse. Just like Freddie Mercury."

"And you're thinking we should just do what? Pick the fight first?"

"That, and I'm telling you—what Wheeler was saying. Fix the world a bit. At least we could help a few thousand people."

My shoulders fall. This isn't the first time Cal has had a bad idea, even if the others didn't involve taking on our batshit crazy parents. It's what he does. Find something that sounds "good" and just do it. No attention to the risks or the actual consequences. And every single time, I've gone along with it.

"Just think about it." Cal squeezes his fingers in and out of tight fists.

I want to tell him he's insane. But instead I close my eyes, thinking back to one of the last times Dad took me on a work trip, before we grew apart.

DAD AND I FLEW TO A LITTLE WHITE BALCONY in Oklahoma City, outside a room with a mouse-haired boy playing with plastic bricks. We stood in the ether, Dad's shoulders thrown back and his hands sending little sparks towards the boy's parents.

"It's against what God tells us is right," the father said. He was a big, red-faced man with twisted lips.

"But, honey, what if he actually gets meningitis?" The mother frowned. "Surely he should get the vaccine."

"We have to hold true to our faith, love," the father said. "God will protect him."

Dad smirked, the cruel proud grin of a demon, as the mother twisted her hands together. "Do you want a turn?" he asked.

I nodded, used to years of following his directions. I spread a wave of calm through the mom, a well-placed lie racing through her brain. "You're right," she said, turning to her husband. "God protects us all."

Two years later, my father showed me the news clipping. The boy had died of meningitis—but not before his swollen brain kept him lying in pain for hours. Dad had laughed. It was the first time I realized he wanted to me to become a monster just like him.

I OPEN MY EYES AND SEE CALLUM LOOKING AT me, almost as if he can see the images that flashed in my mind. I want to hurt my father, the way he hurt that little boy—and the girl, so long ago, in Mexico City. The way he hurt me.

Before I can think better of it, I speak. "This is the worst proposal for a second date." I ball my hands. "But, okay. I'm in."

Cal lights up. "Really? We're—we're going on a date again?"

"Yeah." Feeling better already, I wink at him. "If taking on my dad and my species counts as a second date, then sure."

"Cool," he says, grabbing my arm. "We can figure out plans after class tomorrow. And if we destroy the Talisman, maybe my dad will like you. Or at least not kill you." Cal pauses. "Hopefully."

I sigh.

He leans down, lips brushing against mine sweetly. At least there ends up being a goodnight kiss after all.

PART TWO

If I had to pick my least favorite spots on Earth, our school library would be in the top ten. It's full of humans our age, all of them counting down the minutes until the end of the school day. Some read, some gossip with friends, and there's the group in the back corner with their boring radio tuned to 132 FM.

It's where students go to pretend to do homework while also pretending to follow the library's no-talking policy. Of course, the one good bit is that bored students don't pay attention to what they assume is someone else's homework, so Cal and I can talk freely here about the Talisman.

Cal has his arm around me, and the thrill from the contact is my first thought every time either of us moves. Occasionally, a guy stares at me from across the room. Cal glares at them, making me smile some more.

"This is going to be the most fun since the octopus," I say, grinning at the thought of the trouble that animal got up to after we rescued it from an aquarium and set it free.

I trail my hand along his thigh. His blush makes him even cuter.

"No, since the bonfire at least." He chuckles. To be fair, it's hard to top falling into a fire and seeing how blatantly bad the acting can get before people notice we're not hurt. It's what inspired Cal to audition for Puck in the school play. Didn't get the part, but he was the best Third Sprite any audience had ever seen. "You realize this is actually important, though."

"Of course. But it wouldn't be interesting if we couldn't get caught." I twirl my pen.

"Do you only think about the thrill? You know, if this works, we can make a pretty big difference. Save thousands of lives. Together, we can do anything." He gazes into my face.

"True," I say, still twirling my pen. "Sticking it to my dad would be a first. Even if it scores points for the angels."

His face darkens. He opens his mouth as if about to say something, then pauses as if deciding against it. Weird. He usually tells me everything that crosses his mind. "I just wish we knew where we were going," he says. "The Talisman could be anywhere. Any ideas?"

"Hey, it's rude to make the girl plan the date." I smile and elbow him.

"Don't worry." He grins back. "I bet I'll figure out where the Talisman is before you do."

"You're on." I take his hand.

His eyes shift away from mine. "Do you think it's with *him*? Could he be using the Talisman right now? Like in the story?"

We didn't grow up hearing many of the same stories. But there is one we both know. An implacable shadowy monster as old as humanity, with a thousand arms and no face. Crippling, maiming, killing, each strike strengthening it and increasing its reach. Humans learned that anyone who survived the dark god's curse would never be touched again. So they used this maxim, the brave protecting the vulnerable, until the invisible demon had nowhere left to strike. They stamped the demon out.

The version Cal heard stops there, with the triumphant humans gloating that they had beaten smallpox forever. But when my dad told it, that story was just about how many people his project killed before it ended. He showed me the Talisman he used as a battery: a priceless golden crown with points like rosy thorns representing everything he had conquered and taken from the helpless. I've even used the crown, sometimes, but I don't like thinking about that.

I shake my head. "I don't think he's currently using it. There's plenty of juicy human suffering around here, but not really his type. And he's been mostly living here these days, so if he was using the Talisman, I think we'd know."

"Okay. So if he's not using it right now, and we're assuming he doesn't have it on him, where could he be keeping it?"

I slide my hand further up his thigh before I answer, and Cal's cheeks burn. A human would probably see it as turning pink, but the thing about better visual ranges is that heat means he's literally shining. I should get him embarrassed more often.

"He has to be kicking off some new plan," I say, getting back down to business. "He's probably found somewhere near here to charge up the Talisman, somewhere with the greatest potential for disease, so that it can . . . um, impact more people, so to speak." I know how Dad works. I've helped him out many times, too. "No idea where, though." I tap my pen hard on the table and magic away the sound so we don't get kicked out.

Cal's eyes go wide and his head jerks back up. *Let there be a light bulb.* "I have an idea. And if you're right about it being close to home, we can find the exact address." He flips open his laptop and starts Googling with the hand that isn't around me. It's slow, barely one letter at a time, so I can watch him type: *Pig farms near me.*

Some second date. "Are you sure? Couldn't it be more like spy stuff instead?" I say hopefully. "Mad scientists with secret labs and Russian accents? Maybe he's cooking up a scheme in a lab somewhere."

"I am 100 percent not sure," he admits. "But it's our best odds. If I had your dad's job, and was starting a new project, a factory farm is where I'd be." The arm around me squeezes and his lips part.

"Well, let's go for it." I squeeze him back. "But just for the record, this is the worst second date ever."

As soon as the bell rings, we take flight.

FLYING IS NOTHING NEW. AS A MISBEHAVED demon, even flying in broad daylight isn't totally unprecedented. But convincing Cal to go along with it *is*.

To be fair, we're more like gliding along the ground than legit flying. We're staying low so that if humans see us, they'll think we're a couple of really fast runners in weird costumes and go back to their day. Besides, this is LA. No one notices pedestrians.

It's the kind of half-assed excuse Cal wouldn't normally buy, but for whatever reason, it works today. "I can't believe you're coming with me!" he howls over the whooshing air.

"What, like I haven't been waiting for this for years?" I shout back. He's silent for a few beats, just watching the strokes of my wings. I stretch them out further with each step and enjoy his stares. "I've finally got you committing crimes!"

Maybe that was the wrong thing to say. He stops staring. "Do you have to be like that?"

"Like what?" I have the sinking feeling that I already know the answer.

"All . . . demon-y. Building an identity around taking the wrong side of everything."

"Sure, I'll knock it off. Just tell me you're not into it." I smile again, winking and biting my lower lip.

He groans. "Not the point. It's like . . . angels are annoying, but at least when they say everything is black and white, they pick the right *side*. Most of the time. Some of the time."

I shake my head. "If that's what you think, you really don't get the point of being a demon. It's not about picking the *wrong* side, it's about *picking* the wrong side." Demon propaganda says it's about choice.

"Because that makes so much sense." He lands beside the road and crosses his arms. "At least when angels are obsessed with the greater good, they end up doing good."

I land next to him and let my eyes flash. "Says the person about to commit a crime right this minute. What's the plan? Trespass and theft and maybe even something serious? For the 'greater good,' of course."

"Yes! If this works, it'll save the next Freddie Mercury, and that's *worth* it." It's not a claim, or a statement, or an argument.

411

More like a declaration. Then his voice softens. "But it's not just that it's worth it. I get to spend today with you, you know? It's *fun*."

"See, that's why I'm doing it too. And *that* is what being a demon is about." I take his hand. Choices, right?

Cal looks down at our joined hands. "The truth is, you're right." He forces out the words. "There are things angels don't understand."

"You think?" I snort. "If only someone had told you."

"No, I'm serious. Like, they don't do relationships." His voice is raw. "When strategic goals call for having kids, they appear and say, *I am an angel and you have a destiny,* and they let the human say 'yes, please.' A real attachment would be a distraction from the Great Work." He gives a sad laugh. "I asked Dad if angels are all Jedi and he *asked what a Jedi was*."

I take his other hand in mine. "Well, all the demons I know say if there's anything I want from a human, I should just go for it. And, we're taught that love is an angel thing. Demons don't do it."

"So I guess angels and demons agree on one thing, after all. They'd both be against this." Cal motions to the space between us. The rest of him is stock still.

I look away, my voice a whisper, and find the courage to speak. "Dad was right . . . about love being an angel thing. At least, I've never loved anyone who isn't an angel."

Callum sucks in a shaky breath. Then he grips my waist and whirls me into a kiss that tears down everything we've been taught about angels and demons and love.

DUSK FALLS BY THE TIME WE REACH OUR destination. From the outside, the Everett Valley Farm looks like a warehouse. It's not. We hop fences and fly up to a ventilation opening far too high up to call a window. Then we hold our noses and glide down along a wall into—

"Hell on earth," I breathe. And I know hell.

Pigs are packed as far as the eye can see. Steel bars on the concrete floor form cells lined in the occupants' filth. Their tails are stubs and when their mouths open I see broken teeth. It's tight enough that I can't even count how many pigs are in this cell. It's just a mass of crowded, roiling flesh.

"Conditions like this, plus all the antibiotics in the world. It's the perfect spot for your dad's next move," Cal says.

He might not be wrong.

We duck down to the floor in case anyone is watching. I have no idea how worried we need to be or how often people come by here. From ground level, the stench is even worse and we can see most of the animals have visible injuries. Even the air is heavy and humid, as if this place was designed to be uncomfortable, painful, *evil* in every way.

"Is it here? Try and check," he whispers.

"But what about them?" I wave an arm at the animals around us. "Can we *help* them? You know pigs are smarter than dogs, right? They have emotions, Cal. Pain." And they're right here in front of us. He's supposed to be the angel. Can he possibly be dense enough to ignore this?

"Maybe," he says, sounding doubtful. "We can at least make sure your dad doesn't come back here."

"He didn't do this." But I drop the subject. I go still and close my eyes. A single note rings through the ether and reflects back. Beyond the silent ripples, there's an echo of something similar to my own magic. And that can only mean one thing: my dad has been here.

"That way," I say, opening my eyes and pointing. "Something is over there, or was. We need to get closer."

"Then let's go." He takes my hand and we risk standing up.

We forget about stealth and run. Fly, really, but close enough to be deniable.

In a pen just like the one we left, there are dozens of bodies. Thrown around like a trail of dominoes. One pig after another, all dead. Cal stops and asks, "The Talisman?"

I go still again and call out the same note as before. The echo is still there, but it's just an echo. I stir and answer. "No. It *was* here, recently. He must have moved it. After—after he finished." I look around at his work. Bodies and flies.

Death.

"We've got to go." Cal pulls on my wrist and points to the humans. Employees, cleaning up the mess. Some are moving toward us. Cal starts running. Wings out, but running on the ground.

"Not yet. We're not done here." I run alongside him and whisper a plan. It's fun and it's *right here*.

"Seriously? We're already taking too many risks . . ." Cal gives in.

We make for the front door. This part *feels* scary, but it's safer than the way we came in. Weirdly-dressed sprinters still get less attention than kids flying up a wall.

As we pass the pens, steel gates click open. Classic angel miracle. My part is to give each pen a puff of sulfuric flame for just long enough to start the prisoners running. By the time we make it to the door it sounds like there's a stampede behind us. A slow, lumbering stampede. These creatures have probably never run in their lives, plus there's whatever side effects come with being bred for size. This is not *The Lion King*. But Cal and I are breathing hard with excitement.

"This is the worst idea." Cal grins.

"Most fun since the bonfire, you were right!" I run ahead and pull on Cal's hand.

We flee ahead of the stampede and I watch the pigs disperse. Hopefully some get away. It's exhilarating. All of my favorite things—mischief, mayhem, and Cal beside me.

We hop a fence and run into a grove of trees, disappearing into the darkness. As soon as we're out of sight of any humans,

I jump on Cal and kiss him. I half knock him over, only our wings keeping us balanced. Neither of us has the presence of mind to rise into the air. I can't even keep my knees solid. All I can think about is the feel of his lips on mine.

When we finally pull away, I see his face. It should be bright and clear, but all I see is a black cloud.

"Izzy, I—I have to tell you something."

"*Now?*" I try to tempt him into another kiss, but he pulls away.

"Yes, now. And I'm sorry." His head drops on my shoulder and the air is as thick as gel. "God, Izzy, I'm so sorry."

My eyes widen. "What is it?"

He lifts his tear-streaked face. "This whole thing, it wasn't my idea. My—my dad knows." He chokes.

I step away from him. My eyes are burning so bright I can almost smell brimstone. "No." I bite my lip. "No, Cal. No. You wouldn't do that."

"I'm sorry." He shivers, shrunken and pale. "I wanted to tell you, I did. I just—I wanted to wait until after we found the Talisman but right now I just couldn't—I hate lying to you."

"You're lying now! You'd never tell Archangel Gabriel about this. About us."

Cal shakes his head, looking down. I almost feel bad for him. Or I would, if he wasn't screwing me over.

I cross my arms, wings straight back behind me. Anger comes easily—and it's that or think about his betrayal. "You thought that you could just say you've wanted this—wanted *me*—for years, and I'd go along with whatever you had in mind?" I choke back the sobs. "You used me to do what your father wanted—to get back at *my* father?"

Cal looks miserable. "I *have* wanted this for years! Izzy, I've loved you for years. The Talisman was a justification. Or an excuse. Or something!"

"You know I hate people who lie to me." My tears burn as soon as they form. Salt tracks down my face. "Are you going to tell me it was *worth it*?"

415

"I don't know. Maybe. Lying to you, I feel like I ruined both our lives. But if we don't stop your dad . . ." He takes a deep breath and looks into my eyes. "Izzy, I don't think I can do this. I am really, truly, 100 percent in love with you. But I don't know if I can be with you."

I can't believe what I'm hearing. He tricked me, lied to me—and now *he's* breaking up with *me*? Only an angel could manage to think he's taking the moral high road.

"Because you don't deserve to, you mean?" My voice cracks like lightning. Half anger and half trying not to cry. "You're right. You don't."

"That, and . . . look. I know you've done a lot, with your dad, and it wasn't all your fault. But I don't think I can pretend that's okay, either. Maybe we just both don't deserve . . . happiness."

"Oh, and you're all angelic?" I seethe. "You were working with your dad *literally today*, and using me to do it."

Tears fill his eyes. "I know, but if we'd found the Talisman, then we could have saved tens of thousands of people. All of them as important as us. I know that's angel logic and you don't like it, but it's not wrong. We're not wrong." He's sobbing now and I can see streaks reflecting down his face.

I remain unmoved. "Sure, if that's what matters to you. But I thought I mattered too."

"You do. You will always be my best friend. God, I thought . . . I thought if this worked, I could tell you everything." He closes his eyes.

"You know what my people do to liars." My face is fire and ice and lead. "As for the rest of it—if you'd just been honest with me, no matter what came our way, we would've dealt with it. I thought you said we could do anything. Together." My voice breaks on that last word.

I stretch shaking wings and fly off.

416

I DON'T FLY HOME. NOT RIGHT AWAY. I WANT to be in the air, *free*, not tied between two conflicting causes. I go high enough it feels like there's barely any air to push against. High enough that no one will see, and if they do, my wings are a patch of stars against a clouded sky.

I stay up as long as I can. When my wings start to tire, I drop, reveling in the freefall. Flying when I really shouldn't, swooping down into the places I know are the emptiest. It's the only thing that feels normal tonight.

I make my way back to my house. It's the last place I want to be right now, but it's home.

And as soon as I walk in, I can *feel* it. The note that echoed back at the pig farm, stronger than ever. *A dark whisper.* The Talisman. Its presence courses through my veins. It's like a mass of boiling rage pulsing through all the hair on my body, which is now standing straight up.

I shake my head, barely believing it.

There it is. The Talisman. Unspeakable evil and phenomenal power, right there in the freezer. Between the ice cube tray and a stack of frozen burger patties. We should have guessed. If my dad moved it today, he would've to move it *to* somewhere.

This is good news, right? If I want out of Callum's plan, I can ignore it. Never speak of it again. Or if I want to destroy it after all, now it's found. Fine.

But it's right there, next to the ice cubes. I picture the Talisman, but all I can see is the imagined reflection of Freddie Mercury's face in the gold crown. That was a really sad movie. I can't ignore something that's right in front of me.

I sit on the couch and stare at the fridge for an hour, trying to make up my mind. There's a reason that demons are so messed up. It's not because we're Satanic, although we are. Nor because we like evil, though we do. It's because we're trained that way from birth. I mean, when has a demon parent ever told their kids to do good? Never.

417

My father taught me that bad things were good, doing wrong was the right way, and that killing people was saving them torment. Don't get me wrong, I care about him. He's my dad. But I sometimes wonder if I'm anything more than Child #251.

I dig my fingers into the purple pillows on our living room couch, wondering if I'm anything more to *him* too. Callum. My ex-best friend. My ex-crush. Traitor.

By the time I stop feeling angry, the room looks like it's been through a shredder. Well, that and a fire pit. Standard demonic artwork.

I collapse to the ground, close to tears. Which I shouldn't be, because tears are human. Demons don't cry. It's literally the only thing worse than kindness in our books. I hug my knees, burying my head, and hold back the sharp sting in my eyes.

Maybe it's just because I'm angry at my father. Or because I'm tired of being a pawn in someone else's game. Or for a reason I'm not ready to explore. Either way, sitting there on the floor, I make up my mind.

I'm going to do it, I think. *I'm actually going to do it.*

But that leaves one really, really awful thing to do first, because I can't destroy the Talisman alone. I pick up the phone.

Cal answers on the fourth ring. "I found it," I say in a staccato monotone. *Don't think, don't feel, just say the words you have to say.* "He moved it and it's back here. At home. I'm going to go through with the plan."

"Izzy, I—"

"Don't." I cut him off. "I can't do it alone, but that doesn't mean I want to talk to you. I'm not going to explain myself, and I'm not doing this for you. I'm never doing anything for you again."

"I'm on my—" he starts.

I hang up.

PART THREE

I don't want to see Callum, but I fly to the roof of my house to wait on him anyway. He lands behind me, his wings leaving little sparkles behind him, no doubt to remind the world just how sanctimonious he is. Just like the Archangel freaking Gabriel. His hair looks perfectly windswept too, skin glowing in the setting sun. It's the first thing I see when I turn around.

He hangs his head and his voice is a tremble on the breeze. "I'm so—"

I glare at him, blasting him with energy, and he shuts up, eyes shifting away from me. *Score: Izzy: 1 Callum: 0.*

"I'm only doing this with you because I need your help. I'd rather do it with any other stuffed-up angel instead."

Cal clears his throat. "Thanks, Isabella. I know you don't probably even want me to say—"

I glare at him again. *Score: Izzy: 2.*

"So, where is it?" he asks, abandoning the idea of an apology. "The basement? Your dad's secret underground laboratory?"

"The kitchen," I say.

"Kitchen? Why would he put it there?"

I turn my back on him, allowing my black wings to become visible. I jump off the side of the roof and glide to the ground.

"How long are you going to be mad at me, Izzy?" he calls out from above. I'm not even *looking* right now and I can picture how sad he looks with his wide eyes and soft lips. "I know I messed up, but you're the last Ethereal on earth I'd ever want to hurt. And why would you call me over if you're still angry?" His voice cracks a bit at the end.

I continue walking away. "Because I can't destroy the Talisman. No demon can. Your dad didn't tell you that?" My tone is heavy with sarcasm. "Now you know. And, no, I'm not spilling any other demonic secrets I know, in case you wanted to pretend to date me for them."

Cal floats down behind me and grabs my arm. His grip feels so *familiar*, like it's exactly where his hands belong. "Nothing was pretend, Izzy. I've been waiting an eternity to ask you out. What I felt, I *feel*, is real. I love you."

My heart starts beating faster. The biggest traitor here isn't Callum, after all.

CALLUM'S JAW HITS THE FLOOR WHEN I OPEN our freezer door and pull out a glowing glass jar framed in a solid gold lid and handle. The inside is a mass of seething green, red, and black swirling around a golden crown. I've seen it more times than I can count and I feel my heart speed up. There are parts of me that will always be my dad's daughter.

"Wait, that's the Talisman? In your freezer? With your food?" He looks sick at the thought.

I shrug. "Don't worry, it can't hurt you unless you touch it. You're a freaking angel."

"So, what do we do now?" He's angled toward it, staring.

I hold it out to him. "You're the angel. You figure it out. It'll just absorb anything I can throw at it."

"I think I should be able to . . ." He grabs it from me and then immediately drops it on his foot with a half-yelp, half-squeal, since he can't touch it without burning himself. I smirk. He deserved that.

"Let me hold it and you can hit it from there." I lift it back up and hold it out to him, its weight heavy in my arms.

Cal moves his hands on either side of the Talisman and looks at me hesitantly. He closes his eyes and concentrates. His hands start glowing a little and I hold my breath. The light flickers twice and then dies out, with the Talisman still seething inside. He keeps his eyes closed for a while, trying to get it to work again. After a minute, he just blinks them open, looking at me and placing his hands over mine.

His fingers stroke the back of my hands. I want to move away, but I'm holding the Talisman. His eyes capture mine, blue sparkles that I don't look away from.

"I can't focus, Izzy. I can't do anything. All I keep thinking about is you. I shouldn't have used you. I should have just told you the truth. But I was scared." His eyes are watering. Typical overemotional angel.

"Scared of what? That I wouldn't help you screw over my dad?"

Callum frowns. "This is about so much more than your dad, Izzy. It's not just an angel versus demon thing. Please tell me you understand that. It's about the people who would die from whatever he's got in here if we don't do this." His voice is husky and pleading.

It's so typical for Callum to try to make this about saving people. "I'm not like that. I do things because they're fun and risky and, honestly, a bit evil."

"Then why?" His face falls. "Why are you helping me do this? Just to get back at your dad?"

I stare at him and at the charred living room behind him. For demons, anger is motivation. And I want to tell Callum that it *is* because I'm angry at Dad. For being the type of father who barely knows who I am. Who would rather stick me in a school in LA than admit he's wrong about anything.

But the anger that's beating in my heart isn't focused on that. It's focused on the people I've watched die. I've *made* die. Dad not caring about who he hurts in his work. The forces of evil that leave even the strongest people in this world in agony.

I force the words out before I can stop myself. "Well, at least your dad isn't trying to kill thousands of people for fun."

Callum's eyes snap to mine, a surprised look on his face.

"Yes." I draw a deep breath. "I know destroying the Talisman is about more than just getting back at my dad. Now let's get on with it."

"You mean that?" He looks so *happy*, and I have to remind myself that I'm furious with him.

"Just do it, Callum," I say coldly, my voice firm. "You can do this."

His lips curve up, as if he hears everything I'm not saying, looking so kissable he's the image of a deadly sin. He's still gazing at me, our eyes holding power—as if he's using whatever he sees in me as an anchor. His hands start glowing with a white light, and the mass inside the container becomes shimmery.

The Talisman grows hotter and hotter in my hands. If I were a human or even an angel, I'm sure my palms would be charred to ashes by now. Instead, I just feel the energy absorbing into my skin while Callum makes the contents slowly disappear.

That's when I feel more than Callum's grasp on me. My whole body courses with lightning terror as a hand grasps my shoulder from behind. I turn around slowly, praying—not to God, of course—that it's anyone other than Dad.

"HEY, DAD! YOU'RE BACK FROM CHINA already?" I position myself in front of Callum, the fakest smile in the world on my face. I try to make my voice sound cheery. As if there isn't a literal angel behind me. As if my hands aren't still holding the Talisman. As if we aren't trying to destroy the masterpiece Dad's spent the last century recharging.

Dad's eyes are glowing, which is never a good sign for any demon. And definitely not for one of the Four. His cheekbones sharpen and his horns blast out of the ether. We are as good as dead.

I start backing away, my stomach tossing like clothes in a washing machine.

Dad's eyes narrow viciously. He looks at Callum and then at the open freezer.

"What are you doing with the Talisman?" he roars, his voice running over me in cold waves. "And why is there an *angel* here?" He crumples the fridge door into a scrap of metal, which he throws across the living room. Yeah, I take after my dad when it comes to anger management.

"We were just trying to prevent you from doing your day job. You know, killing people." I infuse as much sarcasm in my voice as possible. *Run, Callum, run.*

The idiot angel doesn't. He steps out from behind me and looks Dad in the eye. Both their faces are glowing bright enough to light up the room.

Dad wraps one hand around my throat, his grip making it clear how easily he could snap me in two. He grabs the Talisman with his other hand. I feel my chest burn.

"Don't you dare," Callum screams, forcing Dad back, white light streaming from his fingertips. His face freezes in a snarl I've never seen him wear before.

Dad stumbles, and I jam my arm into his side. He releases me, and I drop to the floor, rolling away, gasping.

"It's not her I wanted to do this to anyway." Dad chuckles coldly—really, he laughs at everything—and lunges at Callum. A cloud of darkness surrounds them both. The living room glows a deep burgundy, ash falling all around.

I can barely make out two figures. Cal is clearly no match for Dad. Neither am I. But I have to try. Peering through the dust, I can tell that one figure is a dull white—Callum's angelic nature, shining through. I slam myself into the other, but Dad shoves me off of him and grabs Cal's arm, twisting it. Cal might be immortal, but I know that has to hurt.

I hear a sudden snap. Cal whimpers like a puppy, and I feel a rage like I've never felt before wash over me. Cal's snarl is gone, replaced with trembling eyelashes and sunken shoulders.

Focusing my anger on my arms, I form a fiery link between my hands and send it spiraling out towards Dad. It lashes against his face and his shock resounds throughout the room. The muscles in his arms quiver.

I actually hurt him.

"Isabella?" He lifts his hand to his face, dusting off the cinders.

I use my energy to surround him. Before he can retaliate, Callum moves his good arm, mixing his power with mine. Where the light meets the dark, a bond of strength forms, swirling around Dad. Callum moves his other hand to create a pointed staff of light and strides toward him, the brightness growing. He's going to kill my father.

"Callum, no!" I scream, and he stops, staring at me.

I don't know why I've screamed.

I don't know why, unless everything Dad's ever taught me is wrong.

Unless demons can love.

But Dad has to be redeemable. I changed. He can change.

There's been enough death.

I turn to my dad. He's looking at us like he can't believe we've combined our energies against him—as if he can't believe I'd ever oppose him. I shift our energy over towards the Talisman in Dad's arms. As Callum's force joins with mine, Dad drops the Talisman to the floor with a grunt.

It takes a while to undo the century of evil that's been stored in the container. Dad tries to claw it back from us, but he's weakened by the swirls of angel-demon magic. Finally, the Talisman lets out a bright flash that fires around the room and crumbles into the ether.

I FALL TO THE GROUND, EXHAUSTED, AND MY magic fades. Dad's staring at the chars of ash in shock. The crown is gone, the rosy thorns dead, the gold sanded away into a dark brown.

Cal is glaring daggers at Dad. His good arm is around me and he's steeling himself to spring up again.

I don't agree with my father's choices. But that doesn't mean I want Callum to kill him. And I definitely don't want my father to kill Callum.

"Dad, the Talisman is destroyed," I say. "Can you please just leave now? There's nothing you can do here. The world is safe from whatever you were brewing in that mess."

Dad's green eyes narrow as he raises a hand to the singe that is marring his cheek and I feel my heart squeeze. Anger still doesn't get rid of the bond that we share.

His voice falls eight octaves, far below what humans can hear. "I don't know what's gotten into you, Isabella."

I feel my throat close. Why couldn't I have had a dad who wasn't a mass murderer? "I don't want to be your daughter anymore if it means helping you kill people." I shut my eyes. "I don't want to be a demon who watches little girls die. I don't want to be a demon who causes children to suffer from preventable diseases. And if that means I can't be a good daughter anymore, then I don't want that either."

"Then I guess we don't have anything in common now, do we?" Dad uses a pulse of magic to break my bond with Callum's light, and I let him. He draws himself up, walks to the door, and doesn't look back.

Does this mean I'm no longer his daughter? Does this mean he doesn't care about me? The questions swirl in my head as I fall to my knees. I've always tried to be a good demon. But I can't live with the consequences of being good enough.

I try not to wonder why Dad left so easily—whether he'll just try harder and kill us both later—as Callum sinks down next to me and puts his good arm around me again.

425

"Are you okay?" I ask. Tears fill my eyes, a strange sensation bubbling in my chest.

Callum holds his hurt arm close. "Are you okay, Izzy?" His lips tremble as he gazes over my whole body, checking for injuries. "Why did you protect me?" he whispers. "Why did you fight your father?"

I think back to everything I've learned over the years. *Demons don't do kindness and service and friendship.* I can hear Dad's deep voice. *Demons don't do love.*

But those words fade as I gaze up at Callum's tousled brown hair, laced with cinders. "Because of all those things demons don't do."

I don't have to say them aloud. Cal knows exactly what I mean. And he cries too.

A COUPLE MONTHS LATER, THE SUN IS SETTING on the rooftop of our school and I'm nestled next to Callum. It's winter break, so my black wings aren't in the ether and Callum has given up on trying to get me to hide them. He knows it's my one reminder I'm the demon I am. One who might just have a bit of an angelic side. Besides, this way when Cal and I sit together I can wrap one of my wings around him.

Not that Callum's all angel, of course. Apparently, Gabriel wanted Cal to kill me after I stopped him from killing Dad. He refused, and we're still sneaking out to be together. Some things never change.

"Have you heard from him?" Cal asks. He doesn't have to tell me who *him* is. "Do we have to hunt him down and stop him again?"

I bite my lip. "The last I heard from one of Dad's friends, he's back in Asia. Losing the Talisman was a pretty big setback. I think we've earned the right to stop here."

"Pestilence is actually defeated," Callum jokes. "Thanks to doctors and vaccines and a couple of stubborn teenagers."

"Shhh." A demon's true name is never to be taken lightly—let alone my father's. "What if the humans hear you? What if he does?"

"Then we'll deal with him again." He turns to face me. "We can do anything," he says, just like he did months ago, before everything changed.

I take a deep breath of cold air. I'm still sad about the mess of my relationship with Dad. I will always have questions in my heart, but maybe someday, Dad will come back and change for the better. I did.

I lean over and grab Cal's hand. With him, I don't have to worry about which emotions are demon enough to feel. He blushes and I smile.

The pit in my stomach about what Dad's going to do next dissolves as Cal kisses me. His lips are soft and warm against mine.

It's a new year now, January 2020, and the world's going to be okay.

OVER TIME
JOHN KLEKAMP

ONE
ADAM

I could stare at the back of Nate Branham's head all day. The way his coffee-brown hair fades into bronze peach fuzz on his ranch-tanned neck. How that neck slopes into broad shoulders. And how those shoulders flow into biceps that strain the cotton plaid of his shirt.

I'm obsessing, which is dangerous. As a straight-A student in Mr. E.'s class, my name could be called at any moment. And to be honest, walking to the front of the classroom to solve an algebraic equation would be problematic right now. I steal a nervous glance down. Make that impossible.

Usually, I pray not to go to Hell. But at this moment, I'm trying to make a deal with God. "If Mr. E. doesn't call on me, I swear, Lord, I'll stop thinking sinful thoughts about Nate."

I don't need to look down to know God's ignoring me. Why I keep making these promises is beyond my ability to comprehend. In my eighteen years of existence, God has shown Himself to be extremely unreliable.

In His defense, I did make the exact same promise yesterday.

Nate rolls his shoulders and reaches with a calloused hand to scrub the back of his neck. The motion disturbs the air between us, and his familiar scent wafts under my nose. Images of stolen moments in the back of Nate's daddy's pickup flood my brain. I'm definitely going to Hell.

But not today.

The bell rings. Being Friday, and the last period, it's a mad dash for the door.

"Don't forget," Mr. E. calls over the slamming of books and scraping of chairs, "I want your worksheets on my desk Monday."

"My dad has me checking fences tomorrow," Nate says casually as he straightens to his full six feet. "I could pick you up at eight."

My heart skips a beat. Not because I'm keen on repairing fences under the Texas sun, which by June can be scorching. Or the few extra dollars Nate's father will throw my way for helping out. But because of what else these day-long outings usually include.

"I'll ask my dad," I say, still unable to stand. "He usually likes me pumping gas on Saturdays." Dad pays me too, though not as much, which is why he might say yes. "Can I let you know this afternoon?"

Nate shrugs. If our encounters mean as much to him as they do to me, he never lets on—at least not here. "Sure." He turns and heads for the hallway. "Hey, Betty, wait up!" I watch through the door as Nate Branham drapes his arm around his girlfriend.

"Did you have a question, Adam?" asks Mr. E., interrupting my misery.

"What? No," I stammer. "I'm fine, Mr. E., thanks."

That did the trick, though.

I can stand now.

TWO
EVAN

"Tell them no." I'm not yelling, though it's entirely possible Char thinks otherwise. It's noisy in this joint. Plus, venti iced coffees can have that effect on me. I suck a chilly mouthful through my reusable, environmentally responsible straw, one of many products I promote, then put Char on speaker for a sec to snap a selfie of me using it. "Friday's already overbooked." I switch screens and double-check my schedule.

This Starbucks near Times Square is jammed. Did I mention it's near Times Square? Tourists are scrolling through their pics with the Naked Cowboy. No one's giving me stinkeye to take my conversation outside, so I don't. "Yeah, no. I have that sit-in in the morning, a podcast at lunch, the Netflix premiere that night. And, oh, yeah, I've got homework."

Char's been putting up with my bossy-queen tendencies since middle school. While standing behind me in the cafeteria, she correctly identified the vintage of my secondhand Prada backpack. I'd found my soulmate. Today, Char handles all my bookings. I pay her in goody-bag swag. This arrangement has worked well for both of us, though we sometimes get into it over beauty products. We're eighteen, but the way we see it, you're never too young to moisturize.

"Don't forget, you have dinner with Celeste tonight." Char sounds bored. "It's her birthday, remember? And, the swag closet's empty." Bored, but still one step ahead of me like the great assistant she is. "You make enough off your five hundred and—" Char checks the latest count. "Five hundred and sixty-six thousand followers. Go on. *Buy* Celeste something."

Celeste. That would be my mother. Perhaps you've heard of her, Celeste Starr? She was huge in the '90s as Nora, mother to Ethan, the groundbreaking gay character on the beloved teen soap, *Larson's Pier*. Fun fact: Celeste initially turned down the role because, at age thirty-three, she wasn't ready for "mother" roles. But that's Hollywood: Get twenty-somethings to play high school kids and thirty-somethings to play their parents. Celeste did some film work, too. Always busy. Never marrying. But she did carve out a month in her thirty-ninth year to have me, her only child—gay like Ethan. Life imitating art.

If you're wondering where my dad is in this picture, join the club. And, if you know who my dad is, would you let me know? Celeste is annoyingly coy on the topic, but I've narrowed the possibilities down to three: two actors and a director. Any of them could be my father. Celeste definitely has a type.

A barista is trying to catch my eye. I noticed him when I walked in. He seems nice enough and happens to be *my* type: blond and fit, but not like he lives at Crunch. But that's not how I operate these days. Let me see your stats, and if I'm interested, I'll swipe right. A meet-cute in a Starbucks? Near Times Square? Who's got time for that IRL?

"Hello?" Char calls from the other end, getting my head back in the game.

"Right, see if they can wait two weeks." I put Char on speaker again, minimize an Aquaria makeup tutorial, and find the homework I need to finish. "You're the best!" I make a kissing noise at the phone. "And Char, the next jar of skin caviar has your name on it. Ciao!"

I'm a little miffed Char didn't sound more appreciative.

"Hey."

I look up. It's him—the blond barista.

Excuse me while I swipe left.

THREE
ADAM

Apair of coveralled legs stick out from under a robin's-
egg-blue '57 Bel Air.

"Hey, Dad!" I holler.

Mr. Carson's Chevy is just two years old, so it can't be
anything major, or Dad would have it up on the lift. In Eden,
Texas, population: 1,473, everyone knows your business and
what you drive.

I hear a wrench clang on the concrete. "That you, Adam?"
A wiry, handsome man—he's my dad, but it's an accurate
description—wriggles out and smiles up at me. There's a
grease smudge on his right cheek. "How was school?"

If my childhood had a smell, my dad's service station would
be it. I inhale the scent of motor oil and gasoline. For all I know,
the stuff's stunted my growth. I'm five-nine in my Converse All
Stars—five-ten-and-a-half when I can get my blond hair to
look like Fabian's.

"Fine," I say. Nothing much ever happens at Eden High—
unless you enjoy high school football, and being in the heart of
Texas, it's best you do. The Fighting Bulldogs are practically
celebrities. In a dusty town just two-point-four miles square, it's
enough to score the team free cheeseburgers at the Lone Star
Diner if the Bulldogs win. But it's June, and the only things
people are talking about now are the prom and graduation.
"Nate asked if I could give him a hand tomorrow."

Dad retrieves his wrench and gets to his feet. "I suppose Mr.
Branham will be paying you." He eyes the gas pumps out front
and shrugs. "And you'll be full-time here at Shire's Garage soon
enough."

"Yes, sir." The extra cash will come in handy. My parents'
twentieth wedding anniversary's coming up. Since I have an
unspoken desire *not* to be here for their twenty-first, and no

desire to work full-time at Shire's Garage, I'd like to get them something. Mom's easy. Give her a book set someplace she's never been, and she's happy. She'll insist I read it, next. I always do. That's part of the reason I want out of Eden. But Dad's tough, always says he doesn't need anything. "Ten dollars a day," I say. "Usually."

Dad shakes his head and whistles. "Can't pay you that much for pumping gas." He pulls a rag from his back pocket and wipes his hands. "Oh, go on, then. I can handle it."

"Thanks, Dad. See you at home."

THE SPRING-HINGED SCREEN DOOR SLAMS behind me. "Mom, I'm home!"

"In the kitchen." Mom's bent over the stove, stirring something that makes my stomach rumble with hunger. "Chili," she says, seeing me drool. I'll definitely miss Mom's cooking.

An orange furball streaks across the kitchen floor.

"Okra, come back!" Devon, my little sister, comes chasing into the room. "Oh, hi, Adam." She's eight. I pick her up and squeeze her. I'll miss Devon even more. Yes, Devon Shire. Get it? Mom really wants to go to England someday.

"What are you doing to that poor cat?" I ask.

Devon puckers one side of her mouth. "Just put a bonnet on her. We're doing dress-up."

"I see." I spot the cat crouched under the table. "I don't think Okra's a big fan of dress-up. Maybe you could just let her watch."

Devon frowns, then leans into me and whispers in my ear. "Did you find something for Daddy yet?" My little sister broke into her piggy bank to help pay for Mom's and Dad's anniversary gifts. One dollar and thirty-seven cents.

"Not yet," I whisper while Mom narrows her eyes at us. "I'm still looking. But don't you worry. I'll find something."

"Stace is headed up the walk." Mom has a view of our street from the kitchen window, which is open to catch a breeze. She arches a brow at me. I know that look. "I'll bring out some sweet tea."

Stace is propped against the porch railing. Her reddish-brown hair is pulled into a ponytail, and freckles dust her nose and cheeks. It looks like she's wearing lipstick. "I didn't see you after school."

"I had to talk to Dad," I say through the screen door before stepping outside. I lean over the railing, eyeing my bike. It's a one-mile ride to the Branham Ranch, just outside town. I could be there and back well before dinnertime. "I'll be working with Nate tomorrow."

"Oh." Stace frowns, and I can see up close that it *is* lipstick. "You're practically a hired hand at the Branham Ranch these days."

Best friends since the fifth grade, Stace and I have been inseparable. "Two peas in a pod," my mom likes to say. Until Nate.

I break the awkward silence. "Mom's getting us some sweet tea."

"That's nice," Stace says dully.

"Then I have to ride out to the ranch and tell Mr. Branham I can work tomorrow."

"You could call. You do have a telephone."

I *could* call, but it's a chance to see Nate, so—

"Tommy asked Anne to the prom." Stace is staring at the screen door where Okra is batting at flies.

"Oh." I swallow. Why is she telling me this? "That's nice."

"Sweet tea, anyone?" Mom hips the door open, carrying two glasses clinking with ice. She'll have to make more before dinner. "Hi, Stace. Don't you look nice?"

Stace perks up. "Hi, Mrs. Shire. Thank you. I'd love some sweet tea."

"You're welcome to stay for dinner. Nothing fancy. Just chili."

The aroma wafts through the open window, and Stace inhales. "Smells good, Mrs. Shire." But she catches me looking longingly at my bike and says, "Another night, maybe. I've got tons of homework."

We sip our tea between spurts of small talk. "Is that lipstick?" I finally ask.

Stace purses her lips like she's trying to hide the evidence. "So what if it is?"

"It's just—" I shrug. "I've never seen you wear makeup before."

"It's just lipstick," she says brusquely, planting her empty glass on the railing. "Thanks again for the tea, Mrs. Shire," she calls to my mom. "Will I see you at church?" She sounds annoyed. "Or will you still be helping Nate?"

"Um." Am I missing something here? "Yeah, I'll be at church."

This seems to mollify her. "Okay." Stace skips down the steps into the hot Texas sun. "I'll see you then."

I place our sweaty glasses in the kitchen sink. Mom's sitting at the table, her head in a book while the chili simmers. Devon must be in her room. There's no sign of Okra. "I'm going to take a quick ride out to the ranch to let them know I can work tomorrow."

"Again?" Mom looks up from her book, her focus somewhere else. I wonder where this one is taking her. "We have a phone, you know."

FOUR
EVAN

I check the time. If I'm going to find something appropriately dazzling for Celeste, I better get shopping. But first, that venti iced coffee has to go somewhere. I swim against the tide of tourists and get the restroom code from the blond barista. Yeah, it's awkward.

Don't care what the whiteboard says about the last cleaning, every surface gets disinfected. I promote these convenient travel-size wipes too. No, I don't take a selfie.

After taking care of business, I check my reflection in the mirror and sing the alphabet while washing my hands. There's no time to run to the apartment and freshen up, but every jet-black hair on my head is in place, and my olive skin still glows thanks to the mask I demonstrated for twenty-five thousand followers last night.

Someone bangs on the door.

"I'll be out in a minute!" Tourists.

There's nothing around here but foam Statue of Liberty crowns and I Love New York t-shirts. I grab a cab to Soho, but nothing is catching my eye. It's all been there, bought that. I call Char. "You're absolutely certain there's nothing great in the swag closet?" I hear rummaging and harrumphing.

"Nothing the son of Celeste Starr should be giving his momma on her birthday." Char throws out the names of several boutiques in the area, but I'd been to all of them already.

I eye a Walgreens. "Maybe, a really nice card?"

"I'll slap you to Saturn." Char's patron saint is a drag queen. Plus, she loves my mother.

"Fine, I'll keep looking. Where's our dinner reservation, again?"

"Antonio's at seven. Huh. Seems early." Char clucks her tongue. "No, I just double-checked. Seven's right."

"Okay, that's not far. Thanks."

I pocket my phone and look up. Broadway? How the hell did I end up on Broadway?

A half-dozen drag queens totter out of a noodle shop—carb-loading for Pride Month, I suppose. It can't be easy looking fabulous while walking in those heels.

"Oh, my Gawd!" screams an extremely buxom queen, pointing at me. This happens a lot. "Ladies, ladies, do you realize who this is?" She doesn't wait for an answer, squealing, "Evan Starr!"

She reaches into her sequined bosom and pulls out a phone. I move in for a selfie without being asked.

"I adooore your mother. That scene, on *Larson's Pier*, when Nora comforts Ethan after he's bullied—" She clutches said bosom. "Ruins my mascara every time. And you—" She pinches my cheek with her lacquered talons, bringing a tear to my eye. "Are a snack." She steps back and gives me the full up-and-down. "Honey," she says in a Harvey Fierstein baritone, "you're barely legal. Let's just pretend I didn't say that."

The voice-drop: The oldest gag in any drag queen's arsenal, and it always slays.

I snap a group selfie for my own feed. "What's your handle?"

She performs a wobbly curtsy. "The Duchess of Trippledee at your service."

I grab the Duchess's arm to prevent her toppling over, get the correct spelling, and hit send. We wrap things up with a round of air kisses.

Char would have loved this. So would Celeste.

Celeste!

What time is it now? Six-thirty!

Shit's getting real. My eyes dart from one side of Broadway to the other, landing on another Walgreens. But Char's still in my head. *I'll slap you to Saturn.*

"Don't give up," I tell myself. If shopping were a sport, I'd be an Olympian.

Wait. What's this? A shop I've never noticed before. How is that even possible? Its windows are filled with the most fantastical things. Gleaming doodads that would look #hellamazing in your entry hall appear to capture and transform the light. I'm entranced.

No one else on the bustling sidewalk gives the place a second look. It's like the friggin' Leaky Cauldron, and I'm the only one who can see it. More likely, I'm the only one around here with taste. I pull open the door. Celeste Starr, prepare to be wowed.

"Welcome to Time After Time." He's handsome in a bland, catalog model kind of way. Though his suit is too conservative for my tastes. Late twenties. Early thirties, tops. Maybe? He takes a step toward me. His skin is flawless. "My name is Clarence. How may I help you?"

"Hi, Clarence." I look toward the window facing Broadway. A fire truck is stuck in traffic, its lights flashing, but I don't hear the siren. "Uh, I'm looking for a birthday gift for my mother." I look around Clarence's shop, which redefines spare. There's no merchandise to speak of, just a pedestal in the center of the room with two pocket watches under glass. "How long have you been here, Clarence? I've never noticed your store before."

"Just opened today." I find myself staring into Clarence's eyes. They look like ancient pools, dark and deep. "In fact, you're my first customer." Clarence blinks in slow motion. "Your mother, you say?"

"Yes."

"I have just the thing." He lifts the glass and waves me closer. "There are only two of these in the world."

I huff a bit rudely. "Pocket watches?" Just to humor the guy, I bend for a closer look. They're made of gleaming gold—or gold metal, more likely. Identical as far as I can tell, but nothing special. I could open my phone right now and find two just like them on Amazon. What a waste of time. If I hurry, I can still grab a card at Walgreens and make it to Antonio's by seven.

"Pick one," says Clarence.

I look into Clarence's eyes and forget all about Walgreens. I reach for the watch on the right.

Clarence beams. "Excellent choice."

The watch feels warm in my hand—like it's been sitting on a radiator in an old walk-up.

"Turn it over."

I do as I'm told. There's an inscription: "There is no time like the present—"

"And no present like time," Clarence finishes.

Staring into Clarence's ancient pools, I ask, "How much for this one?"

FIVE
ADAM

I lean my bike against the Branhams' impressive wraparound porch and knock on the front door.

"Hello, Adam." Mrs. Branham swings the door open. "Come inside. I'll get you something to drink. Dr. Pepper? Sweet tea?"

I look down at my dusty jeans and sweat-stained t-shirt. "That's okay, Mrs. Branham. But a Dr. Pepper sure would hit the spot."

She smiles and nods. "Well, take a load off, then." She points at a couple of chairs on the porch, then hollers up the stairs. "Nate, Adam's here."

A minute later, Nate walks out with two open bottles of Dr. Pepper. "Hey," he says, handing me one.

"Hey." I take a big swig and grin. "It's okay with my dad. I can work tomorrow."

"Good," Nate says casually, ever on guard when others are around.

One of his daddy's ranch hands tips his hat as he walks by. "Boys."

"So, I'll pick you up at eight?" There's a spark in Nate's brown eyes I rarely see at school, and I wonder what it would be like not to have to hide our feelings—to be able to hold hands the way he does with Betty. "We'll need to check that watering hole, too."

I know what that usually leads to, and it's all I can do to keep a smile off my face. "Right. No problem." I check my Timex, an early graduation gift from Mom and Dad. "I should get going. Dinner's at seven."

Nate nods and watches me down the rest of my soda. "See you tomorrow."

Grinning ear to ear, I mount my bike. I pedal like a madman down the long dirt driveway to Highway 87.

Once you reach the city limits, which I do remarkably quickly, the highway becomes Broadway. I pedal through the intersection with Main Street, Eden's only traffic light, and past a row of small storefronts.

A window filled with the strangest things catches my eye. The objects seem to grab the light, play with it, then throw it back at me, better than before. Usually, when anything new opens in Eden, people rush right over to buy a little something and wish the business owner luck. But I've never seen this place before, and no one has mentioned it.

Dad needs a gift, and the place looks open. I check my Timex. Home is just three blocks away, so there's time enough to browse. I slant my bike against the storefront and head inside.

"Welcome to Time After Time." This guy is definitely not from around here. A suit? Suits are for weddings and funerals. And prom. "My name is Clarence. How may I help you?"

"Hi, Clarence." I stick out my hand. Texas manners. "My name is Adam."

His hand is soft and cool, but his grip is firm. "Adam. From Eden." This makes him smile.

"Yeah, right." Clarence's eyes disorient me. They look too old for his unlined face. "When did you open your shop? I've never seen it before."

"Today. In fact, you're my first customer."

It's not clear what Clarence sells. Whatever he has in the window isn't on display in the store. There's just a pedestal with what looks like a pocket watch inside a glass case.

"I was just looking for a gift for my dad."

"Your father, you say?" Clarence's dark eyes dance. "I have just the thing." He lifts the glass covering and beckons me with a head tilt.

Dad's not the pocket watch type. Not practical. And this one, so gold and shiny, is far too fancy. He'd say, "You shouldn't have," and stick it in the back of his underwear drawer, never to see the light of day.

"It's the only one in the world," says Clarence.

How can that be, I wonder? Texas manners require I take a closer look. It is remarkably gleaming.

"Pick it up," says Clarence, and I do. It feels warm like it's been baking in the Texas sun. "Turn it over."

There's an inscription. I read aloud, "There is no time like the present—"

"And no present like time," finishes Clarence.

I don't know why, but I ask, "How much?"

SIX
ADAM & EVAN

Clarence shakes his head, refusing payment. "And if you're not completely satisfied, you may return it."

"But it's not for me," I protest.

"Whoever holds the watch holds the gift of time. The bearer will always be wherever he needs to be, whatever the time or place may be." Clarence smiles, unblinking. "Whether the bearer knows it or not."

I slip the watch into my pocket and step outside.

I have no idea where I am.

SEVEN
EVAN

"What the actual eff?"

I'm standing next to a bike near what looks like the only traffic light for miles. The light turns red, and an old but very well-maintained car rolls to a stop right in front of me. The driver could be a background player from *The Marvelous Mrs. Maisel.* His window is down, and the guy on the radio is singing about going to Kansas City.

"Hello, Adam." The driver smiles and waves. I'm staring hard, but he's not giving me the finger. What part of New York City is this? He pats the side of his car, a kind of Tiffany blue with Bel Air in chrome script attached to the tail fin. "Tell your dad she's running like a top."

The light changes, and Mr. Bel Air waves goodbye. I see the license plate. Texas?

Did he just call me Adam? And with a drawl?

I whip around to go back inside Time After Time, so Clarence can tell me I'm not going crazy, but he's flipping the sign from "Yes, We're Open" to "Sorry, We're Closed," and turning off the lights.

I jerk the door handle repeatedly and bang on the glass, but it's not me I see in the reflection. Where's my jet-black hair? My olive skin? My clothes? OMG, I'm out in public in dirty jeans and a sweaty t-shirt! I can't be seen like this. What if a fan wants a selfie with me?

The shoes aren't bad, though. Converse All Stars. Classic.

"Hey, Adam!" It's a girl's voice.

This isn't happening. I rattle the door some more and shout, "Clarence!"

"Adam?"

I feel a tap on my shoulder, and I stop acting like I'm trying to break into what now appears to be an empty storefront.

"Who's Clarence?" the voice asks. That's two drawls in thirty seconds.

"Uh." The store is definitely vacant. I slowly turn around. A girl about my age is standing in front of me. Her reddish-brown hair is pulled into a ponytail, her nose and cheeks sprinkled with freckles. She's wearing lip color, but other than that, she's makeup free. "No one?"

"Doesn't your mom usually serve dinner at seven?" She raises her eyebrows and lifts my wrist to my face. It's the first I notice that I'm wearing a watch. A Timex. It's almost seven.

"Um. Hi? Seven, you say?" I'm supposed to meet Celeste for dinner at seven. I've got to text her and tell her I'm going to be late. I pat my pockets, looking for my phone, but the only bulge I find is round. Clarence's pocket watch.

"Like clockwork," she says. "Are you okay, Adam? You look a little flushed."

Flushed? I could hurl any second.

"Here." She pulls the bike upright, looking worried. "I'll walk you home."

"Thanks," I mumble.

She pushes some stray hair behind her ears. The sun is low in the sky, but I can see her tiny ears are lightly freckled, too. "Adam, I'm sorry if I came off snippy this afternoon."

"Oh," I say. "Not a problem." To review: My name is Adam, and I have a bike, a mom, and a Timex. Oh, and according to Mr. Bel Air, I have a dad, too. Wonder what that's like.

We walk in silence for a block and then turn right. It's a dusty place with small homes and old cars and pickups parked everywhere. Televisions flicker in several windows, almost all of which are open—as are many of the front doors. Everyone seems to be watching the same black-and-white movie on Jurassic TVs. There's not a flat-screen anywhere.

"Here we are." She steers my bike toward a white-painted house with a small covered porch and props it against the railing. "You sure you'll be able to work with Nate tomorrow?"

"Huh?"

"Nate. You said you're checking fences with Nate tomorrow. Remember?"

"Oh, right." I nod, playing along. Bike. Timex. White house. Nate. Fences. Got it.

"Adam, is that you?" A woman, pretty despite her depressingly blah dress, stands in the doorway. Something smells good, and I'm suddenly famished. "I was wondering when—Oh, hi, Stace." The woman's eyes cut between us, and she beams. "Out for a walk?"

Stace. Her name is Stace.

Stace gives me a sideways look and seems to sense my anxiety. "Yes, Mrs. Shire. Adam and I just went for a nice walk."

"I'm so glad. Adam, come in and wash up for dinner." She swings open the door and waves me inside. "You sure you don't want to join us, Stace? There's plenty."

I half-wish Stace would stay just to help me navigate whatever the hell is going on.

"No, thanks, Mrs. Shire." Stace turns and waves from the sidewalk. "I'll see you in church, Adam."

Wait. I go to church?

"Adam!" squeals a little girl, hurling herself at me. She wraps her slender arms around my waist. "Can you help me get Okra out of the tree?"

"Apparently, Devon tried putting a bonnet on Okra again," says a man, coming out of the bathroom looking fresh-from-the-shower—my/Adam's dad? "Even after her big brother told her not to." His damp hair is slicked back, and he gives the girl a look of mock reproach.

"Okra," I repeat slowly. Must be a cat. This is Scooby-level detective work. "Sure, I say. Lead the way."

The little girl, Devon—wait, does that mean her name is Devon Shire? What a great drag name. Anyway, Devon, my little sister, apparently, is tugging me toward the back door and a patchwork of grass and dirt. Squinting, I can make out an orange furball halfway up a tree.

I've never had a cat. Or a dog. Or a little sister. And I haven't climbed a tree since I was probably Devon's age.

"Can you get her down?" she asks.

Okra's twitching tail seems to say, "I'd like to see you try."

You know what this reminds me of? That scene in *Pleasantville*—the black-and-white part of the movie, when the fire department arrives, siren blaring, to rescue a cat from a tree.

"Hey, Devon," I say casually. "Let's sit here on the stoop and play a game. I bet if we just ignore Okra, she'll see us having fun, and come down on her own."

"Okay," Devon says, sitting as close to me as any kid has ever gotten, and I've ridden in plenty of cramped subway cars. She must really adore her big brother.

"Let's play the birthday game."

"We've never played that game before."

"Well, then," I say brightly, "this should be fun." I purse my lips, totally winging it. "How old am I?"

"That's not hard. You're eighteen."

"You're right," I say. "Very good. And how old are you?"

She stares at the cat. "This is boring."

"Come on."

"You know how old I am. I'm eight."

"Now, when will you be nine?"

Devon sighs, but Okra is inching closer to the main trunk. "Next year."

"And what year is next year?"

"1960."

I choke. "No, really, Devon. What *year* is next year?"

Devon gives me the meanest side-eye I've seen outside of Char. "1960."

"So, this is 1959."

Devon nods, distracted, "Mm-mmm." Okra is scrambling down the trunk, landing on all fours in the grass.

My heart is pounding.

"Adam! Devon! Dinner's ready!"

Suddenly, I'm not hungry.

EIGHT
ADAM

Clarence motions me to step back, so he can open the door and let me inside.

Thank God.

The craziest thing just happened. The second I stepped outside of Clarence's shop, I had no idea where I was. Definitely not Eden, Texas. In fact, this can't even be Dallas or Houston.

I'm not even sure it's 1959. Where do I start? The lights and noise? Cars that would make my dad's jaw drop? The people?

Okay, the people. I mean, guys are holding hands with other guys. Ladies are holding hands with other ladies. Rainbows are everywhere. And what's with all the face masks? All I can figure is there are a lot of doctors and nurses here. Wherever here is.

And almost everyone is holding a rectangular thing and talking to it.

Why isn't Clarence unlocking the door? He waves at me through the glass, then flips a switch. The lights go off, and a metal grate rattles down.

"What? No! Clarence, let me in! Please." My heart's pounding. What do I do now?

I hear laughter over the traffic and the clatter of high heels. A group of ladies with big hair is coming my way. What a relief. I *am* still in Texas.

One of the ladies points right at me and screams, "It's Evan!" She reaches into the top of her sequined dress and pulls out one of those rectangles. "See!" I'm staring at a picture of this same group of ladies with a dark-haired kid whose outfit is identical to mine. "I tagged you, and it took off. Three thousand likes already." She pinches my cheek. "I bet yours is even bigger."

This makes the other ladies laugh. I notice one of them has a five o'clock shadow.

I rub my cheek, which smarts. "Um. I'm a little turned around. Where am I, exactly?"

The sequined lady scrunches her heavily made-up face. "I've lived in New York City long enough to still consider West Broadway part of SoHo. So, honey, you're in SoHo."

Did she say New York City?

Now, I hear buzzing—or feel it. Is my leg vibrating? Do pocket watches vibrate? But that can't be it. The watch is in my other pocket. I reach in and pull out one of those rectangles.

I hold it out in my open palm like I wish one of these big-haired ladies would just take it already. A picture of a smiling Black girl appears along with a name: Char.

The sequined lady looks at the rectangle and then me. "You going to get that, honey?"

I must look helpless because she reaches over and presses the rectangle.

A voice starts right in. "Evan! I've been texting. Where the hell are you? You're supposed to be at Antonio's." If it's Char, she doesn't sound like she's smiling.

"I'm not Ev—"

"I saw your post." She huffs. "Are you *still* with those queens?"

"As a matter of fact, sweetie," says the sequined lady, "he is." She narrows her glittered eyes at me like she's making a diagnosis. "Now, did you say Evan needs to be at Antonio's?"

"Yes! Celeste is waiting!"

"Celeste? As in Celeste Starr?"

"Yes," Char says slowly, sounding highly suspicious.

"Gurrl, we're on it." The sequined lady taps the rectangle again, and the picture disappears. "Antonio's is just around the corner." She takes hold of my arm. I wince. She has the grip of an arm wrestler. "Ladies, let's move out." Her voice suddenly drops to a manly baritone. "I'm gonna meet Nora from *Larson's Pier!*"

A WOMAN WHO MY MOM WOULD SAY "LOOKS good for her age" sets down a glass of red wine and rises from her seat. "There you are, Evan!" She says this rather dramatically as she glides across the room. Several diners turn to look. "It's not like you to be late." She squeezes the air from my lungs while kissing my cheek. "And who are these gorgeous creatures?"

The sequined lady clutches her ample bosom. "I'm the Duchess of Trippledee, and I can't believe I'm meeting Celeste Starr! You know, I still cry when Nora comforts Ethan—"

Celeste does an exaggerated frown. "After Ethan gets bullied?"

"Yes!" The duchess clutches her heart. "Gets me every single time."

"You know, I was nominated for an Emmy for that episode."

"And you were robbed!"

Everyone in the restaurant is watching now. People have pulled out their own rectangles and are pointing them at us, nodding and smiling. Whatever it is that's happening right now, Celeste and the Duchess of Trippledee are eating it up— almost like they're putting on a show.

"Oh, the pleasure's all mine." Celeste presses her hands together and bows her head like she's praying. "Thank you, queens, for delivering my Evan. It's my birthday, you know."

"You don't say!" With that, the Duchess of Trippledee and her friends lead the entire restaurant in *Happy Birthday*, followed by cheers and applause.

So, I guess these rectangles also take pictures? Celeste smiles for all of them with her arm wrapped tightly around my waist.

"Be sure to tag my son," she says loudly and proudly. "It's Evan-underscore-Starr."

I watch several diners duck their heads and tap on their rectangles as if they've been given a direct order.

"Well, that was fun." Celeste takes my hand and leads me to our table. "Sorry I texted Char to track you down. I was worried."

"Um, that's okay." It's the best I can do.

Our food arrives almost immediately. "I went ahead and ordered your favorite. And don't worry about the carbs. You can run an extra mile tomorrow."

Apparently, my favorite is something called gnocchi, which is sautéed with plum tomatoes, onions, and sausage. It's delicious. In Eden, Texas, the most exotic Italian dish I've ever had is spaghetti with meatballs at the Lone Star.

Celeste takes a sip of wine and sighs. "So, are you seeing someone?"

Gnocchi slips off my fork, splashing red sauce across the white tablecloth. "What?"

She blows out a sad sigh. "You know how I feel about those apps. Love isn't something you order like Chinese take-out."

I have no idea what she's talking about or how long I can keep this up. Clearly, this Celeste woman, and the oddly masculine ladies with big hair, believe I'm her son, Evan. I'm guessing Evan's the guy in the picture with three thousand likes—whatever likes are.

"Sweetheart, you're just eighteen. So, I'm in no rush to marry you off. But you've been out since middle school." I'm chewing a mouthful of gnocchi and wondering what Celeste means by "out." She leans in, resting her chin on clasped hands. "I know Sebastian broke your heart, but I just thought—" Celeste purses her lips. "I just thought enough time has passed and that you'd be introducing me to a new boyfriend by now."

New boyfriend? So, Sebastian is an old boyfriend? I start choking and grab my glass of ice water.

Celeste reaches over the breadbasket and squeezes my arm. "Are you okay, sweetheart?"

I swallow hard, nodding, too stunned to speak. Am I dreaming? My mind darts to the scene outside Clarence's shop—young men holding hands with other young men. Women doing the same. People unafraid to show their love—*who* they love.

Then, I see Nate with his arm around Betty.

Under the table, I trace the outlines of the pocket watch through Evan's slacks.

Two things are clear: I'm in New York City.

And this isn't 1959.

NINE
EVAN

There's a knock at the bedroom door. "Rise and shine," calls Mrs. Shire. She's Adam's mother, not mine. Honestly, I'm surprised I slept at all. The accommodations here are only slightly better than sleepaway camp. Also, this isn't a dream. "Nate's going to be here soon. Breakfast is almost ready." She chuckles through the door. "And if you hurry, there might even be some hot water left for a shower." See what I mean?

"Thanks," I call back. There's no bathrobe in Adam's closet. I dash across the hall in a t-shirt and boxers—and not the cute kind.

You should know, it's weird showering someone else's naked body. Also, Adam has nothing to be ashamed of. I trick Devon into playing another game to discover which of the four toothbrushes I should use. I'm still grossed out, though.

Once dressed, I strap the Timex to my left wrist. Clarence's pocket watch and the Timex agree that it's 7:45. I don't know why, but I turn the pocket watch over and read the inscription. *There's no time like the present and no present like time.* The timepiece feels cool in my hand as I slip it into the right hip pocket of my jeans.

"What are you thinking, wearing that shirt?" asks Mrs. Shire. "You're checking fences, Adam, not going to church."

I look down. "Oh, right." How would I know? I've never lived in 1959 before, and I've never "checked fences" either. I'd Google a video on fence repair if only the Internet were invented.

"Change those shoes while you're at it," says Mrs. Shire. "Your boots are in the closet."

I return to the bedroom, fish a t-shirt out of Adam's dresser, and slip on his boots.

When I say, "I'll just have coffee," I get funny looks from everyone at the kitchen table.

"Since when have you been a coffee drinker?" asks Mrs. Shire.

"Your mother made breakfast." Mr. Shire points a fork at the only empty chair. "Eat."

"But, I don't usually—" I tell myself to drop it. I'm Adam, not Evan. "Right." I sit. A plate of scrambled eggs with three thick strips of bacon appears, followed by a cup of coffee.

"You want sugar or cream?" asks Mrs. Shire with something close to a smirk.

"Uh, no, thanks." Everyone watches intently as I take my first sip—even Devon. I'm guessing Adam isn't a coffee drinker.

According to Adam's Timex, it's eight-sharp when we hear an engine and a horn tap. So, this Nate guy is punctual. Since I keep a busy schedule, I appreciate that.

"Guess that's Nate," I say, standing. I'm just going with the flow here, hoping I can keep up this charade until I figure out how to get back to where—and when—I belong. "Ciao."

"Chow?" Mr. Shire's forehead creases in confusion. "You just ate."

"Um, yeah. I mean, I'll see you later." I turn to leave.

"Adam." There's a gentle chide in Mrs. Shire's voice, and I wonder what careless mistake I've made now. "Dirty dishes go in the sink." She smiles. "And don't forget your hat."

Hat. I'd noticed a cowboy hat on the closet shelf. I place my dirty dishes in the sink and dash to the bedroom to grab it. Catching my reflection in the dresser mirror, I pause. Damn, I—I mean Adam—look good in this thing. I pause again at the front door to see if anyone else wants to tell me what I should be wearing. "Alright, then. I'll see you later."

There's an old red pickup idling out front.

"Hey," says the guy behind the wheel who must be Nate. Damn. He looks good in his cowboy hat too.

"Hey, yourself." I walk around to the other side and climb in. "Um." I twist in my seat.

"What are you looking for?"

"My seatbelt."

Nate lifts his hat and scratches his head. "What's that?"

"Never mind."

I hope Nate drives as good as he looks.

TEN
ADAM

Ever read *The Prince and the Pauper?* Well, as I lie in Evan's bed—the biggest bed I've ever seen, with the softest sheets I've ever slept on—I feel like the pauper.

The rectangle, which I've come to find out is a telephone, vibrates on the table next to the bed. I proudly answer it all by myself.

But this time, Char isn't just a picture on the screen. She's a little movie, covering her eyes and squealing, "Evan, I know you're proud of your pecs, but put a shirt on!"

"Sorry." I adjust the angle, so I think all she can see now are my head and shoulders. "Is that better?"

"Yes, but why aren't you dressed already? You have that Gay Pride appearance in the Village in two hours."

"Gay Pride? In two hours?" I have another question, but I don't ask, "What's Gay Pride?"

Char rolls her eyes. "It's been on your schedule for months."

"Um." I need to get back to Clarence's shop on Broadway. All of this is because of him and his pocket watch. I just know it. "Is the Village anywhere near SoHo?"

"What the—Evan, you were born in Manhattan! You know where SoHo is."

"Right." I'm trying not to panic. I take the phone with me into Evan's closet, which is roughly the size of my bedroom back home. It's overwhelming and only adds to my anxiety. "Char, can you help me, please?" I'm sure I sound desperate.

Char's eyebrows drop. "You're asking me to pick out your outfit?"

"Sure. I trust your taste." Much more than mine.

She eyes the vast contents of Evan's closet and grins. "I'm going to enjoy this." And for the next fifteen minutes, Char seems to get a kick out of bossing me/Evan around—until I grab the wrong belt. "Evan, stop playing. You know the difference between Gucci and Prada." She narrows her eyes. "Did Celeste let you drink wine last night?"

"No." Dad has let me try beer, but wine has never touched my lips.

Char huffs. "Well, get your ass in the shower. I'll meet you in the lobby in thirty."

After first freezing and then scalding myself, I figure out Evan's shower. Water pours down on me like rain from a fixture the size of a hubcap mounted to the ceiling. Also, Evan has a lot of bottles. I have to read every label just to know which liquid goes where.

But I've never smelled better. I comb my damp hair back the way my dad does and fetch Clarence's watch from the bedside table. It's no longer warm to my touch. The pocket watch and my phone both say 7:45.

Celeste smiles at me over a cup of coffee. "Would you like some?"

"Uh, no, thank you."

Her eyebrows climb her forehead. Should I have said yes? Celeste is wrapped in a fluffy white robe in a gleaming white kitchen, exuding what my mom would call great style. "I've never seen you wear your hair like that. You look just like . . ." Celeste's voice trails, and her eyes get misty. I wonder about her unfinished thought as she pads across the tiled floor and plants a kiss on my cheek. "Post lots of pics and have fun."

Char pounces the moment the elevator doors open. "What did you do to your hair?"

"Why? What's wrong with it?"

She tips her head and sucks her teeth thoughtfully. "Actually, nothing. It's a good look."

We take underground trains, and I'm grateful Char's leading the way, so I can take in all the sights. We climb stairs into bright sunshine and rainbows. The air is electric.

If this is Gay Pride, sign me up.

ELEVEN
EVAN

I crane my neck as Nate drives past the row of shops where I first spotted Time After Time. The storefront is still empty. The pocket watch I wish I'd never seen forms a circular bulge in the right hip pocket of my jeans. Damn Clarence and his stupid watch.

"I'm really glad you could make it," says Nate, pulling me out of my reverie.

"Yeah, me too." I wonder how I'm going to bluff my way through this day.

We drive for miles and miles, past flat, open range and distant herds of cattle.

"I don't think there's gonna be a whole lot of fence to fix today. One of Daddy's hands rode the perimeter a couple weeks ago, and everything looked to be in pretty good shape."

"Oh?" This comes as a huge relief.

Nate's cheeks dimple. "But, we'll definitely be checking the watering hole."

"Okay," I say absently, my mind elsewhere. The thing about time travel in books and movies is the lesson. The protagonist must learn some kind of lesson or truth before they can go home. Until I figure out what that is, I'm trapped in a trope.

Nate turns off the highway onto an unpaved road. A cloud of dust billows behind us.

"Right there." Nate points out a sagging bit of barbed wire and pulls over.

Gripping a pair of pliers, one of the few tools I can identify on my own, Nate kinks the barbed wire in several places, tightening the entire section. I pay close attention in case I'm tasked with the next one.

"All set." Nate straightens and nods toward the horizon where tan earth meets the biggest, bluest sky I've ever seen. "There are a few more sections up ahead that'll need fixing, but we should be at the watering hole by noon." A gleam in his eye leaves something unsaid.

Nate tosses his hat onto the seat, so I do the same. We climb in, and he hits the gas—the road all to ourselves. Both windows are down, filling my New York lungs with sweet Texas air.

Ahead, on our right, several cows loiter near what looks like a rusty-sided, above-ground swimming pool. Nate steers toward it and down a bumpy path that has me bracing myself. He parks right up next to the rusty pool and kills the engine.

"At last," says Nate with a sideways glint. He hops out and peels off his shirt, revealing a stark contrast between the deep tan of his muscled arms and neck and the sun-starved pale of his torso. He lofts his balled-up shirt into the bed of the truck and starts unbuckling his belt. "Well, what are you waiting for?"

Through the rear window, I watch Nate drop the tailgate and proceed to strip. Off come the boots and socks followed by his jeans. He's down to his boxers. Then, one swift motion later, they're gone too. I'm looking at a totally naked cowboy, and I'm nowhere near Times Square.

Nate climbs atop the cab, the metal roof dimpling under his weight. "Hey, watch this!"

There's a loud whoop followed by a splash. Is this how you check watering holes?

Now I'm standing on the cab of the pickup, watching Nate splash around in the brown water, my clothes folded in a neat stack on the tailgate. Adam's Timex is tucked safely in a boot.

"Come on, jump!" Nate pushes wet hair from his eyes. "The water's great."

Did I mention the water's brown? But like everything else this day, I'm bluffing my way through. I crouch, then push hard with my legs. "Cannonball!" I holler as I fly through the air.

461

I emerge laughing, wiping water from my face. Nate swims up from behind, but instead of a playful splash or dunk move, he pulls me into his chest and nuzzles my neck.

My head reels. Adam and Nate? He turns me in his arms until we're face to face.

Clearly, this isn't Nate's first rodeo.

Or mine.

How's that saying go? Oh, yeah. Save a horse, ride a cowboy.

TWELVE
ADAM

"Stop gawking!" barks Char. "Honestly, Evan, you're acting like this is your first rodeo."

But it is, and I can't help myself. There *are* cowboys—but also clowns and queens. Lots of leather and chains, too. Hair of every color. People of every color. No shame. No hiding.

Char grabs my hand and drags me through the crowd, pausing whenever someone recognizes me/Evan and requests/demands a picture. She dutifully documents all of these encounters with her own camera—basically taking pictures of people taking pictures of me.

"We're almost there," Char shouts into her camera/phone. "This is insane. Felicia, wave, so I can find you."

It is insane. There's a guy down on one knee proposing marriage to a guy whose eyes brim with tears. Onlookers cheer, and I feel a stupid grin spread across my face.

"It's you," says a blond guy in a green apron. His rainbow nametag says, "Ian."

"I'm sorry," says Char, "who are you?"

"Me? Oh, I'm nobody." He glares at me hard. "Just ask your friend."

Char's narrowed eyes cut between Ian and me. "Uh-huh." She takes my elbow and steers me away. "Did you blow off that Starbucks hottie?"

"Huh? What?"

"I didn't stutter." She rolls her eyes and points. "Okay, you sit here." There's an empty chair behind a table draped in rainbows and covered with all kinds of rainbow hats, rainbow t-shirts, and rainbow pins. I sit, then stand. "Felicia!" Char squeals, hugging a large woman whose head is covered in long black braids. "We can only stay for an hour."

"That's fine." Felicia whips her head in my direction, causing the rainbow beads woven into her braids to click and clack. "Thank you for doing this, Evan. This will really help raise our profile." She runs through my responsibilities for the next hour. "So, basically, I'll handle all the transactions. You just smile and pose for pictures while Char posts everything to social."

Char finds a chair and scoots up next to me. "What's going on with you, Evan? You haven't been yourself lately."

Where to start? "I'm out of sorts, I guess."

Her eyes soften. "Have you been scrolling through pics of you and Sebastian again?" Since I don't know how to answer, I pretend it's a rhetorical question. "Evan, it's time to move on." Her mouth puckers to one side like Devon's. "And not with whatever app the boys are using these days."

Knowing nothing about Sebastian or boys and their apps, I sigh in surrender.

"Is that Evan Starr?" The Duchess of Trippledee is dressed for a night on the town, and it's not even noon. "Sweetheart." She leans into a man with arms the size of tree trunks. "Say hello to Evan Starr. Evan, this is my husband, Ricardo." I notice the duchess rolls her Rs.

Texas manners demand I stand and shake Ricardo's hand. He has a grip like a vise and a torso like a V. "Hi. Nice to meet you, Ricardo. This is my friend, Char, and her friend, Felicia."

The duchess plants her hands on her hips. "So, *you're* Char, the voice on the phone?"

"I am." Char beams. "And you're the queen who saved the day. Thanks for your help."

"I got to sing *Happy Birthday* to Celeste Starr."

"So, you've said," says Ricardo, smirking. "Many times. Since we got up."

Felicia smiles wide. "I'm sorry, but we only have Evan for the hour. So . . ."

The Duchess of Trippledee eyes the pile of merchandise and throws her hands in the air. "Say no more." She pecks Ricardo's cheek. "You run along. The duchess has work to do." She turns to the milling crowd and forms a small megaphone with her large hands. "Okay, dolls, listen up! Everyone here today is selling shit. But our shit shines. Because we have Evan Starr!"

Felicia's smile takes on a fixed quality until she sees a line snaking around the corner.

"Nah-huh." Char wags a finger at five shirtless guys, then points. "See that line? Unless you're Make-a-Wish kids, one pic and move on."

Felicia's rainbow collection is flying off the table. Meanwhile, I'm smiling for so many pictures, I can't feel my face. It seems everyone loves Evan Starr. Except Ian.

"Wow." Felicia is staring at an empty table. "Just wow. Thank you, Duchess."

"Always happy to be of service." The Duchess of Trippledee blows kisses at the three of us, then plows her way into the crowd. "Ricardo?" she hollers, still rolling her Rs.

"Is it too late?" Two guys holding hands stand before us, tiny rainbows painted on their cheeks. They're maybe a year older than Nate and me. "To get a picture with you?" asks the one with dark hair.

"Um?" I look at Char, who sizes them up, then nods. "No, happy to," I say, getting to my feet. I stand between them, the dark-haired guy on my right, his red-haired friend on my left.

"We moved to New York because of you." The redhead's words come out in a nervous rush. His freckled cheeks pinken. "Your *Love in New York* posts." He blinks. Is he . . . crying? "You really put it all out there. The good and the bad. It was very brave of you."

I hear a sharp intake of breath. Char snatches his phone. "Here. Let me do that for you."

"We're really sorry things didn't work out," the dark-haired guy says quietly.

"Smile!" calls Char.

"Between you and Sebastian," the redhead clarifies.

"Oh," I say, confused. "Thank you?"

"All done." Char shoves the phone at them. "Thanks, guys. We really need to get going."

"We're blowing up, Evan." Felicia pulls me into an enveloping hug. "Thank you." The embrace lingers, and I get the feeling this has more to do with what just happened than me smiling for pictures. Felicia then thanks Char, their embrace much shorter.

I feel Char's arm slide around my waist. "Are you alright?" She glances back at the empty table and sighs. "Actually, I'm surprised it didn't come up sooner."

"Me too," I say. If I play this right, Evan's apparent heartbreak could be an opportunity. "What if we walk home instead of taking the train?"

"The train?" Char looks at me sideways. "You mean, the subway?"

"Yeah, I meant instead of taking the subway."

"Okay. But it's a long walk."

THIRTEEN
EVAN

I know I talk a big game about swiping left and right and my preference for no-strings hookups. The truth is, that's what I let people think. "Sebastian, who?" Sure, I scroll through the profiles. But then, I scroll through our *Love in New York* posts. Every single one. Every. Single. Time. Look up masochist, and you'll find my picture.

Our lips part, and when I open my eyes, the intensity of Nate's gaze frightens me so much I swim away.

"Adam, what's wrong?"

"Nothing." That's a lie. Everything about this is wrong. This moment isn't mine to take. I need to get out of this watering hole and back into my clothes before the one part of me that's in disagreement can change my mind. I reach the side of the tank and realize there's no graceful way to climb out of this thing. A cow stares at me with her big brown eyes. I'm feeling judged.

"Obviously, something's wrong." Nate swims to my side and drops his head onto my shoulder. "Is it because I asked Betty to the prom?"

I say nothing but feel my heart sink. This is how Nate and Adam have to live, hiding their feelings for each other until they're twenty miles from town and surrounded by cows.

"You could ask Stace," Nate says hopefully. "We could double date."

Now, I could just cry. I pull away and risk looking into Nate's eyes. "And what then, Nate? Where does this go?" So much for bluffing my way until I can get back to the future.

Nate's smooth forehead knots. "What do you mean?"

I wave a hand between us. "Do *you* see a future where we can be together?"

"What?" Nate smiles incredulously. "Are you nuts?"

"So—" I purse my lips. "You'd settle down. Get married. Have kids."

"Of course." Nate huffs. "I mean, can you imagine? Two guys like us, together?"

"I can, actually. And I wish you could too."

Nate swallows hard. I see the struggle in his eyes. "Adam, this can never be more than what it is right now. You understand that, right? Our lives would be over."

I revert to bluffing. "You're right." I lightly kiss Nate's cheek. "It was just crazy talk."

We help each other out of the tank and get dressed.

As I button up my fly, I feel the hardness of the pocket watch against my hip and fish it out. The timepiece isn't radiating the same warmth it had the first time I held it in my hand. What had Clarence said? "Whoever holds the watch holds the gift of time."

The gift of time.

I sit on the tailgate, flip the watch over, and reread the inscription. *There's no time like the present and no present like time.*

My eyes lock on the last four words.

No present like time.

Scrubbing the back of my neck, I wonder if a stranger in a vanishing gift shop actually did give me the gift of time.

The bed of the pickup truck rocks, pulling me back to the moment. Nate's hopping on one foot, trying to pull up one of his boots.

"That would be a lot easier if you sat down." I slip the watch into my hip pocket and pat the empty expanse of tailgate next to me.

Nate grins. "You've always been the smart one." He abandons the effort, grabs his other boot, and plants his denim-clad butt next to mine. "Are we okay?"

"Of course." But how would I know? I *hope* they will be. When I think about it, Adam and Nate are risking everything for a love their world isn't ready to accept—at least not in Eden, Texas, in 1959.

What am I risking? A broken heart? Embarrassment? Pity?

No one forced me to do those posts. Char even tried to talk me out of it. "Hashtag Evastian? Really?" Adam and Nate had to hide their love from the world. I'm free to put mine on display—an extension of my brand.

That's how much times have changed.

And there it is—the value of Clarence's gift.

I feel the pocket watch warming against my right hip.

I think it may be time to go home.

FOURTEEN
ADAM

Char elbows me. I'm so busy looking for Broadway, I fail to notice everyone around us is crossing the street. "So, do you want to talk about it?"

I'm milking the brokenhearted Evan act for all its worth, buying time for my search. "I guess," I say with my best hangdog expression. Char seems like a truly good friend to Evan, so I feel a bit guilty about my tactics, but I need to find Clarence. At the same time, my stomach is growling with hunger. Celeste only offered me coffee, which I don't drink, and Char was on me to get a move on, so I haven't eaten a thing. "How about we talk over lunch?"

"Lunch?" Char sighs. "Fine. Where do you want to go?" She looks ahead and points. "That Thai place is supposed to be good."

"Antonio's," I blurt, thinking that would put us in the vicinity.

"Antonio's? But you ate there last night."

"I really have a taste for their gnocchi."

"Comfort food." Char nods sagely. "I get it."

Finally, I see a street sign for Broadway and scenery that starts to look familiar. My heart drums against my ribs as we approach the corner where Clarence's shop is located. But the metal grate is down and the interior dark. I read the "Sorry, we're closed" sign as we walk by.

"I think we turn right here," says Char, leading the way. "Yep, there it is."

"Back so soon?" asks a waiter whose face I recall from dinner with Celeste. "This way." He shows us to the same table. The place is dead. It's just two older gentlemen in a booth and us.

I pull Char's seat out for her because that's how I was raised. Her eyes narrow as she sits. "Evan, I'm worried about you. I know you loved Sebastian, but he did you wrong. So wrong."

I nod mutely because the less I say now, the better.

Char opens her right palm over the table, her eyebrows raised. "Your phone."

I hand it over. Char taps the screen several times, then smacks her forehead. "You haven't changed your passcode? It's still Sebastian's birthday?"

I nod mutely.

A grid of tiny pictures appears, and Char huffs a sad sigh. "Evan. It's time. We need to delete these."

"Wait!" I say more loudly than intended. The waiter, poised to take our order, frowns and walks away. Maybe, living in Evan's world for nearly twenty-four hours has made me curious. Or perhaps, this is what Evan would do if he were here. "Can I just see them one more time?"

A sad smile turns Char's lips. She gives the screen a couple more taps, then slides the phone towards me.

Two bright, shiny faces look up at me, their heads touching—nothing but forever in their eyes. I feel my heart catch. Dozens more pictures follow. Kissing. Laughing. Holding hands. More kissing.

At some point, I stop seeing Evan and Sebastian.

I see Nate and me. Kissing. Laughing. Holding hands.

"I *knew* this was a bad idea." Char rummages through her bag and pushes a Kleenex at me. She reaches for the phone. "We're doing this."

My hand seems to move on its own, coming to rest on Char's. "Please. Not the first one."

"The first date." The corner of Char's mouth puckers. "Only picture you never posted."

"Excuse us," says one of the older gentlemen, no longer in the booth. "Is your name Evan, Evan Starr?"

"I'm sorry," says Char politely, "but we're kind of in the middle of something here."

"We'll keep it short, then," says the other man. "We just wanted Evan to know things work out in the end."

Texas manners require I stand and introduce myself. "Hi. Yes, I'm Evan Starr." I extend my hand while Char stares.

"It's nice to meet you, Evan," says the first man, winking. "My name is Adam, and this is my husband, Nate."

FIFTEEN
ADAM & EVAN

"You're back." A knowing smile plays on Clarence's lips. "I trust the watch worked as intended."

"Perfectly." I place the golden timepiece in his cool palm, a look of understanding passing between us. "There's someone I need to talk to."

"There usually is." Clarence turns the watch over in his hand. "You know what I always say, 'There's no time like the present.'"

SIXTEEN
EVAN

"Where *are* you?" shouts Char, trying to make herself heard over the background din of my surroundings.

I smile at the question. "Just picking up a venti iced coffee," I say into my phone. In truth, I've been sitting here for hours, a bundle of nervous energy even before the caffeine hits.

"Well, I've shifted things around like you asked. Check your schedule and make sure there are no surprises."

Surprises. I chuckle to myself. When I got home last night, Celeste was waiting for me. Ambushing might be a better word, but then, Celeste has always had a dramatic flair. "Evan, sweetheart, there's someone I'd like you to meet." Once the shock wore off, my father and I had a very long conversation.

Poking through my phone, killing time while keeping one eye on the counter, I click on the Love in New York photo file. This time, I have every intention of deleting it. Huh. That's strange. Just one pic remains, and I'm happy to see it.

I delete the hookup app and change my phone's passcode. I have no intention of telling Char the new one.

He's here.

I jostle my way through the crowd of tourists, keeping my head down until I reach the counter.

"May I help you?"

"I hope so. My name is Evan, and I was wondering if you believe in second chances."

Ian grins.

SEVENTEEN
ADAM

My head rolls left. I could stare at Nate Branham's profile all day.

"What are you looking at?"

"You."

He laughs at the windshield. "I can't believe we're doing this."

"I can." I spread the map across my lap. "Just eighteen hundred miles to New York City."

The open road stretches before us.

We have nothing but time.

OCEANS OF DUST
LISA AMOWITZ

SEVILLE, SPAIN 1491

G od has a sadistic sense of humor.

Today, like most days, I'd expected He'd get in a few more chuckles at my expense. But parked in the shade of the palm in the plaza, as I sweltered in the upright chair of the wagon my uncle had built to tote me around, I had no idea how the pitiful trajectory of my life would change its course.

Charcoal stick clenched in my fist, I glared at my sister.

"The heat is unbearable today," I said. "Why are you fools playing?"

"It won't be long," Hannah said, dismissing me with a grin. "We will defeat these Moorish dogs quickly and then go home."

I shrugged. There was nothing to be gained by arguing with Hannah. I was here in the plaza at her pleasure. It would have been much easier to leave me behind rather than cart me—her clubfooted, crippled brother—around like goods bound for market.

I suspected she feared if she left me behind, I'd give away her unforgivable behavior. After all, girls were not to play ball, sweat, or run—and neither of us were supposed to be here, in the plaza, at all. The Jewish and Muslim kids who gathered to play were pariahs in this most Catholic of cities, remnants of a heathen past, human garbage the king and queen would soon expunge from their holy nation.

Hannah and I were orphans, twins born to the teenaged Esther Cordova who'd only lived an hour after our birth—right at the very moment the Spanish Dominion vowed to shed itself of Jews like us. We were raised together by a series of aged Tantes, but that was where our similarities ended. Hannah was a golden child born to be noticed, and I was born to exist in life's cracks. She was a beauty, with her corona of rose-gold hair and the grace and speed of a gazelle—the planet around which I orbited. I, her poor, twisted moon of a twin, was her opposite in every way.

Today, Hannah's team of Jewish boys were slated to face off against the Moorish kids who'd beaten every other streetball league in the city. I sat in my cart drawing, unnoticed as always, while my sister sprinted and leapt, my charcoal skipping across the page. When I drew, I didn't have to think about how it might be to dart about like the players did. I didn't have to think about how my swollen joints ached in the summer heat.

In my early years, a block of wood strapped to my shoe had served to even out my mismatched legs. With my crutch, I could hobble for short distances, then climb in my wagon when I tired.

But as my body grew taller, my misshapen foot and leg did not keep pace. By my fifteenth year, I'd become grotesquely lopsided. Every hobbled step was an agony.

And here I sat, the perpetual bystander, watching as Hannah, her blue head scarf a bright dot in a sea of dark-haired boys, feinted, leaped, kicked, and scored. The Jewish boys cheered. The Muslim boys scowled. And I worked rapidly to capture it as best I could. Hannah liked when I drew her.

I could never quite capture the essence of my beautiful, perfect sister. Despite her athleticism and grace, there was always a silence that clung to her—as if a phantom sibling rode the breeze beside her, whispering secrets only she could hear. Occasionally, I'd look up to see a faint shimmer gathering around her, like dust particles in the sun. Then I'd blink and it would be gone. One time, when we were younger, when I was still able to hobble around well enough to chase the balls she kicked at me, I could swear that glimmer swirled into the shape of a boy—an invisible boy that told her secrets and competed with me for her attention.

That day, I was trying—and failing—once again to depict her accurately when *he* leapt from the sidelines into the fray. The charcoal nearly slipped from my damp fingers. Sun glinted off his light-brown curls and kissed his sleek bronze skin. With my crutch, I pushed my wagon closer for a better view of those penetrating black eyes, like the darkest waters of the canal: deep, unknowable, and fixed on the game. My greedy gaze tracked the boy's languid form, those almost lazy movements which belied his speed. My hand skimmed across the paper faster than their feet across the cobblestone plaza.

The players took a break, the sun a merciless eye above us. Hannah trotted over, breathless, sweat soaking through her tunic, to drink water from one of the skins we'd packed. From a distance she resembled every other street boy, but for the head wrap. I wore similar garb, plus the tallis and kippah that marked me as a Jew.

Caged in my unwieldy body, I wore my identity like a badge. Perhaps it was a dare for people to notice me. To proclaim I was there. If so, it was a failure. No one ever saw me but Hannah.

My gaze snapped across the plaza to that boy. He threw back his head and laughed with his friends, but I couldn't help but notice how his glance strayed in our direction.

"Who is he?" I managed to slip my obsessive studies of him behind my other drawings. "He plays well."

Hannah laughed derisively. "*That* one? If he is the best player these clumsy oafs have, they are doomed to lose."

I gazed across the plaza at those long legs, the glistening brown skin of his bare chest. "He *is* very good."

"He's no better than the rest of them, Sollie." Hannah slammed the water skin into my cart. "Save some of that for me. I'll be thirsty after I wipe the floor with them."

"He is as fast as you," I said, my gaze still riveted across the plaza. "And he has trickier moves. You see how he calculates and anticipates what you'll do? He's always one step ahead of you."

Hannah swiped the sweat from her brow. Her opal eyes flashed bright in her overheated face. "What would you know of sport, Solomon? You have never played any game besides crawling after balls in Tante's courtyard."

The cruelty of her jibe robbed me of breath. Surely, she did not understand that those tiny cuts joined together to form a festering wound in my soul. And my pride did not allow me to tell her.

Perhaps it was her way to level the score. She knew I was more cunning than she, and the irony galled her. But my brains were wasted on a lame, sickly boy who would probably not survive into manhood. And she, a girl, was the gifted leader who could never lead.

God's sense of humor at it again.

IT TURNED OUT THE MUSLIM BOYS DID BEAT the Jews. And it was all because of their secret weapon—that beautiful lanky boy with the mop of light-brown curls.

Sweat streamed into my eyes as I gazed toward the fountain where the Moorish boys celebrated their win by splashing and chasing each other. What I wouldn't have done to tear off my clothes and join them.

Hannah stalked back to my cart. Peevish and overheated, I couldn't stand another moment in the blistering sun. "Maybe if you'd listened to me, you'd have . . ."

"Shut up, Sollie," Hannah snapped. She stole a glance back at the boy who'd bested her, now cavorting with his friends in the fountain.

"It's just a dumb street game." My twisted ankle throbbed as if my bones were bits of shattered glass. "I don't know why you get so worked up about it. Can you help me out of this contraption so I can stretch? Otherwise, you'll be carting my corpse back to Tante."

"You know I don't want to be responsible if you fall. Remember when you tripped and broke your nose? If anything happens to you, Tante will lock me in the kitchen to grind fish until I grow scales myself."

"I will not fall," I said. "Now help me out of here before I faint."

Hannah heaved a long-suffering sigh. I knew that sigh—it meant, *I love you, Solomon, but sometimes you are a ball and chain. Am I to be expected to lug you around forever?*

With theatrical disgust, she grabbed the crutch that hung from the side of the cart and thrust it at me. Shifting my weight onto the shorter leg was always excruciating, but I worked hard not to give her the satisfaction of a grimace.

Though the pain shot up through my ankle like a hot spike and hurt like lava flowing through my bones, I hobbled toward the other side of the plaza as quickly as my uneven legs could carry me. I could move fast enough when I wanted to.

And I wanted to see that boy up close enough to endure the pain.

The Moors stopped to watch my halting approach—a rail-thin, milk-pale Jew with a crutch and a too-short leg bent at the ankle like a melted candle. I stopped when I couldn't take another step and called out to them. "Congratulations to you all for-for a great game. My-my sister never loses."

481

There was silence as the boys gaped at me. One of them pointed at my foot and started to laugh. "Your sister? Would you look at that! The Jew girl's brother is a cripple!"

Hannah leapt in front of me, hands on hips. "Take it back! If you insult my brother, I won't play with you swine ever again."

"Sorry," they jeered. "Sorry your brother is a gimp!"

"You're the ones who will be sorry, you idiots!" she said.

It might've erupted into a fight if *he* hadn't broken from the crowd and strode toward me. At close range, I could see the moisture on his upper lip, the strands of gold-flecked brown hair that stuck to his brow.

"Nice to meet you, Hannah's brother. Your sister gave me quite the run."

"You had better moves," I blurted, my cheeks on fire.

The boy's keen dark eyes seemed to look right through me. My breath hitched, trapped somewhere inside my chest. I forgot the blazing pain in my hip and foot, the sweat-soaked tunic that clung to my back.

"I'm Josiah," the boy said.

"And I'm Hannah Cordova," said my sister, stepping between us. "This is Solomon, my brother. He may be—uh—the way he is, but he is very smart."

"Why do you speak for him?" the boy asked. "He seems quite able to speak for himself."

I smiled around my discomfort. Shuffling sideways, I stepped out of Hannah's blockade. "Nice to meet you, Josiah."

"You did play well." My sister adjusted her head scarf and straightened her tunic—her movements feline, not her usual rough gestures.

Josiah swept into a deep bow. "As did you, Miss Hannah."

My heart sank as their gazes locked. The air around Hannah stirred with that familiar iridescent glimmer and its accompanying chill. The stones beneath my feet listed sideways. I clung to the crutch, determined not to prove Hannah right and keel over.

"Were you born like that?" Josiah asked suddenly.

My face went hot. I should have been used to that question. Whether whispered behind my back or to my face, accompanied by disgust, pity, or raw fascination, it was usually the only thing people said to or about me. But Josiah's question was clinical. Matter-of-fact. Instead of making me squirm, I felt seen.

"It's none of your business," Hannah snapped—as always, stepping in to fight my battles. The boy shrugged and let the matter drop. But his name lingered in my overheated brain. *Josiah*. The syllables sat on my tongue, honey-tinged with a hint of cardamom.

For the rest of that summer, Hannah and the boys played hard in the brutal heat. When she wasn't playing, Hannah and I worked out new moves to outsmart Josiah. At night, when my throbbing joints and foot kept me awake, all I could think about was his ink-black eyes.

I didn't worry that, in the Jewish faith, my desire for another boy was a terrible sin. Why would I care to please God after what he'd done to me? I'd never marry anyway. What should it matter if I had no love of girls, if none of them would have a misshapen and pitiful creature like me?

All summer, Josiah's team slaughtered us in game after game. But Hannah was not deterred. Beating them—beating *him*—became her sole purpose in life. And I, glad for a shared goal, threw myself into training her, gratified by her faith in my tactics. Perhaps I saw my sister as my proxy, sending the message that she and I were a team, that I was not just the lame brother she pulled around in a cart.

In a few weeks, my efforts paid off. With Hannah scoring most of the goals, her team triumphed. The boys carried her around the courtyard, singing and shouting, ignoring me as usual. In the mayhem, I spotted Josiah heading across the plaza. Heading directly for me.

"Please accept this on behalf of the Alvarez family." On his open palm was a strange-looking candy. "It was you who taught her those moves, wasn't it?"

The words caught in my throat. I shrugged and popped the candy in my mouth.

"So, were you born like that or not?" Josiah asked for the second time.

I chewed on the sweet, sticky treat. "Yes."

Usually, the questions ended there—but Josiah pressed on. "Does it hurt when you walk on it?"

"I—uh—a little." Face heating, I scanned the plaza for Hannah. I was an onion, peeled of its layers, defenseless.

She must have sensed my distress, for she sprinted across the plaza and planted herself between my cart and him. "Leave him be, you filthy loser!"

"You don't understand," Josiah said—to me, not Hannah. "My papa is a cobbler. Have you ever had a proper shoe fitted?"

I stared down at the thin leather sheath that covered my foot and ankle. Where once it could be wedged uncomfortably into a proper shoe, over the years my foot had swelled to the size of a bread loaf, the few toes curled painfully inward. There was no shoe on earth that could fit such a monstrous thing now. "When—I-I was twelve," I said, almost too soft to hear.

"We have to go," Hannah said, insistent.

"I'm serious. Papa can make you a shoe to help you walk."

"How dare you make jests!" Hannah accused him.

My jaw still working the chewy treat, I looked up into Josiah's earnest eyes.

"I do not make jests," he said, then turned and strode across the plaza, to where his teammates sulked alongside the fountain.

ON OUR WALK HOME, HANNAH WAS SILENT. Bumping along in my cart, the cobblestones jangling and jouncing my sore bones, I considered Josiah's offer. Could he have been telling the truth? And why would he want to help me, a Jew, anyway? Did I dare to imagine how it would feel to walk beside my sister, rather than pulled along behind her in this wretched cart?

Drowsy, my head bobbed as my sister pulled my wagon through the streets of Seville. And I dreamed of myself in our courtyard, chasing balls Josiah kicked, curls pasted to his sweaty brow.

I was jostled awake when the wagon hit a rut. Still groggy, I lifted my head to see an oddly familiar boy pulling our cart, Hannah walking beside him. But I couldn't place him. He was tall and blond, a near mirror image of Hannah, yet blurred, as if his edges were smeared, like one of my drawings.

I rubbed my eyes and murmured, "Who's that?" But when I looked again, there was only Hannah, looking wan and exhausted.

"What are you talking about, Sollie? You must have been dreaming." She continued walking, the cart rattling over stones. I realized with sudden clarity that I'd grown too big for her to pull around.

"When will you take me to Josiah's father's shop?"

She lurched to a stop, the cart bumping into the backs of her legs. "We can't. You know that."

"Why not?"

"He is a Moor!"

I studied those flushed cheeks. The high, pinched quality of her voice. In my life as an observer, I missed little. The blush was not from physical strain. "You like him, don't you?"

"Don't *ever* say that again, Solomon," she said coldly and pulled the cart faster. As it scudded over the stones, jouncing every aching bone, I imagined myself as the unwanted baggage she could never set down.

Did I believe a shoe would let me run, play, or even walk with a steady gait? Or render me marriageable? No.

But I imagined the freedom to get around without relying on others, without being shackled to my sister. Maybe then I wouldn't need to worry that if the escalating violence against Jews forced my family to flee, they'd leave me behind, like the scraps of a half-eaten meal.

In the weeks to come, Hannah's rage did not subside. But I did not stop thinking about Josiah. And how much I needed that miraculous shoe.

IT WAS THE WEEK OF THE FESTIVAL OF VELÁ DE Santa Ana and the city streets were filled with dancing, tapas, and drunken revelers. During those weeks in July, we Jews shuttered ourselves inside our homes lest the merriment turn to violence, as it frequently did.

I was struck with a familiar tug of longing—of wanting to be part of the pulsing life of the city, blending in with the conversos and leaving behind my pariah status as a Jew and a cripple. We Jews were unwelcome guests in Seville, as loathed as the twisted appendage on the end of my leg, a defect on the body of Spain. An infestation the monarchy was soon to flush out.

The long hot week passed in a slow, melting blur. It was too hot for Hannah to practice in the plaza. Instead, we sat together in the shade, plying our basket-weaving trade. When we turned sixteen, we would be put to work in Zaide's factory to earn our keep. Our hermit grandfather, Zaide Yakov, who we saw twice a year, was plenty rich, but insisted we work off the cost of our upbringing.

The Tantes had no use for my sketching ability, but my skill in basket-weaving was highly prized. I was fast and innovative, my weave tight and masterful. But Hannah was dreadful at it, so the Tantes decided that instead of producing baskets, Hannah would be better at selling them. Now, every market Tuesday and Friday, she accompanied them to work the stall, where her natural charms were more of an asset than her clumsy fingers.

The Tantes would not let me come. I'd only get underfoot and require them to wait on me. Instead, they left me at home under the care of Bubbe Balzar, the half-blind old crone who spent three-quarters of her life snoozing in her rocking chair by the hearth and the other quarter demanding I read Torah to her.

Left on my own and given my limitations, I grew immeasurably bored. I'd drawn studies of Bubbe's pruned face more than I cared to mention and had read through every one of Zaide Yakov's books at least twice. I twisted straw for baskets until my fingers crabbed. To break up the tedium, I took to carving a small bit of wood into a little figurine for Hannah, while Bubbe Balzar's snores thundered from the kitchen. Thus distracted, I was startled by the clang of the iron gate that opened to the street.

I had no business admitting visitors. But the doldrum of the day was so unbearable, and my loneliness for Hannah's company so acute, I was eager for any interruption. It took me an interminable amount of time to collect myself, hobble painfully on my crutch to the gate, and peer through the grillwork at the person staring back at me.

I blinked in disbelief. Gazing back at me was a pair of luminous black eyes.

I'd never seen Josiah up this close. But there he was, separated from me only by the intricate scrollwork of the cast iron gate.

"What are you doing here?"

"You never came to Papa's store. So, I've come to you."

For a moment, I was too flabbergasted to respond. "How did you find where we live?"

Josiah laughed. "We have eyes all over the city, my Jewish friend. Your people shut yourselves up behind walls, but we listen and hear everything. The city is a volcano about to erupt. If you open the gate, I will tell you all about it. And I will fit your shoe."

"You can do that?"

"What did you think was in this bag?" Josiah laughed, an easy, buoyant sound. "A cobbler's son begins his training as soon as he is old enough to hold a knife."

I craned my neck to check on Bubbe. "The old crone who is supposedly my caretaker may be blind, but she has the hearing of a hawk. You must be quiet."

"Like a mouse. I won't need long."

Unlatching the lock, I swung the gate inward. There he stood, smelling of lye soap and that undefinable aroma that made me want to press my face to his chest and die listening to the rhythm of his heart.

Josiah scanned the well-appointed courtyard—the vivid bougainvillea blooms clinging to the stucco walls and bursting from the central flowerbeds, the arched portico that ringed the perimeter, the vegetable garden and orange grove. It was a lovely place, and the height of my ungratefulness that I should think of it as my jail.

"You have no idea what is going on out there, do you?" Josiah asked. "Have you not heard of the denunciations? The crackdown on fake Christians and Muslims? The jail within the Castillo de San Jorge is filling up with heretics. And so are the firepits."

I blinked at Josiah. Of course, I knew about the converso families, many of whom joined us in synagogue on the High Holy days even though they'd taken their baptism.

"The *familiares* are rounding up people caught practicing the old ways. In my neighborhood, the Moriscos are reporting anyone caught with a prayer rug."

"Moriscos?"

Josiah frowned and shook his head. "You really do live in a cave, Cordova. Converted Muslims. Most of them are blatant liars, ratting on each other to avoid getting arrested themselves. We are living in dark times, friend."

I swallowed and licked my lips, relishing the sound of the word on his lips. "We aren't friends."

Josiah smiled. "Of course, we aren't. But you and your bad foot put your sister in danger. Because if she has to run, she will not leave you behind. And . . . if the truth be told . . . I like her."

My throat went dry, my heart kicking up a notch. I didn't need to hear about his lust for my beautiful sister.

But I did need the boot.

Josiah strolled around the courtyard and scanned his surroundings. Tired and aching from the strain of hobbling around, I waited at the central table while he found a stool and a small bench, which he brought over to me. I sank awkwardly onto the stool, watching him unfurl a leather sheath and spread his tools on the table.

"Soon you will not tire so easily," he said.

"You have a lot of confidence in your skills. You have not seen the foot in question."

Josiah fixed his gaze on me. "I have every confidence that proper support will ease the strain on your body. You are misaligned and that has worn down your joints. If we fix that, we fix you."

His words sent a tremor through me, not so much at their meaning, but for the sweet tang of his scent, so close at hand. I thanked the heavens there was no sign of the old crone shuffling out of the kitchen doorway.

Josiah slipped the thin leather wrapping off my twisted foot. I did my best not to look at the thing—the raw pink skin, the lumpy mass with its gnarled toes. It looked more like a root vegetable pulled from the ground than a human foot.

"Oh my," Josiah said. "It's a wonder you can bear any weight on it at all. But I can help you. I promise."

I hung my head, my face hot. I could not bear to have my monstrosity exposed. But Josiah peered at my foot, seemingly fascinated by the way it curved sideways, at a perfect right angle to the rest of my leg.

"Someday," he said, almost dreamily, "scientists will be able to fix abnormalities like yours. To open the skin and straighten the bone."

I stared at the top of Josiah's head and marveled at the strands of bronze that threaded his hair. He had to be an apparition, or at least a figment of my addled mind. No one this beautiful could possibly take an interest in me. My shame receded, replaced by an unquenchable thirst.

"Someday," I echoed.

His hands probed the tender skin of the appendage, tracing its monstrous contours, sliding over the crest where only three dwarf toes protruded from the bulbous flesh. I quivered at his touch, a surprising shock of pleasure coursing through me. It was as if years of tangled rope had suddenly been unknotted.

Josiah peered up at me, a broad smile breaking across his face. "You liked that?"

I closed my eyes. "Yes."

"There's tremendous strain on both of your legs as you compensate for the unevenness of your gait. My shoe will put your body back in alignment. I can't promise you will dance, or even walk without some awkwardness, but it will lessen the pain."

Savoring the splendor of those fingers on my skin, I imagined them straying further north to my upper torso, my chest, and yes—I admit it—my groin, which now pressed hard against my trousers.

"Oh my," said Josiah. "You really do like that."

I flushed, wanting to scramble off the bench and dig a deep hole in the garden to bury myself and my sinful thoughts. I was truly a monster, inside and out.

I didn't dare open my eyes—but Josiah took my hand and guided it downward to his groin, which to my utter shock was also hard against the rough fabric of his trousers. "I like you, too," he said.

Helping me from the stool, he laid me down between the bougainvillea, then lowered his face to mine. "You think yourself hideous, Solomon," he whispered. "But you are beautiful."

My heart rammed against my chest. I could barely hear his words over it, barely speak. "In my culture, boys are not supposed to kiss."

"Nor in mine," said Josiah, his lips brushing mine. "But I kiss who I like. And I like you."

He pressed those honey-soaked lips against mine, and the sweet warmth of his tongue darted into my mouth. I was certain my entire body would explode right there in the garden.

"I like—you too," I managed. "I . . ."

Josiah nuzzled me. His hand slipped under my waistband. I will not share that moment, though it is burned forever into my psyche. After shuddering my pleasure, I lay there, languid and slack, the pain receding like distant church bells.

"I must go now," Josiah said. "When I return, it will be with your boot."

"But . . ." I wanted to say, what about this? What about us? *Was there an us?*

Instead, my traitorous tongue snagged on different words. "Do you like Hannah like this?"

Josiah drew back onto his knees. "Yes, Solomon. I like her just like this. Perhaps even more. And one day, I will have her as well. I would marry her, if our cruel world would permit."

The words pierced like a dagger through my ribs. I turned onto my side to hide my tears, but it was no use. They came, shaking and pitiful, soaking the dirt of the garden with my shame.

I felt Josiah pull me upright, a soft hand on my shoulder.

"There now," he said. "You know the way we feel toward each other will only bring more strife to our lives, don't you? Be happy that I love your sister as well as you. For this way, we can always be close."

I swiped at my tears. "What do you mean?"

Josiah brushed a damp lock of hair from my face. "You are my first. This way we can always be together."

I stared, my mouth falling open. "What are you saying? If Hannah loves you . . . you'd still . . . you'd still want to be with me?"

"Why not?" Josiah pulled me toward him. "It is just as dangerous to lay with a Jewish girl as with a Jewish boy, so why not both? Perhaps, one day, despite the obstacles, I will convince her to become my bride."

And so I signed on the dotted line, gratefully accepting any scraps this angel—this demon—this boy would toss to me. I would become his willing slave.

For what other chance at love would I get?

Josiah packed his tools, promising to return in two weeks with a prototype of the fitted shoe. He would then adjust and refine his creation so it would "fit like it grew on the end of your leg."

I could not wrap my head around this possibility. All I could think of was the two weeks I'd have to wait for his return. I seethed with jealousy at the thought of watching Hannah and Josiah compete in the Pzaza. I'd never begrudged my sister her ease, her agility, her beauty, her popularity before. I'd never minded living in her shadow.

Until now.

But as fate ordained, we were not destined to meet for another carefree game. For the night after Josiah came to fit me for my shoe, the Spanish Inquisition began its sweeping widespread arrests. And all hell broke loose throughout Seville. The San Jorge jail began to fill with heretics, holdout Jewish families like mine and Muslim families like Josiah's who had kept their heads down, in hopes the dark forces would leave them in peace.

But we were scum to be converted or expelled from the holy nation of Spain.

For two weeks, Tante Ursula, Fetter Pedro, Hannah, and I cowered inside our home while the fighting and screams raged in the street outside our gates. Then Tante Carmella, Fetter Essua, and their five children moved in, their goats and belongings parked in the courtyard. Next came Old Fetter Tova and his chickens. Then the maiden Tantes and cousins Essina, Vittoro, and their seven children joined us. Last of all came Zaide Yakov.

And so, with our large family wedged into Tante and Fetter's home like canned fish, the beginning of the end of our life in Seville was at hand.

Zaide Yakov treated me like something to step over with his spindly legs when I obstructed his path, for there was often no place for me but on the floor as the agonizing pain kept me off my feet. While the old man ignored me, he seemed keenly interested in Hannah. They'd whisper conspiratorially as she nodded and smiled.

That strange shimmer eddied and flowed around my sister like a whirlpool. As Hannah spent less and less time with me, I focused my rage on it. Her phantom. I had no idea what it was, but once, as I gazed out my window to the courtyard, the shimmer swirled between the orange trees until it took on the contours of a massive, hulking man.

Was I losing my mind?

Most days I languished in my bed, too exhausted to slither off the mattress, largely forgotten unless Tante or Hannah remembered to bring me food, or one of the stronger cousins carried me downstairs. More and more I feared when it came time for them to flee, I'd be left for the Inquisition to burn in the plaza.

I clung to the return of Josiah with his glorious boot. But could he find his way back? Would he? What if his family was swept up in the mayhem and destruction?

Two weeks passed, and the promised arrival of Josiah came and went. I wept, more for the loss of him than for the boot that would supposedly change my life.

One night, as I lay tossing fitfully, there came a rap at the window. Convinced I was dreaming, I forced myself up onto my crutch and dragged myself to the window. There, on the balcony, silhouetted by the moonlight, was Josiah.

"Please," he said, "let me in."

I unlatched the window, and he fell in, almost toppling me— bruised, bleeding from gashes, and barely coherent. I could not fathom how he'd scaled the façade of our home and made it to the exterior balcony.

There was no time to ask how he'd gotten there and why. If I did not do something quickly, he would bleed to death on my bedroom floor. I tore at the lace curtains, the bedsheets, even my sleeping linens, and made makeshift bandages to staunch his wounds. I could not lift him onto my bed, so I covered him and made him as comfortable as I could. I prayed to the gods that had cursed me not to take Josiah.

"Solomon," he said, his voice a rasp. "I brought your shoe."

"Rest, friend. You are delirious."

"Look in my satchel, Solomon. Please."

The satchel rested where it had landed when he'd fallen out of the sky and through my window. I sidled over to it and pulled apart the clasps. Inside the scuffed case were two boots crafted of butter-soft brown leather, one with a low heel, the other as tall as two bricks.

I shuffled back to him, dragging the satchel with me. "How did you . . ." I trailed off. "What happened to you?"

Josiah's breath was ragged. "A family we knew well denounced us and then . . . the *familiares* came in the night . . . and when Papa would not bow to them, they . . ." Josiah faltered. "They clubbed him until he died. When I tried to defend him, tried to stand between them and Mama, they beat me too. They took Mama and my little sister. And when they tried to grab me, I dodged them and ran."

494

Josiah rolled onto his side, his chest heaving with sobs. "I should have fought harder. I should have defended my family."

Helpless to comfort him, I could only rest my hand on his shoulder. Rage coursed through me. "Your playing skills saved your life. Now I will keep you safe."

I knew it was a lie. I could barely look after myself.

Josiah's sobs finally quieted, and he eased himself to a sitting position. "Try the shoes on. Please." There was an eagerness to his tone, an urgency.

"You need your rest."

"No. You must try them on at once."

I sighed and opened the satchel. The ordinary shoe slid on easily. This was a man's shoe. A fine shoe for a nobleman.

The other shoe, which was nearly twice the size of the first one, sporting a heel the size of a paving stone, was nearly impossible to pull on over the tortured skin of my misshapen foot. I stifled a cry as the leather pressed against its ravaged joints and blistered skin, but kept tugging.

I did not have the heart to refuse Josiah. What if he died on my floor knowing his efforts had been in vain? I tugged and pulled until the bulky mass of my misshapen foot traveled through the soft leather like a serpent swallowing a rodent.

Then it was on. And my legs—though one foot still folded in at a wrong angle—now shod in boots with wildly uneven heels, were the same length.

"Try them out." Josiah had propped himself against the bed, his wounds bleeding through my makeshift bandages. "But can you get me water first? I'm so thirsty."

Without thinking, I stood and took the few steps toward the pitcher on the night table. Josiah laughed as I handed him the cup.

"How is your boot?"

I stiffened. I'd been so caught up in tending to Josiah, I hadn't noticed that I'd stood and taken steps. Excruciatingly painful and halting steps, but steps nonetheless. I had walked in his miraculous boot.

"What will I tell my family when they see these boots? How will I hide you now? My family will not let you stay here, Josiah. They hate Muslims."

Josiah smiled through his pain. "Never mind. Lie beside me, Solomon. Keep me warm."

I slid next to him and pressed myself against him, feeling his body quake beneath his bloody clothes. I held him against me, close enough to count his eyelashes, the thick black fringes beaded with tears. He closed his eyes and pulled me closer, until our lips met.

"They will let me stay, my sweet one," he murmured. "When they see you walking, they will understand that by giving you this boot, I have saved your life. No matter their hatred of me, they will in turn, save mine. And we shall never be parted again."

JOSIAH HAD TAKEN A GAMBLE THAT THE desperate Balzars, themselves targets of the Inquisition, would be grateful enough for his gift that they would take pity on him. And it paid off. As the Balzar clan loaded their belongings into the caravan of carts readied for our escape to Portugal, I had miraculously gained the ability to walk. And when we fled in the night to the small town where Zaide Yakov had somehow secured a safe haven to house us, Josiah came with us.

In time, the miraculous boot enabled me to walk with only the aid of a strong stick. Somehow, Josiah had crafted an ingenious design that supported my twisted appendage so that it could more comfortably bear weight. At first there was considerable pain, but as my joints realigned and adjusted to the more normal distribution of weight, I stood upright, propelled by my own efforts. I moved slower than the others, of course, but I was not cargo to be hauled and loaded into carts.

I shuddered to think what would have become of me had Josiah not provided me with the gift of mobility. Would they have left me behind for the Inquisitors to find my rotting corpse? Thankfully, I would never know. For like the rest of our besieged clan, I was too busy with the business of survival.

As we trudged by night through the hills and valleys of Western Spain, this Moorish boy, whose injuries healed quickly, had insinuated himself into our family. The frightened Tantes were charmed by his kindness and his careful repairs of their worn shoes. He tended to their sore feet with special balms and shoe inserts and even helped the younger cousins and Fetters fix broken wheels and harnesses.

Josiah, was, in a word, useful. He worked hard, laughed hard, and never complained. But watching him gravitate to Hannah as he distanced himself from me stung worse than any bodily pain. Had this been his plan all along? To buy his way out of Seville to freedom? I dared not think too hard on that.

After two weeks on the road, we reached the flat, dusty Portuguese border town of Vilar Formoso, recently swelled with desperate refugees from all over Spain and surrounded by resentful townspeople. In the heat of the Inquisition, Portugal was only marginally safer than Spain. Here, dozens of us were jammed into the four fetid rooms Zaide had paid someone dearly for. There was barely a square foot of floor space to call my own.

I breathed a sigh of relief when Zaide pronounced that he had booked passage to the bustling port of Hamburg, Germany and that we'd soon be leaving this wretched waystation behind. But the rest of the family was tired of running. Tired of starving. Tired of trying to keep their bawling children quiet. They refused to join us and renounced their Jewish identity.

After all we'd suffered, I could not blame them. Hannah was infuriated, though we did not linger long enough for her to vent her rage. The following day, Hannah, Josiah, Zaide Yakov, and

I left for Hamburg. It was on that voyage we learned why our grandfather lugged his musty old book collection wherever he went. Within those false-backed tomes he'd stashed a multigenerational Cordova fortune in gems and jewels.

Sadly, the old man never set foot on German shores. After only a few days at sea, he passed in his sleep and after a brief prayer, was laid to rest at the bottom of the Atlantic. Did I grieve? Hardly. To the crusty old coot I was barely alive.

Zaide had booked passage for us under the name of Corvisch, so that we might blend in better in our new home. And after a hasty marriage by the ship's captain, Hannah and Josiah disembarked on German soil as Mr. and Mrs. Hannah and Josiah Corvisch, choosing the less concerning moniker.

Josiah Corvisch and his wife exited the Portuguese merchant vessel with a king's ransom hidden in their crates of books. And I emerged, renewed as Solomon Corvisch, a foppish young man of indistinct ancestry with an oddly-shaped foot.

But the three of us were not the only ones to leave Portugal behind. For within moments of our grandfather's death, the shimmering cloud that had trailed my sister her entire life exploded around her in brilliant hues, like a galaxy around the sun.

HAMBURG WAS NOTHING LIKE SPAIN. PEOPLE jostled together like beans in a jar. I had never been so electrified. People saw me not as Solomon, the lame Jew boy, but as Solomon Corvisch, the artistic kid with an exotic accent. I set myself up with an easel along the waterfront and even began to sell some of my sketches.

Zaide's fortune afforded us a great measure of comfort and status. Josiah opened a small cobbler's shop, and soon word of the quality of his shoes and repairs spread, winning him a loyal clientele. By now, my boot had become such a part of me, my muscles and bones so sturdy, I kept the ornate new cane he'd carved me as a fashionable accessory to the luxurious wardrobe I'd acquired.

But Hannah was restless, wandering the streets with that shadow demon of hers in tow. She'd vanish for days on end—accompanied by that creature, I'm certain—leaving Josiah and me behind . . . together. We picked up where we'd left off. As the fire in my grate dwindled, he'd slip into my room, slide under the covers beside me, and vow his undying love.

How happy I was in those days. How deluded. I was a fool to believe that playing house made Josiah mine, that he was *my* husband.

Looking back, I don't know if his promises and kisses were a means of survival, or if he truly loved us both so much, he could not choose. I only knew I was content wrapped in his arms, lulled by the gentle rhythm of his heart. I spoke nothing of Hannah's vaporous companion to him, and though I sometimes felt it watching me from the shadows like a predator stalking its prey, it was clear that only I could sense it.

One betrayal, my continued tryst with her husband, was enough. Josiah would think me mad, anyway.

Eventually, strife found us in Hamburg. Unrest grew in the bustling streets, not only from the affronted Christian community, but from the friction between Jews from all over the continent—conversos from Portugal, Ashkenazis from the north, Turkish Jews, and Spanish Jews like us, all chafing against each other.

Hannah, though she'd married a Muslim man, was still bitter over the Balzars' wholesale defection and clung to our Jewish identity like a spear. She spoke endlessly of the evil done to us. How we should never forget what the Spanish crown did to our families and our people.

Perhaps she even grieved for Josiah's family more than he. And the creature—the shadow, as I called it—showed itself more and more, a solid, hulking menace.

IN THE SECOND YEAR OF OUR ARRIVAL IN Hamburg, a child—Jeremiah—was born to my sister and my love. I confess, I fully expected to hate the little brat. To envy it as the symbol of the love I wanted to deny and destroy.

Instead, I fell in love.

Baby Jeremiah was Josiah in miniature, and in my twisted heart, my own son. I'd never cared much for children, as they'd recoiled from me and I them. But I could not keep away from Jeremiah. I'd soothe him when he woke crying and bring him to Hannah to nurse. Sometimes I'd feed him goat's milk from the baby bottle Josiah had fashioned from a horn with a leather tip. When his dark eyes gazed up at me with contentment, I was smitten.

One night, as the baby's cries echoed through the second floor of our house and no one stirred to comfort him, I slipped on my boots, grabbed my cane, and clunked as quietly as I could manage toward the nursery.

By the time I arrived at the nursery door, the crying had stopped. I'd have returned to bed, but I could not resist the urge to gaze at Jeremiah's sleeping face. To my horror, a monstrous, stinking mass of dirt and mud cradled the sleeping babe in its filthy arms. And I knew instinctively: this was the shadow being's true form. This was the monster that had haunted my sister since our childhood.

"Put him down at once!" I roared and rushed at it, my cane swinging. "I command you, filth! Get out of this house!"

The creature set the cooing Jeremiah back in his cradle, then turned its flat pebble gaze on me. "Greetings, Solomon. Our meeting has been long overdue."

I pointed my cane before me like a sword. "What are you? Leave now, before I break you into clods of dirt!"

The thing did not budge. If dirt could smile, I imagined it was smirking. "Ah, Solomon. You have known me all your life.

500

You listened to my advice when the others told you that you were useless. But I encouraged you to draw."

"You lie! I have never laid eyes on you!"

"But you have, Solomon Cordova. You gratefully accepted my help. It was I who coaxed the Moorish boy to fashion the boot that changed your life."

"Liar! And it's not Cordova. It's Corvisch!"

"Changing your name does not change your blood. Blood does not lie. Nor do I, Solomon."

"Why do you haunt us? What do you want? What evil are you whispering to Hannah? You are the cause of her strangeness."

"Evil? I am Ash. I have served your family for over a century. My purpose is to protect you."

"Great job you've been doing. Most of us are dead."

The monster bowed its huge head. "For that I am deeply sorry. It is a cruel and sad world that wishes to exterminate your kind."

I chewed on my lip, heart pounding with terror. "Get away from that baby or I'll . . ."

The creature advanced. "Or you will do what, Solomon? Will you tell Hannah that I watch over her child at night as I have watched over the two of you, ensuring your survival?"

"I will tell Josiah that we are haunted by a grotesque demon."

The creature's unblinking stone eyes fixed on me. "If you do that, I will be forced to tell Hannah of your indecency. Of your betrayal of her trust."

My blood ran cold in my veins. "You would do that to me? To Josiah?"

It bowed slightly. "My purpose is to perpetuate the line which continues in this child. Josiah has served his purpose. And you, my friend, are merely a back-up guardian should Hannah die before the child comes of age."

"A what?"

"Hannah is my guardian. Any action I take is at her command. She is determined to protect your people, and I must keep her focused. If she learns what her husband and brother have been up to, it will not go well. She loves Josiah fiercely and deeply. Return to your room, Solomon."

I watched as the thing vanished, seemingly sinking into the floor. Shaken, I trudged back to my bed, my leg aching more than it had in years. I would have to make peace with this demon that saw into my black heart and bore witness to my betrayal. For I had no intention of stopping.

And while the Jews of Hamburg fought and feuded, clamoring for dominance, and Josiah and I made passionate love, my sister rose in strength, her personal magnetism drawing a following. I was certain it was that thing guiding her hand, advising her, like a king's counsel made of mud.

The community of displaced Jews had begun to turn to her at synagogue, where she donned the lace veil of a married woman, walked to the podium, and spoke, at first softly, then her voice rising, of rebellion. Of fighting back. Of reclaiming what was ours. She had become a beacon. Jews from around the continent began to flock to Hamburg to listen to the Jewess of Seville, as they called her.

It was dangerous talk. Talk that had gotten generations of us murdered, hunted, and chased from our homes.

In my heart, I knew it was not her talking. It was that thing spurring her on. And I, her betraying brother, was powerless to stop it.

Life carried on as usual. Josiah working at his shop, me wandering the city drawing and hanging around in taverns, picking up stray men and boys. I had built a life beyond the Corvisch homestead, complete with throwaway men and admirers that were not Josiah, though he was always first in my heart. I had begun to develop a reputation for my art. At my perch along the banks of the River Elbe, people now waited for hours for a portrait. Almost eighteen, I'd grown comfortable, despite the presence of the creature and Hannah's militancy, despite my impediment. I'd become content with the odd life I'd carved for myself.

So when the terrible day came, I was not in the least prepared. That night I'd fallen into bed drunk as a lord and fully dressed, the scent of a lovely rich boy still on my clothes. I woke, gagging, the acrid odor of smoke filling my lungs. If I'd taken another moment to shrug off my boots, I'd never have found them in the billowing darkness.

Staggering into the hall, my cane flailing in front of me, I was unable to see through the thick smoke. "Help! Help!" I shouted. "The baby! Someone get the baby!"

Heart racing, I stumbled down the hall toward the nursery, but a wall of flame blazed up to block me. I tried to turn back, but lost my footing and fell to my knees. Scrabbling along the floor, I groped my way toward the stairs. It was useless; I couldn't breathe or see. Finally, my short, ridiculous life had reached its conclusion.

Something grabbed me by the waist and hefted me off the floor, carrying me as if I weighed little more than baby Jeremiah. Coughing and hacking, I found myself sprawled on the cobblestones outside, tongues of flame licking from every window of our home.

There was Josiah, singed and stunned, dodging back and forth like a maniac. Behind him, cradling baby Jeremiah, was the creature.

"Where is my wife?" Josiah cried. "Where is she? Where is my baby?"

The creature—who was only visible to me—pulled me to my feet, thrust my cane into my hand, then shoved Jeremiah into my arms. Josiah broke into a run toward the burning house, but the creature grabbed his waistband and threw him to the ground. Dazed, he got to his feet, finally noticing that I held his son in my arms.

The creature—Ash, as it called itself—loomed behind him. "Tell the Moor that Hannah is safe," it said.

Still gagging, I tried to choke out reassurance to Josiah, but my words were drowned out by the coach, pulled by a team of horses that came to a whinnying stop beside us. In the driver's seat sat Hannah.

Josiah grabbed the baby from my arms just before I puked and keeled over.

The rest of that night passed in a half-conscious blur, a wild ride through darkened streets with Josiah, Jeremiah, and I nestled amid baskets of grain and casks of wine bound for export in the back of the coach. It wasn't until much later that I learned how Hannah's supposed allies had informed on her to the German authorities. We'd barely escaped arrest. I was too sick to recall boarding what later appeared to be a Spanish warship.

I came to my senses suspended in a swaying hammock, my stomach trying to turn itself inside out.

"Josiah?" I croaked. My throat had been scraped raw, my lungs filled with shards of glass.

"The fire hurt your lungs, Sollie," my sister said, cool hands mopping the sweat from my burning brow. "The sea doesn't appear to agree with you, either, brother dear."

"We're at sea?"

"Welcome to the Lament, our new home. A place where we can at last be free."

"What on earth? Where are we going?"

Hannah's eyes shone like crystals, her hair a brilliant amber in the glow of the small brazier that provided the cabin's only light. "Oh, I don't know. Amsterdam, perhaps? I hear they are accepting Jews as long as we have ample coin."

I groaned and lay back in the hammock. Still alive. Those gods must be having a really good laugh.

When the violence in my stomach at last subsided, Hannah helped me up the rope ladder to the deck of the Lament. It was a massive war ship, its white sails billowing. Before us lay the open sea. I'd have asked how we came upon such a thing, but my gaze landed on the creature, solid as a mountain.

"What is *that* doing here?"

Hannah, who'd gradually shed her boyish wardrobe for clothes more befitting royalty, was radiant in a gown of pale blue silk and gossamer crinoline. Haughtily, she tossed her rose-gold locks over her shoulder. "That's no way to speak to an old family friend, Sollie. Ash saved our lives. And helped us claim this ship. He is our family's sworn protector."

The creature bowed, fading away as if it had been only Hannah and me on the deck all along.

I gripped the rail, too afraid to glance at the empty expanse of sunlit blue. Never had I been this far out to sea, with no land in sight. My gaze drifted skyward, to the single sail that fluttered black against the clouds, and my insides lurched. "Did you *steal* this ship?"

"It is compensation for what was taken from us. We are safe here, brother. Safe from all those who have sought to destroy us." My sister's eyes gleamed with a fervent fire, her voice full-throated as if she spoke in an arena, not the deck of a ship. She faced me, eerily serene. Composed. A stranger.

I took an involuntary step backward, nearly tripping. "Why is it called the Lament?"

Hannah smiled, hands folded at her waist sash. Behind her, a crowd formed a circle.

"Queen Hannah!" they chanted.

"Queen?" I spun around to face them. "Queen of what? You're all mad!"

Hannah's beatific smile did not waver as she lifted her chin to the sky. I searched the deck for Josiah. For baby Jeremiah. But there was no sign of them.

"Like Noah's Ark in biblical times, this sacred ship, Solomon," Hannah said, "is our salvation. It is our holy weapon with which we will mete out retribution for the crimes against the children of Israel."

She stepped daintily onto a crate and pumped her fist in the air, gold hair fluttering like a war standard. Her voice grew louder, deeper, stronger, eerily amplified until it pulsed in my chest. "What has cowering, building fortunes only to run for our lives done for us? We are prey, forever on the run from that criminal enterprise, the Holy Roman Empire, the greatest predator the world has ever known! My people, it is time we fight back!"

The crowd of at least a hundred bedraggled and ragged Jews—men, women, and children—stamped their feet and pumped their fists. And I fell silent, fear silencing my words.

This ship was not meant to retreat from danger. Instead, we were going to sail straight into it.

A hand rested on my shoulder. I turned to face Josiah, his face sallow, those once-bright eyes filled with sorrow. And I understood. He had sought comfort and acceptance among our people, and now he was shackled to us, doomed to meet whatever fate my sister dealt us.

"Come down below," Josiah said. "There is stew cooking in the mess room. You will enjoy it."

I glanced back at Hannah, my chest aching. If not for her pointless quest, Josiah and I could have blended into Hamburg society without a trace. But she had marked us with her thirst for blood. For vengeance.

She'd even marked her own son.

My jaw tensed, rage rippling through my arms to my fists. "It's all because of that thing!" I said through gritted teeth.

"What thing, my love?" asked Josiah as we made our way down to the mess hall. His simple words calmed me. He had no knowledge of my sister's demon. We were here, together on this ship. And my sister, occupied with waging a revolution, might not notice if Josiah slipped into my cabin from time to time.

"Never mind," I said, realizing how crazy I sounded. Had Josiah seen the monster? Or had he seen what the creature wanted him to see? The man who sat in the coach beside Hannah the night of our harrowing escape from Seville. The shadowy boy who played with her in the courtyard.

It had been there all along, manipulating us. Haunting us. Poisoning our minds and deeds.

There was so much resignation in those black eyes, in the sag of his body. My beautiful Josiah, only nineteen, had aged a decade in the past two years of our acquaintance.

But in my hammock, when I pulled him into my arms, the old smoldering hunger awakened. Josiah was the missing half of my soul, the mate nature ordained. My sister was merely the mate society accepted for him.

But I could not leave well enough alone. Instead, I had to slake my unquenchable thirst for reassurance. "Do you love her?"

Josiah's sleepy smile faded, his voice gone gruff. "I know this is not what you want to hear, but even when Hannah pushes me away, I know we were meant for each other."

He looked up, those black eyes wet and shiny as the ocean at night. "Is it possible to love you both equally? You are twins who once shared the same womb. I suppose I am a freak, Sol, for I still cannot choose between you."

I chased him from my cabin that night.

Weeks at sea blurred into months, and soon little Jeremiah was able to toddle around on his own. Increasingly, I became of the mind that Hannah and the creature's only interest was to take as many Spanish galleons and merchant vessels down with us as they could.

And I lived in terror of the day they would get their wish.

Each night, as the sunset painted the horizon in lurid hues, the passengers gathered to hear Queen Hannah speak of our glory, of terrible deeds Spain and then Portugal had perpetrated against our helpless people. How we needed to strike a deadly blow to their empire, which now spanned the seas to a newly-discovered continent.

Into our second year at sea, we'd evaded the Spanish navy and proved ourselves a deadly menace. We'd overtaken dozens of Spanish merchant ships, killed the crews, and emptied them of their goods. And Hannah had come to believe herself invincible, chosen by God as an avenging angel. Little Jeremiah, who was now entirely under my care, celebrated his second birthday at sea.

The Lament, I realized, was a pirate ship. And my sister, its Pirate Queen.

I was sickened by the blood. Sickened how everyone aboard, with the possible exception of Josiah, seemed to revel in it. And that *thing* was to blame. That murderous, cursed being who had brought doom and suffering upon our family.

AFTER I HAD NOT LET HIM NEAR ME FOR months, a distraught Josiah barged into my cabin. For a moment I hoped it was to beg me to take him back.

"Solomon," he said. "I can't sleep at night over fear for her."

My heart sank. It wasn't concern over me that sent him to my room, but my sister. All while it was she who drove us deeper into danger.

"I'm afraid something terrible is going to happen. Tell Hannah she must end this insanity."

"I cannot." I sighed. "I've tried. She won't listen to me."

Josiah stared at me, his expression indescribably sad. "I miss you."

"Then be with me again." I'd been so angry at him, but as always, in his presence my resentment crumbled, replaced by love and desire.

He shook his head. "I can't explain it, Solomon, but I'm afraid if I leave her side I'll . . ."

"Then go now," I said, my voice gone cold. "Go and be with her."

Those words would haunt me for the rest of my days.

WE HAD BEEN CHASING A SMALL SPANISH galleon for weeks. Word was that it bore the confiscated fortunes of Spanish conversos and Hannah was eager to lay claim.

The day was perfect and balmy as we drifted into southern waters. As the sun set, Josiah and Hannah sat on the deck, Hannah peering at the horizon through a looking glass, he absently mending fishing nets. He rarely left her side now, but my soul still ached for him.

The sound split the evening with a thunderous crack. The crew hit the floor, myself included. From my prone position, I realized it was only a single shot. Our cannons fired and the attacking ship exploded, then sank. The crew burst into shouts of triumph.

Hannah did not move from her seat, her face bone white, a bloom of blood spreading across her silk gown.

But the blood was not hers. At the sound of gunfire, Josiah had flung himself across her body and taken the shot meant for her. That single shot had pierced his heart.

HOW CAN I DESCRIBE THE EMPTINESS THAT followed? The hollow gnawing grief that tore at me? Even the child could not console me.

My sister did not leave her quarters for days. The ship drifted listlessly, without destination or purpose. The crew wandered, aimless. Without Josiah as our rudder, our north star, my sister and I became ghosts.

I roamed the ship, my hair unkempt, my beard grown bushy and wild, my clothes soiled. With my rocking limp, I appeared an ogre, the monster people always thought me to be.

If I was a monster, Hannah became a phantom, porcelain-pale and paper-thin.

We were quite a pair.

But slowly, incrementally, Hannah began to change. First, she asked to have her baby, who she'd mainly ignored for his entire two years, brought to her quarters. She was careful to exclude me, as if denying me that last vestige of Josiah.

Had she found out? Had the creature finally told her how—for all these years—she'd shared her husband with me?

ONE NIGHT, QUITE BY ACCIDENT, I SAW THEM. At first, I doubted my eyes.

I had made my way to my sister's quarters to discuss a concern I had over Jeremiah's teeth. Though I'd let myself go to hell, I neglected no detail if it pertained to the child. As an orphan myself, I'd be damned if I'd let Jeremiah grow up in the state of benevolent neglect in which we'd been raised. I indulged his every need.

That night in the captain's quarters, all the lanterns were lit. Long shadows moved across the wall—a couple dancing. Had my sister found a replacement for my beloved so quickly? Was she so fickle?

I did not know her heart. I only knew the bottomless pit of my own grief.

Peering through the paned glass into Hannah's inner sanctum, I nearly lost my precarious balance. For Hannah danced with an apparition—a flickering figure from beyond the grave.

Josiah's ghost had returned. In death, he had chosen to be with her, not me.

Stricken with rage, hurt, and inconsolable grief, I staggered across the deck and climbed down the rungs to the lower level. Tearing through the kitchen, I found a bottle of whisky, polished it off, staggered to my cabin, and flung myself into my hammock. But even sleep rejected me. The thought that Josiah's love for Hannah was stronger than for me would grant me no peace.

Enraged, I tore off my boot, the emblem of Josiah's love, waddled over to the brazier, and lifted the grate. I was about to stuff the offending object into the glowing coals and eradicate every last remnant of him, my false lover, when a tickle in my ear—a pull on my hand—stopped me.

You don't want to do that.

The compulsion had come, unbidden, from the depths of my being. It was not my own thought. I dropped the boot to the floor, sparing it from destruction, and whirled around.

"Show yourself, monster!"

It had to be the creature. It controlled Hannah. And now it was trying to control me.

I had never been more convinced that we, the Cordova twins, were possessed by a demon.

I stormed from my cabin into the narrow hall. Still tipsy from the drink, my gait unsteady and lopsided, the vengeful wrath that burned in my gut drove me forward.

And there was Josiah's form, glowing with a soft corona. But this was not the depleted Josiah. This was the glorious youth who had fitted my boot in the courtyard and forever changed my life.

My anger dissolved. I sank to my knees.

He had come to me. He loved me after all.

But when I looked up again, it was not Josiah at all.

It was the creature, glaring with a malevolence so thick, I could feel its mud fingers crushing my heart.

I rushed toward it, swinging my cane. "How dare you take his form! You made him sacrifice himself. You've been controlling all of us! Driving us forward into this suicidal mission. This is all your doing."

I lunged, but the thing sidestepped me, and I bounced into the rope ladder. Disentangling myself, I charged at it again, until the thing grabbed me by the throat and lifted me into the air.

After toying with me for years, it was finally going to snap my neck like a chicken bone. Maybe I should welcome the relief.

"Solomon," the creature said in its dust-dry voice. "You must not speak of this to your sister. She is cracking from the strain of her loss."

Its fingers pressed against my windpipe and blocked my airways, making it hard to speak. "You murdered him to get him out of the way. I saw you in there, pretending to be *him*. You wanted her for yourself, you filthy demon."

"You are wrong, Solomon. I did not kill Josiah. I merely protected my guardian."

I flailed in vain against its grip. "You've been plotting against us, manipulating us all these years. For what? To be Hannah's lover?"

Almost gently, the creature set me down. "You speak with little understanding of my duty, Solomon Cordova. I am sworn to serve."

I spat at it, the moisture leaving a wet spot on its earthen torso. "Liar. Demon!"

The air shimmered and swirled. The creature vanished and there he was—my Josiah, that warm skin, that beautifully wicked grin—not ghostly, but solid. The wind emptied from my lungs. I staggered back, weak with grief. And yes—with want.

Josiah's form stepped toward me with an outstretched hand. "Lay with me, lover. Lay with me and I will be forever with you as we were that day."

I blinked, my eyes stinging. This was not real. This was a devil tempting me with what I'd loved and lost. What it had stolen.

"No!" Backing away, sweat coating my brow, it took every bit of strength to resist this apparition. This conjuring from hell. "You can't trick me. I will tell her that you murdered her love. That you destroyed him so you could have her for yourself!"

"You won't, my love, or I will confess our sins. How we betrayed her. Your sister loves me more than she's ever loved you. She will pitch you overboard when she learns how you purloined me for your own filthy desires."

Josiah shimmered and morphed into the massive creature—and suddenly, the truth was a searing light in my soul. I saw it all. Understood it all. For this thing was no different than me. "You lie to yourself, monster. You tell yourself your cause is noble. But all you've wanted was my sister for yourself. That is what drives you!"

For a moment, I was certain the creature would break my neck with a single twist. Instead, it deflated, as if I'd poked a hole in its filthy hide and let all the air out of it.

"You are wiser than I have given you credit."

The air shimmered and again, there he was, the youth I'd known on that magical day in the courtyard.

"We are flawed beings, Solomon. Ruled by our own wants. You knew what you were doing was hurtful. You knew Josiah loved Hannah. Yet, you borrowed him, lured him, seduced him to satisfy your own broken soul."

The words stabbed through my ribcage and skewered me on the truth.

"You're admitting it." It took every bit of strength to see the monster behind the image of my heart's true desire. "You killed Josiah to have my sister for yourself."

The Josiah apparition shook his head. "It is more complicated than that. You know what it is to have loved and lost. And so do I."

I shuddered. The lines were blurring. I couldn't see the monster. I could only see my Josiah. My sweet Josiah. "What do you know of loss, creature?"

The apparition stepped toward me. I'd backed up as far as I could go. I could turn and run, take another path to Hannah and tell her everything. But . . .

Josiah advanced. "We can both have what we want, Solomon. We can be together and no one has to know."

My heart pounded in response, though my gut recoiled, sickened by my weakness. Sickened by the bargain I was about to seal. But *yes*, my heart said. *Oh, yes.*

I closed my eyes and Josiah took my hand. We were no longer in the fetid ship, lost at sea. We were transported to my courtyard, the fragrance of flowers mingling with the sweet tang of his sweat. And his lips were on mine, and I melted into them, a moment trapped in amber, preserved for all time.

WHILE MY THIRST FOR JOSIAH WAS QUENCHED, my revulsion at the bargain I'd made festered in me like poison.

But I was too drunk on fantasy to care. Too drunk on whiskey. The only time I allowed reality to creep into my twisted little world was to tend little Jeremiah. Beautiful Jeremiah, with his blond curls, tawny skin, and eyes as bright as the ocean at noon.

I knew in my heart this life was not meant to last. That even the creature sought an end to our fruitless mission. We could not sink enough Spanish galleons to stop the bloodshed and the relentless destruction of our people. Our cunning, our spirit, was no match for their centuries-old hatred.

The morning when the armada became visible on the arc of the horizon, its vast numbers silhouetted against the rising sun,

Hannah rang the alarm bells, summoning the crew to the cannons. But I knew before the approaching ships fired, as the timbers cracked beneath us, that our belle epoch was over.

As crew members fell, their bodies shattered, my sister lay in a bloody heap, a massive hole in her abdomen. I crouched beside her. Would I tell her now? Admit my duplicity?

No. For if she were to meet the true Josiah in the afterlife, how cruel it would be for me to deprive her of peace.

But as the light faded from her eyes and the ship burned around us, my sister had other matters on her mind.

"Take Jeremiah. Teach him—claim Ash . . . so Jeremiah will be the next guardian."

The ship listed, the ocean crashing into its belly. Waves washed over the deck, sweeping crew members out to sea. But I was strangely calm as I clung to the deck rail.

It was finally coming to an end. At last.

"No, my sister," I said. "I will not."

I held her as she died, cradled her blood-caked head in my lap, then closed her eyes as the light went out of them.

The ship, broken beyond hope, was cracking, its sails aflame. Then, crashing through the flames it came, a mountain on two legs. In its giant arms, the creature held the baby.

"You must claim me," it said. "Or it all ends with you."

I breathed in deeply, the acrid smoke scorching my lungs. "Then let it," I said.

Before I could leap out of its way, the creature shoved Jeremiah into my arms, swooped us up, and leaped into the sea. In a blizzard of stars, it whipped around us in a dizzying circle before dissolving into the sea.

It left us there, floating on bits of debris—me and the child, watching as the Lament broke apart and sank beneath the waves.

As for us?

We survived.

But that is a story for another day.

ABOUT THE AUTHORS

LISA AMOWITZ is an award-winning author of three fantasy/thrillers for young adults: UNTIL BETH, VISION, and BREAKING GLASS. She is also a cover designer and Director of Digital Design at Bronx Community College where she has taught for the past twenty-five years. Having successfully raised two creative and independent offspring, she lives with her husband in New York City, making trouble, art, and trying to do yoga every day.

You can learn more about Lisa at lisaamowitz.com.

S.E. ANDERSON is the author of the YA science fiction humor series THE STARSTRUCK SAGA, as well as a YA contemporary novel, AIX MARKS THE SPOT, based on her childhood in Provence. Currently, she is working on her PhD in Astrophysics and Planetary sciences in Besançon, France. Come say hello at www.seandersonauthor.com.

HEIDI AYARBE is the author of four published YA novels, including ILA award-winner FREEZE FRAME, and six non-fiction children's books. She lives in Pereira, Colombia (the heart of Colombia's coffee region) with her husband, daughters, and dogs where she writes, works with local libraries, tells stories, translates stuff, drinks too much coffee, and can't get Cheerios.

EMILY COLIN's debut novel, THE MEMORY THIEF, was a *New York Times* bestseller and a Target Emerging Authors Pick. She is also the author of THE DREAM KEEPER'S DAUGHTER (Ballantine Books). Her young adult titles include the anthology WICKED SOUTH: SECRETS AND LIES and the Seven Sins series, including the upcoming SHADOWS OF THE SEVEN SINS (June 2021) and SIEGE OF THE SEVEN SINS (August 2021), from Blue Crow Publishing. If you liked "Smooth the Descent," check out the rest of the SEVEN SINS universe, including the free prequel novella!

Emily's diverse life experience includes organizing a Coney Island tattoo and piercing show, hauling fish at a dolphin research center, roaming New York City as an itinerant teenage violinist, helping launch two small publishing companies, and working to facilitate community engagement in the arts. Originally from Brooklyn, Emily lives in coastal North Carolina with her family. She loves chocolate, is addicted to tiramisu, and dislikes anything containing beans.

Emily is represented by Felicia Eth Literary. You can find her at www.emilycolin.com.

MADELINE DYER is a SIBA-award winning author. She lives on a farm in the southwest of England, where she hangs out with her Shetland ponies and writes dark and twisty young adult books. She is pursuing her MA in Creative Writing from Kingston University, having already obtained a BA honors degree in English from the "Writing from Kingston University, having already obtained a BA honors degree in English from the University of Exeter. Madeline has a strong love for anything dystopian or ghostly, and she can frequently be found exploring wild places. At least one notebook is known to follow her wherever she goes.

Her books include the UNTAMED series, the DANGEROUS ONES series, and CAPTIVE: A POETRY

COLLECTION ON OCD, PSYCHOSIS, AND BRAIN INFLAMMATION.
   She is represented by Erin Clyburn at the Jennifer De Chiara Literary Agency.

KAYE HART is a volunteer with addiction recovery services by day, writer of the weird and wonderful by night. They live in the UK and spend their time devouring every fantasy novel they can get their hands on. They have an absurd taste in clothes and they don't know how to Internet properly. They can be found shouting into the void at @KayeIsNotHere on Twitter.

JOHN KLEKAMP began writing in high school, contributing features stories to the school paper. Encouraged by his journalism teacher, John pursued a career in television news. After graduating from Northern Arizona University, he worked as a reporter and anchor in the Phoenix, Detroit, and New York City markets, earning numerous awards, including four Emmys. "Over Time" is John's second published short story, and he's thrilled to see it included in this collection. John is married to a super-supportive guy who's learned never to ask, "When will it be done?" Together, they spoil a golden retriever named Dory. John is working on his first young adult novel.
   Don't ask when it will be done.

KARISSA LAUREL is a science fiction, fantasy, and romance author living in central North Carolina with her son, her husband, the occasional in-law, and a very hairy husky named Bonnie. Her favorite things are water sports, Star Wars, Southern cuisine, and Hindi cinema. Karissa serves as an assistant editor at Cast of Wonders, a young adult speculative fiction podcast—part of the Escape Artists family. Most recently, she is the author of TOUCH OF SMOKE, a paranormal romance novel available from Red Adept Publishing. She's also the author of THE NORSE CHRONICLES, an urban fantasy series, and THE STORMBOURNE CHRONICLES, a young adult, epic steampunkish fantasy series. Her short stories have appeared in various anthologies including THRILLING ADVENTURE YARNS 2021 (Crazy 8 Press, 2021) BAD ASS MOMS (Crazy 8 Press, 2020,) THRILLING ADVENTURE YARNS; VOLUME 1 (Crazy 8 Press, 2019), WICKED SOUTH: SECRETS AND LIES (Blue Crow Publishing, 2018), MAGIC AT MIDNIGHT (Snowy Wings Publishing, 2018), LOVE MURDER AND MAYHEM (Crazy 8 Press, 2018), and BRAVE NEW GIRLS; STORIES OF GIRLS WHO SCIENCE AND SCHEME (Brave New Girls, 2017). Her short fiction has also appeared at Daily Science Fiction, Luna Station Quarterly, and Cast of Wonders.

FIONA MCLAREN Raised in the mystical and intriguing wilds of Scotland, Fiona grew up with stories that defied gravity. With her heart corralled by a strapping Greek Cypriot, she now meanders the beaches, hills, and hidden nooks and crannies of the myth-laden island of Cyprus. She works as a full-time, freelance editor with the Reedsy network, alongside other world-class publishing professionals, and she is represented for her fiction by Maura Kye-Casella of Don Congdon Associates.

Fiona supports Epilepsy Awareness, alongside Osteoarthritis and Fibromyalgia Awareness.

RISHI MOHAN is a young adult and adult fiction author. He loves writing about diverse characters, unexpected plot twists, and worlds with a touch of magic. His characters overcome adversity through their passion, humor, and drive to make the world a better place. Rishi is the co-founder of the international free mentorship nonprofit Dweebs Global and lives with his family in Arlington, Virginia. When he isn't writing, you can find him taking long walks and exploring new cuisines.

HRISHIKA MUTHUKRISHNAN grew up in Cary, North Carolina, where she spent eighteen years thinking there wasn't much to the suburbs before she discovered how much her hometown had to offer her. She is currently a senior at the University of North Carolina at Chapel Hill and has been previously published in *Carolina Muse* and The *Indian Standard.* During her summers, she works as a creative writing camp counselor where she and her campers frequently invest in inside quirky jokes. When she's not writing at sporadic moments of the day, she spends it painting and immersing herself in the field of fashion photography.

ANGELA SIERRA was born in Colombia but raised in the US, and defines herself as an American child trapped in the body of a Colombian adult. Though an experienced journalist and columnist for over fifteen years, her first love has always been fiction, a passion she has cultivated as a writer, storyteller, and educator. Her other passions include coffee, chocolate, photography, chocolate, homeschooling, and chocolate. Did she mention chocolate?

UNBOUND:
STORIES OF TRANSFORMATION, LOVE, AND MONSTERS

Published by Five Points Press
Lisa Amowitz (USA), Sarah Anderson (France),
Heidi Ayarbe (Colombia), Emily Colin (USA),
& Madeline Dyer (England)

9 781087 946894